THE
RED PATCH
PRIVATE

Copyright © 2024 Darrell Duthie

Darrell Duthie asserts the moral right to be identified as the author of this work.

All rights reserved. No part of this publication may be reproduced or transmitted in any form or by any means, electronic or mechanical, including photocopy, recording, or any information storage and retrieval system, without permission in writing from the publisher.

Published in 2024 by Esdorn Editions in the Netherlands

ISBN 978-94-92843-128 (trade paperback edition)
ISBN 978-94-92843-104 (e-book edition)
ISBN 978-94-92843-135 (hardcover edition)

Cover design by JD Smith Design
Interior design and typesetting by JD Smith Design

Cover photographs acknowledgement: Canada Dept. of National Defence / Library and Archives Canada: *Sherman tank of the Ontario Regiment pursuing units of the Hermann Goering Panzer Division* Italy, July 1944 (PA-160454)

This book is a work of historical fiction. The names, characters, events and dialogue portrayed herein are either the product of the author's imagination, or are used fictitiously, except where they are an acknowledged part of the historical record.

www.darrellduthie.com

THE
RED PATCH PRIVATE

DARRELL DUTHIE

The invasion of Sicily, July 1943

ALSO BY DARRELL DUTHIE

Malcolm MacPhail WW1 series

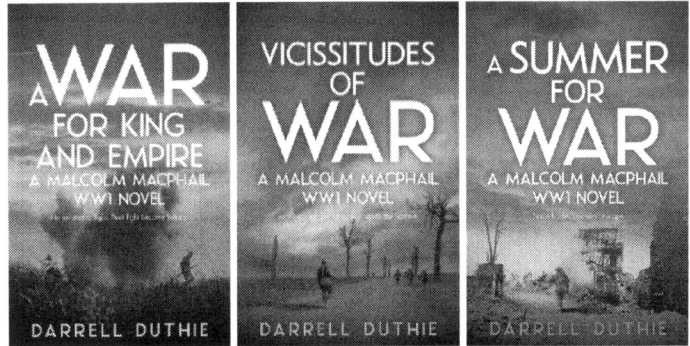

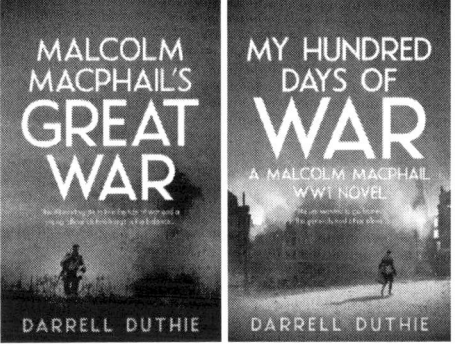

A War for King and Empire – (1915-1916)

Vicissitudes of War – (1916-1917)

A Summer for War – (1917)

Malcolm MacPhail's Great War – (1917-1918)

My Hundred Days of War – (1918)

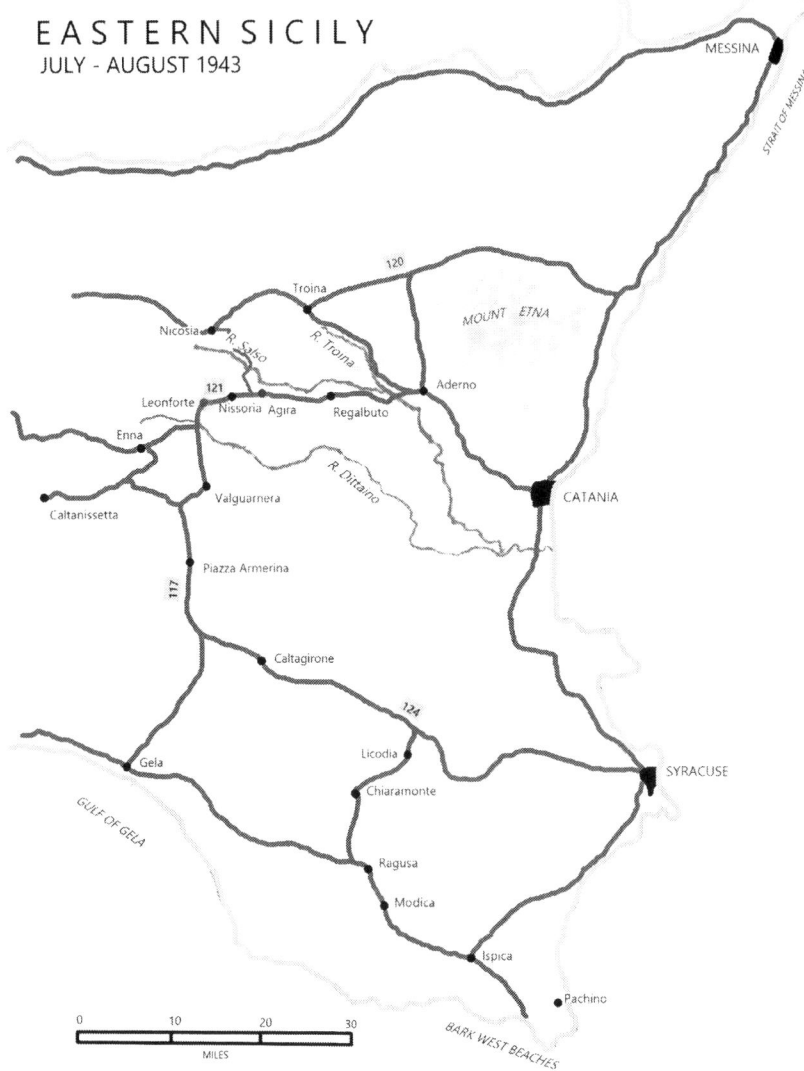

CHAPTER 1

29 April, 1943
London, England

'Not again! How much trouble can one man get into?' said one of the soldiers sitting around a small table. 'It's a wonder he's not in a punishment battalion.'

'Punishment battalion?' His companion frowned. 'I didn't know we had punishment battalions.'

'We don't. Not yet. But Archie may lead to a reassessment of the policy.'

'Look, there he is. Fashionably late.'

A tall soldier had entered the pub, a confident spring in his walk. He had sandy hair, an athletic build, a big grin presently illuminating his lean, chiselled features.

'Private Atwell?' called out the first man.

'Hi fellas.' The newcomer pulled out a chair and leaned back, spreading his legs as if he'd just completed a route march. 'Yeah, nothing to be done about it. The higher ranks aren't for me anyhow – far too much hassle. But do you know what the Captain called me? A "good-for-nothing". Can you believe that?' He smiled wistfully; it was precisely the kind of thing his father might have said.

'All too easily,' laughed the first man. 'Lucky for you, Archie, private's where the totem pole ends. And look on the bright side – you don't have to worry about future demotions.' His two companions chuckled wickedly.

'Only problem is there's this bastard named Battersby in charge of the section now,' spat out Archibald James Atwell. 'Not that it matters. I think they intend on keeping us in England the whole damned war.' Most, and this included his mother – the architect behind the whole scheme involving him and his full legal name, at least if his father was to be believed – had sensibly abbreviated this mouthful into plain Atwell, or Archie. The army administration remained the last known bastion of defiance.

Opposite Archie at the round wooden table, filled with an assortment of almost empty glassware and a well-used ashtray, two soldiers – both of whom had a sleeve of stripes on Archie – grunted at his words. Their frustration at 'missing the war' was evident too, even if it was only expressed in monosyllables, and deep creases of the brow. Unlike Archie they'd missed the Spitzbergen operation. One had been on the disastrous raid at Dieppe the year before, and he wished he'd missed the experience. But, as the evening progressed, speculation about what the future held grew livelier, while the level in their glasses fell.

Had Archie been aware of that morning's events he would have furrowed his own brow – in confusion if nothing else. Almost certainly he would have chosen his words quite differently.

Unbeknownst to him, roughly 10 hours earlier at precisely 0900 hours, in dense mist and generally poor flying conditions, the first of two Hudson bombers of no. 24 Squadron had lifted off from RAF Hendon near London. The light two-engine bomber built by the American Lockheed Aircraft Corporation carried an assortment of very important persons; the manifest revealing that all were bound for Algiers and, ultimately, Cairo. However, the plane's journey was destined to be a short one. Not long after takeoff FH307 crashed in a fiery ball close to Barnstaple and the first staging point on the Devonshire coast. There, after topping up the fuel tanks, the long haul to Gibraltar would have commenced. Pending urgent inquiries to determine the cause of the crash the second aircraft was grounded immediately.

The inquiries were carried out very urgently indeed. The casualty list confirmed that all onboard were lost – including the four-man crew, a rear-admiral and a captain from the Royal Navy, two army lieutenant-colonels (one British, one Canadian), and a Major-General Harry Salmon, the General Officer Commanding (GOC) the 1st Canadian Division.

Archie would rightly have puzzled why his divisional commander, accompanied by a profusion of gold bands from the British navy, was required in Egypt. Egypt was a very long way from the lush fields of Sussex where his division presently found itself. Had he also heard that mere hours later a certain Major-General Guy Simonds, himself only freshly promoted to command the 2nd Division, had relinquished this command and been appointed as the new GOC of the 1st Division he would have realized something was afoot. Particularly, as that same afternoon, Simonds was rushed to an anonymous block of military planning offices in London at 31 St. James Square. Archie may not have been a well-educated man, but even his detractors agreed he possessed a certain dexterity of mind.

Archie's budding suspicions would only have solidified upon learning that tomorrow the new divisional commander would be bundled aboard another aircraft. This too was bound for the Middle East, and the headquarters of the British Eighth Army. But Archie knew nothing of this. The events of that morning, the change of command, and his new commander's immediate travel itinerary were held close to the vest – strictly on a need-to-know basis. And Archie didn't need to know. He would hear much later. The other two, both from different units, would hear later still.

'England's not so bad really,' rumbled Mac DuBois, now holding up his half-full glass at an angle. The liquid was a reddish amber against the flickering of the table candle. In his big hands he held the glass daintily, as a connoisseur might. 'There's not much head, but it doesn't taste bad. *Pas mal. Pas mal du tout.*' He raised the glass to his lips and drank thirstily.

'There's no foam because it's *Fuller's Ale,*' piped up Bill McNaughton, a shorter, moustached man, slender in build. McNaughton had to raise his voice to make himself heard above the hubbub. A group of a half-dozen soldiers were boisterously pushing their way past the blackout curtains and into the pub, already hollering drinks orders to the bartender. 'Ale is top fermented,' he began. 'That's the principal difference between ale and lager, you see. Lager is what you're accustomed to drinking at home, Mac –'

'I told you!' interrupted Archie, looking across the table at DuBois. 'I told you way back when, on the troopship coming over; Bill is going to prove himself invaluable this war.' He made a show of winking at McNaughton. McNaughton reddened and smiled good-naturedly, but didn't continue his explanation. DuBois was grinning broadly.

'Cheers, fellas,' said Archie holding up his glass. 'How's about another?'

'I thought you'd never ask,' replied DuBois. With a soft thud McNaughton set his empty glass on the table, for emphasis. Archie began to wave forlornly in the direction of the bar. There the crew of soldiers had blocked out the view and any hope of being imminently served. The piano started up again, a bevy of voices soon filling the Coach & Horses with a raucous interpretation of "I wonder who's kissing her now?"

'You're wrong though, Archie,' said DuBois through the din. The gravity of his voice was at odds with the atmosphere and the occasion. It wasn't often these three had the chance to meet.

Archie frowned in mock seriousness. 'Wrong? Me?' Firmly he shook his head. 'Unheard of.'

McNaughton, the quietest of the trio, perked up. He was often the butt of Archie's jokes so he was sensitive to the moments when the tables might turn.

'This time you are,' growled DuBois. 'That Hitler fellow is not going away by himself. They'll need us sooner or later. My bet is sooner.'

Archie nodded. 'Maybe. But they've been saying that ever since we arrived. We're trained to the nines, yet all we ever do is march. And Spitzbergen was hardly a real show.'

'Don't forget all the shooting practice,' protested McNaughton. 'Or that exercise we just finished.' He was referring to the one code-named Spartan, completed only a month before. Some said it was to be the culmination of all their training. Archie hoped so, for training had been an exhausting and altogether endless affair.

'Well it can't come soon enough, if you ask me,' said Archie.

'I agree. It's taking a *terribly* long time,' muttered DuBois. Meaningfully he eyed his empty glass.

Archie sighed. 'Oh, all right, I know. My round.' With a grunt he pulled himself to his feet. Just as promptly he collapsed back into the wooden chair. The others gaped at him. But he ignored their puzzled looks, staring instead over their shoulders in the direction of the doorway.

'Now, now, what has the tide washed in?' he said, in a tone they'd heard before. They hesitated, but eventually curiosity got the better of them, and they craned their necks to look. Before they could complete the motion, however – on the periphery of their vision – they caught the glimpse of a dress and the shapely legs of its occupant standing not ten paces behind. Embarrassed they turned away. DuBois fidgeted self-consciously with his collar, his cheeks colouring a little.

'Belay those words, fellas,' said Archie. 'I've decided that England is the place for me.'

'She's a looker all right,' said McNaughton, in a whisper.

Archie was on his feet. 'Miss!' he called out. 'Can we offer you a seat?' The gang of soldiers at the bar had stopped singing and was viewing the situation with more than passing interest. Archie pulled out the chair in question so as to leave no doubt about which seat he was referring to.

'Just a seat?' came the cool reply.

Archie began to stammer. Which was not like him at all. 'And a drink of course –' he managed.

'Fat chance of that,' murmured DuBois.

'Well, perhaps for a moment,' they heard the woman respond, 'while I wait for my friends.'

Her long hair was swept back past the ears, the rolls on the crown curled high in the latest fashion, and it was blond – very blond. That was perhaps the very first thing they noticed. She was their age, mid-twenties at most, quite thin – statuesque some might have said – with fine, high cheekbones and a small jut to her chin that was stern, but somehow not unbecoming. She was unquestionably a beautiful woman. Her lips were painted a bold crimson.

Effortlessly she slipped into the chair beside Archie. 'They should be here soon, I expect. Thank you, gentlemen.' While she went to sit, DuBois and McNaughton scrambled clumsily to their feet as they'd been taught to do in polite company, nearly upending the table and everything on it.

She smiled at the three of them as they stood ogling her in a mist of wonderment. 'I'm Ilse. Please.' She motioned. Awkwardly they sat once again, grinning self-consciously.

She spoke English well, albeit formally. But for all her pains to enunciate like a young English woman of a certain class and breeding, anyone with the slightest ear for it could hear she was plainly not. Rather like DuBois. His accent didn't fit the mold of his appearance either. Not that he cared a whit what anyone thought about him or his breeding. Despite his near peerless command of the language, the subtle Québécois twinges of his upbringing were what gave him away. Ilse's inflections, in contrast, were more foreign to their ears than DuBois's. Her accent was without a doubt Continental. It might even have been German, though they knew reflexively there was no chance of that.

'I'm Archie,' said Archie. 'That there's Bill. And the big fella beside him is Mac.'

'Would one of you have a light?' she asked, conjuring up a Players from her bag, her eyes twinkling at DuBois. DuBois was fast on the draw and he had his Ronson out and in action while the other two were still fumbling in their pockets.

'*Mademoiselle*,' he murmured, leaning over.

She bowed to the flame, then raised her head to elegantly blow a stream of smoke towards the bluish fug obscuring the rafters above. Delicately she plucked a shred of tobacco from the tip of her tongue. The perfect red lips parted and she smiled invitingly, locking her eyes on those of DuBois. 'Thanks. You're French?'

'*Canadien*.'

An awkward silence followed during which Ilse observed DuBois, and DuBois refrained from saying more – even though the occasion clearly demanded it. Disconcerted by her frankness he was attempting to determine the current location of his boots.

Archie cleared his throat. 'Mac's a wee bit shy.' Quickly he added: 'We don't get many opportunities to converse with beautiful ladies. We're a little out of practice.'

Ilse smiled at him. 'I hadn't noticed.'

'Where are you from, if you don't mind me asking? You don't sound English, and you're certainly not Canadian.'

'I'm Dutch, as a matter of fact,' she said, drawing herself up straight.

'Dutch! That's the wrong side of the Channel these days. How did you come to be here?'

'I'm with Queen Wilhelmina's delegation.'

He furrowed his brow. 'Queen Wilhelmina?'

'Yes, the queen of the Netherlands.'

Archie nodded seriously, as if already long acquainted with the queen she was talking about.

'I fled with her and her entourage after the invasion in '40,' Ilse continued. 'I'm one of the lucky ones. But all my family, including my little sister, are still back in Holland. In Zeeland. Perhaps you've heard of Zeeland?'

They looked at each other and shook their heads. Under her unwavering glance even Archie felt compelled to admit ignorance.

'If you had a map, I could learn you some geography,' she said brightly. 'Zeeland is in the south of the country, on the coast north of Belgium. Beautiful beaches in the summer.'

'Teach,' said McNaughton.

Ilse frowned. 'I beg your pardon?'

'In English we generally say "*teach* you",' he mumbled, belatedly conscious he'd nailed the grammar, if not the mood. Under the table Archie kicked him hard in the shin and glared at him.

'Yes, of course,' Ilse replied. 'I must remember that.' At this, something caught her eye. She smiled, waving exuberantly at two attractive young women who were pressing their way through the heavy curtains. Their faces lit up when they spotted Ilse, and beckoned to her that she should come.

'My friends have arrived. So, I'm afraid I must leave you charming gentlemen. We have dinner plans. Thank you for the seat though. And for the education.' At this she gazed first at McNaughton, then at Archie, her eyes lingering for a moment longer on DuBois. 'It was lovely meeting you all. Good luck, boys!'

Ilse had barely turned away before Archie was on his feet. Loudly DuBois coughed. Archie turned back with a mischievous grin, dug into his pocket and strewed a handful of coins onto the table. Then he winked and hastened after Ilse and friends.

'Isn't that just like him,' sighed McNaughton. 'A few nice legs and he's forgotten all about us, and the war. "Can't wait for the action", he says. Ha! Good-for-nothing indeed... He might have suggested that Ilse and her friends sit with *his* friends...'

DuBois sighed. The trio of women, with Archie in close pursuit, was pushing through the blackout curtains. 'Ilse was pretty, wasn't she, Bill?' he said wistfully.

McNaughton nodded. It hadn't escaped his attention the way DuBois had been looking at her. And she at him.

'Well, at least he left us something to remember him by,' said DuBois, thoughtfully, fingering the coins. Then he frowned as he stared at them again. '*Tabernak!* There's barely enough here for a cup of tea for the two of us.' He sighed, then clenched them firmly in his fist.

'What did he do, anyhow?' asked McNaughton. 'To get demoted?'

'You don't know?' DuBois stared at him, a grin slowly spreading until it reached from ear to ear. 'He dinged up a jeep.'

'Is that all? I damn near crashed one myself not long ago. These narrow English roads are plenty treacherous.'

'No, no. He didn't just bump the fender, he ran a brigadier's jeep into a hedgerow – in the middle of the night. Archie at the wheel, another seven of them crammed in back, singing. It was a miracle no one was hurt. They were returning from the local pub, after hours.'

'Ouch.' McNaughton winced. 'He's lucky he didn't get a court martial.'

'It wasn't Archie's brigadier.'

There was a long silence.

McNaughton stared at him, open-mouthed, not sure if he was jesting. 'Serious?'

DuBois bobbed his head up and down. 'Don't ask me how, or why, but one of Archie's superiors put in a good word for him. Otherwise...' He made a slicing motion across his neck. 'It would have been the Tower of London for sure.'

McNaughton whistled.

'And who's this Battersby fellow he's taken such a shine to?'

'He thinks he ratted him out.'

McNaughton grinned. 'Did he?'

DuBois shrugged. 'Who knows? But Archie thinks he did. Now, what do you say, Bill? How about that beer? I'll treat. I don't expect we'll be seeing our pal again soon.'

'Sure, Mac. Why not? No, Archie is off for good. I don't understand why he grouses so much about missing the action, his war is going just fine.'

They both laughed.

CHAPTER 2

9 July, 1943
The western Mediterranean

The tropical kit issued in May was the first of several hints as to their future. Shorts and short-sleeved shirts were met with an outpouring of speculation. Predictably, there was some joking about the thinness of the attire, and it's unsuitability for the fickle English clime. But neither Archie nor anyone else in the battalion guessed their destination correctly. Some postulated Africa, even if that seemed farfetched given that the North African campaign had only just ended with a great victory in Tunisia. Others said the Balkans. Yet others had flung out destinations as far afield as South America, or even Asia. Archie reckoned (or more accurately hoped) it was to be the south of France. He had heard pleasant things about the south of France. One of which was that there weren't many Germans around.

It wasn't until early July that they learned where it was really to be.

Three days out of the port of Gourock on the Clyde, the ship's bag of the *Durban Castle* was opened, and the secrets it contained were disseminated to a chosen few. The next day the Officer Commanding, Lieutenant-Colonel Jefferson, summoned all ranks of the regiment to the aft deck.

Once assembled, the colonel climbed atop the rigging and waved an arm to silence them. 'You must be wondering what this is about?'

A murmur swept over the assembled ranks.

'You know, of course, that except for the neutrals and parts of Russia, Nazi Germany occupies nearly the entire continent of Europe.'

There were nods.

'Now, the powers that be have decided it is high time something is done about it. In case you hadn't already guessed, we're aboard an invasion fleet, and that fleet is heading towards Fortress Europe. Only there's a trick involved; we're planning on going in the back way. Some like to call it the soft underbelly.

'The code name of the operation is Husky. And the 1st Canadian Division has been asked to participate. Not only is the division participating, we have the honour of doing so as part of the Eighth Army.'

A loud cheer went up. Some were still pondering what precisely the underbelly of Europe was, and where that might be. But there was no one who wasn't aware of the exploits of Monty's legendary Eighth Army in the North African desert. A voice called out: 'But where, sir?'

Jefferson was grinning. 'Sicily, gentlemen. The Edmonton Regiment is tasked with invading Sicily. And don't let my words about the "soft underbelly" mislead you. There's going to be nothing soft about it. We know the Italians have close to a quarter of a million men on the island, the Jerries at least two crack Panzer divisions. So it's fair to say we're going to have the fight of our lives on our hands. And the whole world will be watching.'

Archie smiled, and he could see those around him doing the same. Finally, they were to have the chance they'd waited so long for. 'Do what you have to do,' his father had mumbled, upon hearing he had enlisted. 'Just be sure you do the family name proud.' A time was coming when he'd have to show Archie a little more respect.

In the days that followed, the officers and NCOs were kept busy memorizing endless details until their heads swelled, and their temples ached. The men were less busy. Except for when the officers summoned them to share their newfound knowledge, as they did often, or when they were ordered to the daily boat drill.

Today, with the inclement weather, no one was surprised when it took a good bit longer than the record 3 ½ minutes of a week earlier.

Archie stood presently near the aft of the *Durban Castle*, sheltered from the worst of the wind, both hands clasping the port railing in a determined grip. He stared out at the churning grey sea under a sky that promised worse. The big ship shuddered from the force of a breaker, then rolled ponderously off to port before slowly righting herself. Underfoot the powerful engines continued their monotonous pulsing. Breathing deeply of the salt air, Archie turned his face to the sky and closed his eyes. After a blessed moment in which both head and stomach were at peace, a wave of cold spray washed over him, jolting him out of his reverie.

The gale had come up that afternoon. A stiff wind appeared out of nowhere and grew steadily until it was howling, the sea soon tossing wildly, pocked with white crests.

The seventeen-ton passenger steamer hit a big roller dead on the bow. After an initial shuddering protest the ship yielded to the wave and pitched slightly upwards, before tipping, then sliding precipitously down the other side where it wallowed again, this time to starboard.

Archie stumbled and was thrown backwards, almost losing his footing. He was not big – lean really – but hard and wiry, and with all of his strength he dragged his six feet and 175 pounds back up the sharply sloping deck to the railing. There, he bent unceremoniously at the middle and retched horribly. The wind shrieked in his ears. And to think, his war was only beginning.

A big, square-jawed man joined him at the railing. 'Sick?' he shouted, with a smile. The enquiry was a trifle superfluous to Archie's way of thinking.

Archie grimaced, no quick retort at hand. His mouth felt like sandpaper, the bile still coating it.

'Thank your lucky stars we're not on one of the smaller vessels. Some of them are near capsizing.'

'No,' he croaked.

'Damn, that's an armada,' continued the sergeant, admiration lacing his tone. To Archie's dismay Sergeant Matt Evers exhibited no ill effects from either the weather, or the infernal pitching and rolling. If anything he appeared to enjoy it. But then again, Evers hadn't been up late polishing off the evidence from the successful raid on the officers' mess.

Archie gazed out. Off their port side a long line of ships was steadily ploughing forward, one after the other. He knew that to starboard the sight was not dissimilar. Leading the procession and skirting each flank would be the escorting screen of destroyers and cruisers. On the third day of the journey as they'd come upon Eire and its sub-infested waters, they had been a comforting presence, even more after they sank a marauding U-Boat.

Upon reaching the coast of Africa, the number of ships had swelled as newcomers arrived from points unknown. Then, after several days of leisurely zig-zagging under a magnificent sun, the convoys pointed their bows northwards. Soon they veered east to pass through the famous straits of Gibraltar, the Mediterranean beckoning. The sea had sparkled, a gentle roll to it, while the endless blue sky was marred only by the wisp of an occasional cloud. Carelessly, Archie had mistaken the sun for an English one. With his rolled-up sleeves and cap-less head he'd parboiled himself to a painful crisp. He recalled standing at the packed railings one star-filled night, transfixed like the others by the glittering conglomeration of lights at Algeciras in neutral Spain. Beyond was the darkened rock of Gibraltar, the water a perfect mirror. Now this.

Immediately aft a sister ship buried her bow in a wave, her pennants whipping fiercely in the wind. Like the *Durban Castle* most of the other ships were large passenger liners or ferries, hurriedly converted to their new role as troop vessels, a few smaller ones scattered amongst them. Together they carried the roughly 18,000 men of the 1st Division – the heavy equipment and vehicles stowed aboard other, slower transports.

Seemingly undaunted by the stormy seas, the big passenger vessels battled their way forward. Archie felt another wave of nausea pass over him. He put a hand to his stomach.

'Do you think they'll call it off?' he asked Evers. The ship behind disappeared in a wall of grey spray.

Sergeant Evers hesitated. 'I don't know. It'll be touch and go.' But that was wishful thinking. Archie knew no invasion could be attempted in weather as foul as this. There was no two ways about it. They'd be swamped in the little landing craft.

'Christ, let's hope it calms down,' he said. 'Jerries or not, I'll be glad to set foot on solid land. I don't know if I could stand another week bobbing around on this tub. It's a good thing I didn't take the navy up on their offer.'

Evers looked at him appraisingly. 'Funny you should mention that. Despite your reputed "vast" experience with boats, I expect the navy likely shares your feelings, Archie.'

Archie grunted. Then, as he spotted a man coming up from below, the grunt turned to a groan. 'Yeah, well, I hoped the army might offer better opportunities.'

'Opportunities!' Evers shook his head as he followed Archie's gaze. 'You've had opportunities aplenty. Whose fault is it anyway that you didn't take them? Can't fault Battersby for stepping up when you refuse. God knows, I've been to bat for you more times than I can count.' Still shaking his head, he moved down the rail to the others.

After several more minutes taking the air on deck, and pondering Evers's words, the advantages of fresh air were being overcome by altogether too much seawater mixed in. Archie pursed his lips and looked down. Sourly he took note of the state of his tunic. It was thoroughly wet, despite being pressed only this morning after repeated admonitions by the sergeant. He'd have a devil of a time getting the salt stains out. Frankly, he didn't see the value in a crisp turnout given where they were heading. Unlike Battersby. He'd have polished his nose had he thought it would improve his standing.

Brigadier Vokes's recent lecture on the importance of maintaining a high standard of discipline was likely to blame for this outbreak of spit and polish. Fortunately, the brigadier had chosen another ship to carry him and his staff of stiff necks. A good thing too, Archie grinned, for he wouldn't have taken kindly to having his booze stolen. He turned and went below.

He was feeling better, and that was a palpable relief. If he was truly lucky the Blackjack game would still be on. He'd been earning a pretty penny at cards. Most of his mates were proving to be rank amateurs at the game, and it would be a real shame not to take advantage of the pickings when the pickings were this good. The majority of the men were carrying a month or two of pay. Moreover, with few places to spend it onboard, and thoughts understandably elsewhere, the majority seemed ambivalent to their losses. Naturally there were a few exceptions.

Archie heard a curse as he clambered down the ladder.

'What!? You back to scavenge the remains?' snarled a voice. A half-dozen men in shorts were gathered under a single yellow bulb, sitting on wooden crates emblazoned with *Buy Pepsi-Cola*. An equal number stood watching.

Archie laughed. 'You're not still sore about that last hand are you, Dunbar? So how about a gilt-edged chance to earn some back? We'll play Blitz if you like. You even can stake your cigarette ration, assuming you haven't gambled it away already?' Provocatively he arched an eyebrow. 'Unless, of course, Bingo is more your style?'

With anyone from his own company Archie would have been more diplomatic – no need to rile the fellow who might someday be covering your back – but Dunbar was "D" Company; Dog Company to those in the know. Dog Company was always good for a joke. It hadn't always been so back when Archie was in their ranks, but that was ancient history. Besides, Dunbar was an easy mark having already lost a pile on Istanbul being their final destination. *Istanbul!* Whatever was he thinking? Men like him deserved to lose their money. With interest.

Dunbar considered the matter at hand. His gallery of chums were vocally making their preference known.

'Fine,' Dunbar eventually grumbled, to cheers. 'Let's get on with it.'

However, before a single hand could be played, a shout rang down the gangway: 'Pass the word! "A" Company to the officers' lounge. Immediately.'

'Isn't that just dandy...' muttered Dunbar. 'Saved by the bell, Archie.'

'Trust me, I'd rather relieve you of your cigarette ration, Dunbar, than listen to another of Captain Tighe's blasted briefings.'

The officers' lounge – one could see why it had been anointed as such with its big windows and comfy lounging chairs – was recently transformed by the large relief model now prominently exhibited on a table in the middle of the cabin. The model was surrounded by a battery of maps lain out like so many assignments on a schoolteacher's desk, together with a hard-backed mosaic chart outlining the units involved. Some bright soul had turned the chairs so that they faced the table. Not that Archie minded; the view of a raging grey sea was the last thing he wanted to see.

'Alright, pipe down, and grab a seat,' commanded Captain Tighe, as the last of the stragglers trickled in. Tighe was a slender, dark-haired man with the clean-cut good looks of one who should have been captain of the football team had he not been CO of "A" Company. Almost universally, the men respected him. Notwithstanding his carefully-cultivated reputation for contrariness, Archie did too – perhaps even more so in the aftermath of recent events in England.

Tighe had been livid: 'Christ almighty, Atwell. I gave you another chance, didn't I? And this is how you repay me? Brigadier Foulkes is positively steaming.' But despite his consuming anger the captain had still stepped into the breach to defend him. Tighe was okay, even if he had stripped him of the stripe he'd only just received.

'What d'ye suppose it's all about?' whispered Tom Hainsley in one ear. Hainsley was very tall and almost as gangly, cursed with the physical awkwardness that often accompanies such a build. Those who knew him forgave him this foible; for where his feet were prone to tying themselves in knots, he was relaxed and even-tempered, a winning smile for all.

'Hadn't you heard? We're taking on Hitler.'

Hainsley sputtered: 'Ah, c'mon, Archie. Cut it out. I know that…' The sentence died on his lips. One of the sergeants had caught his eye, with a look that suggested imminent hanging from the yardarm.

Now, Captain Tighe was mercifully brief in his instructions. There was little they hadn't heard already; except that a sandbar had been discovered by a daring British submarine. The obstruction was a hundred yards offshore of the beaches. This caused a tittle of consternation as sandbars and landing craft generally don't mix, until the captain explained that it was to the right of Sugar Green, the section where they were to land. '"A" Company is to push inshore as rapidly as possible, towards Pachino,' he concluded. 'We don't know exactly how stiff the resistance will be, but securing the beachhead won't be easy.' A long pause ensued while Tighe looked at the men. They in turn looked at each other. 'Questions?' he asked.

Archie's hand shot into the air. 'Does this mean it's still on, sir?'

Tighe shrugged. 'You'll know for certain, Atwell, when I know for certain.' Suddenly the *Durban Castle* rolled sharply. Were it not for the steel support, which he hurriedly grasped, the captain would have lost his balance. Tin cups, papers, kitbags and other unsecured gear went tumbling and sliding over the deck. Even sitting, the men had to brace themselves. Archie put a hand to his stomach.

'I wish they'd just tell us yes or no,' whispered Hainsley. 'The suspense is killing me.'

At approximately that same moment, at a location far from the coast and the section of beaches the planners had dubbed Bark West – it was in the hilly interior of western Sicily – *Oberleutnant* Manfred Weyers of the 2nd Battalion of the 104th Regiment of the 15th Panzer Grenadier Division, approached his superior officer. He was slightly out of breath for he had walked very quickly.

The officer in question was a *Hauptmann*, a captain, and the commander of 5. Company. Like Weyers he was a veteran of Rommel's Afrika Corps and had fought in its most famous engagements. Both men had escaped the final humiliating surrender in Tunisia; Weyers only because he was recovering in an Italian hospital from a shrapnel wound to his thigh. He was released in time to be expedited to Sicily where the Italians, from the *Supremo Comando* on down, were noisily clamouring for help. When not refusing the Führer's offers of assistance, as they'd done mere months before, the mercurial Italians were masters at crying for help – usually at inopportune moments when help was either difficult to muster, or pointless. Perhaps this time would be different, thought Weyers.

At the shuffle of his first lieutenant's feet over the drive, Captain Biedermann looked up. He was seated at a simple kitchen table that had been carried outside and placed in a spot of shade under a tree. To the other side was a dust-covered *Kübelwagen* painted in desert colours. The car was a boxy, open-air affair with straight sides, four doors, and a sharply slanted windscreen. Such cars were a common sight around Europe, or wherever the German Army was found – which was pretty much everywhere.

The captain was working diligently through a sheaf of papers held down, against the gusts of wind that had come up that afternoon, by a rounded stone the size of a grapefruit. He was anxious to finish before dinner was served. He'd set his mind on a few quiet hours afterwards. Heaven knows when he would have the chance again. In the early evening the air was always cooler, and it was too early for the mosquitoes to begin their nightly torment.

First Lieutenant Weyers saluted curtly. There was no clicking of heels or ostentatious Hitler salute. That was something one did in Berlin; such showy theatrics were thankfully paid no heed in the field. Not in Africa. And certainly not in Russia. Nor even in Sicily, which had its own ways. No fighting man could go to the bother. And Weyers was nothing if not a fighting man.

'You sent for me, Captain?'

Biedermann nodded. 'D'Havet reports that any landings are impossible tonight.' It was not General D'Havet, but simply 'D'Havet', Weyers noted. Which spoke volumes coming from a man as fastidiously correct as Captain Biedermann.

Weyers nodded thoughtfully. He too put little credence in the words of the commander of the Italian 206th Coastal Division, and even less in the abilities of the general's men. But someone in his position didn't say that of one's ally. Besides, even here, far inland, the winds could be felt. He could imagine that at sea they would be stronger still.

'The men are prepared?'

Weyers drew himself up to his full height of precisely 183cm. *Natürlich, mein Herr.* All are accounted for. At your orders the company is prepared to move at a moment's notice.'

'Good,' grunted the captain. 'Very good. D'Havet or no D'Havet, wind or no wind, I have that old feeling in my bones, Manfred. But let's hope I'm wrong.'

Weyers grinned. He knew precisely what feeling his captain was referring to. He'd experienced the same thing himself a few times this war. Including that time at Tobruk when, thanks to the forewarning of a queasy gut, his reconnaissance patrol had so narrowly missed the English one twice their size. It had been a very close call.

The captain nodded briefly, then returned to his papers. Weyers saluted and turned on his heel.

Barely two hours passed. A soldier came hurrying down the dirt track from the direction of the captain's farmhouse. Weyers spotted him halfway down the path. He was on his feet when the man arrived. The message would be for him.

'The general alarm, sir,' he puffed.

'The general alarm?'

'Yes, sir. The captain says you're to muster the men. Our aircraft have spotted multiple convoys converging on Sicily.'

CHAPTER 3

10 July, 1943
Offshore southern Sicily

'Damn!' said the man standing next to Archie, staring out to sea. 'There must be dozens of them.'

'At least that many,' agreed Archie. He could tell the man was keyed up; they all were.

After a succession of near moonless nights, a bright yellow orb was making a momentary appearance. Even without the illumination the many silhouettes, blacker than pitch against the night sky, were easily discernible. The ships were sailing in close formation on a course north-northeast, headed towards land and war, the shores of Sicily not far distant where the two would surely be found.

'It's a bleeding marvel if you ask me. Say what you want about those staff types, they sure pulled it off this time.'

It *was* a marvel, Archie thought. His head pivoted from left to right. More so to think that all these ships, widely varying in size, speed, and the composition of their cargoes, had departed from dozens of ports on three different continents, then converged here at this precise spot, at this very moment, in the early hours of 10 July, 1943. All in accordance with a plan drawn up months before. Little wonder General Eisenhower had not countenanced a postponement.

'Yeah, sure,' allowed Archie, reluctantly. 'But I still say it's a damn sight easier wielding a pencil on the staff than a rifle in the field.'

The man shrugged and turned back to his observation of the fleet. As he did so, Hainsley appeared.

'Hey Tom. What say we go below again, and see if there's a game on? Not many hours left now.'

'No game for me,' said Hainsley. 'I can barely think straight from the nerves as it is. But sure, Archie, let's go below.'

An unnatural quiet reigned. Most were sitting at tables on the mess deck under an unnatural yellow light, a haze of sweat and tobacco smoke. There was little talking. Men cradled rifles and looked straight through their mates to the steel bulkheads opposite, thinking thoughts of a sentimental nature. Sweat trickled down necks and brows. Even the poker game was so listless that Archie chose to plunk himself down instead on one of the benches occupied by a few faces he knew.

He turned to the nearest one. 'Warm, eh?'

'What's that?' came the distracted reply. Followed by, 'Oh, yeah.' Archie gave up the attempt at conversation and began to undertake a study of his rifle.

'That precision instrument you're playing with, Atwell, may be the only thing keeping you alive someday,' Sergeant Craven had told him rather pompously at the range one morning. He was referring to the Lee-Enfield Archie had just neatly twirled in the air like a baton, to a smattering of applause. 'Neglect it at your peril.' Words which they'd laughed mightily about at the pub afterwards. Only now the humour escaped him. He was more than a little uneasy about the coming show, and his own role in it. Not that he'd told a soul of those misgivings – that wouldn't do at all. So he tried not to think about them. But at the moment it was hard not to. Which somehow, in one of those strange meanderings of the mind, led him to recall his two pals back in England, Mac and Bill. He wondered if they too were heading for war. And if they were, were they nervous? He tightened his grip on the rifle, then loosened it. Get a hold of yourself, Atwell, you're turning into a real wilting pansy. There was nothing his father hated more than a wilting pansy.

Mercifully the wind had abated. But even now, past midnight, the water was choppy and in turmoil in the wake of the gale. The

HMT *Durban Castle* eased into her appointed anchorage eight miles offshore, the rattle of the anchor going down penetrating the thin bulkheads. The waiting soon seemed interminable.

After a few restless hours, Archie decided he had to do something, so he made his way back up on deck. His head had barely cleared the ladder coaming when the entire sky lit up. A rumbling roar erupted like nothing he'd ever heard before. He sprang up the final rungs of the ladder, leapt onto deck, hastening to the railing.

An arcing line of flashes and flame marked the southern horizon where the capital ships lay.

In the light of the bombardment the sheer extent of the vast armada revealed itself. So numerous, and in such close proximity, were the ships dotting the sea – big, little, hordes of small assault craft darting busily amongst them – that it seemed possible to walk in any direction without wetting one's feet. Some of the cordon of battleships, cruisers, monitors, and destroyers must have been very close indeed, for in the fire of their guns the deck of the *Durban Castle* was bathed in a light so bright as to be day. This was something important that was happening, and he felt better for the knowledge.

Men flooded up from the decks below, their faces filling with awe as they caught sight of the scene.

'Wow,' whistled Lance-Corporal Battersby, suddenly bumping shoulders. Archie glared at him. He was of medium height, more than a little stocky, with cropped dark hair and a rodent-like face that ended abruptly in a weak triangular chin cut by the slit of a near lipless mouth. The trim brown moustache he'd taken to wearing of late did nothing to improve appearances. He claimed he'd worked in insurance before the war, but no one particularly believed that story, least of all Archie. Regardless, Battersby entertained grand ambitions for his army career, ambitions that only recently had taken a decisive step forward. That the stripe and command of the section had fleetingly been Archie's rankled still. In the excitement Battersby was furiously preening his moustache.

'It was you that snitched on me wasn't it, Miles?' For four months he'd wanted to ask that question.

Battersby darted a glance in his direction. As he reflected his mouth slowly twisted into a smirk. 'The only thing you need to know, Atwell, is that the army says you take your orders from me. Your kind isn't the kind to be trusted with command, anyhow.' He sniggered, then moved off.

Archie clenched his fists into a ball, harsh words forming on his tongue. But now Dick Saunders, also of the platoon, jostled on the left. And someone else was claiming Battersby's spot at the railing.

The big guns roared even louder. For a long while no one spoke, which in itself was worthy of note. Then, as the bombardment fell silent Archie said: 'Boy, I'm glad those were ours.'

Saunders nodded vigorously. 'When d'ya think we're going in, Archie?' he asked. 'Can't be long now.'

'Soon,' replied Archie. 'Very soon.' This assessment missed the mark entirely.

To begin with the battalion was not even assigned to the initial assault; their job would be to land after the beach was taken and proceed inland. On top of which the meticulously planned timetable hadn't accounted for the challenges of weather and navigation. As one hour passed into two, Archie began to shuffle impatiently.

At the sight of Captain Tighe, he accosted him. Few others amongst the ranks would have dared. And had they admitted to that, Archie would have smugly responded with: 'He's just a man, isn't he? Like the rest of us.' There was no need to mention that the captain had spared him from a hanging at dawn, and seemed to regret it ever since.

'Shouldn't we make for the boats, sir?' he asked of the captain.

Tersely Tighe shook his head. 'Hold your horses, Atwell. It's a bit chaotic at the moment – '

'Sir?' Chaos as the invasion began sounded ominous.

The captain declined to elaborate. In lieu of further explanation, Tighe, ignoring the nuisance of Archie hovering before him, raised his head and his voice. 'Go below decks,' he commanded the milling men. 'Get some rest. You'll be needing it later.'

They did as instructed, except that rest came in fits and starts for most. But not for Archie. He was quick in finding a spot next to the bulkhead and dextrously sat down, laid out his gear and rifle, and fashioned a pillow of sorts from his pack. Then he lay down and closed his eyes. Just for a minute or two, he thought. Like his earlier prediction this too proved optimistic.

'Just look at him,' sighed young Postlethwaite, admiringly, shifting positions on the hard deck for the third time in ten minutes. 'How long has he been there? An hour? Two? He hasn't once batted an eyelash.'

'Yeah, Archie could sleep through a hurricane. I don't know how he manages it. I couldn't sleep if I wanted to,' said another.

Harry Dinesen grunted. 'What's an invasion to him? Archie chases off grizzlies at dinnertime before settling down for a night on a mountaintop.'

'Really!?' said Postlethwaite.

Dinesen rolled his eyes.

Then suddenly the ship's intercom crackled into life, and a bosun's whistle blew shrilly. A disembodied voice boomed out: 'Hear this now! Hear this now! Serial one. Serial one. To your boat stations. Serial two. Serial two. Stand by.' Winches and cranes began making an unholy clamour.

Archie woke with a start. Blinking he glanced around. The platoon was gathering, their faces painted lampblack, helmets and web gear fastened, rifles held tightly.

'You waiting for a personally engraved invitation, Atwell?' sneered Battersby, to a few laughs. Ed "Last Chance" Lachance seemed to find it particularly funny, but then he'd tied his star to Battersby months ago.

Archie yawned. 'You were in insurance, Miles. Surely you must have completed a sum now and again? Didn't it occur to you that to get from serial one to serial twenty-three might take a while? Subtraction helps – grade three, remember?' Archie thrust out his legs and leisurely crossed his arms behind his head. 'But don't mind me while you stand.'

Sheepishly a few others of the platoon collapsed to the deck. Battersby did his best to look nonplussed, but after a few minutes he too succumbed.

Soon enough their number was called.

There were nine landing craft a side, dubbed LCAs, with the "A" part signifying assault. Not that anyone would have mistaken the ugly little rectangular box of a boat with a LST, the massive landing craft that carried a whole squadron of tanks in its belly. An example of the smaller infantry version, the LSI, was fastened alongside on the far side of the ship.

Several loaded craft were clanging angrily against the ship's hull in the heavy swell. That was another difference with a LST; had one of those bumped sides with the *Durban Castle* it would have been even odds which vessel survived. The last of the men in front was being winched down the side.

The platoon was waved forward, even as another boat loaded down with men was swung out, before it too was lowered in a whine of machinery.

A curse sounded from ahead, and the file Archie was in came to a halt. Almost immediately a couple of sailors under the sharp tongue of a petty officer pushed their way past. The platoon stood waiting.

Finally, they heard a loud voice proclaim: 'There's nothing to be done, sir, the pongos will have to climb down.'

'Yes, yes indeed,' replied another, more cultivated tone. 'Carry on then.'

There was a *whirr* and a terrible screeching, and the boat was lowered precipitously down the side where it plunged into the water, bow first. By the time they reached the railing the little craft had righted itself and was bobbing faithfully alongside. A couple of sailors were climbing down to it.

'Line yourselves up. One at a time. Quickly now, mates,' came a shout. Then: 'Over you go!'

With a start Archie realized he was next in line. The helmet of the fellow in front had already reached deck level.

'Move it, Atwell. You'll have all the time in the world to pick your nose later.' He recognized Battersby's voice. Sergeant Evers was eyeing him.

Dutifully he clambered over the railing, his hands clutching at the rough scramble netting, and for a terrifying moment his feet bicycled in mid-air before they secured a foothold. He risked a glance downwards and regretted it instantly. The dark sea was boiling, the landing craft wildly tossing and turning thirty feet below. The storm had blown on, but in its wake the sea was troubled.

The little landing craft was not the only thing tossing and turning.

Notwithstanding its seventeen tonnes, the *Durban Castle* was also swaying uneasily in the surf.

As the ship wallowed, the rope netting was flung out to one side. The rough hemp cut into Archie's hands as he gripped it. Reaching the full extent of its swing, the net seemed to momentarily pause in midair, before it swung back towards the ship with a terrifying swiftness. Just in time Archie fended himself off with a desperate jab of a boot. But the effort was insufficient to save his knuckles, which seared in pain as they smacked against the steel plates. But there was no time to think about that. He could feel the boots of the man above tapping on his helmet.

'Keep it going,' hollered one of the NCOs on deck.

Archie threw himself into the descent, but barely made it a few rungs before the netting went flying again. He held on, bracing himself as he'd done earlier. The netting billowed out then snapped back, lashing violently against the ship's hull. Archie winced as his right elbow ran up against the *Durban Castle*.

He looked down. The first soldier, an athletic lad by the name of Aubrey McDonald, was already aboard the landing craft. But Archie was still endless feet from its bucking bottom, and the narrow rows of wooden benches. McDonald and a naval officer were shouting and waving. 'Jump!' he heard.

Archie hesitated, conscious of how very small the boat appeared, in contrast to what seemed like an endless expanse of water churning angrily. It was all too easy to envisage missing the boat altogether, and sinking away in that cold, murky sea. He could swim – like a fish he might have boasted at some other moment – but could he swim in that cauldron?

Again the toe of a boot bumped impatiently on his helmet. Below, McDonald and the navy man were bellowing something important but altogether inaudible. Meanwhile the guns of the monitor nearby were booming in incessant fury. With the salt spray Archie's knuckles ached something fierce. Resolutely he took a deep breath. He followed this up with a hurried look to capture the spot in his mind's eye – to finalize the timing – then he simply let go.

To his surprise Archie landed on something welcomingly pliable, yet firm. He rolled off and got to his feet. He'd had visions of a broken ankle or, at the very least, a frigid immersion in the Med, so this came as a pleasant surprise.

'I said JUMP, soldier. I didn't say jump on *me,* you idiot,' snapped the man underneath.

He glanced down at the poor bugger he'd landed on and noted that save for an olive drab helmet, clearly borrowed from the army, the fellow was otherwise clothed in the blues of the Royal Canadian Navy. None of this would have been particularly noteworthy were it not that the man also bore the epaulettes of a sub-lieutenant on his shoulders. He was nursing his ribs as if he'd taken a broadside at Trafalgar.

'Terribly sorry, sir.'

The officer winced manfully. 'Yeah, well, find a seat,' he said, with a calm Archie found remarkable.

When the craft was fully loaded, or as close to it as the young sub-lieutenant dared given the sea and the loading conditions, they pushed off. Before long most of the regiment, roughly 800 men, were bobbing about on the Mediterranean while the navy tried to fashion order out of chaos.

Their efforts were not an immediate success.

'Christ almighty. How difficult is it to steer for the beach?' muttered Archie, as the waves buffeted the boat every which way. The small craft were being tossed and turned like autumn leaves in a storm.

Then right when all the battalion's craft had been successfully corralled into two lines, and heading purposively for shore, the lead boats swung away sharply to starboard. The other craft followed.

'We're circling,' groaned Archie to Saunders beside him. 'What the hell are we doing that for? Sicily's that way.' Pointlessly he stuck out an arm.

'Oh, my stomach,' groaned Saunders, stumbling over half a dozen others to the gunnel. Archie felt it coming up too. Shakily he got to his feet, intending to join him. However, Lieutenant Wiles intervened with a bark. 'Don't anyone move,' he shouted. 'Stay where you are, Atwell. Sit down. You fools are going to swamp us.'

It seemed a little implausible and Archie could not have cared less at that moment, but he did as he was told and sat, bending his head down to seek the cover of his knees. Between retches he caught sight of the sub-lieutenant in the bow near the steering shelter, also sick. He at least was able to lean over the side. Apparently even the navy was finding the going heavy.

'Jesus,' moaned someone. 'Don't they know Edmonton's landlocked? Couldn't they have found a land battle for us somewhere?'

After two hours of this misery – it was approaching 6 a.m., the shoreline tantalizingly close in the morning sun – and with the platoon unable to take much more, the relieving word was given. Or so they presumed, for the craft abruptly turned towards land, the engine's revolutions increasing. The development was greeted with a weak cheer.

The cheering died rather quickly when a line of red tracer fire from the beach arced its way across the sky ahead.

CHAPTER 4

10 July, 1943
Bark West beaches, southeastern coast, Sicily

The LCA fought its way forward through the water, the flat bow regularly rearing upwards at some unruly wave before slapping down with a thump that sent the boat shuddering and everybody's hands to their stomachs. Spray flew onto the soldiers and wet them down as they hunched miserably on the long benches. Every now and then there was the sound of a machine gun, and red tracer stitched seams in the sky. Then the boat's momentum eased and so too did the turmoil of the sea. Forward there was a discussion ongoing amongst the platoon commander and the navy sub-lieutenant.

Archie saw Lieutenant Wiles, their new platoon commander, raise his arm and point straight ahead – insisting. The naval officer hesitated, then shrugged. They continued their way.

Without warning there was a soft thud, followed by a disconcerting grinding under the hull. The landing craft lurched to a stop. Down went the ramp. Wiles shouted, 'Follow me, men!' and leapt out.

The two sections were already on their feet, every man anxious to feel solid ground again – Jerries or no Jerries. But the lieutenant had vanished.

Then a helmet burst upwards from the sea bottom, followed by the rest of him. They watched as he struggled to stand upright, before wading slowly, heavily, towards shore. It was at that moment that Archie realized they'd been caught by the very sandbar the British submarine had warned about, a lagoon of water seven-feet deep extending before them. Undaunted, the men on the ramp raised their rifles with one arm above their heads, the other pinching their noses, and sprang out. Archie followed the general example.

Briefly he felt himself go under. But prepared, his feet quickly found a sandy bottom, and he stood and began sloshing towards shore. He was conscious of hearing little other than his own exertions. When the water reached shoulder level he raised his head, his eyes darting anxiously from left to right. The enemy would be waiting.

But of resistance on the beach there was no sign. It was, however, a hive of remarkable activity.

Groups of soldiers from the division were regrouping; new units were landing; and supplies were being carried off several landing craft that had cleverly circumnavigated the sandbar. There wasn't an Italian or a German to be seen. Not that Archie regretted it; it was a lark to fearlessly lead the charge on exercise somewhere in England, quite another to do it here.

Halfway up the beach he spotted a familiar face from one of their sister regiments, the Hastings and Prince Edward Regiment – known to one and all as the Hasty Ps – and went to him. The private was resting his arm on a spade while his mates gave the final push to a jeep stuck in the sand. 'Welcome to Sugar Green, Archie!'

'Thanks, Alex. I'm mighty happy to see you fellows. So, where are the Eyeties?'

The man grinned. He pointed at a white stone house set a couple of hundred yards back from the beach. 'Quite a few lying around over there if you want to have a look. A few took off lickety-split afterwards. Course the smart ones had their hands in the air the first chance they got.'

Archie grinned back. Wet, feeling more spent than he ought to have given he'd only crossed a few hundred feet of beach, he knew the Edmonton Regiment had been fortunate. As if to underline that, they came upon a row of Hasty Ps lying side by side in the sand a few feet further on. The assault had not been an entirely riskless business. With almost a morbid curiosity Archie and the rest of the section stared at the bodies as they trudged by, the hazards of war not yet a reality to them.

Off the dunes they moved through a picket line of yellow beach grass and reeds, and encountered a few lonely strands of barbed wire strung amongst them. The ground became flat and hard, covered by thickets of tall, rough grass, and the occasional desiccated palm tree. At the dusty coastal road Archie gathered with a half-dozen others. One of them now raised an arm in surprise, and they looked where he was pointing. Back on the beach, and easily visible from where they stood, a strange-looking and most ingenious contraption was moving ashore. It was a metal-sided boat with wheels – a standard 2-½-tonne truck made amphibious.

'A Duck,' exclaimed Saunders, which was a little less convoluted in the mouth than its real name, a DUKW. They stood watching it.

'We sure could have used one of those. It would have saved the lieutenant his swim,' said Archie, to chuckles.

'What now?' asked Hainsley, gazing around. It was a pertinent question.

Neither Lieutenant Wiles, Captain Tighe, nor even Lance-Corporal Miles Battersby were anywhere to be seen. The army being an institution predicated on the principle of having someone within shouting distance to tell you what to do, this was a novel experience. So they improvised.

Archie turned to the others. 'Let's move on,' he said. He was conscious that they were in the midst of an invasion with numerous objectives for the day. And if his understanding of military doctrine was even remotely correct, standing around in the open was a strategy with few merits. Not that it was obvious where they should move to; there was no sign of the objectives, or even a landmark recognizable from the aerial photographs and mock-ups. 'Perhaps we'll see something further inland.'

'Just like the navy to dump us on the wrong f-ing beach.'

'Oh, stop moaning, Saunders,' came a reply. 'I'm bloody glad they did. I couldn't have survived another minute on that damned boat.' The others mumbled their agreement.

They walked across the arid fields. Some were covered in vines, which generated a few exclamations of pleasure from those in the know. A brief conference amongst them determined that northeast was the likely direction of Pachino, the largest town in this most southerly tip of Sicily, the signpost admittedly a useful clue. They all knew that Pachino was definitely an objective of the day, perhaps the most important objective in the entire region. How the seven of them planned to liberate an entire town would need further reflection. But they were keen. Archie did his best to play along.

Fortunately they were not put to the test. After roughly a mile they came upon a large group from "B" Company and, shortly thereafter, Captain Tighe, Lieutenant Wiles and much of the rest of "A" Company including their missing comrades from the section. Almost immediately the captain put them to work digging defensive positions. The rest of the brigade was entrenching on a 'fortress' hilltop nearby. The expectation was that that the Italians and the Germans would soon try to push the invasion back into the sea, explained the captain.

'What about Pachino then?' mumbled Archie, as he scratched at the hard, dry earth.

'Since when did you become general?' said Battersby. 'Don't you think that's been thought of?'

Archie said nothing. What he bewailed was not so much the strategy, but the impracticality of digging slit trenches in the afternoon sun with nothing more than an entrenching tool. While his tunic, shorts and kit were already bone dry after their recent drenching, he was sweating from every pore. Wincing he looked down at his hands. Cut up from the boarding, the immersion in salt water had done them no good at all; blisters were appearing. He straightened up, and took a gulp of tepid water. It was while he stood there, encouraging the others, that he noticed something in the distance.

'Start digging, Atwell,' snapped Battersby.

'Look there! Don't you see?'

Battersby glanced briefly and shook his head. 'The only thing I see, is you not doing your bit.'

'Fine. If you're too busy commanding the shovel brigade...' Archie hastened over to the company commander standing at a makeshift table nearby. With hands on his hips, and thunderclouds on his face, Battersby watched him.

'Sir?' Tighe was bent over a map. A cough. 'Captain?'

Irritably, the captain looked up, the sweat running down his forehead. 'Yes,' he sighed. 'What do you want, Atwell? I'm a little busy.'

'That building, sir.' Archie pointed at the long, low-slung structure in the midst of the vineyard, a little more than a half mile away.

The captain squinted. 'Yes, what about it?'

'I'm sure I saw some movement there, sir.'

Tighe's eyes narrowed, then came to rest on Archie again. 'Are you certain?'

'Yes, sir.'

Tighe looked again, holding an open palm above his eyes as a visor. 'Corporal Chettleborough!' he shouted at a man standing nearby. He nodded approval at Archie.

'Sir?' replied the lance corporal.

'Take Atwell here, and a few others, over to that building you see in the distance.' He pointed. 'Check it out. There appears to be some movement.'

Chettleborough was taking no chances and gathered the better part of a ten-man section – for the most part from Archie's section. Battersby sputtered at losing half his working party until Chettleborough put an end to the protests by invoking the captain's name, whereupon Archie smiled winsomely. Battersby glowered back.

They formed into file, but Chettleborough soon had them spread out and approach through the vineyard, making good use of the cover. Which all proved very sensible.

As the patrol closed in on the building, "Vino" emblazoned in humungous white letters on the nearest wall, Archie grinned. He'd seen right. Then a machine gun ripped the air.

After the many exercises this was a noise the men knew well, and instinctively they dove to the ground. But somehow, here under a perfect morning sky, the gunfire sounded different, harsher, more insistent – threatening. Several men began to return fire.

Archie lay flat, peeking through the greenery and the vines, trying to catch sight of where the gun was located. There was little point shooting if he couldn't see what he was shooting at. But he couldn't spot the MG. Not until it started up again.

'The big doors at the end,' he shouted to the corporal. 'Where's the Bren?'

'Roberts!' yelled Chettleborough.

Private Ben Roberts must surely have heard but he didn't respond. It was only the throaty staccato of the Bren gun a moment later that confirmed the message was received and understood. This was followed by a second, longer burst, and then the gun went silent – presumably in order to replace the 30-round magazine. Then it opened up again. Archie stared at the wooden doors, still open a crack, but couldn't determine what effect, if any, this fire was having. An uneasy silence followed.

Dramatically the shutters of an upper floor window flapped open. A white flag on a stick poked out.

'Well, I'll be darned,' Archie muttered.

They were Italians. The first man to exit was clearly an officer for he was smartly dressed and bedecked in rows of ribbons and medals – apparently having donned this finery for the occasion of his surrender – and was followed by what appeared to be an entire company of men. Smartly they marched out in file.

'Will you look at them,' marvelled Hainsley. 'They've got their kit bags packed and ready.'

The section was by now on its feet, rifles held casually, but alert, ready for any treachery the Italians might attempt. From their nervous smiles it was soon apparent that treachery was the last thing they had planned; the Italians were only too thrilled to have their war end thus.

Archie went over to the corporal, who was standing with Dinesen. 'Here's your big chance for a medal, Chett. Why don't you go accept their surrender?'

'Oh, one more thing,' he added, as Chettleborough moved away. 'Perhaps I should take a couple of the boys and search that building? There may be some holdouts.'

'Right,' said Chettleborough distractedly, and kept on walking.

Archie turned to Dinesen who was watching with a bemused look. 'Chett's got more weighty things on his mind. I expect he's trying to puzzle out how to say "I accept your surrender" in Italian.'

Roberts was all-in to accompany them, but Archie felt the Bren gun might be a little unwieldy indoors. 'Besides,' he told him, 'not only are you the one that got the Italians to surrender, you and your Bren are the best combination to ensure they don't change their mind.'

There was no point in taking chances. But Roberts insisted. And as the blunt instrument of the section, he was not easily dissuaded. 'Fine,' Archie grunted, unwilling to enter into a discussion he was destined to lose.

Once inside, they split into two parties, and carefully went through the entire building, an endeavour that took a while as it was considerably larger than they'd first supposed. At the farthest end there was even a second storey, where the white flag still flew, with what seemed to be offices. Much as Archie had presumed, it was empty of enemy soldiers. He felt himself a keen judge of character, and nothing about the Italians guarding this place suggested they were of a fighting breed. He hoped this wasn't a sign that the bounty they were guarding was gone.

'What is this place?' whistled Postlethwaite. They were standing in the large hall on the ground floor, dark and delightfully cool after a day traipsing up beaches, down dusty roads, and across fields – all under a broiling sun. Steven Postlethwaite was the peach-faced new fellow, right down to the fuzz covering his cheeks. He'd arrived only in the spring to replace a sick case, barely eighteen, and raring to be a fighting man. Prior to the war, Archie suspected him of never having ventured farther than his family home.

'What do you think, Sherlock?' laughed Dinesen. 'Even if all this doesn't ring a bell. Didn't you see the sign outside?'

'*In vino veritas*,' intoned Archie in mock seriousness, one hand resting gravely on a barrel while the other made the sign of the cross above it. Along both walls large oaken barrels were stacked on their sides, almost all the way up to the rafters. There was more than he could have dreamt.

'*In vino veritas*? What are you babbling on about, Archie?' said Dinesen.

'In wine truth,' interjected Postlethwaite. From the sounds of him the boy had the benefit of a good classical education, if demonstrably not a practical one. 'Ah, the wine cellar, of course,' he added an awkward second later, finally catching the clue. They all laughed.

'I don't know about you fellows, but I've worked up one heck of a thirst today,' said Archie. 'It's not every day you capture a winery. Seems a shame not to sample the wares while we're here.'

This they unanimously agreed would be a terrible shame. Postlethwaite was undecided, but all felt his vote could properly be counted with the majority.

Archie was debating whether to pry out the wooden plug from one of the barrels with his bayonet when Postlethwaite remembered the storeroom with wooden crates – revealing bottles inside.

By the time the Italians were finally regimented and sorted, their weapons accounted for, and kit packs searched, most of the section had helped out with the search inside.

It was a merry band that rejoined the regiment. Chettleborough had a triumphant grin on his face at the thirty-five prisoners he marched in. The prisoners were grinning at their captors, and at each other at this turn of events. The section was simply grinning. Had it not been that Postlethwaite spilled half a litre of red down the front of his tunic, it would have turned out all right.

'You're wounded, son,' said Captain Tighe when he came to the section's newest man. He'd just complimented the corporal, and had begun what was intended to be a congratulatory stroll down the ranks.

'Oh no, sir,' blurted out Postlethwaite. 'Archie… Private Atwell, said that I should soak it in water and give it a good rub.' Then he cottoned on to what he'd said. His face took on the colour of mud.

Captain Tighe reddened, took another step, and looked searchingly at Archie. By way of confirmation – although it hardly seemed necessary – he bent his head towards Archie and took a whiff of what the gentle Sicilian breeze wafted his way. 'Damn it, Atwell!' he exploded.

'By now you should have been a sergeant, at the very least. When are you going to get it in your thick skull that we're at war, and stand up and assume some responsibility? We're in the first hours of the biggest invasion in history. Grow up, man.'

To Postlethwaite's left Dinesen whispered: 'The Captain doth forget that Archie was already a corporal. Four times in fact.'

Postlethwaite's eyes bulged. 'Corporal? Four times?'

Dinesen nodded.

Wearily Captain Tighe shook his head. Then he snapped: 'Get out of my sight.' At a loss to say more, his nose crinkled in disgust. Muttering to himself he turned on his heel.

Corporal Battersby was watching, making no attempt to conceal his amusement.

'Well, you can be thankful of one thing, Archie,' chortled Dinesen. 'At least there was no talk of a firing squad.'

Archie rolled his eyes, and sighed. His thoughts were elsewhere. Never before had he seen so much wine in one place. Impulsively his hand reached for a pocket, his fingers grabbling furiously, fearful he'd lost it. But the big iron key that he had found was still there.

CHAPTER 5

11 July, 1943
Ispica, Sicily

The next morning, the regiment was ordered to take Ispica. As the crow flies – which is remarkably similar to the route of the Strada Statali no. 49 – Ispica was nearly eight miles away, towards the northwest interior of the island.

Archie was one of the very first of the Edmonton Regiment to learn of the orders Lieutenant-Colonel Jefferson had received. It was still dark when a weary-looking Sergeant Evers shook him awake.

'On your feet, Archie,' Evers said. 'You've been assigned to a recce.'

Archie blinked and wiped at his eyes. He made to move but his limbs resisted. Or was it his head? 'A recce? Hang on just a minute, Matt –'

Evers prodded him none too gently with the toe of a boot. 'Don't get all familiar, Atwell. It's "Sergeant" to you. Let's go! And on the double. You're moving out in less than an hour.'

Archie grimaced. He was awake but his head was throbbing something fierce. 'In that case, why wake me now? Give me a few minutes to get the old engine running.'

Evers shook his head. 'I'm going to use a flame thrower on that old engine if you don't get a move on. Captain Tighe's express orders. Because of you I'm up early as well. Besides, it's your own damned fault. Consider yourself fortunate it's not a good bit worse… after that stunt you pulled yesterday. When are you ever going to get it together and make something of yourself?'

'But I can barely move,' protested Archie.

'Oh, stop whining. You'll be in a Bren Carrier. The rest of us sorry types have to walk.'

The need to walk came about in large measure due to the intervention of the *Reichsmarine* and, more specifically, a U-Boat in its employ. It had torpedoed BB3, the *St. Essylt*, off the coast of Algeria, and down with it went most of the regiment's transport. This left the Edmontons, and indeed much of the division, relying upon a means of transport the Romans would have recognized. When he thought about it, though, Archie seemed to recall the Romans having chariots at their disposal. Which was presumably where the Bren Carriers came into it.

Three of the open-top, tracked carriers stood waiting, their motors already turning over. A full complement of helmets was visible over the armoured sides.

'You must be the fellas from the last-chance battalion,' called out Archie, as he approached.

'Climb aboard, Private,' shouted a soldier in one of them. 'Any later and you would have whistled your chance to ride with us good-bye.'

Archie went to the carrier, put a foot on the rear step and, with the assistance of a few willing hands, levered himself over the armoured plating. A Bren Carrier is a versatile vehicle, with many different applications (explaining its official nomenclature as a Universal Carrier), but roomy it is not. The driver, plus an NCO, and a rifleman doing double-duty as a machine gunner was the usual complement. After that its capacity was determined by how determined you were to squeeze in. As the fifth man, Archie had the distinct impression of being wheel number five. Without saying it in so many words, others seemed to feel similarly.

'So,' said the corporal, glancing back at him from his position beside the driver. 'What's your speciality?' Even to Archie's ear he sounded dubious about the possibilities.

'Jack of all trades,' Archie quickly replied.

'How exactly does the melon work into it?'

'Oh, this little thing?' Archie took it from under an arm, and slowly rolled it around in his hands. 'Either it's a top secret weapon, or simply a refreshing snack when it's a hundred and you haven't eaten in hours. Time will tell.' Then he grinned engagingly at the corporal, who otherwise might have thought he was being a smart Alec. With a weary shake of his head the corporal turned away.

The rising sun was firmly in their backs when the three carriers crawled off. They rumbled down a small dirt track and onto the provincial highway, itself more dirt than stones, in Archie's quick appraisal. The driver shifted up and they headed northwest towards Ispica.

'What I don't understand is why we're heading inland,' mused Archie to the other two in back. 'We're going west. I thought the whole point of this invasion was to go east to Messina, then jump the straits to Italy?'

'Beats me,' said one of them.

'They're not paying me to be a general, so I usually leave those sort of details to them,' drawled the other.

'Well, there's some wisdom to that,' acknowledged Archie.

The orders for this modest column, so far as the soldiers themselves knew, were to race forward and ensure any obstacles or hindrances were cleared, and all enemy positions identified by the time the bulk of the regiment followed.

It was a beautiful morning, the sky a dreamy blue in which a remarkable number of airplanes had already been spotted – all Spitfires, American Dakotas or other Allied aircraft heading inland, or returning from it. The air was dry and warm, not yet the sizzling heat of yesterday afternoon. Despite the fumes from their chariot, the soft breeze carried in its folds the most intoxicating of scents, both curiously tangy and salty at once.

Archie was not the only one gawking in fascination at the dry yellow fields and low rolling hills, the rows of vines and stands of olive and citrus trees all the greener for the contrast. They passed one tumbledown stone wall after another, and several simple houses. None could be considered anything more than a derelict shack. Yet therein lay a charm of sorts. It was definitely a long way from the cozy greenery and neat little villages of England, a longer way still from the endless forests of pine and the lakes of blue of northern Alberta.

Riding in a Bren Carrier was certainly the ideal way to tour the island, Archie thought, recalling what Sergeant Evers had said about the alternative. Marching would be an altogether different story, especially in this heat. In a couple of hours it would be unbearable. Perhaps he should see about being permanently assigned to a carrier unit. By this time he had forgotten about the lack of sleep. The locomotive shunting back and forth in his head had kindly moved off down the line. In fact it was disconcertingly easy to forget there was even a war on.

Once they ground to a halt to peer carefully at a distant house through binoculars. Someone swore that he'd spotted something. It turned out to be a mule and its peasant owner. Archie felt good.

After a mile or two, the incline of the road increased; they were climbing slowly but relentlessly towards the mountainous interior. Soon after, they spotted something else, this time of more interest.

The road came to a small crossroads. The lead carrier rumbled cautiously up towards it. One of the men beside Archie picked up his rifle and grasped it firmly in both hands, his finger nervously tapping out Morse on the trigger guard. Archie followed his example. Meanwhile the other man, the gunner, had returned to his station with the Bren, warily eyeing the situation.

On the far side of the crossroads, off to the left, were two smaller stone buildings. To the right behind a metal gate was a larger two-storey building set back from the road, also in white stone and missing any visible windows. The red ceramic tiles on its roof could be seen for half a mile. Along the side of the building was a driveway that appeared to open into a large courtyard beyond. At close quarters none of this warranted more than a cursory glance, but something else did. Predictably, Archie spotted them first.

'Holy smokes, boys! Rein in the horse and stake it down.'

They'd emerged from one of the houses on the far side of the road, obviously alerted by the creaking treads and growling motors. There were three of them, pretty with long dark hair, wearing dresses. Not a man among them noticed the particulars, beyond the length of the hem – short. One of the girls laughed engagingly when she caught sight of the heads gaping in wonderment above the armoured plate. Pertly, all three waved.

'What are we waiting for?' asked Archie, waving back.

'We're on a recce,' mumbled the corporal, dutifully.

'Of course we are,' said Archie. 'But they're clearly locals. They may have seen something. They may even know where the enemy is. We'd be derelict in our duty if we didn't at least have a quick word.'

'D'ya think?'

Archie, serious: 'No doubt about it.'

'He has a point,' said the driver.

They clambered over the side.

'*Ciao!*' called out Archie in his best Italian. It was one of roughly four words he'd once picked up; where, he no longer remembered. He held the melon before him, like an offering. Girls liked gifts. If life had taught him anything it was that.

The three women smiled invitingly at the approaching soldiers. The corporal pushed back the rim of his helmet in order to show off his own twin track of gleaming whites.

Behind they could hear the men from the second carrier, also dismounting. Anxious that they beat them to it, they picked up their pace.

Then in an instant everything changed.

The angry rattle of a machine gun sounded, ripping the seams out of this picture of lazy summer conviviality. The ground around spat dust and dirt, and billowed aimlessly up into the calm air. The MG hammered in their eardrums. All this in what seemed like a flash.

A piercing cry came from the rifleman who'd been in the back with Archie. But no one had time for him, only for themselves. They dove for cover, of which there was none, none save the hard-baked earth covered in white dust. The melon lay on the road, split in two. The girls were gone.

The echo of rifle shots could be heard now. Determinedly Archie lifted his head and began crawling like a madman towards the Bren Carrier – his first instinctive reaction was to move. A line of bullets zipped into the earth only a few feet away. He stopped crawling and planted his face in the dirt, conscious of the need to offer the smallest profile possible. To crawl invited more fire, but to lie in the open was hardly an alternative. Then he heard what might have been the single finest noise of his life up until now; the insistent clatter of a Bren gun.

By chance or design the men in the third carrier hadn't followed the example of the others. *Thank heavens they hadn't.*

Cautiously he raised his head. The embankment of the road was apparently sufficiently high to hide him from the MG's view, and he craned his neck to peek above it. The gunfire came from the big stone building a hundred feet from the road. He watched it carefully. Just under the arch of the roof was a small square hole in the stone. He had paid it little heed earlier, thinking it a home for pigeons. Perhaps it was – once. Now as he watched he saw fire spit from it, the black muzzle lit by the flashes.

Below, near the wrought iron gates of the driveway entrance, there was movement. A squad of Italians was ensconced in the greenery. There were at least three of them with rifles, and they were all aiming at the third carrier.

A little voice began to murmur in his head. He took a deep breath and pushed himself from the ground. Half stumbling he ran down the road towards the carrier. One long step. A second.

There was a *crack*, but he felt nothing and kept running. Then five more steps. He was solidly on his feet by now, and he ran for all he was worth until he piled up against the shelter of the carrier's armoured plate. Then there was a moment to catch his breath and gather his wits, his ears listening to the pattern and proximity of the gunfire. He stepped onto the vehicle's tracks and winched himself up and over the plating. He heard shouting in what was surely Italian.

For a moment he lay still on the vehicle floor, bullets pinging against the metal sides, his heart pounding. He tried to recall exactly where the Bren gunner had stood, and how he'd moved the weapon, and every other detail that might be important. The Italian MG sounded again, closely followed by the Bren from the third carrier. They were duelling it out. He leapt to his feet and yanked at the Bren gun that hung inertly on a swivel. Effortlessly it pivoted around. He pulled confidently at the cocking handle.

The Italians were positioned behind the remains of a wall, sheltered from the third carrier, but not from him. He laid the butt against a shoulder, lined up the sights – hastily, admittedly – and pulled the trigger. Even with the mount the gun's recoil was heavy, but he held it steady as he'd been taught. A quick burst. Four or five bullets. Another look down the sights at the Italians scattering. Then he pulled the trigger until the gun stopped thumping, and even then it took several moments before he realized the magazine was empty. His finger relaxed. His heart was pounding wildly.

Then another Bren opened up. It was from the second carrier. Alarmed by a noise and the sense of movement behind him, he turned in time to see the others pile into the carrier.

His gaze shot back towards the building. Chips of stone were flying from the vicinity of the pigeonhole. Several of the Italians near the gates lay sprawled on the ground. As the second Bren ceased, he saw the remainder of the unit, dressed almost entirely in black – after only a single day on the island it struck him as a most impractical colour – throw their arms up into the air and step cautiously forward. There were more of them than he thought, roughly half a dozen. A loud voice shouted in English to come forward, and they did as they were bidden. There was a nervous moment when, from around the corner of the building, the MG crew appeared, also in black, one cradling an arm. But all four chose discretion over valour.

The sergeant in the third carrier took command. The prisoners were gathered into a group on the road under the watchful supervision of two Brens, and the building hastily searched.

'One dead Eyetie and three wounded,' reported a grinning soldier to the sergeant when the party returned. 'We licked 'em good, Sarge.'

'Harris may think otherwise,' grunted the sergeant.

The man in question, the rifleman from Archie's carrier, had taken a round in the arm, but incredibly he was the only casualty. One sleeve of his shirt was rolled up to his shoulder, a white dressing strapped firmly around the arm in question. He was propped, sitting, against a carrier.

'We were bloody lucky,' said the sergeant, to no one in particular.

Archie nodded grimly. The others, not convinced of the role fortune had played, were in high spirits, still in the exultant throes of their first clash with the enemy. No one mentioned how it all began. What a fool he'd been, thought Archie. His first real encounter with the enemy, and nearly his last.

A vortex of dust appeared coming up the road behind, growing rapidly in size. Soon the form of a jeep was visible at its core. They watched with mounting curiosity as it approached.

At high speed the jeep raced towards them, shuddering to a halt just shy of the column, its dust cloud sweeping over. Out of the dust Captain Tighe stepped from the front passenger-side seat.

'Oh, shit,' murmured Archie.

The sergeant looked at him questioningly.

'My company commander,' he mumbled.

The sergeant spoke with Tighe for several minutes. Then the captain walked over to the carriers, chatting briefly with a couple of the men. Until he came to Archie.

'Blackshirts, I heard,' he said. 'Fanatic buggers.'

'Yes they are, sir,' said Archie.

'I understand there were some girls involved?'

Archie's face was stonily impassive. 'Yes, sir.'

Silently Tighe observed him, long enough for him to feel distinctly uncomfortable. Then he spoke again: 'This is no game, is it, Atwell?'

'No, sir. Absolutely not.'

Whatever Tighe knew, or thought, he wasn't letting on. With a curt jerk of his chin he moved off.

The prisoners were left in the care of two soldiers, one wielding a Tommy gun. Both had accompanied the captain in the jeep, and Harris was helped into their spot in the back for transport to the rear. Archie found himself in the same carrier, in the same battered seat, and with the added responsibility of assuming Harris's place. Which, as the corporal pointedly remarked, seemed only fair.

They set off again. It was only midmorning but already the sun was on a low boil, the metal of the carrier hot to the touch. After a short stretch they climbed to the top of a substantial hill, rounded a lazy corner and, over the tops of the flowering cacti lining the road, were presented with a panorama of Ispica. It loomed before them, perched high atop a sheer cliff hundreds of feet high, a mile away, white houses and the rounded dome of a basilica. It was enough to halt a besieging army in its tracks.

They remained there for some time, studying the village and the valley, and particularly the daunting approaches. Archie refrained from offering an opinion; nobody much appreciated an armchair sceptic.

The corporal dismounted and went to discuss it with the sergeant and the second corporal.

Then with a wave of a hand, they were off. The driver threw it into gear and they barreled down the hill and across the plain, the wind in their hair. The closer they came to the village the more intimidating it looked. When a few bullets pinged off the front armour, they didn't hesitate; the driver brought the carrier to a squealing standstill and turned on a dime. The other two carriers followed his example. All three retraced their path back up the hill. Not to them the duty of conquering the unconquerable.

This too was the opinion of the CO when he appeared to see for himself. Lieutenant-Colonel Jefferson took one look at Ispica across the valley, and had the observer call in a flash bombardment from a cruiser offshore. An ultimatum went by hand into the village. Once *HMS Delphi* delivered her warning salvo, no further arm-twisting was required – a message of capitulation arrived forthwith.

That afternoon, in the sweltering heat, a long file of Edmontons with a weary Archie Atwell somewhere in the ranks – he suspected Captain Tighe of this precipitous transfer from the carriers to the foot soldiers – marched up the steep and twisting road into the village. Despite the surrender he felt a certain trepidation. The greater therefore was the relief when they were greeted by cheering crowds, a profusion of flowers, weapons thrown at their feet by the defenders, and repeated offers of local wine.

Against his better judgement Archie refused the latter. In light of recent events it seemed wise. In light of the next day's itinerary it definitely was.

CHAPTER 6

12 July, 1943
Modica, Sicily

Round about the first light of dawn that morning – dawn being scheduled for 0541, a time that Archie readily described as 'unearthly' to the few willing to listen to his thoughts on the subject – the battalion began a gruelling 12-mile march uphill from Ispica to Modica. At the halfway mark, or so near as not to matter, grit lined his mouth and his feet were aching. Weeks aboard a ship hadn't done his constitution any good at all. He was glad therefore that Sergeant Evers had persevered and insisted he wear the regulation thick, knee-length woollen socks. Initially he'd dismissed them as completely impractical in this glaring heat, until he realized that perhaps they weren't at all. In fact, they might help against the blisters, which were gaining ground faster than the Allied armies in Sicily. Evers was not entirely as dumb as he looked.

As the sun rose, so too did the white dust thrown up by the feet of the column, billowing expansively in the wake of every tank or truck that passed. It slowly settled in layers over the body and coated the face, where it then proceeded to mix with sweat to form a special brand of cement that penetrated eyes, ears and nostrils. Archie rubbed again at the itching eye that was troubling him so. All the while a fiery sun unlike any he'd experienced burnt a hole through the bowl of his steel helmet.

A few industrious souls had commandeered a mule and a cart in Ispica, and luxuriously fitted it out with a parasol, such that they looked more like purveyors of melons than soldiers. But those with wheeled transport were in the minority. The rest of the Edmonton Regiment marched. And tried to look smart about it as they did so. Exactly as their officers had taught, and seemingly still expected despite the weather, geography and general state of exhaustion.

'WAKE UP, Atwell! For Christ's sake, you had a full night's sleep.'

With the supporting arm of a man beside him, he'd closed his eyes for a bit. But he must have stumbled and drawn the attention of some observant officer.

Chastened, he mumbled, 'Yes, sir,' and drew himself up and lengthened his stride.

Then the feeling of relief when they held up at a battered road sign proclaiming *Modica – 5 km;* with it the welcome prospect of collapsing for a spell in the shade of trees, stealing a few drops of warm, heavily purified water from his bottle.

'Atwell, get yourself over to Lieutenant Wiles. He's taking a patrol from "A" Company into town.'

Captain Tighe was once again the prime suspect for this nomination. While there was a part of him that couldn't really blame his company commander, Archie mused briefly how he would act were he in Tighe's boots. The first thing, he decided, was that he would rest his dusty boots and sore feet on the front dash of a jeep instead of marching dutifully alongside the men.

'I'm told Modica is the headquarters of the Italian 206th Coastal Division,' said Lieutenant Wiles conversationally, over his shoulder. Goodness knows where the young, educated and talkative lieutenant dredged up the information. Like the English teacher in Medicine Hat he once was, Wiles was determined to disseminate his knowledge. 'Their GOC, General D'Havet, even won a Military Cross during the first war. The Italians were on our side then. The interesting thing is that it was our own Duke of Connaught, the Governor General, who presented him with the medal. So he has a connection with us.' Wiles smiled at the thought.

'Splendid,' breathed Archie. He had no views this way or that concerning the former Governor General, but he didn't find this short chronicle about the enemy general altogether reassuring. 'So,' he muttered under his breath, 'the intrepid patrol from "A" Company moves in to occupy the city, while an entire division and its war hero general await them…'

The road took a bend to the left, and suddenly they were confronted with exactly what he had feared. A large 30-CWT truck, one of theirs, was abandoned to one side of the road, smouldering darkly. It had been hit very recently. A dead Canadian soldier lay sprawled beside it on the road.

'Sir, look!' shouted Archie. He'd taken in the scene, but what had caught his anxious eye was what he glimpsed at the next bend. 'A field gun.'

He unshouldered his rifle and knelt down.

'Relax, Atwell. Swan's already been this way with a few carriers. He'll have cleared the way.'

Swan. That would be Lieutenant Swan, another of the "A" Company platoon commanders. Apparently Swan was a more valued platoon commander than Wiles if his patrol merited Bren carriers. Of course, they'd gone first, which might explain it. On the other hand, if they'd gone first, what the hell was the point of Wiles's patrol? It was not the sort of question a private asked a lieutenant, however. Archie gulped, and kept his rifle firmly in his hands, not entirely convinced the lieutenant knew what he was talking about; mastering prepositions didn't give one much insight on how to enter an enemy-held town.

They trudged on. To his great relief he saw that the crew of the gun lay on the ground around it. They were Italians. Lieutenant Wiles turned, and looked at him as if to say, 'I told you so'. Archie managed a weak smile in response.

At the next bend they came upon a machine gun pointing straight at them, and when he spotted it amongst the trees a couple of hundred feet ahead, Archie felt his stomach sink. His stride faltered. But nothing happened. 'Come on, Atwell,' came the voice of the lieutenant. The rest marched blithely on. 'Keep up would you?' The MG was sited so as to catch anyone venturing down that particular stretch of road, but of its crew there was no sign. He took out his water bottle and gulped down the last precious inches to celebrate.

Lieutenant Wiles marched on.

Modica turned out to be a sizeable place with more Baroque churches than is healthy for a man, nestled in a deep valley. When they first caught sight of the sprawl of grey stone they could scarcely believe their eyes. Looking down from the surrounding heights Archie wasn't the only one to nod his approval at the obvious advantages Modica's location gave an attacker.

After circumspectly navigating the road downhill, and entering the town by means of a bridge, it was apparent that the good General d'Havet and 206th Coastal Division had drawn the same conclusion about the defensive merits of the topography as the patrol had. Wiles and cohort entered the outskirts of town unopposed. 'They've fled,' said Roberts, with a sigh.

Only appearances deceived. The men of the Coastal Division were in fact out in droves. As they walked into town one after the other appeared, rifle in one hand, a suitcase in the other – the latter flagging their true intentions. Even a nervous Archie had to admit that it was hard to picture a man clutching a bulging suitcase as a threat, rifle or not.

'Hi there,' called out several in good English. 'Welcome,' cried another. There were big smiles. Contrary to the impression left earlier, the enemy appeared overjoyed to see them.

Lieutenant Wiles waved. A few of the men shouted their own greetings.

The narrow streets were lined with white flags. The flags were almost entirely fashioned from pillowcases, bed sheets and kitchen towels. Little imagination was required to picture them in their original use only hours before. But then war demanded sacrifices of all. Beside which, thought Archie, they'd undoubtedly reclaim them by day's end, making it a cheap enough peace offering.

Modica itself was quiet. The streets which had first been empty were now filling with the town garrison which had evidently mustered, now flocking out of every nook and cranny towards them.

'Wait, do you hear that?' exclaimed one of the men. The two files, one left hugging the buildings, the other right on the far side of the street, came to an abrupt halt. Pulses went racing. Small arms fire crackled in the distance.

'Oh, that's miles from here,' said Lieutenant Wiles, dismissively.

'They're celebrating, that's all.' He waved with his arm to indicate that the patrol should move on.

As they did so, more Italian soldiers joined the procession, until it swelled into a crowd that filled the street behind. They were outnumbered twenty to one, but the Italians made no threatening signs, instead talking excitedly and volubly to each other. Lieutenant Wiles groaned out loud when he saw the sheer number of them. 'We'd better collect their arms,' he said. 'We'll set up a depot. Battersby, you separate out the officers…'

Archie wasn't listening. He was smitten. His heart was beating fast, he was in his own world, his eyes fixated on a second storey balcony across the street where a couple of pretty girls were waving at them – at him. A mere glimpse of the dark haired beauty on the right was enough to make him weak in the knees.

He looked round for the lieutenant. Wiles had disappeared into a swarm of Italians, all of whom were talking, most with their hands gesticulating wildly. The men of the patrol were attempting valiantly to fashion some order out of the bedlam. It was clearly a campaign rather than a battle that lay ahead.

Grinning, Archie pushed his way through the Italian soldiers.

The girls hung over the balcony railing. One motioned that he should come in. The other flashed two fingers like Churchill's victory sign, but what she meant was the second floor. Archie waved, pushing open the iron door. Coming immediately to a wooden staircase he bounded upwards.

A door stood ajar and the two of them, one wearing a light dress in a floral pattern, the other clad in a most becoming white blouse with billowing arms, and a short black skirt, giggled as they watched him leap the final steps.

'Come in,' said the one in the dress, the shorter of the two. The taller one, lustrous dark hair falling over her shoulders, motioned gracefully with her arm. She was far more beautiful than he first thought.

'You speak English.'

'We've been to America,' she replied. He could see she was proud of it. 'Are you American?'

'Canadian.' He flashed his most becoming smile.

'I'm Amalia,' she said, 'and this is my cousin, Ginevra. I'm visiting her from Valguarnera.'

Archie nodded. 'I'm Archie, Archie Atwell.'

The girls looked at each other. 'We can offer you tea,' said Ginevra.

'I would love a cup of tea.'

They ushered him towards the balcony where a small round table with metal chairs was set.

'I'll take this one,' he said, choosing the chair the furthest from the railing, and not coincidently out of sight of the platoon down on the street. He set his rifle against the wall, and his helmet on top of that. The girls bustled off. He could hear their excited voices speaking rapidly behind him.

'Would you like lemon, Archie?' asked Ginevra, as she reappeared with a teapot.

'Yes, please.'

She leaned over and carefully poured a steaming trickle of tea into the delicate china cup that her cousin had conjured up. Her hair, smelling of flowers, tickled at his face. She placed the pot back on the table and leaned over him once again, even closer this time. He could feel the warmth of her through the thin fabric of her blouse. She took a wedge of lemon in her long fingers and squeezed it expertly.

'There,' she said, satisfied, straightening up. 'What should we drink to?'

'To an end to the war,' said Amalia.

'I'll drink to that,' said Archie.

The girls insisted that they toast, and so they clinked their cups together. Archie was fearful he might break his – it was terribly dainty – but it ended well, and they all laughed when the ceremony was done.

Afterwards, Archie remembered little of what they talked about, only that the conversation was animated and laugh-filled, and far too short.

Leaning forward he could just make out the street. He saw that the lieutenant had accomplished the near impossible. The Italians were lined up in two straggling columns, one for officers, and the second one for other ranks. Near to the road was an overflowing stack of rifles and other arms. Two of the men stood guarding it, their own rifles held casually in two hands. It was clear that the patrol intended to move out shortly.

Archie pointed at the scene. 'I have to go.' Reluctantly he got to his feet, and reached for his rifle and helmet.

'So soon?' said Ginevra, brushing away a lock of hair that had mischievously fallen down over her nose. She sounded sad.

'I'm afraid so. But I'll be back. I don't know when, but I'll come again soon. That is, I will if you'd like me to?'

Ginevra stood and laid a smooth hand on his shoulder. Her dark eyes sparkled. She leaned up, on her tiptoes, and kissed him. Her lips were velvet soft, but firm. They lingered for a moment, then pulled abruptly away. She smelled wonderful. 'Make sure you do, Archie. I would like that.' Even the way she spoke his name was enough to turn him into putty. But not so much so that he didn't notice that her invitation made no mention of her cousin. He stared into her eyes.

Then Amalia stepped forward, and the spell was broken. She extended a hand as if inviting him to dance. He took it, and kissed it formally, then gave a small bow.

As he exited the building he turned and looked up. Ginevra and Amalia were there, bent over the railing, waving exuberantly. He waved back.

'They're quite something, are they not?' It was an oddly formal voice that he heard.

Startled, he looked around to see who was addressing him. A group of immaculately dressed Italian officers was standing near the building, observing. The man who'd spoken was a few steps away, wearing a monstrously large officer's cap in the Italian style, adorned with a profusion of gold braid.

'I am Major Argenziano. And you are?'

'Private Atwell, sir. Edmonton Regiment, 1st Canadian Division.' He straightened up and gave the smartest salute he knew how. He'd never seen so much gold braid in his entire life.

The Major saluted in return. 'Let me introduce you. We have something to ask of you.'

As he walked towards the platoon Archie spotted Lieutenant Wiles, Battersby hovering a step behind and speaking in his ear. Then Battersby wielded his finger and began stabbing it in his direction. Wiles looked up. He had an irritable look on his face. 'Where the devil were you, Atwell? The Corporal says you disappeared –.' With a start he noticed the group of Italian officers trailing behind.

'Lieutenant Wiles, may I present to you the famous General d'Havet, MC, and his adjutant, Major Argenziano of the 206th Coastal Division. The other gentlemen are from the general's staff. As our commanding officer, I believe they would like to place themselves in your hands, sir. To be followed by a formal surrender to General Simonds.'

General d'Havet, who'd been watching with a most stern expression, must have been pleased by this introduction for his face broke into a broad smile.

Lieutenant Wiles's mouth fell open. 'Ah, yes,' he stuttered. 'It would be my pleasure, sir,' he said, addressing the general. He came to attention and saluted, much as Archie had done. Neither anti-tank gun, MG nest, nor occupied city had perturbed him, but Wiles was distinctly flummoxed at his capture of the first Axis general on European soil.

'It might be best to leave them their small arms, sir. On their honour,' whispered Archie in his ear. Wiles nodded agreeably.

Later, with the formalities complete, the lieutenant signalled the retreat. They climbed back up the hill, only to see one of Lieutenant Swan's Bren carriers growl into view. A hurried consultation took place. General d'Havet and the major were invited to climb aboard, and the carrier quickly disappeared in the direction of the road and the clearing where the regiment was waiting.

Wiles and the patrol resumed their march. No matter, thought Archie, after all the marching they'd done, what was another five kilometres?

Southeast of Caltanissetta, Sicily

First Lieutenant Weyers wiped his sweaty brow with a sweaty palm before once more settling his cap on his head. He would have preferred to have gone cap-less but he had an example to set. Against the blazing sun, it did at least serve some purpose. Though no sooner was the cap on his head when another trickle proceeded to race down his cheekbone. It was not unlike a *torrente,* he thought – an Italian word he'd learned recently, for the bone dry river beds that flooded in a flash. Then these thoughts were swept away as he caught sight of Captain Biedermann observing him from the dark shadows of a Mulberry tree.

'Lieutenant? A moment of your time.' Biedermann beckoned.

Weyers slowly shook his head as he approached. 'I'm not made for this heat, sir.'

'None us are,' replied Biedermann, with a laugh. 'It's a long way from Prussia. But we survived the desert, Manfred, so we'll survive this too, undoubtedly. The men are settled in all right?'

'Yes, sir. They're only too happy to be out of a truck. But some have asked what it is we're doing here.' It had been only two days since the enemy landings in the southernmost corner of the island, the peak of the upside-down triangle that was Sicily. In the early hours of that first day they had scrambled madly to prepare themselves; only to find the preparation for nought as they sat impatiently, every approaching motorcycle raising false expectations of orders that never came. The next day, when eventually they did, they proceeded not southward as expected, in the direction of Gela and Licata where the Americans were streaming ashore, but eastwards towards the island's centre. Weyers had studiously kept his surprise to himself, but inwardly he was confused.

Captain Biedermann shot him an appraising look. 'And you've been wondering that very thing as well, have you not?'

Weyers shrugged. His commanding officer had an uncanny ability to sense what he was thinking. 'Yes. Yes, I have, sir,' he admitted. 'The Americans are pushing inland very rapidly. And they say the British are already at Syracuse on the east coast. And yet...'

'And yet here we are far from the fighting at this critical time?'

Weyers nodded.

'Unfortunately, the battle for the beaches is over. Our allies have not put up much of a fight, but with or without them, the battle for Sicily is only just beginning. General Guzzoni has placed us in tactical reserve. We're to hold the flank of the Hermann Göring division as they fall back on our left. As you say, the enemy is heading inland. And when they do, the 15th Panzer Grenadier Division will be waiting. In fact, General Rodt has ordered that the battalion move several kilometres further south tomorrow to cover the road.'

'Cover the road?'

'Study your map, Lieutenant. There are only so many roads crossing this island and, if the enemy wishes to move northwards, as they certainly will, they will need to come by way of the no. 117. I'm hoping we may be able to give them an unpleasant surprise. What do you think?'

Weyers grinned. 'I think we should be able to come up with something, sir.'

'Good,' replied Biedermann. 'Now, see that you get a good night's rest. I expect at best we have only a couple of days. After that anything can happen.'

CHAPTER 7

12-13 July, 1943
Ragusa, Sicily

Reaching the battalion, the patrol learned that the Italian general and his adjutant were long gone, whisked off to the rear where Major-General Simonds awaited his division's most recent, and certainly most glamourous POW. The lieutenant reported to the captain, the captain reported to Lieutenant-Colonel Jefferson, and when the hurried "O-Group" was finished, the battalion was ordered to its feet. Archie was pleased he hadn't gone to the bother of sitting.

He saw a small force under the command of Lieutenant Snell from the mortar platoon assembling.

'Where are they going?' he asked Sergeant Evers.

'To keep order in town.'

'Say, I'd like to volunteer for that,' said Archie. He would go to his grave thinking of the kiss Ginevra had given him. What a beautiful name for a beautiful girl, he thought.

Evers chuckled. 'Fat chance, Atwell. If you're so anxious to volunteer for something, you can go with them.' He pointed at a column of Sherman tanks parked down the road. Archie recognized some fellows from "B" Company clambering up their steel sides. 'Never too late to prove yourself a soldier.'

'Where are they heading?'

'They're to liberate Scicli.'

'Say again?'

'On second thought, better you stay here where you don't need to read a map.'

It was then that Captain Tighe appeared, and stepped up onto the high ground of the road. "A" Company crowded round.

'We're to advance on Ragusa,' he announced. This name Archie did recognize from the map, but it was just one of many that meant nothing to him. He perked up however when he heard that it was ten miles further north. This last detail was greeted with a chorus of loud groans.

Someone, somewhere, though, had taken pity on the regiment. Maybe it was the thought of their transport rusting uselessly at the bottom of the Med, or sympathy at their bone weariness after much marching and little sleep. Alternatively, it may only have been impatience at some headquarters somewhere; to a man at a desk the pace of the march was never quite fast enough. Lieutenant-General Leese of XXX Corps to whose command they were assigned, had paid them a visit only yesterday. Why, no one knew. Tongues wagged knowingly, nonetheless. Now a squadron of tanks from the Three Rivers Regiment was rustled up for their use (Archie was not certain how many tanks constituted a squadron, but this seemed a goodly number), as well as a sufficient number of trucks to carry the rest.

The Shermans were racing forward. "C" Company and two platoons of "A" Company, Archie amongst them, clung to their sides like so many sea barnacles on a ship's hull. After a mile or two in the dust they bore some resemblance to them as well – coated white and gasping for air.

He tried to think of Ginevra and pleasant thoughts, but the circumstances conspired against him and all that came to mind was the war, and how he longed for fresh air. They'd had little contact with the enemy. All those they'd captured near the coast and at Ispica, and today again, hardly counted. In one respect this was a relief to the troops involved, but anxious minds at Eighth Army headquarters were determined to reel the actual enemy in – the Germans – before they could consolidate.

'Christ, it's hot as Hades,' breathed Archie.

No one replied. The man next to him was clutching to a ring on the turret as if his life depended on it, and Archie doubted whether he'd heard a word. If he had he might have remarked that Archie's comment wasn't entirely accurate; there was a wind of sorts, if only from their motion. Either way it sure beat the hell out of marching; route marches were the bane of his existence.

After three days in Sicily, the English variety were beginning to seem like a casual stroll in the countryside in comparison. Several men had fainted earlier that morning, and the sun wasn't near its brightest.

The narrow dirt road curved right, then sharply left, always climbing, climbing, following the contours of yellow hillsides dotted in speckles of green that one couldn't possibly imagine surviving the heat. And yet somehow they did. Every now and then the road passed precipitously along a narrow gulley, glimpses of a stony river bed far below. After the first such gulley Archie would look away, never having had much of a head for heights. As he liked to say, he preferred to look up the mountain than down it.

The spiralling dust from the column of Shermans was boiling into a gritty white fog. But it was not so unbearable that Archie wished he was propelling himself forward with his own two legs. His feet were mighty sore, and riding into battle on a Sherman tank was fine by him.

As they approached Ragusa, the incline of the road increased, the corners sharper, one switchback beginning where the last ended. The tank commander bellowed something down the hatchway, systematically surveying the hilltops to either side. Not that there was anything to see, not as far as Archie could tell. Even if there had been, the enemy would have surely spotted them first; it wasn't as if they were approaching by stealth.

Rounding a sharp bend, a vista of buildings appeared, covering the slope of the hill on the far side of a narrow valley. Archie held his breath. It was a perfect location for an anti-tank piece, or a machine gun. But there was no precipitous bang or zipping of bullets. Utterly fearless the Shermans barreled forward.

Still climbing the hill, the tanks growled their way through the screen of dust until five minutes later the road levelled off. The hillside across the valley to their right converged into theirs. They turned in that direction. Ahead, a street appeared, lined with buildings. It was early afternoon in Ragusa.

Archie heard gears grinding, motors protesting, a few peeps of the brakes from the trucks behind. The tank commander shouted down into the turret. The column slowed, then ground to a halt. Anxiously, Archie peered ahead, fearing the worst. Positioned near the front of the rounded turret he stood and laid a hand on the big gun to steady himself. He had an excellent view down the road, grey hovels lining it.

He crinkled his nose; Ragusa stank. Four tanks ahead he spotted a cluster of jeeps, and the form of a distinctive olive-coloured helmet worn by a soldier.

'Relax, boys,' he shouted over his shoulder, 'the Yanks have beaten us to it.'

Thus soothed about the nature of the halt, the boys sprang down and went forward to see what was to be seen in Ragusa.

At first sight that was not a great deal, apart from a few jeeps and some soldiers. But as the soldiers didn't include any Germans or Italians in their ranks, the mood was cheerful.

The tanks began creaking forward again, and Archie stepped to one side to let them pass. Then he eased along the buildings until he came to one of the Americans. On the opposite side of the road was an officer, but the appeal of the man before him was that he wore a single stripe on his arm. That would make him a private first class in the American Army. As Archie was also a private, and he certainly felt himself first class, that gave a certain bond.

He smiled at the man. 'Does every one of you fellows get his own jeep?'

The soldier looked at him, his face blank, obviously puzzled.

Given the number of American soldiers, and the approximately equal number of American jeeps, no explanation seemed necessary. Nevertheless, one came in the form of yet another jeep, with a driver and no other occupants. Squeezing past the tanks it puttered to a halt next to the others in a haze of dust that smelt distinctly of gasoline.

'Where's yours then?' asked the American private.

'Some bloody U-Boat sank it,' Archie replied. 'Then they sank the backup jeep, too. Since then, it's been strictly shoe leather in this army.'

At this the private lifted his head to gaze at the big Shermans rumbling past. When he looked back to Archie he laughed.

Archie shrugged. 'Well, with an occasional lift thrown in to break the monotony –' He extended his hand. 'Archie Atwell, 1st Canadians, Edmonton Regiment.'

The American shook it. 'Dan Polowski, 45th Thunderbirds.'

'Thunderbirds, eh? They just call us the "Eddies". You guys see any of the enemy, or did they all take to their heels when they heard who they were up against?'

'Wish it was so easy,' said Polowski with an easy grin. 'But, nah, it's been real quiet. On the radio I heard there was some trouble with a sniper.' He wiped his brow. 'Doggone, it's hot. There are times I'd trade this here jeep for one decent drink. You know what I mean?'

Archie nodded. Then an idea began to take root and he said: 'Yeah, sure. You know… I might even be able to help –'

Polowski frowned.

'With the drinks, that is.'

'Archie!' One of the section had his arm in the air, beckoning to him to return at the double. Sighing, Archie waved back.

'No rest for the wicked,' he said to Polowski. 'Maybe I'll see you again.'

'Find the Thunderbirds and I'll be there. Ciao, Archie.'

Archie would have liked to talk longer to the American. Instinctively he had the feeling that a big opportunity had fallen into his lap. It was the kind of opportunity his father would have greatly relished, even if he'd never especially relished the only son of his first wife. There was also the little matter of the war. Barring the obvious – that the Americans had penetrated as far inland as Ragusa – none of them knew anything about the US 7th Army's progress on the divisional left.

As it happened, the very next day, news about the war did arrive. It came under the auspices of a most unexpected messenger.

The battalion had retired to defensive positions in the yellow hills surrounding the old town. A welcome rest period was granted. 'None too bloody soon' was the heartfelt commentary of Battersby who, for once, successfully caught the prevailing mood.

In the three days prior, from the moment they'd waded ashore, the Edmonton Regiment had travelled some forty miles in the scorching heat, most of it on foot by way of bad roads. Even the strongest were near total exhaustion. As Archie pointed out to his section mates, this made it doubly fortunate that "D" Company was the one to get the morning call for a platoon to occupy Ragusa. The remainder of the battalion was left to laze under the shade of the gnarled olive trees dotting the countryside, to clean their rifles, their kit and themselves, and to chuckle about the fate of "D" Company.

Archie was ambling down the dusty, curving, dirt track from the regimental headquarters further up the hill. There had been great excitement when someone stumbled upon a well, hidden in the weeds behind the ramshackle huts that the colonel and staff were occupying. He was carrying a pail of the precious stuff now, filled to the brim, and therefore concentrating intently, watching his every step lest a drop be spilt.

Consequently, it was all too easy to ignore the sound of the straining engines. All morning trucks and jeeps had shuttled up and down that twisting road bringing equipment, or men, or both. Slowly but surely new transport for the regiment was arriving.

He could hear from the pitch of the motors that the drivers were shifting down to climb the incline, quite steep at this point. They were pushing their vehicles mercilessly. He risked a quick glance. They were nearly upon him, a trio of jeeps, with a dense cloud billowing up behind that tapered into a long stream that must surely have been visible halfway across the island. It was lucky for these lads there wasn't an Axis airplane in the skies. Regardless, they were driving far too fast for the terrain. But that was their business, concluded Archie. They'd discover soon enough the treacheries of Sicilian roads. If they were lucky it would be only a flat tire, or broken axle. Either that or the colonel would pop his head out of his hilltop hovel and coldly enquire who was disturbing his peace.

Archie stood well to one side and waited. His head was slightly bowed as a precaution against the cloud of dust that would soon envelop him. Then he froze as he saw a front tire of the lead jeep battle a rut and lose, the jeep lurching precipitously towards him. But just as he tensed to jump away, the driver corrected expertly, twisting the wheel to the right and stomping even harder on the gas pedal. The jeep bucked to the right and powered on.

Spinning rubber spat out a hail of gravel in his direction. A large piece caught Archie under the leg of his shorts, dead on the shin. He let out a yelp. Reflexively he stepped back, but then nearly twisted his ankle in the narrow ditch. The bucket sloshed to and fro, a wave of water washing over him.

'Christ Almighty!' he exploded, running a quick eye over his shirt and shorts, his shin stabbing painfully. 'Watch the hell where you're going, numbskull!' he roared after them, between gritted teeth.

He glanced down at the metal pail, now half empty, and let it drop it to the ground. Raising his arm in the air he angrily shook a clenched fist at the long-departed jeeps. 'Bloody imbeciles.'

The grin on Hainsley's face as he approached had a uniquely irksome quality to it.

'What are you laughing about? Did you see that? Who the hell do they think they are?'

'You really don't know?'

'If knew, I'd make it my business to find the nearest provost section and report them.'

'The military police? You can't be serious, Archie?'

'Damned right I'm serious.'

'You'd report General Bradley?'

Archie hesitated. 'General Bradley?'

'You know – American general, Commander of II Corps. Omar Bradley... surely you've heard of him? It may comfort you to know that those three stars on his pennant mean he's only a lieutenant-general. That may be relevant seeing as how you're going to report him to the provost section, and all.'

Archie stared up the hill towards the jeeps that had since come to rest in front of BHQ. 'Bradley, eh?' Sure enough, he could see a pennant flying from the hood of the first jeep, though it was anyone's guess at that distance what was on it. However, a welcome delegation was visibly assembled, waiting. That sealed the case. 'What's Bradley doing here?' he grumbled.

'Come to speak with Colonel Jefferson by the looks of it.'

'Hmm.'

'You're a Lucky Lindy, Archie, it was Bradley and not Patton that almost ran you down. They say General Patton carries a pearl-handled revolver. After the way you waved at the general, he might have been sorely tempted to use it.'

This witticism fell on deaf ears or, to be more precise, the small of Archie's back. Without a word of warning, Archie had turned and was walking resolutely up the hill.

'What the devil is he up to?' Hainsley muttered, shaking his head. 'I'll take the pail, shall I?' he shouted after him.

Archie himself had only the vaguest of ideas what he was up to, although at the sight of yet more American motorized transport, creaking cogs were shifting into motion.

One look at General Bradley's well-turned out jeep with its soft cushions, tidy as could be, and watched over by an equally well-turned out sergeant who eyed him warily as he approached, caused Archie to quickly veer off towards the two escort jeeps. He was pretty certain the sergeant was the very driver who'd almost run him down. Yet Hainsley had the three stars on the jeep's red pennant exactly right. Three stars together with the three stripes on the sergeant's creased sleeve, meant approaching him was a veritable minefield. The other two jeeps, however, were surrounded by less intimidating types. They stood lazing around, smoking cigarettes – idle even by Archie's undemanding standards.

'Hey fellas,' he said, sauntering up to the first two men, who were leaning against a jeep. Neither of them looked remotely like a general's escort, a suspicion confirmed by the fact that they greeted him friendly enough.

Archie grinned engagingly: 'Tough work escorting a general.'

'Beats a day job,' drawled one in response. This elicited a snort of amusement from his companion. The man was of medium build, plump, with curly short hair, a carbon copy of the well-endowed cook from "B" Company. 'So, this is Ragusa?' said the man, glancing at the colonel's little hut.

'Not exactly. The town begins at the bottom of the hill. If you have the chance you should take a look, presuming you don't mind the smell. The Eyeties aren't much into cleaning. In case you don't know, this here's the Edmonton Regiment. Arch…' He hesitated, a thought coming to him. 'Battersby's the name, Corporal Battersby. But you can call me Miles.'

'Fred Balanchuk,' said the man, a reply which put a gaping hole in the theory he was somehow related to "B" Company's Ecclestone. 'My sidekick,' and he motioned to the short, lean, olive-skinned man with dark eyes lurking beside him. We usually call him "Shifty", right Tommaso?'

The olive-skinned man rolled his eyes. Balanchuk went on: 'Tommaso Angelico is an awfully big mouthful. Besides, there's very little angelic about Tommaso.' At this Balanchuk chuckled good-naturedly at his mate.

Shifty's smile was a little sour in comparison. He'd likely heard this introduction several times too many. But the nickname fit.

Archie smiled amiably. Even if he hadn't been told the private's real name, the lad looked a good sight more Italian than most of the Italians he'd seen the last three days. Given his name there was a good possibility he might even speak the lingo. That would be useful. Thoughtfully, Archie rubbed at his chin.

'You boys must get around, being General Bradley's escort and all?'

'We're not exactly his escort,' said Shifty, 'We're in transport. And before you ask, those dog faces with the rifles over there aren't with us. But we drew the lucky card today, to drive the general and his muscle around. But, yeah, we've seen some things, haven't we Chuck?' Balanchuk nodded.

'So what's with the visit? Or is it hush-hush?'

Shifty shrugged. Balanchuk spoke up: 'You Canadians are on our right, so I guess the general wants to grease the wheels with your commander. We're tearing up the miles. Wouldn't want your mob getting in the way.' He winked.

'Tearing up the miles? But what about the German panzers then? We heard about the landing.'

'You mean the Herman Görings at Gela?'

Gela was the next bay up the coast from where the 1st Division had landed. Those had been the American beaches. Shifty smiled broadly, putting all his teeth into it this time.

'Nah,' said Balanchuk, 'They didn't get far after the navy got them in their sights. I'm not much for water, but I've gotta give those sailor boys credit. They smashed the panzers real quick. The Krauts retreated, and since then we've done nothing else but chase them like mad. There's no end to what everyone wants – in double time, preferably. For us in transport it's all we can do to keep up.'

'Well, be thankful that doesn't require marching,' mumbled Archie. 'Give me a truck any day.'

'March?' Balanchuk looked at Shifty, and Shifty looked at Balanchuk, and they both stared at Archie. Neither appeared familiar with the word. Seeing the profusion of motorized vehicles at their disposal, they probably weren't.

'Oh, it's an old-fashioned Canadian thing,' Archie said dismissively. 'But, say, are you fellows acquainted with the Thunderbird Division, the 45th? I ran into one of their guys yesterday here in Ragusa. Dan Polowski was his name. Perhaps you know him?'

'Powski you say? No, don't think so. It's a big army. But, sure, we know the Thunderbirds.'

'Yeah, that'd be one coincidence too many. Anyhow, I had a bit of a chat with this Polowski. He happened to mention that he and his buddies were dying of thirst.'

Balanchuk roared with laughter. 'The Thunderbirds are not the only ones dying of thirst in this place!' Even Shifty's face lit up. Archie could see the general's driver staring at them quizzically.

'So, what's the scam?' said Shifty softly.

Damn, the man was quick on the uptake. And for that very reason it was possible this American was precisely the man who could make it happen.

'Scam? Oh, no scam,' replied Archie, laughing. 'I was just thinking that a little inter-allied cooperation might go a long way to alleviate the problems of this island. Or at least one of them. Seeing as you fellows are in possession of most of the available trucks… not to mention a fair share of the thirsty mouths… it could be a lucrative endeavour for the US Transport Corps.'

Balanchuk appeared mystified at Archie's explanation. But Shifty came to the rescue: 'Is it good stuff?' he asked.

'Come on, this is Sicily.'

Shifty grinned knowingly. Balanchuk looked as if he'd missed the last hairpin in the road.

'Listen, it's like this…' began Archie, and he took Shifty to one side. Balanchuk kept his distance and didn't say another word. Archie suspected he'd seen his buddy do business before.

It was a simple enough story. Archie did most of the talking, with Shifty interrupting every now and again to ask a question. But finally he could see he'd hooked him. 'Sure,' Shifty said, he knew some guys who would be interested. The trucks would be no problem at all. They settled on 20/80, which seemed fair enough to Archie seeing as the Yanks had both the trucks and the customers, and all he had was a key. They sealed the deal with a handshake.

Then it was just talking for the sake of talking, a pleasant enough pastime under the trees, especially when set against the more serious alternatives.

'Stop the gabbing,' came a shout.

'What the devil's with him?' asked Archie, motioning at the sergeant. To make matters worse the man was now impatiently waving an arm.

'Stout? Ah, he's okay – for a sergeant. But it looks like we're heading out.'

Sure enough, Colonel Jefferson's front door was disgorging a stream of officers.

They watched as General Bradley shook the colonel's hand. Then he turned for his jeep, while the adjutant and the other officers watched.

'Alright, give me a couple of days to get it organized. Make it four,' said Shifty in one ear. 'You just make sure you're there, Miles. Coast road near the Bark West beaches? 0900?'

'That's it. I'll be waiting,' said Archie. 'Key to the kingdom and all. Make sure you bring a good few trucks. You're gonna need them.'

Balanchuk slid behind the wheel of the jeep, and Shifty made for the second. The dog faces piled dutifully into the back.

Archie stood and watched as the three jeeps cut a tight circle then shot into column and headed back down the road at speed, precisely as they'd come. Clouds of dirt billowed high. He stood at attention while the dust clogged his nostrils and the gravel shot by, snapping a sharp salute when Bradley's jeep passed. He was rewarded by the sight of a bespectacled lieutenant-general touching his brow in response. Balanchuk and Shifty waved as they raced in pursuit.

Archie felt good. The pieces were falling into place. This might yet be his big coup, the chance he'd been looking for to earn some real money, and a little respect from his father. Even he, with all his fanciful tales about running whiskey across the American border in the '20s, could hardly fail to be impressed. On second thought, it was probably wise to leave him in the dark; otherwise he'd be looking for a cut. His second wife was proving expensive.

The brief moment of exultation soon passed.

How on earth was he going to travel from Ragusa to the coast and back? Worse, how was he going to do it without anyone in the battalion noticing? The plan, which had come to him in a flash, was already showing gaping holes. Then a picture of Matt Evers's good-natured features, twisted in disappointment, settled into his head. His good mood evaporated.

And that was before Battersby brought the news he was to spend the evening polishing boots. Given the state of the boots in the regiment the order was presumably meant figuratively. No amount of polish could truly salvage them. Still, it meant more work; apparently another Very Important Person was scheduled to arrive in the morning. 'You'd think we had enough to do fighting a war,' Archie muttered to Hainsley. 'Seems we have to entertain the high and mighty as well.'

CHAPTER 8

14 July, 1943
Ragusa, Sicily

The battalion was gathered in all its finery, a fine word for what was a slightly cleaner, otherwise indistinguishable version of what the men wore every day since wading ashore into Hitler's fortress Europe. Much of their extra kit, including fresh pairs of socks, had sunk with the trucks which were to carry it. They were standing in ordered ranks in Ragusa's station yard, in what was reputedly the new town. The place was a dump.

At 1000 hours, two staff cars rolled slowly into the yard, the first a large open-top job that all knew must contain the celebrated man himself. Indeed, as the car eased to a stop in front of Lieutenant-Colonel Jefferson, Archie spotted Lieutenant-General Montgomery pulling himself to his feet. As all eyes watched, he spoke briefly with the colonel. Then to cheers he clambered up to stand precariously on the very seat he'd previously been sitting on. He motioned to the men that they should gather round, which they did.

'Shit, he's a short Limey,' said someone, as the ranks dissolved, the men pressing forward to surround the General's car.

'Not much of a dresser either,' laughed another.

'Shhh,' hissed a third, reflecting the sentiments of the majority.

Montgomery was short indeed, but wiry, and he wore the sagging black beret, several sizes too large, for which he was famous. Famous too was his Eighth Army, of which the 1st Division and its appendage, the Edmonton Regiment, were now a proud part. Since they had heard that their fate was linked with that legendary formation every man in the division had burst with pride. The Eighth Army was not simply an army, it was the army that had repelled Rommel at El Alamein and turned the tide in North Africa. This was a state of affairs far grander than any had dared hope for when the topic of their future employment had arisen, as it had so often.

Monty stared down at them with a gimlet eye, perched ungainly in the staff car, one foot resting a little clumsily on the seat in front. To Archie he had something of the awkward bookworm addressing a crowd of sportsmen. Yet his sheer self-confidence was so overwhelming that this impression waned quickly. The men were squeezed together into a mass so as not to miss a single word. The general began to speak.

'You Canadians were under my command in England,' he began. 'And I am very glad to have you back with me again.' A murmur of approval passed over the crowd. 'Where are you from?' he asked, although surely he must have known the details exactly.

'Edmonton!' came the shouted reply.

'Edmonton...' A theatrical pause. 'I seem to recall a regiment of mine stationed in an old brewery in England that came from Edmonton.' It was true of course they had been under his command years before, though for most of them it hadn't left much of an impression – in contrast to the brewery. Archie could remember that quite distinctly. 'Would that be you?' asked the general.

'Yes,' came the roar.

Then, *sotto voce*: 'I suppose you'd like a beer?'

'Hell, yes!' shouted Archie. It was fortunate his words were drowned out by those of several hundred others. This time the roar reverberated round the station yard, before echoing back.

Monty paused. A half smile appeared on his lips. 'In due time...' he said quietly, '... in due time.'

He spoke for several minutes more. About how delighted he was to have them in 'his' army. How confident he was that they would uphold the reputation of the Eighth Army. But by that time no one was listening so much to what he had to say, as to how he said it. Short, clipped sentences. A casual tone spoken quietly, but brimming over with vigour and a great deal of confidence. The men cheered rambunctiously when Monty eventually waved, dropped back into his seat and swatted his swagger stick at them as the small motorcade turned and left. The cloud of white dust slowly settled over the cheering battalion.

'So, who's up for storming Mount Etna,' said Archie when the cars were gone. He was speaking to no one in particular. But there were nods and a few exuberant grins from his section mates. Monty's little talk had been a tonic for everyone.

'I'll put you down as the lead man in the next charge, shall I, Archie?' said Sergeant Evers.

Archie twisted round, an uneasy smile on his face. He'd meant it as a joke, and Evers knew that. But you never could be entirely sure with Matt. Since becoming a sergeant he'd turned terribly serious – precisely the reason Archie had no desire to assume the responsibilities associated with being an NCO himself. As his father liked to say, he had plenty enough on his plate just looking out for himself. And while a little bravado in the wet canteen on the ship, or back in England, had seemed harmless, he was beginning to realize it might not be in the middle of enemy territory where "volunteers" were required at a moment's notice. He hoped he hadn't laid it on too thick these past weeks.

Shortly after, his interest was piqued when he passed Captain Tighe in conversation with the lieutenant. He halted and made a show of fumbling in his pocket so that he might hear more.

It appeared that some in Ragusa were less charmed by the presence of the regiment than General Montgomery had been. Tighe was explaining to Wiles that there were reports of several rifle shots in town. The population was said to be restive. 'They might have thought to tell us before. Seems Ragusa is the headquarters of the Fascist Party in the south.' He sighed. 'Heaven knows how many buggers are running around in civvies with a firearm concealed.' Tighe told Wiles to be prepared in case they were needed. Archie hurried onwards, keeping his head down.

The thought of patrolling Ragusa's narrow streets with a target painted on his chest for one of Mussolini's thugs was distinctly unappealing. It was with a measure of relief therefore, when, at noon, not a single platoon but all of "D" Company was ordered into town to keep order. After dinner there was a new development.

A sergeant from "C" Company came upon him and another man dozing away the languorous, cooler hours of early evening in the shadow of an olive tree. Somehow the one brother in arms had lain down curled up against the other with the same idea. While the days in Sicily were scorchers, the nights in the hills had a distinct chill to them.

The sergeant put an end to this cozy state of affairs with a prod from his boot. Feeling it in his ribs, Archie grunted loudly and bolted upright. The other man was not so easily disturbed.

Archie's initial indignation subsided when he saw who it was. 'You scared the daylights out of me, Sarge,' he mumbled.

'Good. Get yourself together, Atwell. The battalion's to assemble. Who's the no-good clod lying beside you?'

The 'no-good clod' hadn't moved an inch, despite the sergeant's less than subtle encouragement. Whoever he was he had veritable steel for nerves, thought Archie, with a real sense of admiration. He shrugged. 'Don't know.'

Curious he gazed down at the man. The sun was setting and in the dark shade of the tree it was impossible to make out details, let alone the fellow's face, which was buried in the grass. There was something oddly out of place though about the cut of his uniform, even if he couldn't quite put a finger on it.

The sergeant was growing tired of waiting, patience never a strong suit of those with a third stripe. The sergeant drew back his foot and let fly. 'Jeez, Sarge, isn't that a bit harsh,' protested Archie.

But a toe of hard leather driven into the sleeping man's side wasn't about to roust this doughty fellow. 'Good for nothing,' muttered the sergeant. He squatted down, and bent over to grab the man's shoulder. Then, as if bitten by a wasp, he recoiled and got to his feet.

'Jesus Murphy, Atwell! Did you know you've been sleeping with a dead Jerry?'

Slowly Archie blinked. He stared down at the man with fresh eyes. 'Dead you say, Sarge? No wonder he was so damned stiff.'

The sergeant just stared at him. Then he shook his head in disbelief, although it may also have been disgust, and cleared out. Which was fine by Archie.

This left him to ponder how it was that a dead German had ended up at this spot, under *his* olive tree. Barring a sudden heart attack, either Polowski's U.S. Thunderbirds or the Royal Canadian Regiment had done him in. Both had laid claim to capturing some part of Ragusa. Unfortunately, despite claiming victory neither unit actually succeeded in clearing the town, leaving the Eddies to tidy house. Was this sudden muster a sign the job was proving more difficult than expected?

Upon reaching the platoon no one knew anything. He was astonished to see half the battalion milling about in general confusion, all the company OCs and seconds-in-command last seen heading in the direction of the colonel's hilltop hovel. In their absence the platoon commanders were as puzzled as the men as to what they should do.

However, rather quickly he spotted Captain Tighe, Major Bury and the others, coming down the hill at a fast trot towards them. The platoon commanders bustled forward. After which the NCOs had their turn. Suitably informed they rushed to instruct their platoons. Then, before you could count to ten, most of the battalion was hurrying to and fro. To what end was not entirely clear, but it was a perfect example of the army chain of command in action.

He turned to Dinesen, who'd appeared out of nowhere, and came and stood beside him. 'Hey, what's with the headless chicken act, Harry?'

Dinesen smiled knowingly. Lieutenant Wiles and their own Sergeant Evers were still missing in action somewhere in the melee, Battersby was clueless – which was par for the course – but Dinesen knew. He'd just spoken with Sergeant Craven of 7 Platoon. 'We're going up against a crack German division.'

Archie gulped.

'They've been spotted in Chiaramonte. They're sending us forward tonight,' he said excitedly.

'Where on this God forsaken island is Chia…monte, or whatever it's called?'

'Chiaramonte. It's twelve miles north of here.'

'Oh, no, not more marching. As if we haven't done enough already

–.' Mentally he was adding up the extra miles, trying to calculate how far it would be to the coast. His math skills were leaving him in the lurch, but even a dimwit like Lachance could figure that marching was out of the question. Unless he was able to commandeer a rare jeep or a carrier, it was a forlorn mission. Somehow, he was going to have to contact the swarthy American driver; he and his buddies were expecting him to display the wares in less than two days. Maybe they could arrange a lift for him. On the other hand, if Dinesen was to be believed, he had bigger worries ahead.

'Ah relax, Archie. They've found some transport for us,' replied Dinesen. 'The PPCLI and the Seaforths are lending us theirs. Finally, we're going into the fight. This is the real thing, Archie.' There was a dangerous gleam to his eyes.

Archie sighed, of two minds about this development. Naturally after Monty's little speech he was as keen as the next man to get into action. But against a 'crack' German division?

Before long the battalion was embussed in a collection of tanks, trucks and carriers. Archie and half the platoon found themselves in a truck immediately behind one of the Shermans. A beautiful summer day was ending as they began to move. They were just entering the outskirts of Ragusa, and would need to pass through the town before picking up the narrow, gravelled road that would take them north to Chiaramonte. Suddenly the column ground to a halt. The men, who'd been chatting excitedly, glanced around in puzzlement; they were barely underway.

'I sure hope the PPCLI and the Seaforths haven't asked for their transport back,' grunted Archie. Three voices spoke at once, each vying to reply.

'Hang on, guys,' said young Postlethwaite, the urgency in his tone cutting through the small talk. He was standing, looking over the cab and down the road, where the tanks of the Three Rivers Regiment were lined up one after another. 'That was a rifle shot!' Like that it went very silent in the open-top 30-CWT truck.

There was a crackle of small arms fire. This time they all heard it. Down the road someone cried out, and there were shouts. Then several rifles opened up. A machine gun stuttered. Archie stood and pushed his way forward to Postlethwaite, joined by Sergeant Evers.

'It's "C" Company,' said Postlethwaite, both fists firmly gripping a steel bar that ran the width of the cab. 'Someone is shooting at them.'

Archie could see men now, sliding off the tanks, and running for the shelter of the buildings lining the road. 'Damn,' he heard Evers mutter, 'snipers.'

'Fascist snipers,' said Archie. Evers snapped a look at him. 'Ragusa's their southern headquarters,' he murmured. But the sergeant was already turning towards the men behind.

'Dismount,' he shouted, and they piled off the truck. 'Watch out for the upper windows!'

A loud *BOOM* sounded from ahead, echoing off the buildings.

'That was a tank cannon,' someone whispered. Every ear was cocked, rifles held tightly. The gunfire had given way to a tense silence. They could see the tank ahead, and the one ahead of that, but apart from the men from Charlie who were standing much as they were, they could determine little else.

Archie had his rifle in his hands and was warily eying the windows and roofs close by. In the lee of the buildings opposite most were already cloaked in an impenetrable grey shadow. Nothing seemed to be moving.

They stood there uneasily, seeing little, hearing little, shuffling from foot to foot and wondering what was taking place. Finally a soldier in front turned to face them, and waved his arm slowly back and forth in the air. 'All clear,' he shouted. 'Pass the word.'

'You heard the man,' said Evers. 'Back in the truck.' They climbed aboard.

There in the back of the 1-½ tonne Chevrolet they sat on the hard wooden benches, pressed shoulder to shoulder, glancing awkwardly about as the light waned, readying themselves for whatever might come next. A pitter-patter of hurried footsteps sounded beside them, and Captain Tighe rushed past, heading down the street towards the vanguard of the column.

'Tighe's in a helluva rush,' said Archie, his words casual, masking the tension he felt as well.

'*Captain* Tighe has a lot of responsibility on his shoulders,' snapped Sergeant Evers. 'Not that you'd know anything about that, Archie.'

At this Archie's eyebrows rose. He hadn't done anything wrong

– not that he was aware of. Certainly not recently. He could see Miles Battersby grinning wickedly at Lachance.

Lieutenant Wiles arrived, and climbed up onto the tailgate. 'They're calling up the Hasty Ps to police the town. Sit tight,' he said.

This left the platoon to do as they were told while speculating on the whereabouts of "D" Company whose task it had been to clear Ragusa. 'Once again the proof is in the pudding why "A" Company is known as Able, and "D" as Dog,' opined Archie.

The decision to reinforce led to another interminable wait, and much muttering. 'I'm beginning to wonder if they called up the right regiment,' grumbled Archie, after a length. Young Postlethwaite looked blankly at him. 'They're hardly *hasty* are they now?' It wasn't exactly uproarious humour, but it helped pass the time. There were a few who grinned.

Finally, officers began shouting, and with a grumbling roar the vehicles restarted their engines, the air soon reeking of fumes. The battalion's first casualties of the war – three dead and four wounded – went largely unremarked at the time; the men were too keyed up, uninterested in sideshows. They rumbled off, into the night, towards the real thing.

CHAPTER 9

Night of 14-15 July, 1943
Chiaramonte and Licodia Eubea, Sicily

The column turned northwards, a heading that with every mile took them closer to the island's mountainous backbone.

Atop the line of hills to the west the final, soft tendrils of sunlight glowed, darkness already tucking itself down into the deep valleys between. Those facing in that direction stared as the last vestiges of light faded. The other half of the truck stared at the men opposite. The heady feeling they'd had setting forth was long gone. Conversation had died out. Archie, not generally one to shy from a little chit-chat, felt little compunction to break the silence. He was still thinking about what Matt Evers had said to him about knowing nothing of responsibility.

Once they'd been equals, he and Matt, both newly enlisted and generally ignorant of things soldierly. If anything, Archie had a foot up on Evers as he could handle a rifle with aplomb, having been out hunting ever since he could remember. But their paths parted years ago. He liked Evers, though he couldn't help thinking Evers resented him for his carefree ways. Of course, Matt had only himself to blame for that. He was the one who had done everything by the book. And what did he have to show for it? Three hooks on his sleeve and a head full of worry. No, he wasn't going to make that same mistake, thought

Archie dismissively. But then he found himself staring at him: calm, dependable, Evers's very presence a comfort to the men.

The column poured through the night, the truck bumping along, the occasional sharp bend catching a few unawares. Those who were sleeping, momentarily startled awake, only to fall back into a slumber as the rhythmic motion resumed.

Approaching Chiaramonte the men who were still awake sensed something was happening from the way the truck slowed to a crawl as it fought its way up the steep road. Excitedly they elbowed their neighbours, and Archie got a sharp one in the gut.

Lachance was looking his way, wearing a cheeky grin. No doubt he'd been the instigator, if not the actual perpetrator. Archie ignored him. Last Chance was almost always best ignored.

Pressed together like sardines in a tin, toes and knees bumping up against those opposite, the men of the section were on edge, a palpable electricity in the night air. Was this to be it?

There was a brief squeal of brakes, and the truck shuddered to a stop.

Still a little dozy, Archie clasped his rifle and rose to his feet. 'Alright, boys, here we go.' He put a foot over the side, found some footing near the wheel well of the truck, and jumped down. A half dozen others followed his example, deaf to the increasingly voluble protests of Sergeant Evers.

'Where the blazes do you think you're going?' demanded a voice Archie vaguely recognized.

The man stood in front of him. 'Evening, sir,' he said hurriedly. 'I just thought…' he began.

'You're not paid to think, Atwell,' said Lieutenant Wiles, a little sourly.

'Sir, what about the Jerries?' one of the men crowding behind asked.

'Yeah, what about the attack, sir?' asked another.

Wiles sighed. 'If the Germans were here, they're not anymore. "C" Company couldn't find any sign of them.'

Archie led the chorus of groans. They'd been training at it for years, travelled halfway round the world to seek it out, and marched more miles in a few days than in half a lifetime; but still the battle was denied them.

'Never fear,' said the lieutenant. 'We're to push on to Licodia. It's very likely they'll be there.' He turned his head from left to right, perusing the assembled men, visibly in search of something. He found it in the person of Sergeant Evers. 'Sergeant,' he said, 'unless you and the section are intent on marching, I suggest you make use of the transport available.'

Evers tensed. 'Yes, sir,' he replied. To the men: 'All aboard,' he shouted.

Without a word, the young, otherwise so amicable lieutenant walked on toward the next vehicle.

'Lieutenant's a little short on sleep,' joked Archie over his shoulder. Then he noticed Evers.

Evers had an exasperated look to him. 'Let's go!' he said.

Rather than waiting with those lined up at the tailgate, Archie scrambled up onto the rear wheel and pulled himself over the side. When facing adversity Archie's father had a firm belief: 'Avoid it, at all cost.'

Archie crashed down onto Corporal Battersby, who'd seemingly taken it upon himself to look after the rear echelon. Roughly Battersby shoved him aside. 'Find your own bloody seat, Atwell. The last thing I want is you on my lap.'

The truck lurched into gear. For a long time it was quiet save for the rattle of the trucks, the grumble of the carriers, and a soft rustling of the wind. Then he felt the lad fidget in the seat beside him.

'Where do you suppose they are?' Postlethwaite asked.

Archie frowned. 'Who?'

'The Jerries, of course.'

'Don't you worry about them Steven. We'll be seeing the Jerries soon enough.' Archie laid an arm around his shoulder. He was a good kid. 'Get some sleep. When we do catch them, you'll be needing it,' he said gruffly.

At the back of the truck, in the corner, Sergeant Evers was watching.

All night the truck bumped forward, periodically shuddering in protest at some manoeuvre of the driver, or vagary of the road. The convoy snaked its way through twisting curves and switchbacks, climbing, descending, before climbing again, always following the narrow, dirt road that in present day Sicily did service as a "highway".

As dawn broke, Archie felt anything but rested. Past 0800 hours, a new morning and a new day had long begun. The column halted.

Upon ascertaining there was no immediate danger, the men of the section sprang gratefully to the ground. There they began to brush away the night's accumulated grime, the endless dust from the vehicles in front that had billowed into the air and settled upon them.

The men were relieved to stretch their legs. They stood beside the road, wolfing down their tasteless breakfasts, washed down with some weak tea, strangely cheerful. Even the news, quickly passed from man to man, that the Americans had taken Licodia a full day and a half earlier didn't come as the disappointment it might otherwise have.

To the west, the Americans were thrusting forward with great speed. To the east, on the far flank of the Eighth Army, along the coast, the 51st Highlanders were fighting for the port city of Syracuse. And transport problems or not, the 1st Division was expected to keep pace in the middle.

After a short rest the battalion embussed once more. The mile-long column motored slowly through Licodia – accurately described as a 'stinking hole' by Harry Dinesen – to the high ground north of the village, and an encounter with the regiment that had beaten them to it.

The soldier walking towards Archie was definitely an American. For one thing he wasn't in short sleeves, for a second he didn't wear shorts, and for a third the green steel-pot helmet was unmistakable. Even if one happened to be colour blind, it was impossible to confuse the particular olive green favoured by the Yanks with their own light khaki. Archie puzzled however at the man's advanced age; most of the Americans he'd met were younger than he was himself. This fellow had years on Colonel Jefferson even, and some whispered the CO was only a couple of years shy of forty. Then he recognized the white cross on the helmet, which explained all.

The sight of the cross set him thinking. It was precisely the sort of detail one might call a sign if you were of a superstitious bent. A white cross was what they buried you under. And perhaps it *was* a sign. Perhaps his days *were* numbered. He shook his head. *Nah*. He wasn't superstitious. Besides, as his buddy Mac DuBois always liked to say, you can never predict when you're going to get it. And Mac's pa had been in the last war, so surely he would know.

The chaplain was a couple feet away, nearly abreast of him. Unsure whether he should nod or salute, he crossed himself instead, and tried to look suitably demure. Archie was no Catholic, and anything but demure, but it seemed appropriate. The chaplain nodded in return and raised a friendly hand in greeting.

Archie grinned back. 'Hi, Father.'

The chaplain had no sooner passed than someone off his right flank called out his name. 'I thought it must be you. If I didn't know better, I'd think you were following me.'

Archie whipped round. The soldier was a few steps behind, helmet pushed back at an unsoldierly angle, hands parked casually on the hips. He was wearing a sloppy grin. Archie recognized him instantly.

'Following you? Hardly.' Archie laughed, extending a hand. 'Following orders more like. I should have known it was your crowd that snatched Licodia; the mighty Thunderbirds… the division of the endless jeeps.'

Private Dan Polowski bowed. 'At your service. Liberators of Licodia Eubea, the 157th Regiment, 45th Thunderbird Division. Colonel Charles Ankhorn in command. Welcome straggler.' Then he nodded his head in the direction of where the chaplain had disappeared. 'I saw you making friends with Father Barry. He's a good man.'

'Barry, eh. I was wondering who actually captured Licodia. You were in Ragusa at the time, weren't you, Dan? Don't tell me; the good Father put the fear of the Lord into the Jerries and you roared up in a jeep when they had their hands in the air?'

Polowski turned grim. 'Consider yourself lucky you missed the experience, Archie. We lost sixty guys, dead or wounded, taking this shit hole.'

Archie winced. 'Sorry.'

'One of our half-tracks was roasted by some dick with a flamethrower who thought he'd be smart and play possum in a tank wreck.' He shook his head. 'All fair in war, I guess. But it was pretty bad. A lot of us can't wait till we meet those Hermann Göring bastards again.' The threat was left unspoken. Then again, words couldn't have matched the message in his eyes. Archie nodded. He wondered if he would ever feel that way about the Germans. All his many musings about the war suddenly seemed a little trite.

'Hey, Dan, do you have a moment? It's lucky I ran into you. There's something I've been wanting to ask.'

The two soldiers shuffled off, heads down, hands deep in their pockets. The conversation became more animated.

'So,' concluded Polowski, with an easy-going charm. 'You've got the goods. The boys from the US Transport Corps have got the trucks. And God knows I've got the thirst. Only you're sixty miles from the coast, with no transport, and stuck in the middle of a war. So you want me to pass the message back to some shady character you just met that you need to reschedule. Does that about sum it up, Archie?'

Archie nodded. 'You don't sugar coat it, do you?'

'I don't know how it is in your army, but in this army they'd probably shoot me if I went chasing off without permission for a day or two – especially if they knew I was chasing after what *you're* chasing after.'

'Don't think my army's much different,' said Archie glumly. 'That's the problem, you see. And in my case there's a list the length of your arm of eager volunteers prepared and willing to do the shooting too. I wouldn't have asked otherwise, but I don't see much choice.'

'So it's probably just as well,' replied Polowski, grinning. 'Look, I know a guy who knows a guy in signals. I'll give it a try, Archie. I can't promise anything, but I'll do my best. What's his name?'

'Angelico. Private Tommaso Angelico.'

Polowski frowned. 'You sure he's not with the mob?'

'Mob?'

'Mob, mafia, call 'em what you like. Lucky Luciano ring any bells?'

Blankly Archie stared at him.

'Man, you Canucks are something else. I didn't think such naivety was possible. Don't you know that half the gangsters in America are from Sicily? I'm beginning to think you just signed up to go into business with them. If I was you Archie, forget about your pal Tommaso. Forget about the whole thing, and keep your head down. You don't want to get mixed up in a racket with some Mafiosi. Trust me.'

'No?'

'No. Listen, I would have loved a few of those bottles, but I'm going to forget I ever heard anything about this, and I advise you to do the same. The Krauts are bad enough, Archie. You don't want to get on the wrong side of some crazy Wops. Don't forget, this is their island.'

CHAPTER 10

15-16 July, 1943
Licodia Eubea and Caltagirone, Sicily

The battalion was dug into a defensive position in the hills north of Licodia Eubea, not far from Polowski's 157th Regiment.

The American Seventh Army was on the Edmonton left, the British Eighth Army on their right, and the Eddies found themselves as the vital hinge between the two. 'It's down to us Canadians to supply the grease and keep the peace, it would seem,' commented Dan King. This colourful description probably came to mind as the third man of the section's gunners was up to his elbows in the stuff cleaning his Bren.

Nor was Archie convinced their role could be described as an especially peaceful one. The elements of two German divisions that were rumoured to be arrayed in front were unlikely to let them pass with a mere smile and a wave. Nevertheless, he too had heard the rumours about tension between the Yanks and the Limeys in the Allied high command. Not being in the high command, the Canadian role was limited to following whatever orders the other two came up with. It was not entirely dissimilar to being a private, as he explained to King. While this division of responsibility may have bothered some, it didn't bother Archie – his immediate concern was closer to hand. He'd been assigned sentry duty.

'Ah, come on, Sarge,' he had pleaded with Evers. But to no avail. Evers was resolute.

An hour of his stint had passed when the sergeant turned up out of the blue – or rather out of the pitch dark – and caught him gazing up at a sparkling pasture of stars.

'The night shift, Sarge?' he began, seizing this new opportunity to turn his fortunes around.

'Look at it this way, you can't very well gaze at the stars during the daytime, can you?'

'I'll be useless tomorrow.'

'Nothing new about that,' replied Evers. 'Buckle up, Archie, and stop the grouching. If the Jerries do appear, let someone know will you? Relief's in three hours.' Without a second glance, and thereby neatly avoiding the chance for a rebuttal, Sergeant Evers disappeared into the gloom.

Close by, cloaked by the darkness and a wizened old tree, Evers came upon Captain Tighe. The two talked briefly. When they were done Tighe sighed.

As the hours passed, Archie kept himself awake in the time-honoured tradition of sentries everywhere. He would walk a few paces in one direction, then turn on a dime and walk back the very way he'd come, all the while trying to match his earlier footsteps – for the sport. It was in one of these turns that he spotted a body of men approaching far down the road. They were soldiers, there was no doubt of that. At the sight of them his drowsiness evaporated. He suddenly recalled what Evers had said about the regiment standing in the front line.

He squinted, concentrating intensely. And soon he recognized the group for what it was. When they were within hailing distance, he cleared his throat and stepped into the middle of the road, his rifle held before him. In his firmest and deepest tone he called out: 'WHO GOES THERE?'

'Who the hell do you think it is?' came a reply from the ranks. 'The tooth fairy and entourage?'

This response wasn't entirely unexpected. They were marching in ordered double file. If that wasn't enough, Evers had even mentioned the possibility. And now he could see them plainly.

A second, deeper voice growled: 'Stand aside, soldier, the Hastings and Prince Edward Regiment is passing through.'

'Ah, the Hasty P's,' said Archie. 'I wondered when you fellows would finally turn up.' But he took the advice proffered. They wouldn't hesitate to overrun him given half a chance, if only to do their nickname proud. 'Hey, you gave the Jerries hell at Grammichele!'

'Is that you, Atwell?' asked the deep voice. Then, slightly louder: 'It's Archie from the Eddies, boys.'

'Hi Archie,' said a couple of the men as they brushed past. He greeted those he knew, and many whom he didn't. The group was in high spirits. It had been a tight scrap in the little village, but they had come out on top in the division's first real engagement. The faces were tired but bright.

Not long after, Archie's sentry duty came to an abrupt end; the regiment was to move north to the state highway no. 124 and follow it to Caltagirone.

It was the next town along the highway from the hilltop citadel of Grammichele. This made it a logical place for the withdrawing Germans to regroup, especially as it was also the headquarters of the Hermann Göring Division.

'What's going on?' he asked, when his relief arrived with the news.

'Jerries have been spotted,' said the man, 'lots and lots of Jerries.'

'But 1st Brigade is already heading that way,' protested Archie. 'A bunch of them just passed here.'

'Don't ask me. All I know is that those are the orders. Word is we're to attack. The battalion's already mustered, and the CO and Brigadier Vokes have gone ahead to recce.'

'You don't say,' Archie replied. Perhaps this would be it, their first clash with the Germans. He hoped they would have some transport. While on the map Caltagirone looked deceptively close, if Sicily had taught him anything it was that distances were deceiving. What was an easy mile on paper all too soon became an exhausting three in practice. Compared to that sentry duty wasn't half bad.

Unfortunately, as they fell into file, there wasn't a vehicle to be seen.

That the march was not to be treated cavalierly was soon apparent.

The steady slog uphill for some fifteen miles took the better part of the night. A little past dawn a weary battalion arrived at the forming-up area southeast of Caltagirone.

The nervous excitement Archie had felt at the thought of the attack had long since given way to other emotions. 'Christ, my feet are killing me,' he muttered as he came and stood beside Hainsley. 'And I'm starving.'

'Here,' said Hainsley. Brusquely he thrust an orange into Archie's hand.

'What's this?'

He smiled. 'Breakfast.'

Archie began to peel. Then over Hainsley's shoulder, across the plain to the northeast, he saw something else and whistled. Illuminated by the rising sun, a massive mound lay on the horizon like a dark cloud. But from its pyramidal form it was clear that it was no cloud. 'That can't be,' he said.

Hainsley turned and followed his gaze, squinting into the sun. 'Oh, but it is. That's the famous Mount Etna, alright.'

'That has to be fifty miles away.'

'If not more,' agreed Hainsley.

The two of them stood for a moment in the brilliant morning sunshine, unspeaking, staring at the mighty volcano known as Etna. Their eyes wandered to the broad valley floor below. Not far from this vantage point, certainly less than a mile distant, the wrecks of two German tanks smouldered on the acrid yellow plain, wisps of dark smoke staining a picture perfect sky. If a reminder was needed, the war was close at hand.

Archie brought the orange to his lips and took a bite. 'Hey, that's tasty, Tom,' he said. 'Thanks.'

'Only good thing about this island,' opined Hainsley, 'the fruit. Enjoy it. Oh, and about the attack –'

Archie stopped chewing.

'It's cancelled. Seems 1st Brigade has already cleaned house in Caltagirone.'

The enemy had decamped, leaving only the remains of their tanks to tell the tale of the sharp rearguard action hours before.

In the absence of the enemy, or fresh orders, the Edmontons were left momentarily to their own devices. Archie decided to take advantage of the lull to wander up the road in the direction of town. Not that he was especially interested in seeing the sights, rather he was in search of an olive grove, though a single tree would suffice, under which he might lie down. He was tired and sore, and every bone in his body was reminding him of the night's exertions. Rounding a bend, the town appeared before him.

Caltagirone covered the high plateau ahead, and at the sight he halted. Between the bombers flying out of North Africa, and the retreating Germans, the place was a ruin, fires still burning, rubble crowding the streets. Sergeant Evers stood in the middle of the road several feet ahead, staring as he was. He went to him.

'What a mess,' said Archie, whistling. 'Glad I don't have to clean up.'

Evers turned, and nodded. 'True. But someone had better get at it. And quickly, too. Otherwise we won't be going anywhere.'

A thought came to him. 'Hey, listen, Sarge. Seeing as we're not in any battles or anything like that, I wondered if you might put in a good word for me with the Lieutenant? I was hoping for a couple of days leave.' Polowski's warning about the mafia was pretty far-fetched and, even with a day or two, he could probably salvage the whole venture. Then there was Ginevra as well.

'Leave!? We're in the middle of the biggest invasion of the war, and Private Archie Atwell would like a little rest and relaxation? Are you nuts!?'

There was a long silence.

'Does that mean you'll think about it?'

Threateningly, Evers raised an arm. 'Take a hike, Atwell, before I find something hard and sharp to beat you with.'

For some reason Archie kept walking. He came upon a bulldozer from the divisional engineers filling a massive crater in the centre of the road that effectively blocked it. A little further along, a second bulldozer could be seen clearing a path through the rubble of the town proper, a platoon of Italian prisoners helping. With the road out of action, the regiment was going nowhere.

He yelled up to the man in the dozer: 'What happened?'

The man stared at him, then cupped a hand behind one ear. Archie tried again, but to no avail. The man took his foot from the pedal and the roaring of the motor subsided. Archie pointed at the crater and questioned with his arms.

'Jerry engineers,' shouted the man. 'They've blown every road into and out of this place. Mined and booby-trapped some as well. So be careful.' Archie waved at him. The man waved back then put his foot down and began throwing the levers of the machine about. The bulldozer belched black smoke and lurched forward. Then he spotted the perfect tree. It would be a good while before the mess was cleared. He had all the time in the world for a nap. Or so he thought.

However, the obstacles of the fleeing Germans proved but a temporary setback to the pursuance of war. New orders found their way to Colonel Jefferson; a makeshift route through Caltagirone was fashioned by the engineers; and miracle of miracles, the service corps conjured up transport for the entire battalion.

Meanwhile, Ginevra was leaning towards him, a saucy look in her eyes, her lips parted ever so slightly. Archie was attempting to reach out and grasp her, but a terrible hubbub was distracting him from his goal. Irritated, he levered open an eye. When his mind processed what his eye saw, he bolted upright. A tank was crawling past not fifty feet away, loaded down with men. There was an entire column of them.

'Rise and shine, sunshine,' called out one of the mounted soldiers. His buddies whistled. The soldier was from Charlie Company, and Archie recognized more than a few. Without their extra gear, relieved of gas capes and small packs, they were saddled up for a long journey on their iron steed. Archie sprang to his feet. Further back a long procession of trucks was following in the wake of the tanks, big 3-ton Bedfords and a potluck assortment of others, including several whose provenance was most definitely Italian.

Archie stood watching as they rumbled past. Until he spotted the familiar faces, whereupon half the platoon shouted: 'Archie! Get your ass onboard!' He put on a sprint. With a big grin he pulled himself up over the tailgate and claimed a spot on the wooden bench. He was on the verge of saying something when a familiar face opposite persuaded him otherwise.

'So nice of you to join us,' growled Sergeant Evers. 'It appears you weren't aware, Atwell, but this isn't the Rotary Club ladies' tour of Sicily that you signed up for.'

'No, Sarge,' Archie mumbled. There were some snickers and several outright chuckles, none as irritating as the cackle from Battersby. Evers stared at Archie, daring him to say more. Archie turned away and pretended to be engrossed in the jolting antics of the truck behind.

Thus mounted, the Eddies skirted the worst of the craters and the piles of stone debris. They went charging up route 124 through San Michele di Ganzeria, where the entire population turned out with an exhibition of their finest white linens hanging from every window. Italian soldiers lined the road, some waving white flags. But their offers to surrender were ignored. There was no time. The column rolled on.

At the junction with the no. 117 they met more Americans who had come from the south and Gela. They paused briefly, then turned north towards Enna and the centre of the island. The Edmonton Regiment had become the vanguard of the division and of the corps.

This role didn't appear to warrant a supply of adequate maps – at least not judging by Lieutenant Wiles's frustrated contortions with his. Neither was there much in the way of plans or even defined objectives. In fact, they had little to go on save a naïve self-confidence that it would be them that brought the Germans to heel, and few seemed bothered by what would happen then.

Two villages to the northwest, in the hills near a town called Piazza Armerina, the men in the gun pits could hardly be called naïve. In appearance they were lean and bronzed, tan shirt sleeves rolled up to past the elbow, their field caps worn at rakish angles. They went about their duties with a confidence one might have called casual, perhaps even arrogant. But then the casual observer wouldn't have known of their long experience in Africa. The second battalion of the 104th Regiment of the 15th Panzer Grenadier Division was completing its final preparations. First-Lieutenant Weyers was very proud of his men.

After the rearguard action at Grammichele and Caltagirone, the battalions of the Hermann Göring Division had passed through yesterday heading for new positions, most likely on the Catania Plain and the coast where a breakthrough could not be permitted. To Weyers's eyes the withdrawing units were weary and worse for wear, their ranks visibly thinned, although these observations he kept studiously to himself. Not that it really mattered. Weyers set his mouth. From this moment forth it would be up to the 15th Panzer Grenadiers to hold the castle gates against all comers.

They'd had three days to ready themselves. Plenty of time, really. And Weyers was quietly pleased with the results. Especially now that Captain Biedermann had also expressed satisfaction. Unusually for him he'd been rather effusive.

Nevertheless, as Weyers stood awaiting the car with the battalion commander he couldn't help but revisit the many preparations in his mind. The rifle and machine gun pits were well dug, and cleverly hidden on the heights to either side of the road – all except the one in the house; one couldn't very well conceal a house. Though the thick stone walls of the place did provide other compensations. He'd inspected each position personally. The crossfire from the MGs would be withering.

Further back there were mortars that were also sited on the road, although thankfully they weren't his responsibility. He preferred the enemy he could see to the one identified by coordinates on a map. But equally he was glad the mortars were there. As well as a couple of self-propelled guns, there were also several Italian 90mm pieces, and a handful of 75s, dug-in in a direct line-of-sight at various spots. They would surely come with tanks, so the Pak 40 anti-tank guns were a godsend. No, he thought, any approach along the road was a devil's errand. But if the enemy intended to pass through Piazza Armerina there was no escaping the road.

The battalion commander's Kübelwagen shuddered to a halt in a mist of dust. The ground was bone dry despite the early hour, and later it would be worse, impossible to move a step without a gritty white cloud swirling. Captain Rudolf Struckmann threw open the back door before the car even rolled to a complete stop, and energetically sprang out, his eyes darting from left to right. It was highly unusual for a man of his modest rank to command an entire battalion. But then not many men in the Wehrmacht could claim the honour of wearing a Knight's Cross of the Iron Cross suspended from their collar.

Weyers touched his hand to his cap. 'Welcome, sir. Captain Biedermann asked me to give you his apologies. He intended to be here to greet you himself, but his duties called him away at the last moment. He asked me to show you the defences we've prepared, however.'

'No matter,' replied Struckmann. 'The Captain was entirely right: duty first. Please, lead the way, Lieutenant.' He had already turned away, gazing contemplatively up the hillside.

Weyers led his commander up the incline to the first of the positions he'd so painstakingly chosen, even to the extent of staring carefully down the barrel of the MG-34 once the men had securely mounted it on a tripod. Struckmann now leaned over that very gun, and swept it back and forth with oiled ease, much as Weyers had done, making his own estimation of the lines of sight. He looked down at the metal ammunition boxes stacked close to hand in the pit.

After a moment the captain muttered, '*gut*'. Weyers knew it shouldn't have mattered. He was simply doing his duty, but he felt a glow nonetheless. Struckmann was most decidedly not a commander whose credentials were confined to paper, not like others he'd had. Weyers pointed his arm downhill, to the waiting staff car. But the captain insisted he wished to see more. They walked rapidly, clambering up and down steep slopes, across treacherously narrow goat paths, and through rough grass littered with stones that clattered downhill as they went. It took them nearly an hour to see all that 5. Company had prepared.

'You've done well,' said the captain. They were standing once again on the road. 'I'll be certain to tell Captain Biedermann when we speak.' He stared at Weyers, and his eyes seemed to bore into him. 'You are entirely familiar with the orders, Lieutenant? You may need to move quickly.'

Weyers nodded. 'Yes, sir, I am. The company is prepared.'

'Excellent. Then good hunting, Lieutenant.' With that Captain Struckmann sprang into the Kübelwagen. To Weyers it seemed the man had as much energy as an hour previous. Which was remarkable, for while the temperatures were cooler than they would be in a few hours, this was surely not Struckmann's first inspection these past days. The captain carried a great weight on his shoulders; there were many who would be watching what happened here: not least Colonel Ens and General Rodt of the division – perhaps even Field Marshal Kesselring himself.

There had been no hint from the captain when, exactly, the Tommies were to be expected. But there was little doubt it would be soon. No matter, he thought. Everything that could be done had been done. Then he went in search of a mug of coffee – with any luck it might be the real thing, not the *ersatz* he was all too accustomed to. Later there would be no time. He smiled to himself, pleased at Captain Struckmann's reaction. For the moment his tiredness was gone.

CHAPTER 11

16 July, 1943
Approaches to Piazza Armerina, Sicily

The column was racing northeastwards, their destination a simple dot on the lieutenant's map labelled Piazza Armerina.

In the vanguard, the tanks of the Three Rivers Regiment were churning up a veritable dust storm. Dutifully following was a procession of the first dozen carriers and trucks, and their choking, spitting regimental cargo.

Archie's section, in a 3-ton Ford a little further from the front of the column, was spared the worst. Though he too could feel the grit on his lips. Remorseless, the midday sun glared down from a canvas of dazzling blue. Despite a breeze of sorts, and a wind thrown up by the truck's motion, it was stiflingly hot.

Archie wiped at his forehead. Nor was he the only one doing so. The section all wore helmets, tilted low to shade their eyes, various pieces of cloth draped behind so as to cover necks and ears, lending them the appearance of some rag-tag army from Arabia. Sweat trickled down faces and necks, and streamed in rivulets under shirts of light-woven Aertex. But all heads including Archie's were focused forward, foregoing idle chat to carefully observe the road and the hills they were passing, blue mountains rising menacingly not so many miles distant.

No one had expressly told them so, but vaguely they were aware they were playing a dangerous game, even if it seemed a strangely carefree one chasing down a retreating enemy under a brilliant blue sky. However, they knew a moment would come when the enemy stopped his retreat. And even the typically garrulous Lieutenant Wiles did not venture an opinion when that would be; or what would happen when they did.

Three miles from Piazza Armerina, the convoy rounded a bend.

The narrow dirt road swept down from the long ridge it had been following, straighter than any arrow. Archie shivered, an odd sensation of nakedness coming over him. Several hundred yards ahead the road could be seen to narrow further, straddling the steep hill to the left, a gully of unknown depths off to the right. There it began to climb sharply once more. After only a few days Archie had learned the hard way that all roads in Sicily inevitably led uphill. *Thank goodness for the transport.*

For no apparent reason the column abruptly slowed, then halted. Their own cloud of dusty exhaust came rolling over them.

Archie grasped his rifle and nervously shot a glance around. Hainsley, he noticed, was staring at something behind him. He turned. Many hundreds of yards away, where the road curved round the hill, a stone farmhouse could be seen perched on the hill. Above it a puff of white smoke floated in the air. A signal!

A group of soldiers was already dismounting to make their way forward to investigate. The column began to creep forward once more. The vanguard was nearly at the hill.

There was a huge *BOOM*.

A geyser of dirt blew skyward in front of the lead Sherman further up the road. A machine gun began to rattle, followed by another, then yet a third. Suddenly men were shouting. The turret of the tank swiveled in the direction of the hill. Others behind were quick to follow the example.

'Dismount!' a voice commanded. Archie and the others leapt from the truck. Before he jumped he caught a glimpse of "C" Company, terribly exposed on their iron steeds, now hastily abandoning them.

'Why don't the tanks fire back?' asked Postlethwaite.

'Look for yourself man,' growled Battersby. Postlethwaite blushed. Archie didn't blush but he turned to look again in the direction of the tanks for he'd wondered precisely the same thing. After a fresh glance, Postlethwaite, too, established the answer to his own question.

'Darn. They're too close in. They can't elevate their guns high enough,' he said.

Archie whistled. 'Yeah, and they can't go forward, and they can't go back because the road's full. They're stuck.' A thought came to him. 'It's an ambush. We'd better get off this road, boys.'

Others were arriving at the same conclusion and the regiment scrambled to find cover, away from the column of trucks lined up like so many ducks in a row. Nor was this analogy lost on the truck drivers. A few were taking matters into their own hands. Engines revved noisily. A few lurched off the road, and bumped and rattled into the adjoining fields of dry yellow grass.

There, a few stands of olive trees and shrubs were scattered. From common sense, as much as any training, the men on foot gravitated towards them.

Without warning a shell landed with a bang close to the road. Ten seconds later a second went off, followed closely by a third and a fourth. Mortar fire, thought Archie grimly. Another round fell and one of the trucks, slow or unable to extricate itself from the column, went up in flames. The machine guns continued to rattle.

Sergeant Evers stood with his binoculars surveying the hill. 'There's an MG in that house,' they heard him say.

Archie pointed. 'Look, Sarge.'

One of the 6-pound anti-tank guns had been uncoupled from its truck, and was being wheeled into a firing position in the grass. Evers hurried towards the gun, his arm preceding him, waving in the direction of the hill, speaking volubly. It was his self-assuredness that Archie marvelled at. They'd both joined at the same time, arrived in England together on the very same ship, but now it was Matt who was the steady hand everyone in the platoon and company looked to when in doubt. Since coming to Sicily Archie found himself doing exactly the same. Prowess at card games or dazzling a pretty Scottish lass didn't count for much here. It was entirely his own fault of course. Lieutenant Wiles and Captain Tighe had given him every opportunity. And with every opportunity he'd made a mess of it. He'd never particularly felt much regret until recently.

Slowly the barrel of the anti-tank gun elevated, and he perked up at the sight. A shell was rammed into the breech. Behind the armoured shield the crew crouched in position. Their NCO stood further back beside Evers, both with their binoculars raised, seemingly oblivious to the MGs and the snipers, even if the shot was a long one. Then the NCO lifted his arm into the air, like the starter at a race.

It was strangely still for a spell as they made their adjustments, then the arm of the gun crew's NCO chopped downwards, and from the gun issued a sharp thunderclap. The barrel recoiled and the gun rocked back and forth on its thick rubber wheels. Half a hundred watching eyes saw a momentary puff of smoke appear on the hillside, and the sound of the shell's detonation echoed back towards them.

The breech of the gun was thrown open. Tendrils of smoke billowed forth, and before they dissipated another shell was thrust in and the breech slammed shut. The commander's arm rose, then fell. *BANG*.

Archie held his breath and watched, but with the naked eye the fall of the shell was undetectable. Quickly the gun crew reloaded and fired again.

At first glance it appeared as if this round, too, was a miss. However, a second glance revealed smoke, pieces of stone, and masonry flying about. A satisfying *BOOM* resonated back. When the air cleared the front wall of the house revealed a gaping hole.

Archie whistled softly. The others had their arms in the air. Young Postlethwaite was cheering wildly.

Nearby, a detachment of men rushed up, weighed down with gear, and he saw that it was a 3-inch mortar and ammunition they were carrying. They began to set up.

A large explosion drew all eyes back in the direction of the road. This time a shell had fallen in the rear, the column largely dispersed save for a few stragglers. One of them, a truck, was emitting thick black smoke. Behind it, the other sorely needed anti-tank gun was tipped on its side in a mangled heap.

Colonel Jefferson and Major Cromb of Charlie Company appeared, trotting across the field. They came from the direction of some trees, where they'd evidently been observing. Captain Tighe emerged and went to them. There was a *bang* as the mortar crew got off its first round.

'What the hell are we waiting for?' said Battersby. Lachance muttered his agreement.

'A plan, perhaps?' said Archie, cocking an eyebrow. There was nothing to be gained by rushing towards the enemy like a posse of mad hatters. All the exercises in England had taught him that. Battersby frowned but said nothing. For all his experience with actuarial tables and the like, Battersby was not a man easily mistaken for a "thinking man's soldier"; which was why the comparison with a mad hatter sprang to mind.

After a half-dozen rounds the mortar crew in the field was preparing to shift position to avoid counter fire. But the Germans, as they had been all afternoon, were a step ahead, and lobbed one at the detachment from 3 Platoon.

The enemy bomb exploded with a sharp blast. As the dust settled Archie spotted the crew lying sprawled about, their own mortar toppled. One of the men screamed for a medic. Archie knew the 8cm *Granatwerfer* to be highly accurate, but this last effort was only possible with the most careful siting and direct observation. Mortars didn't aim themselves.

Suddenly Lieutenant Wiles was in their midst. 'A Company is to take the hill,' he said breathlessly. Then to Sergeant Evers: 'Assemble the platoon and follow me.'

At this stage the plan was anything but clear as Archie assumed his position in file with the others. The lieutenant led them across the road, walking quickly in the direction of a second hill, a half mile east to their right. Archie could see the other platoons moving roughly parallel. Then it came to him what it was the colonel envisaged.

'Of course!' He spoke louder than he intended for Postlethwaite, in file ahead, turned and looked.

'What's that, Archie?'

'Oh, nothing.'

But Postlethwaite's curiosity was not so easily dismissed. He swivelled again, this time pausing his step so that he might come closer. It was only that Archie put a hand on his back to propel him forward that the men behind didn't stumble into them. 'Where the dickens are we going? The Hun is on that other hill?'

'I think the whole idea is to outflank them. But watch your step and keep your eyes peeled. Evers will hang you out to dry if you ruin his attack formation.'

'Attack formation?'

'Hmm. And there may be mines ahead.'

'Really!?'

Archie sighed and wearily shook his head. Mines were the least of their concerns.

The sun was at its midday fiercest. The long grass brushed over their short puttees, scratching against bare legs, while sweat poured down already sweaty brows, but not a man was heard to complain. They trotted down a mild incline until they reached a creek bed, and for the sheer novelty of it they stomped with their boots through the pitiful trickle of water that was fighting a hopeless rearguard action against the summer heat. Then the ground begin to climb sharply.

'By section,' shouted Sergeant Evers. The file disintegrated, and shook itself out into an extended line two sections abreast of each other and began swarming up the hill.

The little group around Archie moved cautiously from tree to shrub, to a large outgrowth of rocks baking in the sun, treacherously hot to the touch. They knelt down to prepare their next move, but Battersby, with Lachance tagging along in his wake, came surging forward.

'Off your ass, Atwell. The enemy's that way,' he snapped. They moved on. The crest of the hill was in sight not a hundred yards further up an open grassy slope. And still there was no sign of the enemy.

Far in the distance a machine gun rattled, such a commonplace sound from the training schemes that no one paid it any heed. Then the ground around Archie began to spit dust and dirt. He ran for it, no thought in his head except that he should make for the next stand of trees near the crest, an instinctive rush that took no time at all.

As the others collapsed down beside him, his breathing slowed, and he was conscious that he was oddly clear headed. He hadn't felt fear and that surprised him a little; it was a relief, if truth be told. However, this seemed no different to what they'd done endlessly in practice, with instructors firing above their heads. The machine gun had to be a half mile away, if not further. Granted, a half mile was child's play for a modern machine gun, but aiming was a very different matter – even with a tripod. In a long 10-second burst of 150 rounds you might get lucky. But hitting a moving target as it moved laterally across your view was not easy. He'd tried himself at the ranges, so he knew.

'Where are they?' asked Roberts, the Bren gunner, crawling up beside him. The gunfire had died away as suddenly as it had come.

'My money's on that hill to the north,' Archie said, indicating with his finger. 'Are you going to shoot back, or what?'

Roberts shook his head. 'Pointless. I can't even see them.'

The view from this spot was superb. They could make out the twisting white ribbon of the no. 117 downhill to their left, the road all but deserted. The battalion had extricated itself from a tricky situation. To the north was the fortified knoll, the first of many hills that formed a cauldron around a long valley that ran off to the north, capped at its furthest end by the cragged form of a hilltop village. That would be Piazza Armerina – elevation 2366 feet – if the lieutenant's map was to be believed.

Closer to hand Archie's gaze fell on something else. Emboldened by the absence of bullets pricking the air, he pulled himself up and went forward to investigate. It revealed itself to be a pit, neatly concealed, and dug on the very edge of the hill. The pit was empty and he clambered down into it.

While once occupied – and not long ago either was his estimation – he was disappointed to find little evidence of the Germans save a well-trod dirt floor and a parapet that may, or may not have been, used recently. *But wait!* Reaching down, his fingers clawed at the dirt, and came up with an object pinched between thumb and forefinger. He shook it, then grinned.

'Sergeant!' he bellowed at the rest of the platoon who were coming up. He waved for good measure.

Evers acknowledged with his own wave, and strode towards him. He was puffing more heavily than Archie would have expected for a man who, a month earlier, had led the charge up, down, and across the better part of the British Isles. But then again, a couple of weeks at sea hadn't done Archie's condition any good either.

'Have a look at this, Sarge.' Archie held up a square piece of green carton a little bigger than a deck of playing cards.

Evers took it in his hands. 'E-C-K-S-T-E-I-N,' he read slowly, mouthing out the black lettering. 'Jerry cigarettes. Well, well… so they *were* here... Must have pulled back when they saw us approaching.'

Archie nodded. 'I bet this was an observation post. Probably for those sons of bitches directing the mortar fire.' There was no need to state the obvious; had it been an MG position the two of them would have been preoccupied with something other than a piece of trash.

Evers looked up and his eyes widened as he took in the panorama. 'You're probably right,' he replied. 'I'm going to fetch the lieutenant. He'll want to see this.'

Before he could do so, Archie made a croaking noise, and extended a finger towards the hill to the north of the road. The lines of men who had been making their way up the hill were scattering. There were puffs of smoke visible. The sound of the explosions came washing over them. 'Losing his O-Pip hasn't done much to crimp Jerry's mortars.'

Evers shook his head. 'No. Be thankful you're not in "C" Company, Archie.'

Archie turned away from the hill and saw a couple of officers approaching. Lieutenant Wiles wasn't one of them, but he saw Captain Tighe, and there was another figure whose bearing was unmistakeable. For those at the bottom of the totem pole it paid to be able to spot your battalion commander at great distances.

Hastily he moved to make room for his betters. They were now jumping into the pit themselves.

The two officers greeted Sergeant Evers, and Tighe gave a curt nod in Archie's direction. To his surprise Lieutenant-Colonel Jefferson nodded as well. 'Hello, Atwell.'

'Hello, sir,' he mumbled.

'Isn't that something,' whispered Evers in one ear. 'The Colonel knows your name.'

Archie frowned. This was neither the time nor the place to ask Evers what he was driving at. If he thought about it he would have realized the colonel didn't know every man in his command, only those of importance. And the troublemakers.

Meanwhile the colonel's attention was elsewhere. He too was admiring the view, a pair of binoculars clamped to his eyes. 'Quite the sight,' he marvelled to Captain TIghe. 'This will do very nicely, Pat.'

Tighe nodded. Then over his shoulder he shot the two of them a meaningful glance. Hints were not something the army did well – why hint when all that was required was bellowing an order? But it did the trick; Evers looked at Archie, and Archie looked at Evers, and they made their retreat.

'Just so it's completely clear,' growled Evers as they walked, 'don't even think about stealing a midday nap, Archie. You may not have realized it, but what happens here is not only of interest to the Colonel and Brigadier Vokes. General Simonds, General Leese, and even Monty himself are watching. Word is the Eighth Army is having the darnedest time trying to move along the coast road to Catania. So, it's up to us on the left to find a way around. But first we have to outflank that hill.'

It was all Archie could do not to roll his eyebrows at this latest pontification from Evers. The three stripes *were* going to his head. Then he thought of Battersby who, with a single chevron, carried himself like a minor deity, and reconsidered. 'Sure thing, Sarge,' he sighed. 'Just say the word. I'll be ready.'

CHAPTER 12

Late afternoon, 16 July, 1943
Hills south of Piazza Armerina, Sicily

Lieutenant Weyers of the 15th Panzer Grenadiers lowered his field glasses as he heard the soldier scrambling up the last few metres of stony incline towards the plateau and the gun pits. He sat on a low boulder set back from their trenches, facing east-southeast. He leaned forward with both elbows resting on his knees for stability, surveying the scene. Behind him on the back side of the hill, was the narrow line of the no. 117 a couple of hundred metres downhill. In front, the expanse of a dry yellow valley ringed by tree-speckled hills stretched out, forming a most impressive vista. Roughly a mile to the north, and balanced on an even higher hill, was Piazza Armerina. If the enemy wished to reach that, they would have to pass here. And they clearly wanted to; he'd already spotted them in the distance.

Expectantly, Weyers looked at the young soldier bounding towards him. The lad, whose face a month earlier was as fair as his hair, was bronzed a deep tan. He was bathed in sweat.

'*Und?*' Weyers asked softly. To the uninitiated the question was innocuous, but both officer and soldier knew he was referring to the enemy – and the enemy's dispositions more specifically. Snaking along the base of the hills, like so many ants, small groups of them were visible working their way up the valley towards the village. How many they'd come with, and what they were planning was not entirely clear. He hoped the soldier had returned with some information he could use.

'They've abandoned the road, sir,' the soldier began, nervously gulping in air. He'd been with the 104th Regiment and the 2nd Battalion only a short while, and was still very much in awe of his superior officer.

Weyers grinned. He knew that already. The defences he'd established had done their work.

'They're moving by foot through the hills. *Ein ganzes Battailon, mein Herr. Sie sind Kanadier.*'

'*Kanadier?*' interrupted Weyers sharply. 'A whole battalion. Are you certain?' He felt a shudder run through him. He hated Canadians.

The soldier nodded. They were quite definitely Canadians, he replied. One of their officers had been taken prisoner a little earlier. 'They all wear red patches on the shoulder, sir.'

Violently Weyers's right foot snapped forward, kicking at the earth. With the toe of his boot he dislodged a stone from the sun-baked earth and it arced high before dropping into the mortar trench, where it catapulted off the back of the helmet of one of the men. The man swivelled round, eyes flashing. Upon spotting Weyers he quickly looked away.

The runner didn't know what to make of his lieutenant's agitation. He swallowed.

Weyers motioned that the soldier should proceed with his report, but his thoughts were elsewhere. He listened with only half an ear to the mixture of facts, conjecture and outright speculation that so often passed as battlefield intelligence. Almost everything he knew already. All but that one thing. When the boy had said his piece Weyers impatiently waved him away.

Ironically, the lieutenant's father was never bitter about his fate, not even during that horrible period nearly fifteen years ago when he lay shivering in bed, wracked by fever. But his mother was. And that bitterness only increased with the passage of time. It was from her that Weyers eventually learned what happened that September day in 1918 when the Canadians stormed the Wotan Stellung. By mid-morning his father had lost a leg from the shells, and very nearly an arm as well, his health precarious to the day he died. 'It was war,' his father said philosophically, whenever young Weyers asked about it. But to a boy – he must have been only seven or eight at the time – it was not his father's words but his mother's, so oft repeated, that remained with him. Ever since, Weyers loathed the Canadians.

He raised his field glasses to his eyes. 'There!' he shouted to the men in the pit. His heart was pumping. 'On the hill!'

Across the valley, a dozen men in an extended formation were sweeping up the slope of the hill towards the crest. It was just under the crest, on a terrace, that Weyers had sited the position. He heard rifle shots as the attackers were spotted. Their momentum appeared to waver momentarily, but then they pressed on. Weyers lowered the glasses. '*Schnell!*' he roared at the machine-gun crew.

The soldiers in the pit were not to be rushed, not even by an officer – these were men who knew well what they were doing – and Weyers was momentarily embarrassed he had shouted. Slowly but deliberately a soldier nestled the sharply-curved wooden butt of the MG-34 firmly up against his right shoulder. His left forearm pivoted at the elbow and swung across his chest so that the hand would support the butt from under – useful when firing 800 rounds a minute – and stared down the sights. A second man crouched beside him, surrounded by metal cases. Out of one such case extended an ammunition belt that led to the machine gun. A third man at the parapet held binoculars fixed on the hill opposite. Then the first soldier's finger reached for the trigger and he squeezed it. Weyers lifted his glasses. The second crew opened up an instant later.

The clatter of MG fire not far ahead sent them tumbling to the ground. It seemed as if they'd done little else that afternoon; walk a few steps until a distant spark from a scope or a pair of binoculars flashed, or a fleeting movement on a slope opposite caught someone's eye. Or, worse, bullets began whistling round. In every case they dove madly for cover. Under the circumstances they'd been extraordinarily lucky; only Roberts had been hit. After several anxious moments – he was the best of their three Bren gunners – they collectively breathed a sigh of relief when it was declared a mere scratch. Through it all, Roberts was the stoic one of the lot. They'd outflanked the hill only to discover the Germans had pulled back to another.

After briefly studying the lay of the land, Colonel Jefferson had ordered the battalion up the valley without delay: their objective a prominent feature not far from Piazza Armerina. Able was to lead, Baker was on the flank, Charlie was in support. And Dog was probably still trying to keep order in Ragusa; in differing circumstances it was a hierarchy Archie would have been all in favour of. They followed goat trails, or no trails at all, hugging to one side of a hill or another, encountering without fail German positions in all the places one might expect them. There was a wearisome efficiency to the enemy's defences.

'Damn it to hell. Where are they *this* time,' hissed Lance-Corporal Battersby. 'Do you see anything?' This last was addressed to Archie who was lying brotherly, in body if not in spirit, at his side. The two men were at the head of the section, the section at the head of the platoon, the platoon at the head of the company.

'You mean the Jerries, Miles?' Archie replied. Battersby grunted. 'A better question might be: where are they not? That way we'd know which way to go.'

Battersby grunted again, louder. A spitball went flying.

Archie glanced over his shoulder. Hainsley and another man (Lachance he thought) were lying flat on their bellies fifty feet back. The rest of the section was spread out further behind on the narrow path they'd been following near the base of the hill. Spotting Archie, Hainsley raised an arm, and then began furiously jabbing a finger in the direction of the opposite side of the valley. But the sound had clearly come from ahead, and Archie shook his head, frowning. Hainsley kept jabbing. So he looked closer.

It must have been nearly a mile. Certainly too far with the naked eye to see a bunch of Germans hunched behind a machine gun in a camouflaged hole peering down their sights; Hainsley's eyes were good, but not that good. Archie scanned the sky above the hill hoping to spot a few puffs of smoke, or even some birds circling overhead. The latter would be a real clue where the Germans were. But he saw nothing, nothing except… wait… there were men moving on the hillside!

That was what Hainsley had meant. He felt a shiver of anticipation run down his back. At last – the enemy.

But then, on closer inspection, he saw they weren't the enemy at all. He raised a thumb in acknowledgement. He nudged Battersby with his elbow and pointed.

'Look, some of our fellows. Must be "B" Company.'

At that moment a machine gun, somewhere directly ahead, began to rattle furiously. It was the same one they'd heard before. The specks on the hill opposite scattered – all but one. A single speck lay immobile, a tiny dark spot that he found impossible to draw his eyes away from, having seen him move only moments before.

'Should have known,' muttered Archie.

'Should have known what?'

'They have two positions. One on this hill, and another on the far side. They're covering each other. Can't you see? Oblique fire. We need to do something. Those guys are going to get chewed up.'

'Wonderful, Private Clausewitz. But if you're right, we'll get chewed up ourselves if we move. No, we'll wait it out here. The rest of the platoon will be up soon. There's a Forward Observation Officer around here somewhere. Once he gets forward, we can call up the artillery to deal with them.' Archie felt the vein in his temple pulsing. Admittedly, the combination of the FOO and the self-propelled guns of the Royal Devon Yeomanry had dealt neatly with several machine-gun nests earlier. But Archie was certain Captain Graham was miles away; the German artillery and mortars were proving troublesome, and they would necessarily be the first priority.

There was another burst of machine gun fire, then the distinctive bang of a mortar. On the hill opposite the mortar round went off with a deep thud, accompanied by a wisp of white smoke. Through the smoke men could be seen retreating down the slope in search of cover. The attack was failing.

'Christ, Miles, our boys are going to be dead by then.'

'I'm not going to risk my neck on some whim of yours,' snapped Battersby.

Archie gritted his teeth and muttered: 'Leave your neck out of it then, but we need to do something.'

'Easy for you to say. I'm the one responsible for the section.'

'Congratulations. But if you keep your head down while Baker Company is shot to pieces someone is going to ask questions.'

Battersby turned to stare at him through hard beaded eyes. 'Fine,' he muttered, at length. 'You want to play hero, Atwell? You and your buddy Hainsley can take the lead. Move out.'

'Gee, thanks, Archie,' grumbled Hainsley when the two of them set off down the track a moment later. 'Battersby's a nasty piece of work, but you didn't have to bring me into it. Knowing him he probably hopes you and I run smack into the middle of the Jerries – just to prove he was right.'

Archie glanced behind. Battersby was impatiently waving them on. It wasn't altogether reassuring. 'Likely. At least I've got us some extra firepower,' he said, fondling the Tommy gun cradled in both arms. He'd very nearly had to wrench the thing out of Battersby's clutches. His trusty Lee-Enfield he left behind in reluctant exchange, every pouch of his webbing now weighed down with ammunition. He grinned. It was certainly not light. Not with all the extra ammo. Especially not in this blistering heat.

'You should have taken a Bren, Archie. The Thompson's useless beyond a hundred feet.'

'What, and lug a brute of a Bren around? This thing's heavy enough as it is.'

Shortly thereafter Archie came to reconsider his words. Rounding the curve of the hill, and emerging from behind an outcrop of rock, he halted, dropped precipitously to one knee, and raised a hand in warning. Hainsley, a couple of paces behind, crouched down and shuffled forward to join him. The merits of having a Bren gun were staring them in the face – several hundred yards distant.

Up the hill two machine guns were spitting out their latest deadly lashing. A wisp of smoke curled up into the dazzling blue sky, the enemy dug-outs plain to see carved in the hillside. The Tommy gun would be as useless as Hainsley predicted. While a Lee-Enfield's odds were better, duelling it out at ten rounds a minute with a couple of machine guns firing at forty times that rate was work for a madman.

'What now?' said Hainsley. 'Two steps up that hill and they'll see us.'

'Come with me. We'll fetch someone. I have an idea.'

'Another idea? Swell… just swell…' Hainsley's mumbled words went unheard. Archie was already on his feet retracing their path back to the section.

A moment later he slowed his pace as the goat path they were on crossed over a narrow gully jammed with rocks. Thoughtfully, he looked up its length, which gave Hainsley the first inkling of what he intended. He would have asked the specifics, too, were it not that Archie was five paces ahead striding purposively forward.

'Look,' Archie said, his voice rising, 'it's the only way. With a few men we should be able to sneak up their flank and hit them from behind. They won't be expecting us so close in.' Battersby shook his head dismissively, as if he didn't remember a thing their instructors had taught.

'Hainsley and I will do all the work –' Archie's words trailed off, examining the faces clustered behind. 'But we'll need Dinesen, as well. All you have to do, Miles, is wait till you hear shooting, and then shout "fire". Can you manage that, do you think?'

There were broad grins from the section. Archie's saucy disrespect would have repercussions they knew. Battersby wouldn't be Battersby if he took this lying down. Especially if it didn't work out. But they were fighting a war and, to a man, they agreed with Archie. Sensing the mood Battersby shrugged indifferently. The face he presented to Archie was less congenial: 'It's your bleeding funeral, Atwell,' he hissed. 'So don't stand there gawking. Get on with it.'

It was all Archie could do not to wipe the smirk from his face with a fist, but he restrained himself, turning instead to Roberts and King. 'I'm counting on you two.'

King nodded gravely. 'Good luck, Archie. We'll cover you, won't we, Ben?'

Coming to the slide they'd seen earlier, Archie, Hainsley and Dinesen began to scramble up the loose rocks. They were conscious they should do so with a minimum of noise, but that was easier said than done. They were all too aware they had to hurry. Several times the machine guns on the hill began buzzing. They seemed so terribly far away, even if they were not. Every now and then a mortar banged.

Through it all the sun beat down relentlessly.

'What's he got against me?' Dinesen asked, panting, as he paused to wipe his brow.

'To the contrary,' said Hainsley. 'He's got a bee in his bonnet, that's all. That's Archie for you.'

'Christ. Couldn't he have picked another bee?'

'That's the point,' said Hainsley. 'He picked you. You should be pleased, Harry.'

Dinesen grunted, and slung the Tommy gun over his other shoulder.

Archie was paces ahead. A metronome in his ears was pounding a beat no one else heard. He didn't understand it entirely himself. Normally he couldn't have cared less what happened to "B" Company, but he did now. Perhaps this was what war did to a man.

Methodically, deliberately, the party climbed the stony bed of the gully – the going easier the further they went. As they reached the head of the slide the gully became ever shallower. It was now barely waist level and they bent over as they climbed, acutely conscious they were virtually in the open. Without warning Archie stopped and knelt down. Cautiously, the other two picked their way towards him and went down on their haunches. Sweat stained their tunics. They were breathing heavily.

'What's wrong?' asked Hainsley softly, pushing up the rim of his helmet so as to better see.

'Shhh, listen. I thought I heard something.'

They cocked their heads and listened. They were on their own. There was nothing the rest of the section or the regiment could do if the Germans stumbled upon them now.

Eventually Dinesen broke the silence. 'Don't hear anything.'

Hainsley shook his head. 'So, what's the plan, Archie? You do have one, right?'

Archie nodded, and as the other two looked on, he brushed smooth a square in the dirt and began to draw with one finger. 'Alright, we're here. Roughly halfway to the top. I reckon that the Jerries are a few hundred feet to our right, and dug in just below the crest. Here.' He stabbed a finger in the dirt. 'That's a mighty fine position. Unless, of course, someone comes from behind.' He grinned.

'Archie, they'll have someone watching.'

'Likely. But remember the action is in front. Not a lot to see looking the wrong way. Besides, they'll be expecting a lot more than three men.'

'Let's hope you're right,' mumbled Hainsley.

'We'll climb to the crest and then move in behind them. Get as close as we possibly can. Before they're any the wiser we lob a few grenades. After that… well, I was looking forward to putting this bad beauty into action.' He petted the Tommy gun, nodding at the identical one Dinesen clutched under an arm. 'Their MGs on the other hill won't be able to do a damned thing – even if they somehow see us.'

'And the balls-up factor?' asked Dinesen. Back in England they'd laughed about the balls-up factor. It became a veritable sport for the Eddies to compile the myriad ways some plan hadn't gone as planned. The most fun was identifying who, of the many officers and NCOs responsible, was responsible. The faces were deadly serious as Archie considered his answer.

'If it's a balls-up, we'll do what we can and scram. But look at it this way, Harry. If they're shooting at us, they won't be shooting at "B" Company.'

'Great. Next time you go looking for someone to play sitting duck, count me out, Archie.'

As they continued up the hill the gully petered out, leaving only a smattering of trees, thick patches of gnarled shrubs, and tufts of yellow grass to conceal their approach. The three men moved slowly and deliberately, until that cover vanished too. Then so too did Archie.

Anxiously, Hainsley and Dinesen swept the ground with their eyes, their hearts pounding. Finally, Dinesen spotted a pair of boots ten feet away, sticking out of some greenery. Hainsley crawled forward to see what the problem was, for a problem it would surely be.

'You nearly gave me a heart attack,' he murmured as he came closer.

Archie whipped round and put a finger to his lips, then pointed ahead. The green shrub had effectively swallowed him, and Hainsley fought his way through the tangle until they lay shoulder to shoulder.

From Hainsley emanated a noise that sounded much like he'd swallowed his tongue. Neither of them had ever seen the enemy at such close quarters.

The Germans certainly weren't hundreds of feet away, as Archie had confidently predicted, nor were they below them. They were virtually next door, on the far side of a low pile of rocks, dug in on a terraced precipice, a hundred feet below the crest. At best fifty paces separated them.

They were nearly twenty strong. Dressed in faded tan, the Germans were concentrated around three holes they'd dug. Each small trench was separate from the others, and the first two were laid out close to the edge so as command the valley. A mortar and crew could be seen in the third hole, set further back, and invisible to any observer looking from afar. And, wait, what was that?

A lone soldier stood erect, removed from the others, overlooking the entire position from the rear. His boot was resting jauntily on a large boulder. To his eyes he held binoculars. There was little doubt he was searching for "B" Company on the hill opposite.

Archie peered down the sights of the Tommy gun at the man. He stuck out like a sore thumb wearing a field cap instead of the grey bucket helmets of the others. There was something about his bearing and the uniform, though, and suddenly Archie realized what it was – the man was an officer!

The effective range of a Thompson submachine gun was hotly disputed, but it was widely held that at anything less than a hundred yards you really didn't have to be much of an aim. Archie was confident he was better than that. His trigger finger was certainly sorely tempted. This would be his first blow at the Germans, and it would be extra special to bag an officer. Reluctantly he lowered the weapon. He needed to think it through. There were, after all, only three of them.

Then to his dismay, and for no reason he could ascertain, the officer pivoted to his right and seemed to look straight at them.

Archie squirmed and twisted, and tried to back away into the shrubbery, until the utter futility of it convinced him to play possum instead. He could hear the crackle of branches as Hainsley retreated. The lens of the German's glasses were unwavering. He felt naked under the stare, the sweat dripped unchecked down his nose.

Decisively the officer lowered his binoculars. All but certain what this portended, Archie raised the Tommy gun's barrel and squinted a bead at him. The plan was already in disarray. Controlled, his finger squeezed the trigger. A single shot. With any luck the enemy might not hear it above the racket from their own MGs and the mortar.

The officer crumpled. For a gratifying moment Archie thought he'd succeeded, until he noticed the German hugging the sides of the boulder. He began hollering like a man possessed. In frustration Archie squeezed the trigger again, the wooden butt pumping satisfyingly against his shoulder, the boulder taking a beating. But soon he checked his fire, kicking himself for wasting precious ammunition and calculating what might be left of the twenty-round box magazine, the officer now the least of his worries. As he switched out the magazine, he caught a glimpse of Hainsley scrambling away on all fours towards a shrub of his own.

'He must have seen me,' puffed Dinesen, coming in for a hot landing behind him.

'Spread out,' Archie snapped. He didn't want a lucky MG burst catching them all. And he still entertained some hope that the Germans might think they were with more than they really were. But he didn't say any of that for his thoughts were a step ahead. He rolled on one side, his fingers rooting furiously around in a pouch for a grenade.

The terrace was a hive of activity – orders being shouted, men running. Suddenly near the first MG position there was a bang and two of the soldiers in the open went down. Out of the corner of his eye he could see Hainsley on his knees, a second grenade held like a baseball pitcher before he released it. Good man, he thought. 'The machine guns, Harry!' he shouted to Dinesen, who'd since claimed a modest shrub of his own. 'Aim for the machine guns.'

But already there was return fire. Several of the Germans were peppering the area with rifle fire. While its volume was impressive the inaccuracy indicated they hadn't yet established the party's exact location.

Dinesen's Tommy gun began chattering. Archie's hand had closed round a grenade and he held it now in his palm, the lever squeezed in. He pulled the pin with his teeth, and his arm swept back. Still lying prone on one side, eyes fixed on the furthest MG nest, he let fly. Hainsley's grenade went off at that very moment, showering the first of the MG pits in a blast of dust. Then a dozen paces further Archie's landed as well. There was a satisfying bang. It was a good bit short of what he'd intended, but the chaos in the German position seemed complete.

First appearances, however, deceived. The men of the 104th Regiment (although he didn't yet know them as such) were no rank amateurs, and certainly not prone to panic at the first sign of difficulty. Through a cloud of dust Archie made out the machine gun in the first pit being manhandled from a spot overlooking the valley to a position overlooking them. The second machine ripped into action, firing downhill – that would be the rest of the section! He thought he heard Brens.

Pairs of infantryman were taking up station behind rocks, shrubs and other spots of cover. They had the appearance of a pack of circling wolves, waiting to pounce.

Damn that, thought Archie. Quickly he tossed another grenade, spit the pin out, and with barely a glance to inform his aim threw a second. There were more bangs. Dust billowed, and shouts rang out, and the rifles continued to crack.

Off his left Hainsley was working the bolt of his Lee-Enfield with abandon. Dinesen's face was tense, concentrated. Short, quick bursts came from his Thompson, every shot meant to count – just like they'd been taught. The three of them may not have been in Africa, but they weren't rank amateurs either. Archie put the Tommy gun to his shoulder, took careful aim this time, and noted with satisfaction that one of the Germans manhandling the machine gun went down.

A whistle pierced the tumult: two long blasts. At first Archie was confused what it signified. A bullet crunched through the shrubbery perilously close. Then he saw the mortar crew emerge from their pit, doubled over with weapon and accoutrements in hand, and head hastily northwards. The German fire redoubled. With an angry chatter the redeployed machine gun fired. Archie pressed himself flat in the dirt, his face rubbing it. All around bullets were whizzing, branches were cracking, as the MG-34 raked their little line of greenery. In the warm afternoon air, the dust hung heavily.

The MG cut out. After a few seconds it started again, then went quiet. This time it stayed quiet. The rifle fire died away. Cautiously Archie inched his head up in order to look. Through the branches he saw movement on the terrace. Not daring to lift his head any further he squinted. Were they, or were they not pulling out?

He lay listening. It was quiet. Then Hainsley shouted: 'The buggers are leaving!'

'Keep your head down!' he barked, a little churlishly perhaps, but this wasn't the moment to let down their guard.

It was excellent advice. Barely had the words passed his lips when a flurry of stick grenades tumbled out of the sky. A loud crack immediately in front of him sent his ears ringing. He felt the concussion, but lying prone had escaped the deadly flying shards. Initially, he was concerned the grenades were the prelude to an assault, but they proved to be the Germans' final move.

'Damn,' enthused Dinesen, as he lifted himself to his knees, his helmet lying upside down in the grass. They watched as the last of the German file disappeared over the crest to the north. 'We did it, Archie! We did it! Who'd have thought, eh?'

Archie stole a glance at Hainsley. He was sporting a toothy grin.

CHAPTER 13

16 July, 1943
Piazza Armerina, Sicily

'That's the last of the company, sir,' said Lieutenant Weyers to Captain Biedermann. The two men were standing beside the road leading out of Piazza Armerina watching a loaded Opel Blitz disappear to the north. The last vestiges of the sun were disappearing as well, the purple-tinged hills turning a shade of black.

The captain glanced at his watch. '2100. Very good, Lieutenant, a successful withdrawal. It's a pity, though, we didn't hold them a little longer. Frankly, I thought we might.'

Weyers frowned.

'No, no, you misunderstand. Captain Struckmann was most complimentary. And I couldn't have done better myself. Those Tommies moved a lot faster than anyone expected. But whatever made them attack you on that hill in such force? It was unfortunate.'

Weyers shrugged. He'd wondered that very thing himself. Of course, he knew that the enemy had been fewer than Biedermann thought, but his superiors had made their own calculations and suppositions. And from long experience he figured there was no profit to be had in undermining them.

Those damned Canadians. They had scaled that cursed hill and caught him and his men completely off guard, something Weyers had sworn wouldn't happen. From that moment on there was only one sensible thing to do. His orders were very explicit, and rather unforgiving in that regard – pull his men back in order to fight another day. Sicily might be a lost cause, but the enemy was going to have to fight tooth and nail for it all the same. The 15th PzG Division would see to that.

He gritted his teeth. Then he thought of the soldier he'd caught in the open with his binoculars, and sadly no rifle to hand. But what preoccupied him was the recurring vision of the man in the greenery who ever so coolly had raised his weapon, brought it round so that the muzzle pointed at him, and fired. When it was all over the men had exhibited great admiration for the hole in his cap; it would do his reputation no harm at all. That was not the first time he'd stared down death, but *Verdammt* that was close. Too close. A chill went through him.

'Manfred?' said Captain Biedermann. 'Are you quite all right?'

'Yes, sir, I'm fine. Too little sleep, I expect.'

'Come. Let's be on our way,' said the captain. 'We have a great deal of work ahead. You can sleep a little in the car.'

Lieutenant Weyers nodded, and moved to one side in order to hold open the rear door of the Kübelwagen. Biedermann stepped in. Weyers liked his commanding officer. He could be a trifle stuffy – as was to be expected of a Prussian aristocrat from Memel – but he was a sensible sort, good with the men, amiable and supportive of his officers. And the captain was right, there was work to do.

Weyers walked slowly round the rear of the car, took a last lingering look at Piazza Armerina, and got in beside Captain Biedermann.

17 July, 1943

From his modest podium atop the steps of what not long before had been an Italian corps HQ, Captain Tighe was holding forth: 'Five enemy dead, at least that many wounded, and a captured machine gun. You and the section opened the approaches to the town, Corporal. The

Seaforths reported it completely deserted last night. Even the PPCLI agreed.'

The men laughed. The rivalry between battalions was sometimes fierce.

'All thanks to you,' he continued. 'You and the section did excellent work, Battersby. I'm recommending you for a medal.'

Lance-Corporal Battersby was beaming. 'Thank you, sir. Couldn't have done it without the men, sir.'

At the far end of the file of "A" Company, Archie gagged. Those closest to him swore that it was closer to a retch, but afterwards he claimed he was merely clearing his throat. Nevertheless, it was as well the captain didn't hear a thing.

'Yes,' said Captain Tighe, 'you're entirely right, Corporal.' The company CO turned his eyes to the men of the section. 'Well done to all of you. It was a strong position, but what pleases me most is that you took it without a single casualty. Not a scratch! When I told Colonel Jefferson he was very complimentary. I'm pretty certain he'll tell you that himself, shortly.'

If there had been a regimental band present this was the moment it would have begun to play. Of course there wasn't. Some joked that the band had gone down with the divisional transport, to which others responded that it was the vilest luck to lose both your ride and your music in one fell swoop. If there was one place you needed both, it was Sicily. Captain Tighe, in any event, had exhausted his repertoire of stirring speeches. A small band of wide-eyed Sicilian boys were the only bystanders as the rows of Edmontons came to attention, turned right, and marched smartly away with a unmistakeable spring to their step.

'Couldn't have done it without the men, sir,' parodied Archie, his forefingers clamped to his nose.

'Oh, come on, Archie,' said Hainsley. The two of them stood, taking stock of the high ground overlooking the town. There the battalion was to rest and reorganize. 'You know what he's like. Battersby would take credit for the sun rising each morning if anyone believed him. Captain Tighe's no fool, though. He knows better.'

'Hmm. Yeah, well, sure doesn't seem that way to me. You were there, Tom. Aren't you even a little angry? Battersby didn't do a bloody thing.

We took all the risks, and did all the fighting, and he twisted it to his own advantage – now he's the one getting all the credit?'

'Sure, Archie, it's damned unfair. But I'm just thankful the three of us made it out okay. Remember, you've got the respect of the guys who matter. They know exactly what happened. Hell, the entire regiment will know it in a day. Battersby will be the laughingstock of the 1st Division.'

'Perhaps. Just don't underestimate Battersby. He's got his sights set on being far more than a section corporal. Mark my words. Napoleon may have been an intriguer, but he's no match for Battersby.'

'Was he really?' said Hainsley. 'Napoleon, an intriguer? Are you sure about that? I never imagined emperors needed to do much intriguing.'

Archie sighed loudly.

'You're just grumpy because they didn't let you sleep out.'

'Didn't give me any breakfast either,' said Archie. Of course, there was another matter troubling him; he had missed the rendezvous with the Americans at the winery. Well, easy come, easy go, he thought. No, it was more than that. And it wasn't because he feared the mobsters Polowski saw lurking behind every tree. What a fool he'd been trying to follow in his father's footsteps. As if he'd ever amounted to anything more than a hill of beans. Meanwhile, Battersby, who was no one's idea of a good soldier, was basking in glory for something *he'd* done. But Hainsley was right, the others did look at him differently since Piazza Armerina. Thoughtfully he fingered the key in his pocket. Then with a savage flip of his hand he threw it away.

'I saw a melon patch not far from here,' said Hainsley. 'Why don't we go do some plundering? The captain promised us we could rest today. I'm positive no one will miss you for an hour or two – not with your current sunny disposition.'

They walked a ways down the hill under a blistering sun to a little stone hovel, and proceeded to stomp all over the peasant family's garden plot in search of melons. The woman of the house was shrieking bloody murder from the back door.

'What's with her?' said Archie. 'The place is a pig sty, the garden's a shit pile. Surely she can miss one tiny, little melon?' Neither the local populace nor the allied armies were entirely reconciled to the other's presence in Sicily.

'Grab something, will you, and let's go,' urged Hainsley, studiously avoiding the woman's stare. Later, as they plodded up the road again, Archie reached out an arm to offer a crudely carved slice of melon. Hainsley shook his head.

'Why not? It's delicious.'

'I'm not really hungry,' he replied.

'Your choice. But this would have just rotted. Didn't you see that dump?' Archie took a huge bite, the juice dribbling down his chin, and he grinned. But after a few more bites the melon lost its taste. The memory of the woman and his boorish behaviour kept replaying itself in his mind. He tossed what remained of it into the shrubs.

Had the peasant woman heard, she might have found some solace in learning of the denouement of the midmorning raid on her garden. Soon thereafter Archie was sitting on a groundsheet under a tree, doubled over, moaning when he thought no one was listening. He felt as if he'd singlehandedly gone up against a division of Panzer grenadiers.

'Gyppy gut,' pronounced Saunders authoritatively, when he arrived. Saunders had little in the way of formal medical training, but his mom was a nurse, and Latin names intimidated him not in the least; most importantly he had a knack for the work. The others in the platoon were only too happy to have someone in the position who knew more than they knew themselves, which was close to nothing. 'You ate something from a garden didn't you? And didn't wash it?' he asked.

Archie nodded. 'I feel awful. You might have warned me.'

Saunders snorted. 'Would you have listened? Actually, it's kind of obvious when you think about it. Fly lands on manure pile; fly decamps to somewhere nicer, say a lovely little melon patch; big, dumb, hungry soldier bumbles along…'

Archie groaned.

'Let's just hope that it isn't dysentery. You'll know soon enough; if your crap's full of blood you've got a problem, Archie. Meanwhile –' Saunders rummaged around in a pouch. 'Take this. It's salt and a few sugar cubes. A lick of salt, a cube of sugar every so often, and drink lots: water or tea. No alcohol. That includes wine, Archie. No wine.' He frowned in emphasis.

At the reminder Archie's head began to throb. It was all too much to bear. He'd finally done something right in the army, but his superiors were none the wiser thanks to Battersby. And here he was keeling over from the cramps, and the opportunity to make a bundle had slipped through his fingers. And it would have been a bundle, too, recalling the bottles stacked from floor to ceiling. He still wondered if Polowski had it right when he called them Mafiosi. But, either way, now it didn't matter. He let out a deep sigh.

Saunders mistook the sigh for something else. 'I'm serious, Archie. Gyppy gut is no laughing matter.'

'You don't have to convince me.' He winced as another cramp surfaced.

'Buckle up, eh. Half the battalion thinks you stormed that hill by yourself. Wouldn't do to let them down now, would it?' With more force than he intended he slapped Archie manfully on the back.

'Bastard.'

18 July, 1943

'Move it you lump of coal.'

With a grunt Archie tugged away one corner of the towel he'd been using to shade his eyes from the sun. 'Piss off, Miles. Can't you see I'm sick?'

'When are you finally going to get it, Atwell?' demanded Battersby. 'I'm the corporal, you're the private, and when I tell you to move, you'll damn well do it. Do you think Hitler calls it a day because some dick of a private says he has a touch of a belly ache? We've got orders to continue the advance.' None too gently he prodded at Archie with his rifle.

'Jesus! Take it easy, Hitler. I *am* sick.'

At 0700, precisely as promised, an impressive column of trucks, carriers and assorted other vehicles drew up bumper to bumper on the Via Generale Gaeta, Piazza Armerina's main thoroughfare. As the Edmontons waited for the order to embus, a lively discussion broke out as to who this Italian general was that no one had ever heard of adorning the street signs.

'Must be Roman,' someone said. 'All the famous Eyetie generals are Roman, aren't they?'

'Nah, definitely not Roman,' said Borden, 'not with a name like Gaeta.' Doug Borden's father was a professor of languages so this lent some weight to his words.

'When was the last time the Eyeties won a war, anyhow?' enquired another. 'Must be from then.'

Borden shrugged. There were frowns all round as the group ruminated on this. 'The Great War,' said Hainsley, finally. 'They were on the right side of that war. But I never head of a General Gaeta in the Great War. One thing's for sure, whoever he is, this Gaeta fellow is in no danger of being replaced anytime soon.'

'No,' said Borden, laughing. 'And definitely not by a general from the Sicilian campaign. They're all POWs. Don't get me wrong, I'm not complaining. It's a shame the Krauts don't take an example from the Eyeties, though. Say, where's Archie? He'd have something to say on the subject.'

'Seeking relief where he can,' replied Hainsley, with a wink.

'Again?'

Hainsley nodded. 'He's got it pretty bad.'

There were understanding nods. Gyppy gut was becoming a minor epidemic. 'Better to get rid of it now than later off the back of the truck, I suppose,' offered Borden.

Then one by one the engines of the assembled vehicles slowly went dead, which rendered that particular wisdom rather irrelevant. They weren't going anywhere. Groaning the men sank to the ground.

By early evening the Edmontons were still "standing by", with nary a sign of any forthcoming advance. The men were restless and impatient, the novelty of sitting for a few hours long since stale. Archie was the only one amongst them who was pleased at the turn of events. The idea of jolting around in a crowded truck for hours on end filled him with dread. He still felt thoroughly miserable.

It had been dark for several hours when finally they were ordered to mount their vehicles. Expectation awakened, it was all the more disappointing when nothing happened, at least until Hainsley clambered up over the tailgate.

'Ah, there you are,' said Archie. He was glad to see him, and equally glad for something to relieve the boredom. 'Where did you race off to? Monty was asking for you, was he?'

'Not exactly.' Hainsley blushed, and sat down beside him. 'The Captain promoted me.'

'Really?'

'He made me the new section corporal, Archie.'

For a moment Archie forgot his unruly insides. 'Congratulations, Tom. They couldn't have picked a better man.' A pause while this startling new development sank in. Then other implications bubbled up. 'What about Battersby?' he asked. 'Don't tell me they demoted him, did they?' A row of gleaming teeth shone through the gloom.

'Oh, no,' said Hainsley, brightly. 'Nothing like that. Battersby is taking over Evers's position as platoon sergeant. Matt's off to bigger and better; he's "B" Company's newest CSM. I understand they needed a new one.' Then he realized how it must sound, and his voice petered out.

'That snake Battersby is a platoon sergeant… *our* platoon sergeant? You can't be serious?'

Even in the darkness Hainsley was unable to meet Archie's eyes. He looked away. 'Sorry,' he mumbled.

'No, good for you, Tom. At least one decent thing came of this. And you deserve it. Best man in the section.' He said the words, but he had a hard time putting much enthusiasm into them.

Modestly, Hainsley looked away.

Archie's bowels were throbbing, and now so too was his head. It was his own damned fault. He was the one that had thrown away that last promotion, and the others before it. Acting as if he didn't care, as if the responsibility was unwanted. It was a sham he knew. He hadn't fooled anyone but himself. These past weeks in Sicily convinced him of that. But of all the rotten luck, running into a general in the middle of the night in the middle of nowhere! There was barely a ding in Brigadier Foulke's shiny bumper, and no one had interrogated him about what he was doing racing around the English countryside after midnight. Battersby had managed to turn it all to his own advantage. And now he'd pulled the same trick again. Platoon sergeant! Archie held his head in his hands.

One small salvation, at least the bastard had picked another truck to ride in – he couldn't have faced him at that moment.

The trucks and carriers started their engines. After a short pause, the column jolted into motion. It was past 2300, more than sixteen hours since they'd first mustered.

As the truck grumbled forward, Archie heard someone say the plan was to cut the Jerry communication lines further along the highway. The Americans on their left would deal with Enna, although tomorrow would bring a new day, with very likely a new plan; the Germans obstinately not playing the role assigned to them. He simply hoped he'd make it through the night without an embarrassing mishap.

'The stupid thing is, Archie, if we hadn't captured that hill,' said Hainsley in one ear, 'if YOU hadn't captured that hill, they would have passed Battersby straight over.'

Archie grunted and looked away, staring out the back past the flapping canvas. A few flickering yellow lights here and there, and Piazza Armerina disappeared from view. Good riddance, he thought. Feeling his bowels shift, he laid a reassuring hand on them.

CHAPTER 14

18 July, 1943
Valguarnera, Sicily

First-Lieutenant Weyers stood beside the road in the hilltop village of Valguarnera watching a dust-encrusted *Zugkraftwagen* 251, a half-track, rumble past towing an 88-millimetre gun. In its wake a vapour of white dust spewed upwards, swirling in intricate patterns before slowly settling on a coughing lieutenant and his equally discomforted company commander. Weyers spat. He could feel the grit in his eyes and nose, and even between his teeth. It was late afternoon. He was hot, and tired, and in the foulest of moods. And to think it had begun so promisingly less than two days before.

After departing Piazza Armerina the withdrawal of the 2nd Battalion of the 104th Regiment was short in duration. The men were barely in the trucks before they ground to a halt. Under a star filled sky, the sergeants roared orders to dismount. The 1st Battalion joined them later that day, and together they prepared for the Allied advance.

Taking the road in a north-easterly direction from Piazza Armerina, twelve miles distant, lies the mountain village of Valguarnera, perched 2000 feet above sea level. But to get there one must first traverse an impressive pass, the Porta Grottacalda, where a high ridge sweeps down from the northern mountains, and the road wends its way where it can, cliffs to either side. To the west towers an even taller feature, the square-shaped Monte della Forma. Together they form a formidable natural barrier to the interior of Sicily, one Weyers's men had taken excellent advantage of.

Initially Weyers had thought it would be the Americans that came. They were racing across the island's interior to join their forces spreading like an ink spot in the west, the British still stymied on the coast. But in the end, it was the accursed Canadians once more. They had come in force. If the intelligence reports were to be believed, they threw in the better part of three battalions.

Weyers's men and a mixed bag of others held the pass for an entire day. Then as the weight of the attack became too much, they slipped down the road a couple of kilometres towards Valguarnera, with orders to hold fast again. And should have held fast. Would have held fast had it not been for the morning's developments.

In a billet in Valguarnera, he was awakened early by gunfire, shocked at the sound. By God, he thought, it seemed virtually in the town itself. Yet the enemy was kilometres away so that was impossible. A mad scramble followed, and an hour or two of frantic chaos, of orders and counter-orders before the situation became clear. East of town a convoy of six trucks with reinforcements was taken under fire, a hundred men or more presumed lost. West of town a growing pyre of their own burning vehicles blocked the road to the front lines. To add insult to injury, every counter-attack had failed.

Hastings & Prince Edward Regt. read the shoulder flashes of a man they'd captured, which was so much unintelligible gibberish for someone schooled in Goethe. But Weyers had made it his business to be schooled in the ways of the enemy as well. And no matter how fantastic the explanation, the only one possible was that this regiment with the unwieldy name had marched by night over hill and ravine, and surrounded Valguarnera by dawn.

'Surely there must be another way?' Weyers asked now, addressing his commanding officer.

Captain Biedermann shook his head. '*Nein*. We risk being cut off. The Canadians are behind us as well. They may not be in force, but it's better to leave immediately and stand firm later, than risk not being able to leave at all. You know the General's orders.' He turned to examine his young first-lieutenant. He was a fine officer, and it would not surprise him if one day he was leading a division. Weyers was obviously upset. Biedermann laid a hand on his shoulder and smiled: 'Tomorrow brings a new day, Manfred.'

To Weyers's ears this sounded frightfully obvious. But his captain was not a captain by virtue of years spent behind a desk, and he understood his meaning. It was a question of being sensible, however much every sinew in his body cried out not to be.

Under his breath he cursed. The good Lutheran Biedermann didn't care for curses, and shot him a stern glance.

'*Indianerkrieg*,' he muttered.

The captain stared at him, puzzled. 'Indian warfare?'

'Yes, sir. Mining the roads and blowing the bridges mean nothing to these soldiers. When we sleep, they climb the hills and traverse the gullies in the dark, and attack us from behind.'

'Yes, I see your point, Lieutenant. They're wily opponents indeed. We'll need to be more cautious in future. But go now. However before you go, you must remember one thing –'

'Sir?'

'It may not have appeared that way today, but we are the ones leading them by the nose. Not the other way around. Do keep that in mind.'

At this Weyers felt a smile coming, and he nodded, his good spirits returning. Captain Biedermann had a knack for putting things in their proper perspective.

19 July, 1943
Valguarnera, Sicily

It was a long and tiring night for the section. The truck slowly bumped and rattled its way over the tortuous road from Piazza Armerina, the hard wooden benches only adding to their misery. Uniquely amongst them one man slept soundly through it all, even when Dinesen playfully poked a pencil in his ear. When they drew to a final halt after almost three hours, the air cool, and the sky still a bluish-black, harsher measures were required to wake him.

'Damn, Archie,' said Hainsley. 'We thought you were gone for good. You feeling better?'

Archie wiped at his eyes before probing his stomach, at first cautiously with two fingers, and later more vigorously with all five. 'Much. That was just what the doctor ordered, a decent sleep.' The others shook their heads in mystification at how it was possible, and carried on lining up. All three platoons of "A" Company marched brotherly together to Valguarnera, arriving near dawn.

At first sight Valguarnera wasn't much. But there was one attraction.

The regimental anti-aircraft platoon, having time on its hands as a result of a near total absence of enemy aircraft to shoot at, had taken possession of a cement water tower. The tower was riddled by bullets of various calibres. Whether this too was the handiwork of the Ack-Ack platoon was not clear. Suspicions were not allayed, however, when they saw that it had been transformed into a makeshift shower bath – to the great delight of "A" Company, who happened upon it. Two dozen men lined up to await their turn, while a handful of lucky ones cavorted under the irregular trickle, to the laughter of all.

'Ssst.' At the sound Archie glanced round. He didn't see anything odd, only the boys horsing around under the water tower, making an awful ruckus.

'Ssst.' There it was again, louder. He trawled his head lazily from left to right. It was far too early, and already far too warm to put much energy into it. Again he saw nothing. He shook his head. Had all the rattling in the truck rattled something loose?

'Archie!' A woman's voice called. A few of the boys whistled. Archie spun round, his lethargy now a thing of the past.

A woman was standing in the shadow of one of the buildings near the road, a hundred feet from the water tower and the field, where prancing, naked men were making total idiots of themselves. His eyes widened for he recognized her immediately. She was wearing the identical dress that she had worn in Modica. He strode towards her, a cacophony of whistles following.

'Amalia! What the devil are you doing here?' He was grinning from ear to ear.

'I live here,' she said. 'I told you that.'

He slapped a hand on his forehead and laughed. 'You did. Yes, you did tell me. I completely forgot.'

'No matter,' she said. Her face was serious. 'It's Ginevra.'

Archie's heart leapt. 'Has something happened?'

'Yes and no. Come. It's best she tell you herself.'

He felt the relief wash over him. At least now he knew nothing tragic had happened. 'So, she's here? But… how did you know I would be?'

She cocked her head, and the traces of a crooked smile emerged. 'We wanted to surprise you. We heard your battery would be coming to Valguarnera. The Edmontons, yes?'

'That's right. The Edmonton battalion.'

'Here it is. Come in.'

She led him through a weathered wooden door that looked as if it dated from the early Middle Ages into a dark hall. It was very cool inside. The walls and floor were clad in polished stone. He could just make out a narrow spiral staircase down the hallway. Amalia pointed up.

He took the metal stairs two at a time, then stood on the landing looking left and right. Amalia pushed past him and opened a door. 'This way, Archie.'

A woman was sitting at a small table in what looked like the kitchen. At the noise of their entrance she looked up. Her face was red and puffy. She had obviously been crying.

'Ginevra!' He'd smelt the perfume of her coming through the door. It was impossible, but she looked lovelier than he remembered, her reddened eyes and dishevelled hair faintly comical on so striking a woman. It was all he could do not to smile. And she was fine, that was the most important of all. Although, of course, she wasn't fine.

She looked at him and her eyes brightened. He went to her and stood a foot away, laying his hands gently on her shoulders. She put her head up against him, and after a quick moment pulled it back and tried to smile, but she couldn't. She nodded up at him, and placed a smooth, cool hand on one of his. 'Archie. Thank God you've come. We didn't know what to do. You're the only one who can help. Amalia told me she would find you, but I didn't believe her.' She glanced at Amalia, who bobbed her head in agreement.

'Oh, she found me alright. She's a resourceful woman Amalia. What's happened, Ginevra?'

'It's my brother, Lazzaro. The *Tedeschi* have him.'

'Tedeschi?' Archie had never heard the term before.

Ginevra gave a half-hearted Hitler salute.

'Ah, the Jerries.' Archie's voice became serious. He pulled out a chair and turned it to face her, the chair legs squeaking in protest as they dragged over the floor. Taking her hands in his, he said: 'You'd better tell me everything, Ginevra.'

Shortly after the regiment had left Modica, the two girls had talked things through. Amalia – clearly the tactician of the two – was confident that Archie at some point would come through Valguarnera. There was that. And, besides, Amalia had to go home sometime; a companion was welcome. So, seeing no particular reason not to (the war evidently not being of overriding concern) they set off, first via Caltagirone, and then on to San Michele di Ganzeria where Amalia had an uncle, and Ginevra a brother. That part was easy, they said, restrained smiles at the memory. They had borrowed a lift from the army trucks – Archie could only imagine the heady moments for the soldiers in back as these two clambered over the tailgate. Then, with the loan of a little horse – at this point Ginevra turned to Amalia and there was a rapid fire exchange of Sicilian. A pony, perhaps, Archie suggested. They both nodded. Yes, it was a pony, said Ginevra. With the pony from Amalia's uncle, they made their way overland to Valguarnera, following small roads and paths. Amalia drew a wiggling route in the air to illustrate. Neither of them made any mention of the battle that must surely have been raging several miles to their left on the hills surrounding the state highway. Was it normal, Archie asked, for two girls alone to travel through such terrain in Sicily? They shrugged.

But where was Ginevra's brother in this story? Ginevra held a finger to his lips to hush his questions. The brother had come with them, of course. Archie raised an eyebrow. Lazzaro's unit was at San Michele di Ganzeria. The soldiers had attempted to surrender to the passing Canadians, but were rebuffed each time. Archie didn't interrupt but he remembered the Italians well, standing by the road waving, the regiment plunging on with no time to spare for the millstone associated with a hundred prisoners.

Her brother had said he would try to surrender again at Valguarnera. More likely he hoped he could simply melt away, reckoned Archie. But Valguarnera was where it went wrong. The last of the Germans were retreating. They spotted him in his uniform in the street, and snatched him into their truck. Archie could picture how it had really gone. A last convoy rumbling through the streets, a sharp-eyed NCO looking out the back spotting an Italian soldier walking alone, then a shouted command, the truck slowing, and an invitation to come aboard in that characteristic tone that invites no dissent.

There was silence. The story had ended.

'What direction did they go?'

Both women pointed north. It could hardly be otherwise.

'Did you see a unit name on the trucks or the soldiers?'

They looked at each other, then shook their heads. Even if they had it would have meant nothing to them. It was too much to ask.

'Oh,' said Archie, with an easy smile. 'That can't be all?' He laughed. 'You really needn't worry, Ginevra. The Jerries aren't interested in a simple Italian soldier. The Jerries trust only the Jerries to do the real fighting. All they'll do is dump your brother with some Italian unit when they get the first chance, and the Italian Army will assign him some menial work like digging trenches, or directing traffic. In a couple of weeks the battle will be over. After that, there won't be a Jerry left on Sicily. Your brother will be home free.'

'He will?' She may not have understood the expression, but she sure understood his tone.

'Yep. Count on it.' It was certainly possible. Stranger things had happened. He'd gotten carried away, though, with the conclusion that the battle would be over in a couple of weeks. Based on recent experience that was wildly optimistic. And naturally there were other scenarios; but none of those would reassure Ginevra. 'I'll need his full name,' he said, speaking firmly. 'I may be able to find him if we take him prisoner. Then I can let you know he's all right. Do you have a photo perhaps? That would be useful. I can show it around the regiment.'

She was composed again. The tears were gone. He saw the hope creeping into her features. It didn't hurt that Amalia was squeezing her hand, and beaming at her. 'His name is Lazzaro Parisi,' she said, pronouncing it slowly, syllable by syllable. 'The Tedeschi won't hurt him, will they Archie?' She put her hand out onto the table, and pulled something back towards her, turning it over. It was the picture of a dark-haired man in uniform. It had been lying in front of her the entire time.

'No, of course not.' Dismissively he waved the notion away. 'Italy and Germany are allies. They would never hurt him.' He smiled. 'Parisi, you say. That would make you… Ginevra Parisi, would it not?' He reached out and picked up the photograph, carefully slipping it into his breast pocket.

'Yes, Archie Atwell, I am Ginevra Parisi.' She blushed. He could have swept her away then and there.

A noise from the street distracted – the stomp of marching feet.

He stood and went to the window, a finger extended to part a crack in the heavy curtains. A column of soldiers was passing in the sunlight. He sighed. 'I have to leave.'

At the door he turned and kissed her fiercely on the lips. She responded, but then drew away almost immediately, and pointed towards the stairs.

'Lazzaro will be fine,' he said.

'Thank you, Archie. Thank you.'

He turned to move away, and felt her pat him on the bottom, twice, very quickly.

He raced down the stairwell. The last image he had of her was as he craned his neck upwards, and caught a brief glimpse of a smiling face, plucks of silken black hair hanging before it, a hand of farewell extended.

CHAPTER 15

20 July, 1943
North of Valguarnera, near the Dittaino River, Sicily

When the shooting started Archie and the rest of Able were half a mile behind Dog. "D" Company had the job of establishing a beachhead at the spot where the no. 121 highway crossed over the Dittaino River. After days spent waiting for the engineers to repair deep pits blown in a road, or to accomplish the impossible from the remains of a tottering bridge, few in the division were oblivious to the need for seizing every potential obstacle with alacrity. At the very least they needed to do it before a German engineer had his way. The bridge over the Dittaino was the next such obstacle.

'Finally a chance for Dog to do its bit,' opined Archie, although above the rattle of distant gunfire there was little chance anyone would hear. The platoon was marching in extended file, several feet between them, and he was feeling good about himself. Sweet memories of Ginevra were swirling in his head and, apart from a painful relapse yesterday afternoon, his Gyppy gut seemed all but banished.

As the last of the brigade's battalions, the Edmontons had passed through Valguarnera, and carried on down into the Dittaino Valley where, shortly before midnight, they were given orders to resume the advance. Now, at the sound of MG fire the column slowed its march, and came to a halt. They could see Captain Tighe standing erect to one side, an Emperor's imperious hand in the air.

'Hold up,' bawled Sergeant Battersby, down the ranks of the unmoving platoon.

Archie turned to Hainsley. 'As section corporal, shouldn't you be assisting our fearless leader in carrying out this intricate manoeuvre? There may be someone who hasn't yet figured it out.'

Hainsley sighed. 'He's just finding his way, Archie, that's all.'

'Is that what he's doing? I could help him with that. Perhaps you could pass along the message that the Germans are straight ahead.'

'I didn't mean it like that, Archie.'

It was still very early, a quarter to five. To the east it was brightening quickly, revealing a long, high ridge to the north, whose peaks jutted out like citadels in the sky.

The gunfire quickened. A large blast sounded from further down the road, somewhere near the river. Then the shellfire also intensified. Just as Archie was beginning to regret his mildly callous remarks about "D" Company, a series of flashes dotted the distant hills: counterbattery fire.

'They were quick about it,' said Hainsley. 'Thank heavens for the arty.'

The watercourse of the Dittaino was notable for the absence of any water – no river Thames this. Several hours later when "A" Company was ordered across downstream from the bridge this proved a blessing, especially for those who couldn't swim, and even for those who could but were encumbered by a 3-inch mortar tube strapped to their backs. A jumble of slippery stones and boulders made up the broad river bed. The riflemen clambered across with relative ease, curses emanating from the mortar platoon. Once on the far bank the company was directed to spread out, to consolidate the beachhead.

"B" Company was already on the far bank digging in. As Archie came ashore, he glanced to one side and noticed a sergeant bent over, talking to a couple of men in a slit-trench. The sergeant looked up. To his surprise the man waved. Archie rubbed at his eyes.

'I'll be darned,' murmured Archie when everything came into focus. He threw up his own hand in greeting.

Sergeant Evers stood and walked towards him. To Archie's further astonishment he appeared to be smiling. Matt hadn't smiled a lot this past month, especially not since the landing, and certainly not at Archie; the worries of command, no doubt.

As he approached, Archie called out. 'Congratulations! You'll be running this company before long.'

'Thanks, Archie. I've missed you clods.' A full-fledged grin. This immediately gave way to an expression more serious, and Archie kicked himself for being so obtuse. Of course, there'd be a good reason for the bonhomie.

'You should know I put your name forward.'

Archie's surprise must have been painfully obvious.

Evers continued: 'I recommended you as platoon corporal to replace Battersby. Don't ask me why. Lieutenant Wiles was agreeable enough – you know how he is – but I'm afraid Captain Tighe wouldn't hear of it. Not on any account.'

'No?' While Captain Tighe's reaction wasn't entirely a surprise, this unequivocal dismissal still hit hard. Archie liked Tighe. He respected him. But the feeling was clearly not mutual.

'No, the Captain flat out refused.' Evers shook his head resolutely. 'You can hardly blame him, though, can you?'

Archie shrugged.

'He's always thought well of you. In fact, I think he still does, but you've stomped on his toes one time too many. On mine, too, for that matter. But I've become inured.'

'Thanks, Matt, all the same.' A pause. 'So it's hopeless? Promotion? Being something other than a private?'

'Come on, Archie. Do you even care? I mean, *really* care?'

Archie bobbed his head up and down.

'You'd be responsible for ten others. It's a little more than a stripe or two, and a new title.'

'Yes, I know. Honestly I do.'

'Good. I'm glad I wasn't mistaken in sticking my neck out for you again.' Evers fixed him with an appraising stare. Finally he nodded. 'I'd like to say it's not hopeless. After all we're in a war. But you're going to have to do a lot more than polish your boots, and return a salute now and again to change the Captain's mind. A heck of a lot more.'

'What about Piazza Armerina, then?'

'Exactly. Something like that. Why do you think Battersby was promoted to sergeant? He forced the entrance to the village.' Evers stared at him, expectantly. Archie suspected he knew more than he was letting on. When Archie began to sputter he held up a hand. 'Yes, yes, I know the whole story, Archie.'

Archie sighed. 'So if I can force the Allied path to Messina there's some slight chance for me?'

A chuckle from Evers. 'Something like that. But it's not hopeless, Archie. Concentrate on being a good soldier, not on what Battersby is up to. The good news is you may soon have your opportunity. No shortage of opportunity in a war.'

Archie frowned. Sergeant Evers extended an arm and pointed northwards where two particularly high blueish-grey peaks were visible not four or five miles distant.

'Do you see those two mountains? Well, Monty wants us to bypass the Germans on the plain by swinging left through the interior. The only way to do that is to first pass the castle gates. Those two mountains, Archie, are the castle gates. No way past on the road without capturing them both, and there are no other roads. You've heard about Leonforte I'm sure. That's on the mountain to the left. The town runs all the way up the mountain to the very peak, more than 2000 feet high. Assoro is the feature on the right – from where the Jerry guns were firing at us earlier this morning. That one's nearly 3000 feet in elevation, up a bugger of a road, with a sheer cliff on the far side.

'We can't get to either mountain without moving across this valley, where the Jerries can see us picking our noses, if they're so inclined. And make no mistake about it, both hills will be swarming with Jerries. My bet is they won't surrender easily this time. So it may interest you to learn that Lieutenant-Colonel Jefferson's orders are for the Edmonton Regiment to move on Leonforte. You wondered about a chance, Archie. Well, there it is.'

'Hmm.' He stood thinking, his face taut.

'Buck up. Don't think I would have told you any of this if I didn't think you had the right stuff deep down. I've always thought so, even when you and I were both privates. I even figured you'd be the one to get ahead. But you need to get around to making something of yourself, and soon. For some strange reason young Postlethwaite is positively in awe of you. But you're going to have to prove yourself to the rest of us, Archie. You've let too many people down, far too many times.'

He paused. Then raised an eyebrow. 'The question is: just what are you going to do about it? Otherwise, the next time Captain Tighe speaks of you in public it'll probably be from on high after a few of the boys have tossed a shovelful of gravel your way.'

Archie didn't respond. He'd had a lot of lectures in his life. But never had anyone spoken to him like this – forcefully, but as equals. Thoughtfully he stared at the high, cragged mountain on which stood a fortified town called Leonforte.

21 July, 1943
Leonforte, Sicily

No one in the platoon, the company, or even in the battalion had experienced anything like it. It thundered in their ears, and thumped in their chests, an unprecedented concentration. It was 2100, a certainty of timekeeping that required no wristwatch, merely a foreknowledge of the artillery scheme. Down in the dusk of the Dittaino valley that they had left behind, the barrels of the divisional artillery coloured the fields in a glow of yellows and oranges, while the moody grey sky ahead flashed and flamed as the detonations from the 25-pounders rippled up the hill slope towards Leonforte.

The deluge of shells did the waiting troops a world of good. Archie could see it on the faces around him. For that meant the waiting was finished, the attack had begun, and the shells would surely take their toll on the waiting enemy.

When Brigadier Vokes's orders had arrived late that afternoon they were a surprise. The Seaforth were supposed to lead, but the Eddies promptly mustered as required. With Lieutenant-Colonel Jefferson at their head they'd marched, with helmets on and rifles slung, in a long column down from Mount Stella to the highway, where they began the steady climb towards the mountain fortress. Each step had seemed higher than the last, nor was this a trick of the mind as the road rose steadily from the river bed of the Dittaino until, reaching the hill proper, it gave itself over to a series of switchbacks. Emerging from one such bend in the road, the setting sun casting long shadows, Archie had glimpsed the form of the Leonforte feature looming, and Matt Evers's parting words came to him.

He was thinking about what he must do when Sergeant Battersby suddenly roared. 'That's it, boys. The attack's begun. Remember, keep moving.'

"A" Company began to move. Rounding another bend, Archie momentarily held his breath as the full extent of the mountain appeared, a veritable cliff towering above them. Then through the gloom, a few paces distant, the ground to their left fell away. After a few more steps a deep ravine revealed itself, separating the company from the base of the hill on the other side. The road continued, dangerously skirting the ravine, until it reached a narrow bridge where it crossed over the gulley. Then it curved back on itself in a hairpin turn to begin climbing the hill in the opposite direction. To Archie's mind, and surely influenced by Sergeant Evers's earlier description, the terrain bore a distinct likeness to that of an ancient castle set on a cliff, a deep moat guarding the approaches. From an invading army's point of view, the only difficulty with this comparison was that the drawbridge was visibly out of action; there were at least two gaping holes in the stone bridge. Strictly speaking, there was more hole than bridge.

Great, thought Archie. What now? Engineers or not, it would take hours to fix.

As if reading his thoughts, Sergeant Battersby's voice rang out: 'Follow the captain.' Battersby was standing to one side, waving the platoon forward in Captain Tighe's footsteps. The captain had precipitously veered off the road and plunged out of sight into the ravine.

'Leading by example, are we?' Archie asked Battersby, as he came abreast of him. Ahead Lieutenant Wiles had disappeared following in the captain's footsteps.

Battersby squinted, the light admittedly dim, then spoke: 'Someone has to ensure the weak of mind don't get lost, Atwell.' Dramatically he winked.

'Thoughtful of you, Miles. Only, who's helping you?'

In small groups, Able followed by Dog, they descended into the gulley. The men gingerly picked a path down the rock strewn slope, sliding here and there where the gravel was loose, catching long socks on the wiry shrubs and nicking many a bare leg. At the bottom they moved quickly and soon began to scale the steep and rocky incline on the far side. The going was harder, but the men were fired up and aware of the need for haste, the bombardment scheduled to end soon. With the help of his mates, each man, loaded down with gear, weapons and as much ammunition as he could carry, pulled himself from one stony ledge to the next. Sooner than any expected they found themselves on the continuation of the narrow road, now facing uphill, a sheer cliff to protect their right, and the enemy somewhere ahead.

Tom Hainsley stood waiting for the rest of the section on the road. He waved when he spotted Archie.

'Town's just up the road,' he said.

'To think we're doing the Seaforths' work for them,' grunted Archie, breathing heavily. It was only a quick hand from Doug Borden that had saved him from a nasty fall. He'd taken far too much ammunition.

'Say again?' said Hainsley.

'Didn't you know? General Vokes wanted to send the Seaforths in this afternoon. That is until some genius in the artillery dropped a 25-pounder on their battalion HQ. A short, apparently. After that the gusto to storm the mountain was understandably lacking. So… out the Seaforths, in the Eddies.'

'You're pulling my leg.'

'Nope. Cross my heart. Heard it from a fellow I know. You're in the high command now. Surely you were briefed, Tom?'

Hainsley smiled. 'I'm a lance corporal, Archie, not a blooming general.'

Fortunately any concerns about the enemy hearing their approach, marred as it was by much clanging and considerable cursing, were allayed by the enthusiastic barrage of the brigade's support battalion, the Saskatoon Light Infantry. The farmers from Saskatchewan let off such a clatter of mortar and MMG fire, interspersed with a few smoke bombs, the entire Eighth Army could have marched into Leonforte unheard.

In any event, "A" Company had not fired a single shot before it approached what very much resembled the gates of a castle, followed by a jumble of stone buildings that clearly marked the beginning of town. A line of red tracer shot down the centre of the road.

'Keep right,' an officer at the front shouted. It may even have been Captain Tighe. The air reeked of cordite and smoke from the bombardment. Every man was clasping multiple weapons, stepping quickly, and gawking anxiously about. The Germans, however, were nowhere to be seen. In the distance, a man screamed in pain, and this only served to heighten their apprehension.

Passing a mid-sized church, grand Roman-style pillars in its façade, a few men crossed themselves. Past the church the road swung right where it doggedly headed straight up the hill. 'Keep right, fellows,' said Lieutenant Wiles. 'Able has the right half, inclusive of the road.' He was standing at the junction, directing traffic and taking stock of the platoon, with a map in hand. Judging by his expression, the weight of the world was on his shoulders. Archie, who at any other time might have joked about this, nodded politely at him.

It took some time climbing the steep streets, but "A" Company made it through the better part of town without difficulties. Off their left they could hear shots every now and again. "D" Company was having a tougher time. Then Archie spotted what looked like a train station, not far from what appeared to be the crest of the hill.

At that moment, the trouble began.

CHAPTER 16

21 July, 1943
Leonforte, Sicily

'Follow the tanks,' First-Lieutenant Weyers instructed his men. The men dutifully fell into twin files behind the Panzers and began moving down the hill. All three battalions of the 104th Regiment were fighting together, so there were many new faces that Weyers didn't recognize. But that was of no concern, for they all knew what was demanded of them, and the Canadians were terribly naïve if they believed they were going to march in and seize Leonforte with barely a fight.

Captain Struckmann, in briefing the battalion officers last night, had made it very clear that the 2nd Battalion would not be disappearing into the dark on this occasion; Leonforte was to be held. It had to be held. The Allies were not to be allowed to slip around their right flank on the Catania plain. That would be a catastrophe for their forces who had ground the British to a standstill.

The enemy bombardment was impressive enough, but Weyers's men in the town had kept their heads down and for the bulk of the company waiting on the reverse slope of the mountain, the bombardment was entirely inconsequential. Now it was time for his grenadiers to show what they were made of. While he would have brushed away any such suggestion, Weyers still harboured bitter memories of the clash at Piazza Armerina. None of his superiors had faulted him in any way. To the contrary. But he faulted himself. This would be redemption, he thought grimly, a chance to settle old scores. Both for him and for his father.

Abruptly the first panzer in the column roared. It was nearing the centre of town. For an instant the flash of the gun lit up the narrow, darkened streets, an echoing flash and a *THUMP* from the detonation coming an instant later. Then the zipping burst of an MG erupted, from one of the strong points, or the machine-gun nests carefully sited on multiple rooftops. This was followed by the sound of more MGs and what must surely be rifle fire. The latter would be from the enemy, Weyers reckoned. He removed his side arm from its holster.

Deliberately they moved further down the hill, following the main street, the tank commanders warily eying the path ahead from their iron pulpits atop the darkened turrets. The commanders knew the dangers of such a vantage point, but they also knew the dangers of navigating a Panzer in confined quarters where an anti-tank gun could appear anywhere. Dutifully Weyers's men fell in behind each Panzer; to them the task of rooting out the infantry hidden and lying in wait. Weyers joined the last group of men who were in file behind the third tank. He had chosen this position not because he shied away from leading more prominently, only that his role demanded a broad overview, one not possible in the forefront.

'There,' shouted *Oberfeldwebel* Friederich von Steinen, at the sound of another cannon shot, pointing ahead. Weyers nodded to his staff sergeant.

An uneasy dusk had turned into the darkest of nights in Leonforte. The narrow, twisting streets were menacing. At intervals violent flashes bathed them in lurid colours, all manner of ordnance rocking the still of the night. Lieutenant Weyers's eyes were fixed on the street ahead, and the buildings to each side. An impatient finger twitched on the trigger guard of his Walther.

'Damn it,' cursed Archie as the sound approached. 'Another tank. God, I loathe tanks.'

'A Mark III, I'd wager,' said Hainsley with a touch too much boyish enthusiasm for Archie's taste.

Archie and a handful of others were crouching on the lower floor of a two-storey building that abutted the long main street, butterflies fluttering in their stomachs. The deep growl of an engine signaled the tank's approach. Its tracks clanked and rattled ominously, until the whole building took to shaking as the massive beast rumbled past. Even inside, the air reeked of dust and gas fumes. Archie rose onto his knees just far enough to be able to peer through the filthy window pane, then almost immediately sank to the ground again. 'Infantry,' he said, and held up two palms and ten fingers for the inspection of Tom Hainsley.

'Any more tanks?' Hainsley asked, with a frown.

He wasn't entirely certain, his glance had been only a cursory one. But he would have noticed another Panzer – they weren't exactly inconspicuous. He shook his head.

Hainsley nodded and beckoned to Dan King, the third of the section's Bren gunners. 'We'll let them pass, then you get that thing into action,' he whispered. 'Saunders, make sure you keep those magazines coming.' He took a deep breath. 'On my signal, boys.' And he stared round at his small squad as he clearly felt a corporal in charge ought to.

All told there were six of them, the rest of the section having melted away to whatever wall, building or length of dark shadow they could find after the first tank caught them unawares. The rest of the platoon and the company had similarly vanished when the firing began. In retrospect it had been a bloody near thing. Another few seconds, another few steps, and the entire section following along at the very end of the company would have waddled across the tank's path, right as it fired its 50mm missive of high explosive. Fortunately, Hainsley had warned them in the nick of time.

Hainsley went to the window and glanced in the direction of the tank and its escort of soldiers. 'Now!' he shouted. Archie stepped forward and set about energetically smashing out the window pane with the butt of his rifle. Then he stepped away to make room. Without a word King moved into the gap and laid the bipod of the LMG on the window sill, settled the butt comfortably against his shoulder and leaned forward. The Bren gulped for air, the sound of the burst very loud in the room.

Archie squinted past King; the ordered squad of Germans, caught from behind, was visibly buckling. Unrelenting, King returned his finger to the trigger and kept it there until the Bren would fire no more. He wrenched out the curved 30-round magazine set atop the MG and let it fall to the ground with a clatter. Saunders passed him another, which he clicked into position with an oiled ease – an ease that came from having done it a thousand times before, the skill suddenly very useful. Between King and Saunders, they had eight magazines in the basic pouches of their webbing, and probably at least that number spread amongst the others.

Hainsley pushed forward to see the situation for himself, vying to get his own rifle into action. Archie peeled away and hastened to the heavy wooden front door, which he cracked ajar, fully intending to join in the slaughter with his rifle. Only, before he could do so, he spotted something. And at the sight of it his knees went wobbly.

'TANK!' he roared.

He said it with a half turn of his head. Although with the Bren and a handful of rifles banging away, it was doubtful anyone heard the warning. A third Panzer – Hainsley had it entirely correct, for the squat tank filling the road was indeed a Mark III – was coming around the bend to the north at an aggressive clip. Even more worrisome was the realization that the tank had spotted them for the barrel of its cannon was turning in their direction.

Transfixed by the sight, Archie let the rifle slide to the ground. Then, coming to a decision, he turned and leapt towards the pile of packs in the middle of the room. There he seized a curious-looking long, metal tube which was leaning against the packs. A new wonder weapon some called it, and while they were the very devil to operate, it was the only weapon they had that stood a chance against a Panzer. It was known as a PIAT. And it was loaded, for he'd loaded it himself.

Hainsley saw him and shouted: 'Archie! What are you doing?'

Archie didn't respond. He was halfway to the door with the PIAT in his arms, and not a second to spare. He barreled through the doorway and across the street, where a low stone wall offered refuge. The tank couldn't have been more than 50 yards away by this time. A suitable range for a PIAT he thought as he lifted the weapon's rubberized shoulder piece to his shoulder, and rested the barrel's bipod on the wall. Archie didn't trust its accuracy much beyond the range his mother could throw a bunched up dishcloth – though admittedly she was a heck of a shot.

Ironically, the minimum aperture on the sight was for 50 yards. But there was no time to raise the sights. Not that he needed to. It was dead in front of him. Archie squinted down the tube, and with two fingers pulled at the trigger.

With all his energy focused on the tank, the recoil took him by surprise. The projectile hit the Panzer squarely under the turret. Through some quirk of chance too infinitesimal to calculate it had lodged itself in a viewing port, the driver's port. Almost too good to believe. But nothing happened. The seconds crawled by. Still nothing. He heard shouting. The tank squeaked to a halt.

Archie pulled himself to his feet and began to run, sprinting for the narrow alleyway set back from the stone wall, expecting at any moment to hear a blast. An enemy light machine gun sputtered angrily, and rifles crackled. Bullets whistled through the air. Sill there was no explosion. The turret of the tank began to slowly revolve.

Archie threw himself into the plunging darkness of the alley, away from the terror of the Panzer and the fury of its infantry escort.

A flash of light penetrated down the alleyway, accompanied by the crash from a heavy cannon firing. Almost immediately there was a tremendous blast, bringing with it another flash of light. It was then he realized they hadn't been firing at him.

Archie kept going, not knowing what he should do, only that remaining still was a fool's errand if the soldiers followed. He had failed, failed miserably.

He came upon an intersecting street and ducked down it. There, in the dark alcove of a building, he stopped and squatted down amongst the trash, the stench overpowering, safe for the moment. He listened for his pursuers.

Hearing none he relaxed, and sank into a pile. But above the sound of his own breathing, and the beating of a heart that might very well have been his, was the crackle of small arms fire. There was a shout in German. They would be rooting out the survivors of the section. The blast had been for them.

The fear rushed up unannounced, catching him in a sudden vice, a constricting net thrown over. His breath came fast and shallow. Facing down the Panzer he had felt nothing, only a glorious clear headedness and the blood coursing vibrantly in his veins. But now he was immobilized.

Get a hold of yourself, Atwell, he told himself. You were the genius who said you'd make a fine soldier.

He had to do something he knew. Hainsley and the others would be wiped out. Helplessly he stared at the PIAT still clenched in two fists of white knuckles. But the thing was as useful as scrap metal without bombs, and the bombs were with the packs. Although, for all the good the bombs were, he would have been better throwing the bloody contraption like a spear. Then, thinking of the numbskulls who'd come up with such a dud of a weapon, his mind was suddenly racing again. And he cursed at the memory of the rifle he'd let fall, and a Tommy gun leaning equally useless against the packs.

His hand rooted frantically through the pouches of his webbing, his fingers closing excitedly around a spare Bren magazine before he recognized what it was, and released it. Then a moment of joy as he felt the hard apple of a grenade, followed by a second in the same pouch. His spirits lifted. And, of course, he had a bayonet!

He pulled himself to his feet, and considered leaving the PIAT behind. However leaving weapons behind hadn't worked out well in this battle, so he took it. The Jerries didn't know the damned thing didn't work.

Where the alleyway met the street, he paused. To his relief he saw that the tank had moved on. But a dozen soldiers in bucket helmets remained and were clearly preparing an assault through the smashed façade of the building Hainsley and the others occupied.

Lurking in the alleyway, there seemed no other choice than to toss a grenade and hope the Germans would be intimidated by that, or perhaps the sight of him brandishing a PIAT. Then, down the steep incline of the street, a tank's gun sounded. Evaluating his chances, Archie lifted his head. The sparkle of machine gun and rifle fire that enveloped the town was building to a new crescendo.

One of the Germans – an *unteroffizier*, or maybe even the real thing – heard the commotion, too. He began to shout as only a German of a certain breed and authority can. The soldiers turned and began to regroup on the street. As a parting gift a soldier in grey casually lobbed the stick grenade he was holding into the building, and turned away. The detonation was short and curt, a whisper of white smoke came curling out through the broken wall. But neither the soldier nor his comrades in the troop stopped to look or listen; they were already trotting down the road in two files, 9mm Schmeisser sub-machine guns and Mauser carbines resting securely in their arms.

Inside the room the scene was unrecognizable. The packs still lay in the heap where they'd been dumped, but the front wall had all but disappeared, the ceiling leaned ominously, and the floor was carpeted with a knee-high debris of wood, stone and plaster. Instinctively Archie stepped through the rubble to what had once been the window.

'Archie,' called a voice. He turned and squinted at the dark shape a few steps away and was astonished to see the fine-etched features of Dick Saunders lying in the debris.

He went to him. 'You old devil, Dick! Are you okay?'

'I'm not exactly sure,' replied Saunders, as Archie leaned over. 'I thought we were done for. Here give me a hand. We'll see.' He winced as Archie pulled him out from under the wooden beam where he'd been pinned, and stood wobbling precariously, proud as a peacock that he still could. 'Man, was I glad when I saw you. I was expecting a Jerry. Leg's a bit sore, but the rest seems okay.'

Archie frowned at this diagnosis, which ran counter to pretty much everything he saw before him. Saunders looked a shambles. But he was no doctor.

'Trust me,' said Saunders, his voice growing in strength. 'Who's the medic around here, Archie? I'll survive, eh.'

'What about Hainsley? King? McDonald? Dinesen?'

Saunders shrugged and pointed at the rubble of the front wall which had once lent a defined barrier between room and street. 'Don't know. McDonald and Dinesen got out the back a couple of minutes ago. I told them to beat it and get some help after the Krauts started tossing grenades. The buggers had a Panzer, Archie.'

Archie sighed. 'Yeah, I know.'

'Sorry, I'm still a little groggy. Of course you do. You've got some balls on you, Archie, I'll give you that. Facing down a Panzer with a PIAT.' He shook his head.

They found Hainsley soon after, near where Archie had left him, close to the window. He gulped. Hainsley was covered with the rubble you might expect when a 50mm high explosive shell meets a stone wall at close range. 'Tom!' he shouted when he saw the body twitch. Hainsley groaned, his eyes firmly closed. 'Come on, let's get you out of here,' he said. Hainsley's eyes fluttered.

Saunders went down on his knees to help, and together they dug furiously at the pile of stones and wood. When their excavations were complete they stood. A final yank, Archie grasping Hainsley firmly under the armpits, and they pulled him free. Hainsley's right arm hung limply, the rest of him coated in dust and debris and what looked like blood. However, his face was untouched, though deathly pale.

'Thanks, Archie,' mumbled Hainsley, blinking. 'Here, let me sit for a bit.' His legs gave out and they let him sink to the ground. Archie leaned over with concern.

'I'll check him out,' said Saunders. 'You look for Dan.'

Dan King turned up too, although his own mother wouldn't have recognized what protruded from the avalanche of debris. There was a blood-stained bush jacket, limbs and neck cruelly twisted, a gaping wound to his head with the blood still fresh. King's eyes were open but glassy. Archie knew there was no need to call over Saunders.

'Oh, damn it to hell,' he mumbled. He'd never seen death so close. There were less than a dozen men in the section, and now one of them was dead. 'Why the hell did you have to go and do that, Dan?' he said. He felt as if he'd taken a blow to the stomach, the air sucked from him, his mind paddling through an impenetrable fog.

A moment passed and he sensed Saunders hovering behind. Then he heard a deep gasp. 'Jeez… Oh Christ…' Archie felt a hand laid on his shoulder, and there was a long silence. 'Come on, Archie. We have to go. We can't stay here.'

Archie dragged himself to his feet. As he did so he noticed King's Bren lying in the rubble. Against all odds it looked in working order. He stepped forward and snatched it up. Quickly he looked it over. He even broke off the magazine, only to see that it was full. 'Right,' he grunted, and slung the canvas sling over a shoulder so that the gun hung freely from his right. He went to the packs, leaned over and picked up a rifle – his own he thought – and slung it on the other side.

'You'd better take the PIAT,' he said to Saunders, and was intending to say more but his voice broke. He looked away lest Saunders see what he preferred he didn't.

'It's not even cocked, Archie,' said Saunders, staring not at him but at the PIAT. 'Do you think…?'

'Sure, I'll do it. You're in no state.'

Unshouldering the Bren and the rifle, he took hold of the metal tube and flipped it around so that it was resting on the ground on the shoulder piece, the tube vertical. One of the principal flaws of the PIAT was the hit-and-miss nature of its cocking system. Theoretically, it was supposed to re-cock itself after firing, but all too often it had a mind of its own.

'Bloody thing. Not only doesn't it work in the clinch, you have to be a muscle man even to load it.' He stood with both feet on the shoulder piece and bent over the tube, grasping the trigger guard halfway down with both hands. He pulled up, then gave a quick twist to the right. Gritting his teeth, he pulled again as the steel spring inside fought back until rewarded by a *click* as the sear locked into place.

'They don't make it easy, do they?' said Saunders.

'Here,' replied Archie, 'It's all yours. Don't forget to take a few of those bombs… if you cross your fingers one or two may actually work.'

They stuck to the back streets, moving slowly for Hainsley's benefit, hoping to find others from the battalion, conscious that three men stood little chance against a company of Germans, let alone three Panzers. In the meantime, the gunfire had died away, but the streets were eerily deserted. Archie had begun to fear the remnants of the battalion were thoroughly routed and had fled. The sound of small arms fire came as a relief.

'They're ours,' Archie said excitedly. Saunders looked sceptical. 'Can't you hear? That's a Lee-Enfield, or my name's Miles Battersby.' Wanly, Saunders smiled. 'I'll go ahead. You and Tom follow. But keep a good distance between us, just in case. Do you think he'll manage?' He motioned in the direction of Hainsley who was nursing an arm, distinctly wobbly on his feet.

Saunders nodded. 'I'll see that he does. Not much choice is there?'

'No,' Archie replied with a grimace. 'And don't forget about that modern marvel you're carrying.' He wondered if it came down to it whether the PIAT would be of any use at all; Saunders was struggling mightily with the three cardboard containers strapped to his back, each one containing a bomb. Simply unloading the whole rigmarole would take five minutes. And it was even odds whether Saunders had recovered from the ill effects of his encounter with the Panzer. It was a ragged trio he was leading, but there was no time to worry about that. Archie strode forward. The shooting was intensifying.

Where the street emptied onto a small, octagonal square, the situation became clearer. Directly in front of him, on the other side of the square, perhaps a hundred feet away, two streets came together in a triangle. In that triangle was wedged a large two-storey building, although a second glance revealed it to be three houses side by side. A small band of Edmontons was making a fighting retreat in that direction. He was in time to see the last two soldiers, presumably a rearguard, hastily turn and disappear through a doorway in a hail of flying plaster. A heavy wooden door clanked shut behind them.

A quick glance to the right revealed a parallel street that entered onto the square. Several figures lurked in the gloom, and doubtless there were more hidden from view. It was impossible to make out their uniforms, but settling down on one knee he bent an ear round the corner, the sort of game little boys played. Archie wasn't especially familiar with German, but whatever language they were speaking wasn't English, nor was it Italian. Besides, the Eyeties were all too busy surrendering to be lurking in darkened streets. So that left the Krauts. It could hardly be otherwise. Softly he spat on the ground.

Then, across the square, he noticed movement in another street. Archie looked closer. Damn! There was a whole crowd of them lined up against the buildings, awaiting their orders. Two soldiers were positioned at the street corner itself where it met the square. They were lying on the ground with a machine gun and a steel ammunition box, and a clear view of the houses. A third man came and knelt behind them on one knee and raised a pair of binoculars. The bastards were intending an assault.

Across the square the MG-34 began to zip, joined by another closer by that he hadn't noticed. A whistle squealed. From both streets men in tanned camouflage and bucket helmets surged forward.

At the sight Archie rose, a sudden rage boiling within him. His hand reached for his pouch.

CHAPTER 17

22 July, 1943
Leonforte, Sicily

First-Lieutenant Weyers heard the MGs go silent as he tucked the whistle back into his breast pocket. Pistol in hand, he lifted his arm and began waving the waiting lines of men forward. He knew there was a risk to the tactic; on the other hand there couldn't have been more than a dozen of the enemy, and all told he had nearly thirty Panzer grenadiers amongst his two squads. So it seemed a risk worth taking. He certainly didn't want to allow this group the time to settle in properly, sight their weapons, and turn the place into a redoubt – not when the counter-attack was progressing so well. No, it was a question of hitting hard and fast. A short rush and they would have them.

He motioned to the last men to hurry, and when they thumped past, Weyers went in pursuit. An enemy machine gun sounded from ahead.

Without warning there was a flash of light and a muted *BANG* in the square.

The fall of the grenade couldn't have been more than twenty metres from him. Weyers recoiled from the sheer surprise of it as much as the sight or sound. Surely they were too far from the houses for the enemy to be tossing grenades?

One of the first men in the formation went down in a sickening clatter of gear. A second grenadier grasped at his leg, cursing, and the entire squad behind slackened their pace. Seeing this hesitation the second prong of the attack, coming from the street to the right, slowed and began to spread out, sudden uncertainty setting in.

Then the throaty rattle of a machine gun burst sounded on their flank, almost behind them, the MG unmistakeably a Bren gun. He'd heard them often these past days in the hills.

Weyers felt the sour bile of fear rising up in his throat. He glanced about. What the devil was going on? They'd been tricked. From the building ahead he now heard another MG join in. Rifles were cracking. Damnit!

Like any experienced warrior, Weyers's eyes took instruction from his ears. He snapped his head around to the left from where he had first heard the MG. And sure enough, leaning against the corner of a building abutting the square and half hidden in its shadows, a single man in a bowl helmet was visible with an LMG gripped in his hands. Most unusually he was shooting from the hip, at almost point blank range, enfilading the long file of Weyers's men. One man, two… then a third went down. The machine gun barked and flashed. Their own MGs crews were impotent, cloaked as they were by their own men in the square. The platoon was being cut down – his platoon!

Angrily Weyers turned towards the soldier and thrust out his arm, the Walther extended. His index finger pulled furiously at the trigger. Too furiously it was to prove, for the trio of 9mm bullets buried themselves in Leonforte's extensive stonework. And the enemy soldier still stood, a half silhouette, sheltered by the building. Seemingly impregnable, he was firing one quick, short burst after another. He pivoted towards Weyers.

In the gloom it was a near impossibility, but it did seem as if their eyes met for a brief moment. Then the Bren coughed angrily. A salvo of bullets whistled round Weyers. Right when he was prepared to sigh in relief that they had missed him, a burning pain shot through his arm. Reflexively he dropped the pistol, only to regret it an instant later.

'*Scheisse,*' he muttered, clutching at his arm. The men were scrambling in all directions, away from the killing ground of the square. A few were down on one knee and returning the fire from the houses. But it was a futile business without cover.

The enemy soldier knew what he was doing; Weyers had heard spoken of these specially-trained mountain troops the Canadians were employing. He had turned back towards Weyers's grenadiers and was again firing short two or three-bullet bursts. Oddly, Weyers couldn't make out the man's compatriots, although undoubtedly they were ranged behind. Then as suddenly as he had appeared, the man vanished, and the fire from the flank did as well.

'Von Steinen!' Weyers yelled. For a certainty he knew his trusted first sergeant was somewhere in the melee, although he couldn't pinpoint where. '*Zurück!*' he shouted. '*Zurück!*' One of the MG-34s was noisily dueling it out with a Bren in an upper floor window of a house.

'*Jawohl, mein Heer.*'

Von Steinen understood immediately. There was nothing to be gained from continuing the action. The only sensible course was to use this lull to pull back and regroup, lick their many wounds. Of all the infernal luck, thought Weyers. The Canadians were reeling, only pockets of resistance left. His men would have made short shrift of the group they'd cornered if this second enemy party hadn't come along. Or had it been planned? The tables were well and truly turned; they were the ones caught between hammer and anvil.

The Panzer grenadiers needed little encouragement and withdrew as quickly as they were able, melting away into the warren of streets surrounding the square.

Archie cursed as he saw the German officer duck out of sight with the last of his men. His breathing was heavy, although he had done nothing more than switch out one magazine of the Bren for another. He darted a renewed glance at the square. The Germans were gone.

But wait! There were still two soldiers to be seen. Both had their hands in the air. Yet while ostensibly surrendering they were crouched low and backing away. Archie raised the muzzle of the Bren, and watched. It was true they had their hands in the air, but in point of fact they weren't doing anything different than the others, which was to flee. The only difference was these two were banking on some perversion of the laws of war to get away with it. To hell with that. They'd mown down King and Hainsley without a second thought. The bastards! Archie put his finger to the trigger, and the gun thumped satisfyingly.'

When it was done the all-consuming rage dissipated, the red mist that had smothered his every thought evaporated without a trace.

Grimly he surveyed the square, now dotted with bodies and equipment. He would have felt better had he been able to finish off that arrogant looking officer – he had a suspicion it was the very one he'd seen with the tank. As to the tank, there was little he could do about that. But he wouldn't forget it either. He was still angry at what they'd done.

A little later when the coast seemed clear they made for the houses. Crossing the square an object on the paving stones caught Archie's eye and he bent to retrieve it. It was a pistol, the pistol the officer had dropped. He stuffed it into his webbing. With a new magazine it might prove useful.

'Eddies,' he shouted, as they approached the thick wooden door of the first house.

The door cracked open and the three of them wasted no time in slipping through the opening. Behind the door, a few steps back in the gloom, stood an officer, waiting.

'Atwell!?'

'Yes, sir.' The officer's broad, ruddy face sharpened into focus as Archie stepped forward.

'Evening, sir,' said Archie.

'Good evening, indeed,' said Lieutenant-Colonel Jefferson.

There was a commotion behind, and he turned and saw Saunders relieving himself of the box with its three PIAT bombs. Hainsley was at his side nursing his arm. 'You've brought some others,' said the colonel.

'Private Saunders and Corporal Hainsley, sir. We're all "A" Company.'

Solemnly Jefferson shook their hands, put a gentle hand on Hainsley's shoulder, and slowly looked at each of them. 'Just the three of you?'

'It could have been worse, sir.'

'Yes, I'm sure it could have been.' The colonel shook his head. 'Pity though,' he added. 'I was hoping there might be a few more like you. But I'm happy you're here.' He rubbed at his chin, and they saw his eyes sparkle. 'I think it's fair to say that the three of you saved our proverbial bacon. Another ten minutes and the Edmonton Regiment would have needed a new commanding officer. A new headquarters' staff, too, I dare say.'

'It was Archie's doing, sir,' said Saunders. 'I was just the pack mule.'

The colonel smiled, and once again he looked at Atwell. Previous glances from the colonel had usually been tinged with a certain disapprobation, disgust even. That was missing now. 'You all deserve a reward for your gallantry. Only I'm afraid that may not be possible –'

Archie felt himself frowning.

'You see, Atwell, there's a good chance we won't survive the night. The Regiment is scattered over Hell's half acre. I'm hoping that doesn't mean the Jerries have got them. And we have nothing to hold back the Panzers.'

'Oh, but Saunders does,' said Archie pertly. 'That's a PIAT he's carrying, sir. In theory it can stop a Panzer cold. Although in my limited experience prayer might be as effective.'

At this the colonel raised his eyebrows. 'Some day you'll have to explain that to me, Atwell. But for the moment the PIAT is most welcome.'

'Sir!' A crisp-looking lieutenant arrived at the colonel's side. The lieutenant nodded congenially at the three soldiers, a most unusual look for a staff officer destined for higher things, and confronted with three lowly and decidedly scrubby enlisted men he didn't know from Adam. He too was aware of the close call they'd had. He turned to address the colonel.

'Nothing, sir. There's no reception at all with the wireless. Brown says he's tried everything he can think of, but he's never seen anything like it. The no. 18 is normally reliable gear, according to him. He's on the roof top as you suggested. He says that at this elevation we should easily be able to raise brigade. He'll keep trying though.'

'Yes,' said Jefferson. 'Yes, tell him to do that. And see that someone has a look at Corporal Hainsley, would you?'

Jefferson turned back to them. 'So you see, gentlemen, our problems are manifold. Oh, don't look so downbeat you three. You don't really think I'm ready to wave the white flag just yet, do you? Besides, that wouldn't be fair given your performance outside my front door. No, we're going to do what the general sent us here to do.' He grinned, and for all his tiredness and accumulation of worries it was a grin that could have won over an army, and Archie – a tough customer by his own reckoning – felt himself won over as well. He'd always been a little sceptical why some men were made colonels, but it seemed there were good reasons after all.

'Have something to eat and drink, although I'm afraid rest is out of the question under the circumstances,' said the colonel softly, before he left.

Roughly a half hour later – Archie had his mouth full of cheese at the time – there was a new disturbance. Anxiously, he swallowed, and listened to the sound of boots in the hall. It turned out to be two platoons from "C" Company. The colonel's meagre ranks were swelling.

'Atwell?' said a man, appearing before him. 'The colonel wants to see you.'

He found the colonel standing in the cellar. Curiously, a young Italian boy of about ten was with him. He had just handed the boy a piece of paper, which was now being unceremoniously stuffed into the lad's shorts pocket. A soldier at the colonel's side was speaking a few words of Italian to him.

'Does he understand?' he heard the colonel ask.

The boy's head went up and down.

Gravely the colonel shook the boy's hand, and patted him on the shoulder, and the boy was off.

'You wanted to see me, sir?' Archie came to attention.

'Yes,' replied Jefferson. Then he noticed the puzzlement on Archie's face. 'I sent a message with him. We desperately need reinforcements, but we still can't reach brigade. I'm hoping that young lad may be able to.'

There was little Archie could say to this, so he said nothing. As omens go it wasn't much if the battalion's fate rested on a single Sicilian kid. Expectantly he stared at the colonel.

'I hate to ask, Atwell, after all you've done, but I'm shorthanded as you can see. And with the wireless out… I desperately need someone to reconnoitre. Would you? Check out the lay of the land, see what the Jerries are up to and, above all, herd any of my stray sheep in our direction?'

It would have been simpler merely to give an order, but that was not Jefferson's way. 'I'll do it, sir,' said Archie.

'It'll be dangerous.'

Archie shrugged. 'No more dangerous than remaining here, sir.'

The colonel smiled.

CHAPTER 18

22 July, 1943
Leonforte, Sicily

'Remember, Dick,' said Archie, 'if you're tempted to use that PIAT, you need to pull the trigger extra hard. And once you do fire, keep the trigger pulled a good long while. The bloody thing won't re-cock otherwise, and then you're truly up the creek without a paddle. The Bren's a safe bet either way. Unless it's a tank. In which case I wasn't kidding with the Colonel about the praying bit.'

'Stop fussing, Archie,' Saunders sighed. 'I did all the same training you did. My leg may be tender but I can pull a flipping trigger. So bugger off, eh. We'll try to hold the fort until you return.'

Alone in the streets of Leonfòrte, Archie's bravado dissipated almost as soon as the door thumped shut behind. Beyond the obvious dangers associated with marauding groups of Panzer grenadiers and the occasional Panzer Mark III, the town was built in the form of a scythe, no street straight for long. Losing one's way was no idle concern. On top of which, being on a hill meant that most were built at sharp inclines, so one moment he was panting uphill, and the next being propelled downward, all the while trying to avoid holes, protruding cobblestones, and other hazards in the dark. He was well aware that an encounter with the enemy was apt to end poorly, so he moved deliberately, hugging the sides of the buildings, sticking to shadows where he could.

Dawn was only a few hours off but the battle for Leonforte was still in full flight. At intervals bright flashes lit the sky. Small arms and mortar fire echoed off buildings and carried into the surrounding hills. Panzers muzzled their way through town, uncertain where resistance was located, hell bent on finding it. The air reeked of gunfire. Where he heard a machine gun or the slamming of an '88 close by, Archie skirted the fracas as best he could.

Stumbling upon one such furious exchange, unable to discern friend from foe, he ducked into a nearby building in the hope he might find a peephole through which to safely learn more. Once inside he stepped warily down a hallway that was cool and very dark. Then he froze. Voices.

He hesitated an instant, cautiously unslung his Lee-Enfield and took it in both hands. He tiptoed down the hallway to the end until he reached a door half ajar. The sounds from the battle outside were deafening. Suddenly the voices spoke again, softly.

Gently he pushed at the door with a boot. Then he plunged through the doorway and stood poised, the rifle held steady in both hands. He was grinning.

Inside the room there was a sharp intake of breath. Then a voice said: 'Jesus! You scared the living daylights out of me. I might have shot you.'

Two Eddies were sprawled on the floor beneath the window sill, backs to the wall, their rifles stacked several feet away.

Archie chuckled. 'It's a good thing you didn't. Colonel Jefferson wouldn't have liked that one bit. And, of course, you would have needed something to shoot me with... But never fear, the Colonel will be happy to see you boys.'

One of the men stood.

'It's you?' Archie said, scarcely able to believe his eyes.

Battersby took a step towards him, the glimmers of a smile emerging until, belatedly, he saw who it was. 'Atwell? What are you doing here?'

Archie groaned as the second man also stood. 'Lachance? You too?

I might have known. Well, no matter – the Colonel didn't strike me as particularly fussy about the reinforcements he received.'

The reinforcements themselves saw it rather differently. In fact, it took some considerable convincing, and liberal use of the colonel's name, before Battersby was prepared to take Archie at his word, and listen to directions how to reach current battalion headquarters. Hearing himself, Archie couldn't help thinking he was overdoing the rhetoric – 'desperately needed' was not a term he usually associated with these two.

'I don't like it one little bit,' muttered Battersby finally, as he collected his rifle. 'You lurking around in the streets like this. There's a battle going on. Why aren't you in it, Atwell? I wonder what the Colonel will say about that.'

Which was a mighty odd thing to say after his explanation. Especially as he'd found the two of them squirreled away in a house, while others were fighting tooth and nail practically next door. 'I think you'll find the Colonel will be more interested in why one of his platoon sergeants plus companion, were holed up in the dark with their heads between their knees,' Archie replied. 'I'll mention it to him, shall I?'

Lachance had an awkward look about him. Battersby simply scowled. 'Not if you know what's good for you, Atwell. But it doesn't matter. You're nobody. No one listens to a private.'

The firefight down the block had ended by the time they were on their way. Archie glanced after them. Battersby was right; even if someone did listen, no one had seen what he'd seen. He headed downhill.

If the Germans were in control in the south, it bode poorly for their chances of capturing Leonforte. The engineers trying to span the ravine couldn't very well do that if the Germans were pouring fire at them from the town's outskirts. And with no bridge, no reinforcements. Forget capturing the town, he and the rest of the battalion would end up in the cemetery up the hill, or in a POW camp.

A few streets further, Archie was cheered to encounter a half platoon of Eddies. However, his repeated entreaties to accompany him to HQ were ignored. The men under the command of a young lieutenant rushed on; apparently there was a Jerry machine-gun nest they were intent on destroying. He couldn't say he faulted them their choice.

To the northeast, above the towering crest of the mountain at the far end of town, the sky was softening. Dawn was approaching. Archie had just glanced behind when ahead he spotted a lone soldier making his way up the street in his direction. The broad-rimmed helmet tipped him off as a fellow Eddy, but even at a distance the man appeared curiously edgy.

He was shooting his head from left to right, and brandishing a pistol that followed the movements of his head. Something about the scene was not quite right. So instead of greeting him as he'd intended, Archie slowed and edged into the gloom of a building doorway to watch. Silently he reached for the Lee-Enfield. The rifle lacked the show-stopping clamour of a Tommy gun, but it was far more accurate, not to mention subtle. If the man was indeed an imposter as he suspected, then Archie had no wish to alert his comrades. On that thought Archie re-slung the rifle and eased out a bayonet.

As the man approached Archie heard his boots shuffling on the paving stones. Then the man was abreast of him, and it was clear his unit insignia was all wrong. It was no battalion he knew. Archie jumped from his hiding spot, his left arm closing like a vice around the man's neck while his right drove the point of the bayonet up against his side.

'Who are you?' he demanded to know.

The man gasped, then began squirming. He turned his head a fraction so that he might see Archie. 'Brigadier Vokes sent me,' he wheezed.

Archie's heart missed a beat. Had he got it all wrong? 'Vokes? Brigadier Vokes? Which brigade then?' he challenged.

'Second Brigade,' the man replied. 'Vokes is GOC of 2nd Brigade.'

'And you are?'

The man motioned that he should loosen his hold, which he did. This was when Archie noticed the lieutenant's flashes staring him in the face. Normally he kept a wary eye out for them. Even without the epaulettes it was blatantly obvious it was an officer.

'I'm Carson,' said the man, breathing heavily. 'Lieutenant Carson of the Reconnaissance Squadron.'

Archie let his left arm drop to his side, and spirited the bayonet away.

'Oh, I'm terribly sorry, sir. I was afraid you might be a Jerry dressed up like one of us. You hear about such things…'

The lieutenant put a hand to his neck and smiled bleakly. 'Well, I'm glad I'm not. I was afraid I was a goner. You damn near squeezed the life out me. What's your name?'

'Atwell, sir. Archie Atwell. I'm with "A" Company.' Then the words flooded out of him. 'You see the wireless isn't working, sir, and we're scattered in small groups all over town. It's pretty chaotic, the Germans are fighting for every building.'

'The Brigadier's heard nothing, and naturally he feared the worst. We all did, frankly. That's why he sent me. But some of you are still here?'

'Yes, sir. We're still here. I'm not sure with how many. The battalion got split up when the Jerries counter-attacked, and we're spread all over. That's what I was doing, trying to round up some of the men. Perhaps we should move a little out sight, sir.' Then, as he ushered the lieutenant towards the darkened doorway, he spotted a boy out of the corner of his eye. He was running across the street towards them. Anxiously Archie looked up and down the street, but saw nothing untoward. He smiled when the boy came closer. It was the very lad who'd been speaking with the colonel not long before.

The boy ignored Archie and planted himself in front of Carson. Sicilian, only ten, and already he knew who mattered and who didn't in the army. 'Signor,' he said to Carson, and saluted. 'For you. From colonel.' And he pulled out the piece of paper that the colonel had entrusted him with.

'What's this?' said Carson, mystified, as he held the crumpled note in his hand.

'It's on the level, sir. I saw Colonel Jefferson give it to him myself.' Carson seemed perplexed by this explanation. 'Aren't you going to read it?' asked Archie.

'Yes, of course,' replied Carson. His eyes flew over the page, then he looked up, first at Archie, then at the boy, who was watching him with a most serious look. He read it again, more carefully. 'He's asking for help,' he said finally. 'Colonel Jefferson says you need reinforcements.'

'Yes, sir, we do. But above all, sir, we desperately need anti-tank guns. We've nothing to stop their Panzers.'

'I understand. I'd best get going then.' Carson glanced down the hill as if already plotting his route.

Archie cleared his throat.

The lieutenant frowned. 'Was there something else?'

'You wouldn't happen to have something for the boy, sir? He's done his duty very well. I'd do it, but I think he'd appreciate it more coming from you.'

'Ah, yes, of course. How silly of me.' The lieutenant made a show of going through his pockets, but slowly a frown formed. Then his face brightened. His hand flew to a breast pocket, emerging triumphant with an opened packet of cigarettes. These he pressed into the boy's outstretched palm. 'Well done,' he enthused. The boy beamed as he admired his trophy, and raced off with a jaunty wave.

Archie raised an eyebrow.

'Oh, he'll sell them,' said Carson breezily. 'Worth more than money to most of the locals. Tell your colonel that Brigadier Vokes will think of something. But impress upon him that you most hold on. Hold on,' he repeated.

Dutifully Archie replied, 'Yes, sir, we'll hold on.' The assurance seemed to satisfy Carson.

Without looking back the lieutenant trotted quickly down the street. Archie hoped the haste of his mission wouldn't blind him to the dangers; he would make a fine prize for some ambitious young Panzer grenadier. And Carson had to make it to the rear if there was to be any hope of them surviving the day.

Several times on his return journey Archie narrowly escaped the fire of a machine-gun post on a rooftop. On another occasion, hearing shouts and the patter of many boots on the paving stones, he dove headfirst through the broken window of a building and lay holding his breath until a squad of enemy infantry blundered past at the double a moment later. The painful cuts and nicks were a small price to pay.

Later, past dawn, Archie found the colonel. He was ensconced in the cellar that had become the de facto battalion HQ. That it was a wine cellar, and a visibly well-endowed one at that, would have greatly interested Archie were it not that the colonel and staff were present, as well as two company commanders.

But Jefferson had no time to receive him. He was distracted by another matter. Outside a fresh hailstorm of gunfire was erupting.

Suddenly, in a noisy rush of gear clanging against walls, and boots missing steps, a soldier tumbled down the cellar stairs.

'Sir!' the soldier shouted, flush with excitement.

Every face turned towards the interloper, the tension in the cellar tangible, to a man grimly aware of their predicament.

'Shermans, sir! In the lower town. And a column of quads behind with anti-tank guns, plus a company of men. They're racing like the devil. The lieutenant thought you'd want to know.' He stood panting.

The colonel's weary face brightened, and he cocked a sprightly eyebrow. 'Did he now?'

The man's information was otherwise sparse, but the column was reported to be over the ravine. Which meant they were in town, which meant that the engineers had miraculously conjured up a Bailey bridge during the night – against all odds.

'A flying column,' said the colonel thoughtfully. He glanced in Archie's direction and Archie imagined that he saw the glimmer of a smile in those weary, baggy eyes. Then, to his surprise, the colonel dipped his head ever so gently. The moment passed quickly. Officers and men were already parading in front of Jefferson, clamouring for attention and for orders. Archie slipped unnoticed up the cellar stairs.

The first contingent of their sister battalion, the Princess Patricia's Canadian Light Infantry, came upon the Edmonton Regiment's current tenements at 0945, several whistling loudly at the contents of the cellar. They were preceded by the sound of heavy weaponry, the 75s of the Shermans and a harsher crack which Archie knew to be the high-velocity anti-tank guns, and many, many machine guns.

The battle itself went on through the day and into the evening as the Princess Pats pushed further up the hill, flanking the small railway station to the northeast, heavy losses being incurred when they drove the Panzer grenadiers from the nearby peaks. But when the peaks fell, so too did Leonforte. The German mountain stronghold had crumbled.

Three battalions of the 104th Regiment of the 15th Panzer Grenadier Division, including a downtrodden Lieutenant Weyers with an arm in a sling and his heart drooping behind, put their tail between their legs and pressed into the available transport. Kittyhawks and Spitfires would dog them mercilessly.

All of which was lost on Archie. He could barely keep his eyes open, so when that afternoon Lieutenant Wiles appeared behind him and told him he might rest, he curled up in a dark corner and slept.

CHAPTER 19

23 July, 1943
Assembly ground in the hills near Leonforte, Sicily

There was little ceremony, but none in the platoon expected or wished for that, not after the long, bitter fight at Leonforte. They'd lost a few of their own, and it was only by divine providence or happenstance that the casualties weren't far worse. The PPCLI who had come to their rescue had taken it on the chin. Tom Hainsley, in any event, was deemed sufficiently fit for travel, a result of which he was now jostling around in a truck packed with others, heading for the coast and a dressing station. Archie had watched him leave, waving, enveloped in a cloud of white dust.

Lieutenant Wiles moved slowly along the ranks. His face was drawn and weary, no eye for a missing button, or a weapon uncleaned, both sins of which there were many. For the sake of the platoon and his own dignity, he pulled himself erect. 'Men –,' he began awkwardly. Teacher or not, the lieutenant was never one for speeches. 'You did well. The captain couldn't be here. He asked me to tell you that's he's proud of you. But as you know, the battle has left us short-handed.'

Archie sucked in his gut and threw back his shoulders in emulation of the lieutenant's posture. He suspected that Colonel Jefferson would have said his piece, and perhaps even another officer who'd been there. It was not beyond the realm of possibility that Lieutenant Carson of the recce squadron had even put in a good word for him, despite the rocky beginning to their acquaintance.

These few weeks in Sicily had changed him, and for the better, he thought. While his father had certain virtues to commend him, the lone cowboy act wasn't one of them. It sure hadn't got him anywhere in life, and Archie had come to see that his version of the same was no better. It had taken him a damnably long time to realize it.

Lieutenant Wiles walked solemnly down the line of men heading towards Archie. But then he stopped short.

'Congratulations, Lance Corporal,' he said with a winsome smile, extending a hand to Private Lachance. Lachance, slow on the uptake, frowned. It was only after someone thumped him on the back, and whispered in his ear, that a smile burst forth and he shook the lieutenant's hand. At that it was Archie's turn to frown.

'The section's yours, Corporal Lachance,' said Lieutenant Wiles. 'Report to the Quartermaster for your stripe.'

Lachance laughed engagingly. In front of the assembled platoon Sergeant Battersby was beaming, a rank of mildly crooked teeth leading the charge. Given half a chance Archie would have put a boot to them. Fortunately for Archie, standing in row lent him no such opportunity. He was left to unobtrusively suck the remnants of breakfast from his teeth and boil at the injustice. He wished he'd told someone about the two of them at Leonforte. Too late now. Lance-Corporal Lachance stood beaming off his left.

'Not so glum,' growled a voice, a little later. Archie was sitting on the remains of an old, stone wall, methodically chipping away at the ground with his toe.

Surprised, he looked up. 'Sarge!'

'I heard all about it,' said Sergeant Evers. 'Mind if I join you?' Without awaiting an answer Evers slid in beside him.

'Seems I can't do anything right these days,' said Archie. 'I tried, you know, Matt. I really did.'

Evers nodded. 'Sure, Archie. I heard that, too. Concentrate on doing your duty, and your time will come. And when it does come you'll know you truly deserved it.' It was the sort of wisdom Archie would have once scoffed at, but now he listened silently.

'But listen,' Evers said, changing the subject, 'I was really sorry to hear about King. First man killed in action in the company, I reckon. Rough luck about Hainsley, too, but he'll be back in no time.'

'Yeah, They didn't stand a chance. Bloody Panzers.'

Evers nodded knowingly. Then: 'Did you hear about the Hasty P's taking Assoro?'

'Did they now?' Archie's interest was aroused. Enquiringly he stared at the sergeant.

'Yep. All 3000 feet of it. They ignored the road and scaled the Western cliff instead, all the way to the top. By night no less! Ha! The Jerries in town were pissing their pants the next morning, let me tell you. Imagine rolling out of bed, sticking your head out the window for a breath of fresh air and a gander up the mountain. And getting a burst from a Bren about the ears. A damned fine feat, I say. Maybe even as fine as the Eddies at Leonforte.' Evers grinned. 'Well, a close second at least –'

'What now?' asked Archie.

'Now we're off to Agira, and later to Aderno. The Jerries on the plain are putting up a nasty fight and Monty's most anxious that we throw them a stiff left hook. I expect we'll have a day or two to reorganise. Then we'll be on our way. The rest of the division's already on the move. The fighting's not going to get any easier, I'm afraid.'

'No, I didn't think it would.'

Evers laid a sympathetic hand on Archie's knee. 'Don't quote me on it, but you deserved the section. However, it seems your old pal Battersby has taken a real shine to Lachance, and the Lieutenant was either too busy or too preoccupied, and just nodded it all through. Stiff upper lip, Archie. I can't do anything more for you. But the army never overlooks a good soldier. Not for long in any case. Trust me.'

Which was all fine and well when you were already a company sergeant-major, with the next stop a lieutenancy. Not that Matt didn't deserve it. But meanwhile the improbable duo of Miles Battersby (rumoured insurer), and Last Chance Lachance (confirmed good-for-nothing), reigned supreme in "A" Company. Colonel Jefferson had seemingly forgotten all about him. And Captain Tighe, somewhat understandably given their mutual history, had no desire to be reminded. As to Lieutenant Wiles, he was just oblivious to Archie's bruised feelings. And there wasn't a damned thing Archie could do about any of it. At this rate he was destined to remain a private until some Jerry put a bullet in him. Given Matt Evers's assessment that they'd be back in the brawl in a day or two, that might not be long either.

24 July, 1943
East of Nissoria, Sicily

Hauptmann Weyers could scarcely believe his eyes. He lowered the binoculars. 'They're a half hour late,' he said disdainfully. Despite the harshness of his tone, he was grinning. His arm was still in a sling, making the use of binoculars terribly unwieldy, and the sun had burned mercilessly all afternoon as it had every day this fortnight, but this was his first battle in command of the company. And, pleasingly, the Canadians were now walking straight towards them. To have such luck!

'They should have followed their artillery barrage in when we had our heads down,' agreed the *Feldwebel*, crouching beside him. The older sergeant continued to watch through his glasses as he spoke. 'The boys in Nissoria did well to hold them as long as they did, sir.'

Weyers nodded. It was astonishing what a tank or two, an 88, a couple of machine guns and a few riflemen, well placed, could accomplish. Save for a single Panzer and the 88, both unfortunate losses, the bulk of the men were now safely withdrawn. No one could have believed that Nissoria was only five kilometres from Leonforte and Assoro. It was a leisurely stroll of a couple hours, even in this blistering heat. Yet it had taken the enemy nearly two entire days to reach this point. But then, grinned Weyers, Captain Struckmann had ensured that their stroll was not made easy.

The weight of an entire division was bearing down upon them. But there were no roads for a brigade, let alone an entire division, so they would necessarily send forth a single battalion, as was their custom. Yet even so that battalion would need to squeeze together in a narrow file in order to follow the funnel of the highway through the hills.

When Struckmann surprised him yesterday, promoting him to

captain and command of the company after the tragic loss of Captain Biedermann at Leonforte, he had made clear that Weyers's first task would be to turn the two hills east of Nissoria that flanked the road into a chokepoint; an impossible bottleneck for the forces arrayed behind. And when the time eventually came, which Struckmann assured him it inevitably would due to the firepower massed against them, he should be ready to fall back to the next line of hills 1800 meters further, and repeat the exercise. '*Ja, mein Herr,*' Captain Weyers had correctly replied. He recalled clicking his heels in the excitement of the moment, much to his morbid embarrassment later.

Weyers guessed now it was likely a single enemy company leading, or perhaps two. They had started up the modest incline of the road. Progressively the incline increased as the road went uphill, tracing a path along the slope of the ridge that headed towards the first line of hills. There the bulk of his forces waited. To one side of the road the land fell gently away to a broad valley of stunted green shrubs and yellow grass, offering precious little cover for an attacker. He stood on the other side, in a freshly dug gun pit, almost 100 metres up a steep bank, and close to the ridgetop. A funnel indeed, thought Weyers, as he watched.

He had first noticed them several minutes before, as they darted from the hovels of Nissoria, and even imagined he saw their red patches, although that was hardly possible at such a distance. Their numbers were swelling, and already they were moving – the need to push forward no doubt instilled by their commanders. They appeared to be forming an irregular skirmish line. Beyond the infantry, Weyers could make out the sounds of clanking, and the low growl of the mechanical drives of their tanks as they navigated the town streets. They'd throw a flanking infantry screen out into the valley, and send the tanks up the road to force a passageway, he figured. Nothing he hadn't prepared for.

There was no need to involve himself further at this stage; his officers and *Unteroffiziere* knew what was expected of them.

He had been anticipating it, but the first round from a mortar startled him nonetheless. He heard the clap, and observed as the bomb burst in a geyser near the Canadian lines. He thought he even saw soldiers fall. A nearby machine gun began to rip, the tempo harsh and exacting. One of the spanking new MG-42s, of which he wished they had more. Fresh mortar bombs began plunging into the line of the enemy advance.

He lowered the binoculars so that they dangled round his neck, before tucking them securely into his tunic. Then he wished the sergeant and MG crew good luck, and scrambled down the steep bank to the road where he began walking up the half kilometre stretch to the large house with its red-plaster walls.

The Casa Cantoniera was located at the highway's highest point, on the saddle of a ridge that extended from the northern hill to the southern one. From a second floor window of the Casa there was a virtually unimpeded view down the road towards Nissoria, across the valley. Several of his men, seeing the potential in this vantage point, had been anxious to place a machine gun or two here. He'd refused them, sending them away with the explanation that while the temptation was great, the enemy would certainly spot the building, and target it with his artillery and tanks. An MG-34 in a window would be sorely tempting fate. No, better to employ the house as an observation post; and even then he would need to be wary. He waved over a signaller and the observer, the latter bringing with him his map and fine scissors telescope.

On the reverse slope of these hills, out of sight of enemy observers, were the company's supporting mortars. Additionally, Weyers had a handful of the deadly 88s with their high velocity rounds, these placed on the Monte di Nissoria, roughly a kilometre to the rear. Finally, there was the trio of Mark IIIs buried up to their turrets in key spots. It was not an especially large force, but sufficient.

Weyers's eyes returned to the scene near the town. The Canadian commander had split his forces as expected. One group was moving through the valley with the presumed intention of flanking his position, while the second had similar designs on the other side. This latter detachment appeared to be heading all the way around the ridge, hoping in so doing to catch them unawares. They hadn't counted on Captain Struckmann. 4 Company had been placed beside Weyers's men for just such an eventuality. The gunfire intensified.

Some minutes passed. The attack was proceeding slowly. Then the voice of Weyers's adjutant crackled through on the receiver. He was asking for another round of mortar fire on the same target.

Weyers was in time to see the bomb fall, precisely as Lieutenant Baumgartl requested, close to a platoon-sized group of enemy soldiers who subsequently scattered – the best way to describe the enemy advance through the valley. Small groups of men obstinately pushed forward, frequently going to ground in the underbrush after a fresh hail of machine gun fire. The attack was disjointed, uncoordinated. It would not be long now thought Weyers.

'Sir!' The observer was gesturing towards Nissoria, a tone of urgency in his voice.

A column of the enemy's Shermans had appeared with the clear intent of advancing up the road. They were moving very fast.

'Patience,' Weyers said to the man, 'Patience. Give them a moment. With any luck we should get more than one.'

The observer spoke briefly into the radio set, before looking at him again, expectantly.

Weyers held the glasses to his eyes, unmoving. The first of the squat tanks reached the open stretch of road. 'Now,' he said.

The observer spoke into the radio.

CRACK. An 88 on the hill fired. Momentarily the leading tank disappeared in a fog of smoke and dust. When it reappeared, the crew was spilling out of it, flames licking at their heels, black smoke billowing high.

Another 88 barked, and another Sherman brewed up.

The remaining tanks were of no mind to take the battering unanswered. Their turrets turned and fired at the gun positions on the Monte di Nissoria and the two hills.

Then with a start he saw a blast near the top of the ridge astride the highway. He swivelled to see better, the smoke clearing. The MG position where he had been not long before had taken a direct hit. A handful of men were scrambling away.

On the road, a tank from further behind in the column was edging its way past the burning wrecks of its squadron mates. Once clear its cannon boomed angrily – to what effect Weyers could not see – and the tank jolted forward, engine revving, others clanking impatiently in its wake.

Weyers could feel the sweat running down his face. He lowered the glasses and rubbed at his eyes. 'Thank you,' he said to the observer, who had offered him a water canteen. He drank thirstily of it.

If the tanks were able to reach his position at the house, only a couple of hundred metres distant, there was a considerable danger they would cut off a good portion of the men on the ridge and overrun his support line behind. Then there was a grave risk that their momentum would take them through the next two lines – still lightly defended – all the way to Agira. And were Agira to fall… Weyers shook his head. They had to be stopped.

There was little, however, that Weyers could do. His dispositions were made. The company was fighting well, the artillery and mortars coordinating superbly. Suddenly he knew the terrible loneliness of command. It was one thing to be in the fight yourself, he decided, it was quite another to be removed from it with the men trusting him to see them through.

Wisps of dark smoke swirled above the ridge and the road. He could even smell it. The small arms fire, which had come in intense volleys, was all but continuous. It made for an almighty clamour, yet the rifles and machine guns were overshadowed by the crack and roar of heavier guns echoing around the valley.

Then just as he was beginning to fear the worst, another enemy tank shuddered, and came to a standstill. Its crew clambered out. At this new obstacle to their progress the column behind the tank stopped. Weyers clenched a fist in relief. As if sensing a wounded prey more anti-tank guns joined in. The tide had turned.

The battle was reaching its denouement when, at the sound of creaking stairs behind him, Weyers turned. He was in time to greet a dust-covered officer from 4. Company emerging up the stairwell, with a flush face, and eyes only for the view.

'Well?' said Weyers impatiently.

The lieutenant grinned, his white teeth all the whiter set against the grime of his face. 'I count 10 tanks destroyed, sir.'

'Yes, that's my count as well,' said Weyers, allowing himself a weak smile. 'But what about their infantry?'

'The ones who haven't retreated appear to be digging in for the night. The captain says to tell you your left flank is secure, sir.'

'Who are they?' Weyers asked.

'Royal Canadian Regiment,' replied the officer, referring to a slip of paper, and enunciating the syllables slowly and distinctly.

Weyers grunted. He thought of his father at the Wotan Stellung near Arras in northern France, almost precisely twenty-five years earlier, and felt strangely pleased with himself. It had been a long day, but not an unsatisfying one, even if there was work still to be done; mopping up pockets of the foe left behind; dealing with their own casualties, preparing for tomorrow's fight. For the Canadians would come again. Of that Weyers was quite certain.

That evening Major-General Guy Simonds, GOC of the 1st Division, was apprised of the day's action. Shortly thereafter, accompanied by aides, he returned to the map table to plot a new plan. The entire Eighth Army was at a standstill, anxiously awaiting the division's progress in these hills. And Simonds knew well that General Montgomery, the man who had turned Rommel's army in the North-African desert, was not a man who abided excuses. Within the hour a fresh battalion was marching forward in the darkness, across stony ground. Later, some would mutter the new plan was not so much a plan as a wish.

CHAPTER 20

25-26 July, 1943
Highway no. 117 to Nicosia, Sicily

None of these events reached Archie's ears, or indeed the ears of any others in the Edmonton Regiment. For the moment the developments from a scant few miles away hardly seemed to matter, for the regiment had but a single task – to secure the divisional left. In practice that meant holding the junction of the no. 117 and no. 121 against all comers. It was there that the highway split and the two went their separate ways. The 117 branched off to the north towards Nicosia and the German-held interior, while the 121 swept eastwards in a long curving arc through the objectives of Nissoria, Agira, and a succession of others, before reaching the coast. From the north the Germans could hit their flank, so preventing that was what preoccupied the Eddies.

It was not by chance therefore that Archie and a dozen others found themselves several miles to the north, somewhere on the twisting highway no. 117.

'Jeez that feels good.'

Archie was in the first of the two Bren carriers, racing up the road at speed, a refreshing wind tussling his hair. It was a welcome relief after yet another day of scorching heat. The carriers were accompanied by a posse of motorcycles, Nortons mainly, as part of a mixed night patrol under the command of a lieutenant from the 4th Reconnaissance Regiment. The lieutenant's adjutant for the patrol was none other than their own Sergeant Battersby. 'Keep your eyes peeled,' growled Battersby over one shoulder, from his position in the pulpit of the carrier. 'And put on your bloody helmet, Atwell.'

'Keep your eyes peeled? No kidding, it's a recce,' murmured Archie, as he sank back down, and planted the steel bowler on his head. 'Do you suppose he came up with that all by himself?'

'Nah,' said Dinesen. 'Weren't you listening earlier, Archie? That's what the Lieutenant told us before we left. Good thing Battersby was here to repeat it, though.' He winked. The other two were grinning.

Archie grunted, now recollecting the little speech from their earnest, if occasionally out of his depth, platoon commander. Among other things, Lieutenant Wiles had advised them to watch out for the Americans. 'They ought to be coming up on your left,' he'd said. 'So not too quick on the trigger finger, fellas. If you do see them, let them know you aren't a bunch of Jerries – otherwise you'll be eating a late dinner of lead.' They'd all chuckled at that, although in the present gloom distinguishing friend from foe was no laughing matter. In fact, it was a concern that even under a full moon they weren't able to distinguish much of anything on the surrounding slopes.

The small column slowed as the incline steepened. Ahead, a hairpin turn beckoned. In a rattle of gears the driver shifted down. Then they were round the bend and picking up speed, no longer climbing, shooting instead down the back slope of the hill. At the sight of another sharp turn looming in front, the driver geared down reluctantly.

Bing.

The first round ricocheted off the front armour, no one recognizing it for what it was. But the staccato zipping of a machine gun soon alerted them. Miraculously, Sergeant Battersby, standing like some present-day Roman emperor in his command perch on the left of the Bren carrier, escaped unscathed. Somewhat belatedly he now collapsed in an undignified pile behind the waist-high plating.

Behind the carrier, one of the motorcycles swerved wildly before skidding out of control, the rider unceremoniously catapulted into the berm. He was fortunate that the road had broadened after the curve, sparing him a treacherous tumble downhill.

Archie lifted his head and peeked forward, searching for what he'd seen an instant before. 'They're on the knoll, straight ahead,' he shouted, then sank down again. Where the road came to the next hairpin turn was a dark, jutting embankment, a hillock actually, the road curving around it and miraculously clinging to the blasted rock face. Flash suppressor or not, Archie had spotted the telltale flickering of the MG's latest burst coming from that rise.

To his credit the carrier driver didn't hesitate. With a lurch the vehicle surged forwards, the motor roaring. They pounded down the road towards the hill, the sound of gunfire intensifying into a crescendo. A hailstorm of bullets hammered against the front armour. But they were oblivious to it. And as the German fire waned, Borden, the Bren gunner, replied in kind and the gun's throaty pulsing only added to the heady mixture of danger and excitement.

This was not what the Germans had foreseen when they dug their clever position. The MG nest dominated the long stretch of nearly straight and open road with its paucity of cover, and endless opportunity to rake an advancer with fire. It had seemed ideal. But then the Germans had reckoned upon a foe more like themselves. They certainly hadn't accounted for an enemy willing to take matters rashly into his own hands, and to do what considered theory might call folly. Therein lay the Eddies' advantage. And, besides, there was no other choice; to stop, turn and retreat would be suicide. Pell-mell the carrier raced forward.

'Oh, damn,' said Dinesen softly, as the realization dawned on him what the driver intended.

The hillock came rushing towards them, the speed of the Bren carrier only increasing. Then, where the road turned sharply to the right, the carrier simply kept going straight.

For a moment they felt as if they were flying, and they might well have been. The carrier hit the dirt wall of the ditch and passed over it, only to come to a shuddering halt moments later as it slammed into the steep slope. The motor stalled.

'Get the buggers,' shouted Archie, his blood coursing. Then, all they could hear were their own voices as the four soldiers sprang from the carrier and began to rush up the incline. They'd done this sort of thing time and again in the Scottish Highlands.

Once again they were fortunate the Germans had not foreseen such an eventuality. The German MG was positioned such that it had a perfect view of the most exposed stretch of road. With small adjustments the elevation of the barrel could be raised or lowered several degrees. But that was not enough to cover the rocky slope leading up to the slit trench. The gun simply couldn't point that low. It was as good as useless.

This conclusion dawned soon enough upon the stunned MG crew once they had recovered from the shock of a tracked carrier hurtling towards them. Several grabbed rifles and began to fire indiscriminately. By then the roaring madmen were upon them.

With a bellow Archie jumped into the waist-high trench, a screeching McDonald close on his heels.

Immediately ahead a German rose and turned to meet them, lifting his carbine in their direction. But he was too slow. Still moving Archie fired the Lee-Enfield from the hip, and the man went down. There was a *crack* in Archie's ear and a second German fell. The rest of the defenders were now before them in the wide pit that housed the MG. There was no time, or indeed room, to chamber a new round with the bolt action. One of the Germans fired hastily in Archie's direction, and for an instant he thought he was done for, but he felt nothing.

He plunged on, his momentum carrying him. In the first chaotic minutes no one had thought to fix bayonets for this eventuality. He knew precisely what he had to do, however. With a violent thrust he speared the rifle muzzle into the face of the first man he came to. The man cried out, his rifle dipping. Archie let go of his rifle, grabbing for the man's neck with both hands. The two of them tumbled to the ground. Archie pulled himself on top of the man and viciously dug his thumbs into his neck as far as they would go. The soldier was a handsome man, deeply tanned with strong defining features and jet black hair. But his eyes were now starting to bulge grotesquely, specks of saliva forming in a corner of his mouth.

'That's okay, Archie. Steady on.' He felt a heavy hand come to rest on his shoulder. Then the hand shook him roughly when he didn't react. 'They've surrendered, Archie. It's okay.' Archie felt his hands go limp and he rolled off the German, and stared at him. The man lay inert, not a muscle twitching. Right when Archie was thinking that he had killed him, the soldier wheezed and started to cough. His unsteady hand reached for his throat. It had been a very near thing.

'Here. Let me help you.' Dinesen was standing above him with a grin that could have stretched from Pachino to Messina, a hand proffered. In his other hand he held a rifle.

'Thanks.' Archie felt wobbly as he got to his feet. This wasn't like any exercise he'd ever been on.

Borden was standing back from the trench, a Tommy gun cradled in both hands, a watchful eye for the prisoners.

'Where'd you get that thing?' asked Archie. 'I could have used that.'

'It's Battersby's,' said Borden. 'He left it in the back. Figured he wasn't using it.' He smiled. 'Almost as good as a Bren. A little light perhaps, but it worked a charm on this bunch. One look and they had their hands in the air. Lucky thing too, for you, Archie.'

Quizzically Archie looked at him.

'Didn't you see? One of them had a bead on you.'

'Thanks, Doug.' Archie glanced at the Germans, for the first time seeing them as the men they were. There were three all told, not including his wrestling partner who was making a valiant attempt to sit. All had their hands in the air. McDonald was roughly patting them down. At Archie's stare all but one, the most senior of the group judging by the chevron on his sleeve, averted their eyes.

'*Kamerad*,' said the man holding Archie's stare, looking at him plaintively as if hoping for some confirmation of this.

'*Kamerad* to hell,' growled Archie. 'If you bastards had your way we'd all be dead. Bugger off.'

The soldier may not have understood English but he understood the tone. He looked away.

'Hey, relax, Archie. They've surrendered,' said Dinesen. 'We won.'

'Tell that to Dan King.'

For all the violence the entire affair was surprisingly bloodless. One German was dead, another nursed a wounded arm, while the remaining four were unharmed save for one very sore neck. The Eddies hadn't suffered a scratch. All in all it had taken no more than a couple of minutes.

Which was almost how long it took before support in the form of

Sergeant Battersby and four soldiers from the second carrier arrived on the scene.

'Ah,' said Battersby, a satisfied look about him as he stepped forward to survey the trench and the prisoners. He cleared his throat. 'All right you lot, don't stand about picking your noses. Get those prisoners down to the carriers. We're on a recce, in case you'd forgotten.'

There were sighs. Archie spat demonstratively on the ground. Then he picked up his rifle and went to help shepherd the prisoners down the rocky knoll.

'No, Atwell, you stay where you are,' said Battersby. 'Dig the dead Jerry a grave.'

Archie shot him a look that would have felled any other man, but Battersby ignored him.

'You'd better be quick about it, too, if you want a ride home. We won't be here long.'

Archie lay the rifle against a large stone, took the entrenching tool from his webbing and half-heartedly clawed at the earth. It was rock solid. With much effort he finally managed to scratch a furrow deep enough to shelter the better part of a finger. At that pace digging a grave would take the entire night. How the Germans had endeavoured to dig both a trench and a gun pit was beyond him. He looked over his shoulder. Battersby and the others were carefully edging down the hillock's slope. Archie stepped into the slit trench.

'Might as well do something useful,' he mumbled to himself as he knelt on both knees beside the dead German. Ignoring the nasty stain on the man's chest he began methodically digging through his pockets. There he found various papers, a picture of a plump blond with curls, and a modest wad of bills clipped together. The money he stuffed in his own pocket and, after a quick perusal of the papers, placed them back in the German's tunic to rejoin the blond. He was about to stand when a thought occurred to him. He put his hands under the body and rolled it over onto its front. It was bad enough having to bury the Jerry in the first place without him staring at him the whole time.

'Well, well… what might this be?' Strapped to the man's belt, hanging down behind his leg was a scabbard with frog, and the hilt of a knife sticking out. Slowly he slid it out. In the moonlight the blade glittered menacingly. Ever so cautiously he applied a finger to the edge, before jerking away. He whistled softly. The only problem was the scabbard was not coming voluntarily. He smiled. 'You bastard. You probably think this is a great laugh.' Then he rolled the man onto his back again so that he might remove the black leather belt. The belt he screwed into a tight roll and put in a pouch, followed by the scabbard and knife. Then he got to his feet. With both hands he began vigorously scraping the entrenching tool along the sides of the trench. Battersby was probably itching to leave without him. The sooner this was done the better. Within a couple of minutes he had gathered enough dirt to cover the man in a thin dusting of the stuff. Good enough, he thought. No one could say he hadn't tried.

Back on the road there was a buzz of activity. In addition to the band of motorcycles, and the two carriers, he saw three jeeps, one behind the other.

Scrambling down the last few feet of the knoll he sprang over the ditch.

'Hello there! Where'd you come from?' asked one of the group of Americans who was standing by the jeeps. The Americans wore streaks of lampblack on their faces, helmets tilted at various angles, and each was holding a weapon of the Tommy gun variety.

'Burying some Jerries,' replied Archie.

'Best place for them, six feet under,' said the soldier, with a thick, southern drawl. He shot a spitball in the direction of the hill, so as to leave no misunderstanding how he felt about Germans. Archie nodded.

'We heard you fellers making a helluva racket. Got here as fast as we could. Good thing they warned us we might run into some Canucks.' He patted the Tommy gun.

'Good thing indeed,' said Archie with a grin, 'Wouldn't have done much for inter-allied cooperation shooting up the Edmonton Regiment. Especially as we're clearing the road to Nicosia for you.'

The man smiled.

'So how goes the war?'

'The war?' The soldier grunted. 'The plan is to take Nicosia. But, hey, did you hear the big news? About Mussolini?'

Archie frowned. 'Mussolini?'

'He's out! Gone.'

'Out?'

The Americans all began to nod vigorously. 'You bet, it was on the radio not long ago. The Wops dumped him. Looks like Italy's out of it now.'

Archie shook his head in wonderment. 'Isn't that something,' he said, 'I suppose all we can do is hope.' Not that he put much faith in hope; the Italians in Sicily had long since given up the fight, but their German allies unfortunately showed little inclination to join them.

'The Edmonton Regiment? You boys are from the Edmonton Regiment?' said another of the Americans, stepping forward. His manner and his speech was all-American, but he looked Italian.

Warily Archie nodded. No American he'd ever met knew anything of the Canadian Army, let alone recognizing something as obscure as the name of an individual regiment.

'Ain't that something,' said the man. 'A couple of boys in the transport corps who I know have been looking all over for one of yours. Guy with a funny sounding name…' The man rubbed at his chin. 'Battersby,' he said finally. 'Yeah, that's it. Miles Battersby. Do you know him? These friends of mine are awfully keen on getting in touch.'

Archie risked a fleeting glance at Battersby who, together with the recce officer, was involved in an animated discussion with a handful of the Americans. Posing as Battersby with the two drivers had been inspired. At least now half the American Army in Sicily wasn't hunting *him* down. They'd probably gone to a great deal of trouble to show up on the coast road with a half-dozen trucks, ready to fill each to the brim – promises made to all and sundry – only to find nothing. On the other hand, one look around and they would have discovered the winery themselves. There weren't many buildings with VINO painted in ten-foot high white letters.

He pointed at Battersby. 'That's him over there, the chinless wonder. Don't let appearances deceive, he's a real nasty piece of work.' Archie shook his head. 'If I were you I'd warn your friends to stay clear. Tell them to find someone more amiable to talk to.'

'You don't know my friends,' said the man coldly, staring at Battersby. He waved over one of his pals, a wiry, olive-skinned man with dark eyebrows. 'There he is,' he said, pointing. 'Take a good look.'

The man's eyes narrowed, humourless. After a moment he said: 'Got it.'

'Hey, thanks. Appreciate it, buddy,' said the first man.

Archie took a deep breath as they walked away. Perhaps Polowski's theories weren't so crazy after all. The two privates from the transport corps had seemed harmless enough, even the short, Italian-looking one. But these fellows, on the other hand… It would serve Battersby right if they searched him out for a little chat. His scheming ways had fooled half the army. But this crew might prove more of a match.

CHAPTER 21

26-27 July, 1943
East of Nissoria, Sicily

'Pfff.' Captain Weyers snorted, then waved a dismissive hand when the inevitable question came about what would happen now that the loyal support of the Italians appeared uncertain. 'Somehow we'll manage,' he blithely replied, to looks of astonishment from a couple of his young stallions. 'Come now. Who amongst you has not moped about the roads being clogged at inconvenient moments? Or precious supplies being consumed by our dear allies, who then surrender themselves and those very supplies to the Tommies? Or worse?'

There were knowing smiles. A chuckle or two could be heard from the small band of officers and NCOs that surrounded the company commander. The unprofessionalism of the Italians was a recurring topic of amusement, and often scorn. Where the North African veterans could, on occasion, find a word of praise for their allies, those whose sole experience was of the Italian army in Sicily were resolutely negative. One man, however, didn't share in the joviality. Oberfeldwebel von Steinen was by nature a cautious and conservative man, and an experienced warrior. It was all fine and well to belittle the Italians, he thought, but defending their country without them would be a dangerous game.

'Ah, Walther, not so glum now,' said Weyers, placing a friendly hand on his shoulder. 'I know what you're thinking, but the Italians won't surrender. Berlin would never allow it.' He smiled. 'No, never.'

Expressionless the staff sergeant nodded.

Weyers couldn't imagine what he would do without him. Von Steinen had been a bulwark two nights ago when the enemy launched their assault, mere hours after the first, and it was he who had so diligently gone from post to post and ensured that everything was as it should be. Yesterday Von Steinen had personally led the defence at the Casa Contoniera, the red house, the crucial centre of their first line. And for a third time they had beaten them back. Evening had come which meant the next attack was surely imminent.

The bulk of his company was now entrenched in the second defence line, the one the Canadians called "Tiger", a name which had made him smile when he first learned of it. No matter how tired they were, the men straightened their backs and proudly grinned at each other when he told them. Then Weyers's thoughts were disturbed by something. He cocked an ear to listen.

An instant later the soft calm of early evening was shattered. As one, the group of officers turned their heads to stare to the west. A rolling thunder had come up, a tempest of shellfire that grew to a storm that neither wavered nor abated.

'What is that?' whispered one of his young officers, hardly older than a boy.

'That, Lieutenant, is the enemy trying again,' said Weyers, grimly. 'And, so to hear, taking no half measures either.'

Two kilometres away across the bowl of the tree-spotted valley, in the direction of Nissoria, the heights of the first ridge line were marked by billowing explosions and plumes of smoke.

Weyers sighed. It would be a difficult night. The battalion had held off an entire brigade for days, but he knew well that his regiment, his battalion, and his company were being ground away, as surely as the pounding of the ocean inevitability turns rock to sand. But he was not a man taken to bouts of doubt or anxiety, and he contemplated the coming hours with a calm assuredness. It was this assuredness that his officers assumed in their turn, and the men in theirs. A quiet confidence permeated 5. Company.

To Weyers's surprise, he noticed that his hatred for the Canadian enemy had faded these past weeks. Grudgingly he could feel respect for his foe, where once he had felt none, for his dogged tenacity and unorthodox tactics if nothing else. And that respect had done much to soften the painful memories of his father. For if his father had died at the hands of such men, then surely there was honour in that?

'*Mein Herr!*' shouted an officer.

Weyers turned. 'I'm coming,' he said. It was time to throw them back.

Base area west of Nissoria, Sicily

Sometime before this, Archie was shuffling on his feet. He unshouldered his rifle for the umpteenth time, only to sling it over the other shoulder – anything to relieve the boredom. Sentry duty was never a favourite pastime and naturally Lachance, almost certainly at Battersby's instigation, had seen to it that he was the section's volunteer for the night; the army's concept of volunteers differing rather markedly from the definition the dictionary offered. The sun was retreating quickly, a gentle breeze coming up in its place.

'You fucking bastard,' hissed a voice in his ear. An arm slipped around his neck from behind and seized him in an iron vise. 'What the hell are you up to, Atwell?' Through the thin cotton of his bush jacket he could feel the point of something very sharp pricking in his side.

'Miles, is that you?' wheezed Archie. 'Hey, let go, would you? I can barely breathe. I'm on sentry duty. But you know that of course.'

'I met some Yanks today, Atwell. Wop Yanks.'

'How nice for you. Friendly bunch, the Yanks. Let me go, Miles.' He was having trouble breathing.

'These weren't.' The arm clenched tighter.

'No?'

Archie felt the point jab into him. He almost cried out, but saved himself the ignominy by biting down hard on his lip. It must be a bayonet Battersby was holding. It sure hadn't taken the Americans very long to find him. 'Take it easy, Miles. That hurts.'

'No, they weren't friendly at all. They roughed me up pretty bad. In fact, it was all I could do to convince them they shouldn't slit me wide open. They asked a lot of questions.'

'What the devil are you on about?'

'That's what I wondered at first. They kept going on about these four big deuce-and-a-halfs they'd arranged. Drove them halfway across the island to the coast, apparently, and had to pay off some MPs for the privilege. The way they told it some Canadian was going to deliver them a warehouse full of vino. Vino, they said. Not wine. Vino. They were mighty peed off when he didn't show. They were even more peed off when some British provosts stumbled upon their little convoy and started asking questions. They figured they were set up. Now two of them are in the brig, and their friends are looking for revenge.'

'That's quite a story, Miles. But it doesn't explain why you've got a bayonet sticking in me. Not setting much of an example as the platoon sergeant, are you? Vino is Italian for wine, by the way. And you did say they were Wops. No mystery there.'

Archie winced as the bayonet probed further.

'Always have to be the smartass, don't you? I have a good mind to push this all the way in and be done with it. Stranger things have happened in this shithole, with all these Krauts and Eyeties about.'

At this Archie held his breath. Battersby was on the edge more times than not, but now he was completely off his rocker. But to kill a fellow soldier from his own regiment!? It was unthinkable... although not entirely unthinkable. For when Archie thought about it, strange things did happen on this sun-baked island. The worst of it was he'd probably get away with it, too.

Battersby continued. 'You know, the funny thing is I wouldn't have put it together except for that word 'vino'. I got to thinking about it afterwards. That's when I happened to think of that winery near the beaches that you plundered. Then I knew exactly what happened. Which is a damn lucky thing for me because I swore to those Yanks I'd get to the bottom of it.'

'Jesus Murphy, Miles, there were a dozen of us, besides me. And we didn't plunder anything, all we did was sample a few of the wares.'

'Yeah, sure. But you're the only one of the lot who could come up with a scheme like this. You're always trying to make a buck. And you're going to own up to this one, Atwell. Then you and I are going to go 'liaising', as they call it, and you're going to bloody well empty your pockets in front of the Yanks and tell them I had nothing to do with any of it. Whatever happens after that is your business.'

'Hey, you two! Stop horsing around. We're moving out. Get yourselves in file.'

Archie and the sergeant both turned at the sound of this commanding voice. A long column of men in single file was approaching, two officers in the lead.

'But,' stammered Battersby.

'No buts about it,' replied one of the officers. He held a map in one hand and what looked to be a compass in the other, and both were deserving of more attention than the two strays from his platoon. 'FALL IN!'

'You're going to pay for this, Atwell. Oh, are you going to pay –' hissed Battersby.

'Yes, sir,' chirped Archie. He was only too glad at this unexpected reprieve. Without hesitation he practically sprang toward the line of men, and pressed himself into their midst with an apologetic smile. 'Sorry,' he mumbled amiably to the man whose toes he'd pranced upon.

The officer grunted to Battersby; 'You too, soldier.'

Battersby neatly saluted, mumbled 'yes, sir,' and when the officer looked away he threw his hands out in exasperation. Then grumpily he claimed a spot in the column. Hastily the men made room when they spotted his chevrons. No one said anything.

Within several minutes any proclivity to speak was rendered near impossible by the crashing of what they would later learn was the entire divisional artillery plus a regiment of the Royal Artillery in action, an awesome roar the likes of which Archie had not heard before, not even at Leonforte.

By the time they filed round through the outskirts of Nissoria heading north, the sky was dark, and the curtain of shells from the 25-pounders was stepping out to the east. Off to their right flashes could be seen and small arms fire heard coming from the ridge east of town, the "Lion" line that the Germans had hitherto defended with such infuriating success.

The 'fighting patrol', for that was what the man over Archie's shoulder had told him this platoon-sized group of men was, continued north. Fighting patrol or not, it was clear they wouldn't be joining the tussle for the ridge; they were following a small road that wiggled its way across the dry hills towards a prominent dark pyramid in the distance, the bluish hues of the hill visible for miles. That would be the Monte di Nissoria, thought Archie grimly. It seemed a fair guess the patrol was meant to clear it.

The narrow road, more a track, ambled down from the heights on which the town was built, and then skirted the edge of the valley heading away from the fireworks. Passing a line of pine trees along the roadside they lost sight of the fighting altogether. Soon the road began to climb again, by which time the ridgeline was out of sight. What happened there would not be their concern apparently.

There was a tap on Archie's shoulder. 'Hey, you're not "D" Company, are you? What are you doing here?' asked the man behind.

Archie shook his head. 'No, not "D" Company. You'll have to ask your Lieutenant why. He was the one who was so fired up about bringing us along.'

'Lieutenant!' The man snorted. 'That's no lieutenant. That's the company commander, Major Bury. Lieutenant Dougan's the one behind him.'

'Major Bury? Really? Oh, great,' Archie moaned. He was beginning to think he'd escaped the flames only to land in the fire. He knew Bury from a time long ago from his own time in "D" Company. Worse, Bury knew him. Their acquaintanceship hadn't ended well. Luckily Captain Tighe had taken him in.

'If you stick to the shadows perhaps he won't notice you. Hey, aren't you the guy that emptied Dunbar's purse back on the ship?'

'Don't let it get around,' said Archie. 'I'm unpopular enough as it is.'

'I wouldn't worry about that. Dunbar's bark is worse than his bite. Besides, knowing him, he wrangled the money out of some other poor bugger's pocket.'

'Quiet in the ranks!' snapped a voice, sotto voce.

The sotto voce was a hint; the more senior the man the less likely he felt the need to raise his voice. Hint taken both Archie and the other man went silent.

As dusk turned to darkness the platoon marched steadily onwards, a long file of men, quiet except for the soft shuffle of their boots on the dry ground. It was no longer easy to make out any landmarks for every hill seemed identical. Major Bury, however, was of another mind for shortly after passing a dilapidated grey-stone hut, and a low stone wall to announce it, they came upon a junction with a second track. This one was more overgrown and uneven than the last. They turned on to it, the black nucleus of the Monte di Nissoria looming ahead.

Then almost as soon as they had turned, they veered off into a rocky field, and soon were following a tortuously twisting goat path through the outcrops. Of course, thought Archie, Bury was leading them around the hill. But if the Monte di Nissoria wasn't their destination, what was?

The night was deathly quiet except for the occasional sharp burst of small arms fire far away. Once, a tank cannon thudded.

They walked on, pausing briefly to take swigs of warm water from their canteens and shake out their weary legs.

Then, after making their way up yet another hill along a treacherously narrow, rock strewn path, the file halted without warning. The men stood one behind the other, peering into the gloom. Archie strained his ears for an indication of why they had stopped. Finally, a murmur echoed down the line.

'Fix bayonets,' said the man in front of Archie. 'Pass it on.'

As the patrol obeyed there was a rustle of gear. Archie slipped out his own 8-inches of steel and pushed it into place with a *click*, twisting it to lock into place. The spike bayonet of a Lee-Enfield no. 4 was deceptively modest, not especially long, no thicker than a finger in width, and lacking the obvious menace of a sword bayonet's sharpened blade. But it was wickedly effective all the same.

The man in front began to shuffle forward and Archie followed. His senses were tingling, nervous fists clamped firmly round the rifle stock.

Coming to a small plateau on the hillside the men moved onto it, slowly encircling their commander and the platoon lieutenant who stood waiting.

'There's a Jerry post ahead,' said Major Bury, when they were assembled, his voice low and even. Lieutenant Dougan stood beside him. Unusually for officers both were holding rifles. Archie couldn't help but notice theirs had bayonets attached too. 'We're going to get as close as we can, and then we'll charge. Bayonets only. There's to be no shooting. I repeat: no shooting. Any man that makes a noise is going to have to deal with me. Is that clear?'

There were nods and a few soft murmurs of assent.

'The first ten men will come with me and the Lieutenant. The rest of you will follow with the Sergeant the moment we've gone in.'

Bury glanced round at the men. Apparently satisfied, he stepped to one side and motioned that they should file past. When it was Archie's turn he kept his chin buried in his chest, and his helmet tilted well down, although he could have sworn the major took a long, second look as he passed. 'Alright,' he heard Bury say, almost in his ear, 'That's ten.' Then the major hustled past to assume the lead.

Exiting the small plateau the path began to descend. After passing a sheer rock face, it curved sharply to the left to follow the contours of the hill. Without really being able to see much at all – it was more the sensation of open spaces beyond – Archie knew they had come to a valley. Shortly thereafter the path bent to the right. This time it headed almost straight downhill. After a few steps in that direction the cause of all the commotion was in plain sight.

At the bottom of the slope, the dark ribbon of a tree-lined road delineated the furthest extremity of the hill. Halfway between the road and the patrol was a clearing on a bluff. On it was built a trio of farm buildings, and what looked like sand-bagged dug-outs overlooking the road in both directions. Archie thought he saw something else. He blinked for he was uncertain whether his eyes were playing tricks in the dark. However, after another few steps, he was convinced they were not. There were two of them, he reckoned, standing together by the smaller of the buildings. They appeared to be looking south down the road. Lest there remain any semblance of doubt, the fireflies of their cigarettes was enough to remove it.

The major's pace slowed and the file behind emulated his measured, steady steps. This was no time to let down their guard. Yet for all their care, it still seemed a tremendous racket that they were making. With a start Archie noticed it diminished considerably when he held his breath.

Suddenly he saw one of the figures move. A voice, level, not raised, pierced the calm of the night. The second figure shifted position. Then they heard: 'Peter? Peter, *bist du da?*'

Peter didn't respond, but Major Bury stepped up the pace.

'Alarm, Alarm!' shouted the German, after a spell.

'Charge!' shouted Bury. They stumbled down the hill, moving fast but wary of their footing on the rock strewn path. On the bluff new figures were emerging from the buildings. Roused unceremoniously from their sleep, the enemy appeared confused.

A single rifle went off with a loud *crack*. Then the second sentry also fired, not at them, but rather as a warning. More shouting followed, louder still, multiple voices joining in.

They were truly charging now as the ground levelled out, feet thumping loudly and gear rattling. Archie felt a deep pounding in his chest that matched that of his feet. His head pulsed in unison.

When they reached the farmyard a dozen or more Germans were milling around the grounds in confusion, apparently oblivious of where the danger emanated from. But someone in command had spotted something. An order was shouted. Hurriedly, the soldiers began to assume defensive positions.

Major Bury roared, the lieutenant roared, and the men duly followed their example. Archie contributed a blood-curdling Indian cry from his boyhood days as they rushed into the yard like men possessed. The major thrust wildly at a German, narrowly missing him, and the soldier stumbled backwards. Bury plunged on.

And then the man, helmetless, was in front of Archie, his rifle held sideways with both hands. Archie thrust the Lee-Enfield rife forward, and caught him high in the chest. The bayonet slid in effortlessly, and he yanked it free with a grunt, the soldier collapsing to the ground. Without a second look he ran on.

It was a wild scrambling melee. Several of the Germans were gathered in a small group near the doorway of one of the buildings, evidently having just emerged, and Archie could see Major Bury and another man rushing towards them.

A German stood against the wall of the building opposite. He had his rifle to one shoulder and was pointing it in the major's direction.

The piercing cry came from deep within him. Archie ran as fast as he could. The man, startled, looked up from the sights then whipped his head to one side to look. Archie was not ten yards away.

The German, panic visible on his face, brought the rifle down from his shoulder and twisted it around towards Archie. His quick reflexes were what saved him. The wooden stock of the rifle hit the barrel of Archie's outstretched weapon with a heavy thud, batting away the thrust just in time. But Archie kept going. He barreled into the soldier, pinning him against the stone wall of the farmhouse.

'*Kamerad*,' said the man, looking plaintively at him.

Archie was breathing heavily, his thoughts a violent tumult. He stared at the man, disbelieving. Then hearing voices, he turned. The platoon was spilling into the courtyard. Here and there a dishevelled German stood with hands held high. A sudden clatter demanded his attention and he snapped his head back to face the soldier. The man had let his rifle tumble to the ground. He was wearing a weak grin.

'Sure,' said Archie, 'Why not. But get your hands in the air like the rest of them. And don't be thinking for a moment we're pals.'

The man frowned.

Archie mimed with his arms, and the man's own arms shot up.

As the sun's rays finally peaked over the hills to the east, the weary fighting patrol of "D" Company was afforded a grandiose view of the Salso Valley and the surrounding peaks. As was often the case, the topography provided the answer as to why the campaign was proceeding as it was; the harsh and rugged terrain, with limited ways to cross it, conspired against the would-be attacker.

Before them Archie could see the broad valley – he'd been right about that – of the Salso river that ran down from the mountains of the interior to the eastern coast. Sandwiched in between this lazy flow – now in mid-summer all but dry – and one of the seemingly endless chains of hills they'd been fighting through, was a narrow road. Having reached the road, Major Bury solemnly informed them their task was henceforth to close it.

The humble dirt highway at the foot of the hill was not merely the sole and, therefore, critical artery between Agira (besieged by the Canadians) to the south, and Nicosia (besieged by the Americans) to the north, it was important for other reasons as well. In particular, it was one of a dwindling number of escape avenues for the Panzer grenadier regiments still fighting to hold Agira. Since every man in the division had learned the hard way that a German on the flight today was a German behind an MG-34 tomorrow, preventing the Panzer grenadiers from slipping away into the hills had become a priority for everyone from Major-General Simonds on down. Which may have gone some way towards explaining the paucity of prisoners that morning.

The men not yet assigned a task stood collecting themselves, sipping at canteens that were already past the half-empty mark, and reliving the events of the morning with the others, when machine gun fire erupted.

'Where's it coming from?' cried a voice.

'By the bridge. Right by the bridge.'

Sure enough, down the hill and to the left, a hundred yards from where the road crossed over the Salso on a low, stone bridge, Archie could make out two trucks where previously there had been none. Small groups of men were visible moving through the trees. It had not been more than ten minutes since a section accompanied by Lieutenant Dougan had headed that very way.

'Brens,' murmured Archie, 'they're Bren guns.' His first thought had been that the lieutenant and his men were ambushed, but that now seemed unlikely.

'Come on,' bellowed the platoon sergeant. 'Follow me.' Archie and half the platoon scrambled down the steep slope of the hill to the road in an unholy rush.

The machine guns rattled on for a minute or two, then abruptly ceased.

Reaching the road the explanation for the commotion was soon obvious. Two trucks, visibly German, were pulled off to one side. Evidently, they'd been coming from Nicosia, on their way to Agira. One was emitting smoke, and even at a hundred yards both had the unmistakeable look of having been raked by machine-gun fire. A couple of Eddies were cautiously edging around them.

As Archie approached with the sergeant and the others, Lieutenant Dougan came striding up, a Bren cradled in his arms. 'Jerry reinforcements for Agira I expect. We got a couple but they scattered. They could be a mile away in the meantime. You'd better send a few men out, just in case, Sergeant.'

Archie turned to the man beside him, the same one he knew from the trek through the hills, already a close acquaintance. 'Damn John. Those officers of yours are real bruisers. First a bayonet charge. Then shooting up a convoy. Not many officers could pull that off. And me thinking that "D" Company were all misfits.'

John grinned, and it appeared as if he might have something to say on the topic of misfits when a shadow settled across his face, his eyes flitting nervously.

'Although using a bayonet or a Bren is one thing,' Archie blundered on, 'but holding back a Panzer is another entirely. Believe me, I know what I'm talking about. If the Jerries send a tank or two this way… well, I hope the Major has a good plan.'

'The Major intends to make clever use of the Hawkins grenades and the PIATs we've brought with us,' said an even voice behind him.

With a certain foreboding Archie turned.

'Major,' he flustered, and quickly saluted.

'Atwell!' Major Bury's dark eyebrows furrowed into a frown. 'What the blazes are you doing here? I thought I recognized your face earlier, but I knew it couldn't be. Yet here you are.'

'Well, sir, you invited me along as it happens. On no uncertain terms, if you'll recall. Me and Sergeant Battersby.'

'Battersby? I suppose he's also from "A" Company?'

'Yes, sir, he is.'

A glimmer of enlightenment now pushed away the puzzlement on his face. Bury chuckled. 'Ah, that was you two. Well, we can always use an extra man or two, even if one of them is your sorry self.' Archie blinked, but held the major's stare. 'You made it sound as if you've some experience with Panzers, Atwell?'

'Yes, sir, I have.' There was little point in elaborating on how it had worked out. After the Spitzbergen expedition Bury thought little enough of him as it was.

'Good. I'm going to put that to work. Does that experience extend, by chance, to using a PIAT?'

'Yes, sir, I'm afraid it does. Although it's been a decidedly fickle relationship until now.'

Bury grunted non-committedly. 'Well, Atwell, let's hope for all our sakes that you're able to win her over in short order.'

'Yes, sir.'

'Sergeant?'

Miraculously the sergeant appeared at his side.

'This here is Sergeant Page.' Then to the Sergeant: 'You'll be happy to hear I've found an experienced PIAT man for you. Would you take the good private from "A" Company over to the bridge? Atwell will be needing a projector and a supply of bombs.'

'Ah, excellent, sir.' The sergeant smiled amiably at Archie.

The novelty of all this good cheer made Archie think perhaps he'd been wrong; "D" Company didn't seem so bad after all. Maybe he should look into switching boats again. Then he remembered precisely what it was Bury had volunteered him for.

'Sir! Look!' A corporal was motioning at the farmhouse up on the hill. They could see a man waving from one of the upper floor windows.

Bury reached for his glasses. 'I put a couple of lookouts there,' he said. 'There must be some movement on the highway. You two had better get going, Sergeant.'

Archie squinted down the straight stretch of road in the direction of Agira.

'Do you see anything?' asked the sergeant, already turning to leave. 'I can't see a thing.'

'Dust,' replied Archie. 'I'm sure I see dust.' While he didn't want to cry wolf, there was nothing that threw up a whirlwind of dust quite like a tank.

CHAPTER 22

27 July, 1943
Agira–Nicosia road, Sicily

'The Major sent a runner. The Sergeant says to tell you there's two, maybe three Mark III or IVs, and at least one truck behind,' said the man. 'You ready?'

'I sure hope so,' replied Archie. His heart was pounding something fierce, and his brow was bathed in sweat, on this occasion not from the heat. If only he'd kept his mouth shut with that soldier, earlier. 'I guess we'll see soon enough,' he added.

'Wait for the signal then. Good luck, eh.' Keeping low the man crossed back over the road and began to climb back to the top of the bluff on the north side of the bridge where a section of Edmontons were hunched over two carefully sited Brens and an assortment of every rifle and Tommy gun they could lay their hands on. As the sergeant had hastily explained, it was Bury and Dougan's intent that this force be the cork in the bottle. Given the terrain involved, it seemed an appropriate tactic, even if Archie had a few qualms about serving as a cork.

The German post they'd overrun lay astride the road, overlooking it like some ancient guardhouse. Half the platoon was now dug in there. To the south was Agira, to the north Nicosia. From the direction of Agira the narrow road proceeded in an arrow straight line for almost a mile until it came to the two immobilized German trucks in the shoulder. There it narrowed further, as the neck of a bottle will, when it reached the small bridge over the Salso. After the bridge the road swept sharply right, which would force any vehicles to a crawl. The enemy trucks had been caught just after crossing over.

It was on the far northern side of the bridge, with the bluff at his back, that Archie now crouched in the berm in a tangle of wiry shrubs. Every part of him itched, and to move was to be scratched even more. He hoped that some small recompense for the toll to his bare legs and arms would be the concealment the shrubs provided. Increasingly though he had his doubts. With the long metal tube of the PIAT tucked between his knees and protruding upwards like a chimney stack, he felt some kinship to the proverbial ostrich with its head buried in the sand.

It was on the bridge that the officers had decided to place their cork. A logical enough place given that there probably wasn't another crossing of the Salso for miles. The bluff on the northern side was an added advantage. From its heights there was a clear line of sight down the road in the direction of Agira. Of course that advantage was muted if the traffic came from the north. Likewise, there wasn't a great deal of cover worthy of the name if a Panzer started throwing its weight around.

'Damn,' muttered Archie to himself, as he sat pondering this.

Within moments there was the sound of motors, the deep throaty tanks audible above the others, an ominous cacophony of rattles and clanks foreshadowing the German column's arrival. Archie popped his head up to take a final look. He groaned when he saw the tracked vehicles, white dust billowing everywhere.

Archie forced himself down as far as he could; he was going to have to rely on his ears, for he didn't dare gawk about anymore. One glimpse of him would give the game away before it began.

The platoon at the farm dutifully held their fire as the convoy crawled past in easy range. The unsuspecting Germans drove on, seemingly not spooked by the sight of their abandoned trucks. The noise grew louder, until it seemed deafening.

This being a rear area the German commander had understandably dispensed with a forward screen. So instead of a tank or a motorcycle it was a large half-track that led the way, a tank conveyor towing what looked very much like a Mark IV. Behind, shrouded in white dust, was at least one other Panzer moving independently. Maybe more. The half-track's treads clanked terribly as they ground over the bridge, and soon Archie was breathing in the monster's exhaust of gasoline and dust as it powered past, the tank rattling and groaning in its wake. He heard the half-track's engine roar louder as it climbed up off the bridge onto the dirt of the road and into the curve.

BOOM! The ground rocked and a second detonation followed a moment later. The no. 75 Hawkins grenade. These looked not dissimilar to large metal flasks, typically buried, and reportedly very effective at dealing with tanks. Archie had never seen one in action before. But these had worked perfectly. A blast of hot air blew over him, carrying with it a hailstorm of dirt and debris, which rained down on his helmet. Out of the corner of his eye he could see that the track of the tank was completely blown off. The half-track, too, appeared to be struggling.

Then he heard renewed clanking, and he knew that it was the second Panzer following the first. It too had reached the bridge. It had to be now. Signal or no signal.

Wrestling with the shrubs that clutched at him, Archie wrenched himself free and rose first to his knees, and then to his feet, the projector cradled in both arms. Protruding above the guardrail his upper torso was now completely exposed to any crewman hanging out of the tank turret, or even to a soldier staring ahead from the truck behind. He stepped into the road and went down on one knee, tucking the PIAT's shoulder piece up against him.

At the sight of the chaos ahead the second Panzer, squat and menacing and painted in desert colours, threw up its rear like a horse kicking, and screeched as the driver applied the brakes. A cloud of dust came blowing over. The tank was already half on the bridge. It seemed literally in front of him.

He stared down the tube through the sights. The tank's cannon was pointed straight at him. He had his two forefingers on the PIAT's large trigger, and forcefully he pulled it. As he'd been instructed he held the trigger taut, and was aware of the powerful spring unleashing, sending the bomb hurtling on its way. The propellant ignited a split second later. As the hammer of the recoil punched him in the shoulder he watched as the bomb hit the Panzer's front armour. It couldn't be, he thought. What were the odds? He'd hit precisely what he was aiming for: the turret. A weak spot someone had told him.

There was a loud bang and a flash, and smoke swirled. And out of the smoke the tank, its driver obviously incapacitated, growled slowly towards him, its metal tracks devouring the few yards that separated them. The main gun drooped dispiritedly, and smoke was issuing from the top. But still the tank came.

'Oh, shit.' He clambered to his feet.

Then there was a bright flash and a deep roar, and he felt himself flying through the air, thinking this must mean he was on his way to heaven – which wasn't half bad for the son of a drunk from Wetaskiwin.

'Wake up,' intoned a calm voice, 'Wake up.'

'Slap him on the cheek again, Fred,' said another more excitable tone. 'I think he's coming around.'

'Give him a moment.'

Archie blinked. 'Lay off the slapping, would you? Fred knows best. Where am I?'

One of the soldiers, the excitable one, sprang to his feet. 'Sir, he's woken up,' he hollered. 'He seems to be perfectly fine.'

'Fine?' Archie grunted. 'I'd like to see how you bloody well feel when the Panzer Corps runs *you* over.' As the world came into clear focus, he saw that he was lying on the ground on a rubberized ground sheet, under the shady branches of a tree, a brilliant orb of a sun managing to peek through the foliage. His helmet lay beside him, exhibiting a crater that rivalled one of Mount Etna's.

A shuffling in the dirt announced a new arrival. 'Come now, Atwell. Buckle up. From what I understand of your little faceoff, the Jerry Panzer was the one that got the short end of the stick. So if anyone should be complaining…'

Archie blinked again. 'Sir?'

'Yes, it's me,' said Major Bury. 'The Lieutenant's here with me as well.' They stepped round so that Archie could better see them. 'Would you like some water?'

'Yes please. But I'd first like to see if I can still walk.'

'Allow me.' Bury held out an arm and Archie grasped it. With the major on one side, and the lieutenant on the other, he got to his feet. With the exception of a stiff back, a sore leg and what felt like a thousand nicks on his face and arms, he seemed okay. Compared to that last night in Greenock before they'd shipped out, he was positively fit.

'Huh,' he murmured appreciatively, stretching both arms while he took a baby step. 'Isn't that something? It all seems to still work.'

The officers smiled. 'We found you in the shrubs.' Bury pointed. 'Cushioned the blow I expect. The Panzer however wasn't so lucky. Perhaps you'd like to see it?'

'Yes, sir, I would.'

Without another word the major strode up onto the road, and Archie hobbled after him. 'Have a look.'

It took Archie a moment to take it all in. He saw the bridge with the bluff looming over, the big half-track and the tank below – both damaged. Closer to hand were the two abandoned Borgward trucks, now joined by a third that had almost reached the bridge. This one had its cab in the ditch and was missing a front wheel. But the centrepiece of the scene was on the bridge itself. Occupying the middle of it was a charred Mark IV Panzer, a spiral of oily black smoke curling out of it. Unlike the wrecks Archie had seen earlier, the smoke came not from the commander's turret hatch thrown wide open, but rather from the hole in the tank's body where the turret had once been. As to the turret, it rested upside down in the river bed.

Softly Archie whistled. 'Damn. Isn't that a sight for sore eyes?'

'Isn't it just,' said the major. 'We figure either the ammunition or the fuel brewed up.'

'I was worried it might not go off, sir. That bloody bomb. Or that the front plate would be too strong.'

'Well, it did. And it wasn't. And now there's nothing bigger than a man that'll get past that god-awful mess you just made. The bridge is closed for good, Atwell, or at least until someone can get a dozer up.' Bury's voice dropped. 'Or maybe another Panzer. Jerry will no doubt attempt that.'

'What happened to the truck, sir?'

The lieutenant smiled. 'He saw you and suddenly decided he wanted to go the other way,' said the major. 'Only he ran over one of the Hawkins that we planted in the shoulder. A lot easier planting them there than on the road itself, and not so easily spotted.'

'What now, sir?'

'More of the same, I'm afraid. If they haven't figured out we're here, they will soon. We'll have to hold them off until reinforcements arrive.'

'Atwell! I've been looking all over for you.' To Archie's amazement, a perturbed and sweaty-looking Sergeant Battersby swept in from behind. He went to stand at Major Bury's side and addressed him.

'Hello, sir. I just wanted to tell you, you needn't worry anymore about this man. I'll take him off your hands straight away.'

'You'll do what?' Major Bury frowned. 'Hang on to your horses for just a moment, Sergeant. You must be Atwell's companion from "A" Company?'

Battersby nodded. 'Yes, sir, that's correct. I'm Sergeant Battersby, sir, Atwell's platoon sergeant. I hate to trouble you with it, sir – you being so busy and all – but there's been a bit of a mix-up.'

'A "mix-up"?'

'Yes, sir. Exactly that. No harm intended. But you see, it was Private Atwell's fault –'

Bury raised his hand to cut him off. 'This "mix-up" was Atwell's fault?'

'Yes, sir. You see, Atwell's not much of a soldier, never has been. Heaven knows I've done my best, but I'm afraid he still strays from his duty all too regularly, sir. As a matter of fact, when you and the platoon came along, I was tutoring him, hoping to teach him the error of his ways. Only one thing led to another and, well… here we are. I'm terribly sorry, sir, if we've gotten in the way.'

Bury raised his eyebrows. 'Hmm.' There was a long pause, and he appeared to be thinking. 'I must confess, Sergeant, I didn't notice you were here until this very moment. No, no, hear me out. But I have observed Private Atwell on two separate occasions in the past couple of hours. And I feel entirely confident in assuring you that not only has Atwell done his duty, he is – contrary to what you say – a damned *fine* soldier. Which makes me wonder, frankly, what kind you are?'

Battersby reddened. 'I can imagine you might think that in the confusion of the moment, sir. Atwell is very adept at appearing to be busy even when he's not. But with your permission, sir, I'd like to escort him back to the regiment.'

At this Archie had the impression more steam was coming out the major's ears than smoke out of the Panzer on the bridge. 'No, you bloody well don't have my permission, Sergeant. Both of you are staying here. In the event you hadn't noticed we're miles behind enemy lines. I have only a single platoon at my disposal, and we have no other support. Speaking of which, there must be something useful you can do.'

He turned to Dougan. 'Can you think of something? Have the Sergeant clean rifles for all I care. But put him to work,' he snapped. Then he stalked away, still muttering to himself.

'Follow me, Sergeant,' said the lieutenant.

'Fancy that, Miles,' murmured Archie, feeling greatly emboldened, 'no midday snooze after all.'

Battersby bristled. 'When this is done, Atwell…,' he hissed. 'You haven't heard the last of me.'

But then Dougan whisked him away without further ado. Archie caught a few words about undertaking a recce down the road.

This left Archie to take the major's advice about having a drink. He was absolutely parched. While he glugged down the better part of a water bottle, he amused himself by watching Battersby being introduced to a gaggle of soldiers. They were standing down on the road, going over their equipment. He looked back in the direction of the bridge and felt a smile break out. Captain Tighe and Lieutenant Wiles would look differently at him after this. Hell, the entire company would.

Owing perhaps to his mishap – one couldn't very well call it an injury when nothing was injured – Archie was told he might have a short rest. It had been a very long night, and in some respects an even longer morning. So with no further prompting required he sought out a spot of shade under a tree beside the German trucks, and lay down. He closed his eyes.

It was approaching noon when a loud commotion caused him to open them again. A sizeable group of bronzed men wearing shorts with Lee-Enfields slung over their shoulders was coming down the hill from the farmyard. 'Platoon from "C" Company,' he heard someone say.

Not long after, one of Dougan's men approached Archie. 'The Major is looking for you.'

'Ah, there you are, Atwell,' said Major Bury. Even after the morning's aerobics Archie was still a little surprised at the warm familiarity with which the major greeted him. In times past Bury had usually looked straight through him – except when he was wearily shaking his head, a look of immense frustration on his face. 'We've received some welcome reinforcements.'

'So I see, sir.'

'They couldn't have come at a better moment,' added the major. 'A second platoon is supposed to arrive this evening, which will give us the better part of a company. That should suffice in closing the road to the Jerries, eh? Dougan will make sure of it. He knows his business. So in good conscience I can finally head back to the Regiment.'

Archie nodded, not accustomed to company commanders sharing their motivations, or much of anything for that matter.

'I'm going to take you and that Sergeant of yours with me. You've done your bit. And I imagine they've been scouring the hills for you both.'

'Yes, sir, I expect they have. Although Captain Tighe may not be overjoyed at my return.'

'Any problems, let him speak with me. I'll be happy to vouch for you. Hell, if he doesn't want you in his company, I'll take you back in a jiffy.' He laid a reassuring hand on Archie's shoulder.

'Thank you, sir.' He threw back his shoulders. It was a little silly, perhaps, but somehow Archie felt redeemed. After all their shared history, nothing Bury could have said would have meant more than those few simple words. There might yet be hope for him in the Edmonton Regiment.

'Now, where's that Sergeant of yours?'

'I don't rightly know, sir.'

'Dougan?' Bury waved over the lieutenant who was conversing with his opposite number in "C" Company.

'The Sergeant I sent you, where is he?'

Lieutenant Dougan looked puzzled. 'I've been wondering that

myself, sir. He went with a bunch of men down the road towards Agira to reconnoitre. They really should have been back by now.'

Bury sighed. 'Down the road, you say?'

'That's right, sir. No more than two miles, I told them. Too dangerous otherwise.'

'I see.' Bury took a deep breath and turned to Archie. 'It looks as if you and I will be taking the road for a spell. For no more than two miles though. After that we're heading into the hills. Let's hope we see them, otherwise your Sergeant is plum out of luck.'

CHAPTER 23

27 July, 1943
Nicosia road, three miles north of Agira, Sicily

The Kübelwagen slowed as it raced down the hillside of desiccated yellow grass, the valley of the Salso to their right, a sharp bend only metres ahead. The brakes of the truck behind squealed noisily. It was late afternoon and Captain Weyers was hot and tired, and more than a little perturbed. He sat slumped in the rear passenger seat. The visor of his cap was low against the glare of the sun, and his eyes half closed; he was rethinking the recent battle for what was probably the tenth time that day.

At a little past nine o'clock this morning he had given the order. And with that the Tiger *Stellung* was abandoned, much as the first line had been late the day before, even if the latter had required no order. After the enemy's assault, orders were superfluous. Everything now depended on the third and final line of fortifications arrayed before the medieval town of Agira, and its critical road junction.

There really had been no choice, he told himself. He had hoped to contact Captain Struckmann earlier, but under the circumstances that hadn't been possible. When eventually he did reach the battalion commander, Struckmann quickly agreed; there was no alternative but to withdraw. Weyers's company had lost more than forty men in the past two days, and at least that many in the weeks previous. He had never before experienced a bombardment more intense, neither in Russia, nor in Africa. Nor had he seen his men – veterans nearly all – so dazed and bewildered. It was a question of time after that. He worried that his company and the battalion, perhaps even the entire 104th Regiment, was so weakened it might not fight again.

'We are not the only ones,' Lieutenant-Colonel Ens had told him later, brushing away his worries; 'others will hold Agira'. The colonel ordered the regiment north, their role unclear. What Weyers did know was that where the Canadians were forcing their way eastwards along the highway no. 121, the Americans were doing the same ten kilometres to the north. And what could they possibly accomplish there? They needed a rest and reinforcements, and neither seemed likely. But then it was not up to him to conduct the campaign, only to do what he could with the men and material he had. And miracles were always possible – his mother had lived years in the hope of one.

Weyers felt the car round the corner – 'it corners like a boxcar on wheels,' he'd once joked with his driver – then, without warning, Corporal Schumacher stomped on the brakes. Weyers was thrown forward, and the staff car shuddered to a halt. '*Scheisse*,' he snapped, 'what's going on?'

The driver pointed through the windshield. Ahead a truck, an Opel Blitz, identical to the one following but with its canvas tarp in place over the cargo bed, stood parked incongruously in the middle of the road. Immediately beyond it the road curved again.

There was a squeal that went on and on, followed by a bang and a loud crunching noise, and the car jolted abruptly forward. Weyers swivelled to look. The Opel Blitz behind, containing almost half his remaining company, had successfully navigated the bend, but not the sudden stop.

Under the blazing stare of his commanding officer, the driver of the truck hurriedly put it in reverse. In his haste to extricate himself from the situation, he backed it up all the way to the last bend. Weyers groaned loudly. But the truck driver had seen something. And later his action would prove fortuitous indeed.

Barely had Weyers turned back to the scene in front, when a starburst appeared in the middle of the windshield. Another that followed nearly shattered the glass completely.

'Get out!' he yelled to Schumacher. The crackle of small arms fire was unmistakeable. 'Get out!' Crouching down so as not to offer the enemy a target, he threw open the rear door. Pausing, he coiled himself for the effort, and then leapt out the door and onto the road, where he deftly rolled the final metre into the ditch. His winded driver landed in the grassy furrow a moment later.

'Did you see how many?'

'No, sir.'

Regardless of their exact numbers the enemy was not concentrating on the two of them, but rather on the truck up the road where Weyers's men were spilling out. Judging from the volume of their fire they couldn't be that many. He hoped not, for it was a well-chosen spot for an ambush.

The gunfire intensified. Weyers recognized the clipped burst of an MP40. The machine pistol was not an ideal weapon at anything other than short range, but in the absence of better its 500-plus rounds a minute would serve nicely to keep the enemy heads down. Which appeared to be precisely the intention of Sergeant von Steinen.

For an instant he could see his staff sergeant, standing near their truck, furiously directing with one arm, a rifle held in the other. A small party started cautiously leap-frogging their way along the ditch side of the road. On the other side, a larger group was spreading out through the trees and shrubs, where the cover was dense. Von Steinen had arrived at the same conclusion he had; they would need to outflank them.

That this was not to be a wholly riskless manoeuvre was soon apparent. Weyers saw one of his men make a sprint across the road, then go down. He caught the briefest glimpse of a Tommy with a rifle slipping out and away from underneath the stranded truck.

In frustration he clenched a fist. There was nothing he could do. Not yet. He held a pistol in one hand, but unless the Tommies were exceptionally foolhardy the only sure result of using the Walther would be to attract their attention. He was all too well aware that he'd never been much of a shot with his left, and his right was only just out of its sling. He would need to wait.

Finally, although it couldn't have been more than a few minutes, he saw the first of his men crawling up from behind. 'Von Steinen!' he bellowed in the direction of the trees. 'Are you ready?'

'*Noch zwei Minuten,*' came the reply.

'Fine,' he shouted, glancing at his wristwatch. Then to the men behind: 'You heard the Sergeant. We have two minutes.'

The two minutes they put to good use. Under the cover of fire from von Steinen's men they crawled a little closer, fortunate there was a low stone wall abutting the adjacent field affording extra protection. Their little group was now an even half-dozen. It was not many, but one of the men had helpfully brought a machine pistol, so rounded up they were stronger. 'When the whistle goes, put that truck under fire,' he told them. 'Then we go in.' The burly corporal commanding the squad nodded.

TWEEEET. At the whistle a deluge of gunfire erupted, including from at least two machine pistols. A flurry of stick grenades clattered down near the truck. As the explosions cleared, Weyers got to his feet and sprinted ahead. The truck was wreathed in white smoke. But of the enemy, there was no sign.

'Check the back,' commanded Weyers over his shoulder. Still encountering no opposition, he moved forward, edging warily along the truck's side. When he reached the cab, the driver's door hung open and he darted his head in to look. Nothing. For some reason the motor cap was also open. But there was nothing untoward that he could see. Nor could he see any sign of the enemy. Two soldiers drew up, brandishing their rifles. In response to his questioning look they shook their heads.

'It's the damnedest thing,' he said, when von Steinen appeared. 'They appear to have fled.'

It was strangely quiet. Both men looked at each other. With a start, Weyers saw an expression come over the sergeant's face. He knew instinctively that von Steinen had reached the same conclusion at the same moment he had. 'Back!' he shouted. 'Get back.' Von Steinen began barking orders.

But by then, of course, it was too late.

The rifle fire came bunched in a tight volley. The shots were still ringing in Weyers' ears when a sub-machine gun stepped into the fray.

Von Steinen standing to his left let out a piercing curse. Meanwhile the handful of soldiers caught in the open near the truck were scattering, while the two that were no longer able to, just lay there.

'The shed,' said Weyers, 'They must be in that shed!' Further down the road, squatting in the field, were four stout walls of grey stone under a wooden roof. Perhaps it was a shed, although it may simply have been the ruins of two centuries previous. Either way, Weyers had seen movement. He extended his arm holding the P38 through the driver's side window. The truck's open door was a lucky break. 'A machine gun,' he shouted. 'Bring up a machine gun.' But his cries were lost to the shouting of men and the zipping of bullets, and the sheer impossibility of complying.

In frustration he looked to his side at von Steinen. His staff sergeant was pale, pressing a bloodied hand to one shoulder, and in obvious pain though doing his best to conceal it.

He gritted his teeth. It was not to be. So that left a single option. 'Get the men back to the truck,' he commanded. 'And have it turned around. We'll keep you covered until then.'

Von Steinen stiffened. Weyers could sense a protest was forthcoming. 'No, just go,' he said. 'See that the men are out, but leave me a couple. I can handle it very well, Friederich. Trust me. Just round up the others and ensure that you're ready for us.'

Grimly von Steinen nodded.

Weyers didn't see him leave. He was too busy watching the Tommy who, like some rabbit he'd once hunted as a boy in the forests of Prussia, had sprung from the bushes down the road. Then the truck door shuddered, and Weyers hastily shrank away as a sub-machine gun stitched a seam in it.

When again he was able to look, the man was mere metres from the truck. He was running bent over with a pistol extended in his right hand, and something else in the other, the tell-tale red formation patches on his sleeve. Weyers's eyes caught those of his opponent. For an instant his heart seemed to do a somersault. It was him! He was certain of it. The one from the square in Leonforte who had caused so much trouble. With a snarl that surprised even him, he raised his pistol.

The soldier slowed, crossed his arms in front, and with the one supporting the other, fired his own pistol. Two rapid shots went *pinging* off the truck. A miss! But they were sufficiently close to cause Weyers to hurriedly duck away behind the by now sorely tested truck door. It was odd though. Weyers could have sworn the pistol had the exact same sharp report as the Walther that he carried. But of course that couldn't be. Then he bobbed up and saw the man bounding forward once more.

Weyers loosed off a quick shot – too quickly as he'd done no more than point in the soldier's general direction. Then he lost sight of him. Only to spot him an instant later bending down on one knee, his left arm sweeping gracefully forward. Suddenly Weyers knew precisely what it was that he had in his other hand.

'Back! Back to the truck,' he shouted. The handful of men left by von Steinen as a rearguard were kneeling or standing near the truck, valiantly returning the enemy's fire. Obediently they backed away. 'Now, run,' he screamed. And they did.

The grenade went off with a soft bang, the concussion muffled by the truck's undercarriage. Then he stepped away, and as he did so there was a deeper boom, and flames began licking at the truck.

Weyers turned and ran on past the Kübelwagen. He would have cursed had he the breath for it; his few belongings lay strewn on the rear seat. He kept running.

Behind him there was a sound much like fireworks. He presumed the truck's gasoline tank had exploded, and likely its cargo bed was now following.

Up the road the *Opel Blitz* stood idling near the bend, the passenger side door flung wide open. Von Steinen was frantically beckoning to him. The four men of the rearguard were clambering in the back. Weyers ran the final few metres and sprang aboard.

The truck's engine roared, and with a jolt they were away. The truck clawed its way up the incline of the hill, slowly at first, but soon with considerable speed.

There was a deathly silence in the front cab.

Finally, Weyers spoke. 'The Troina road. We'll have to take the Troina road. We're supposed to be in Nicosia, God dammit. That's almost the last road north that's left. What are they doing here, anyway? *Scheisse!* Silence. 'No one said a thing about the enemy being here, did they?' he asked. The driver didn't reply. His eyes were firmly fixed on the road. Sandwiched in between them was Sergeant von Steinen. Von Steinen was an old veteran. He knew when to keep his trap shut.

'How's your arm?'

'I'll survive, Captain.'

The captain sank back in his seat. 'What a fucking mess.'

'At least there's the prisoner.'

Weyers looked over at von Steinen. 'Prisoner?'

'Yes, sir. We were able to capture a Canadian sergeant. He's in the back with the men.'

'We did? Where was he?'

'They found him in the back of the Opel, apparently, hiding behind some boxes of brandy.'

Weyers grunted. 'Well, well, that's something, I suppose. Not much. But it is something.'

Then he reached for his cap, his prized cap with the bullet hole in it. Only to discover it was gone. '*Verdammt!*'

CHAPTER 24

27-28 July, 1943
North of Agira, Sicily

Lieutenant Wiles had assumed the colour of a beet, but not from the sun. 'Missing? What do you mean Sergeant Battersby's missing?'

'I'm afraid that's all I know, sir. He was with the others at the truck when the Major and I found them, but somehow during the skirmish he vanished. Afterwards, we looked everywhere, but there wasn't a trace of him.'

Wiles sighed. 'It's one heck of a story, Atwell, I'll grant you that. The two of you disappear without a word for the best part of two days, then when you show up you tell me you were abducted by "D" Company. Whereupon you add that you fought two mixed battles. And to top it off the Sergeant has gone missing… I've have had three patrols out searching for the two of you since you disappeared. And there's a war on in case you hadn't noticed.' The lieutenant sounded somewhat riled.

'It wasn't exactly an abduction,' murmured Archie.

'This is no time for semantics, Atwell. I've a good mind to report you as absent without leave, and you can explain it all to the provosts at their leisure, and yours… while you rot in a cell. I don't have time for this.' He looked away, his eyes focused on something over Archie's shoulder. 'Captain?' he shouted.

Had it not been for the errant eyebrow that refused to line up like the other, Archie would not have known that Captain Tighe even recognized him when he approached, so studiously blank was his face. The captain nodded at Lieutenant Wiles.

'As you can see, sir, Atwell's turned up. According to him Sergeant Battersby has gone "missing", however. He has quite a tale to explain their disappearance. Tell him Atwell.'

Once more Archie related his experiences of the past 48 hours, this time to the captain. When he was done, he added: 'Major Bury said he would vouch for me, sir, if required.'

'Major Bury? Did he now? Alright, Atwell. When I have a chance, I'll speak with the Major. It's a tall tale for certain, but a short conversation with Bury will resolve the matter nicely.' He frowned. 'Be certain, Atwell, I *will* get to the bottom of this.' Then he turned his attention to Wiles. 'See that he's tidied up and ready. He's a disgrace at present. The rest of the platoon is prepared and equipped?'

'Yes, sir.'

'That only leaves a replacement for Battersby doesn't it, Andy?'

'That it does, sir.'

'Well, there's not a lot of time, and I don't like the idea of mixing things up at the last moment… No, let's postpone that decision, shall we? Tell the men we'll be moving out in an hour.'

'Moving out, sir?' said Archie, after the captain had left. 'I'm not sure I'm in any state for a route march. I'm dead on my feet.' Which was no exaggeration; every part of him seemed to ache. On top of it all he was exhausted. He was so dreadfully tired.

'March? Who said anything about a march? The Brigadier has given us orders to attack the Grizzly line tonight. So if you're already feeling dead you needn't worry about what happens. And if you don't get out of my sight, Atwell, I'll shoot you myself.' Wiles glowered, almost taunting him to make a rebuttal.

Archie gulped, and took a step back.

'You heard the Captain,' muttered Wiles. 'Go get yourself together.' Then off he stomped.

At 2000 the regiment assembled, and immediately thereafter set off northeast in a long snaking file in the direction of the two hills,

Mount Crapuzza and Cemetery Hill, that anchored the northern part of Agira's defences.

The platoon had been agog at Archie's surprise reappearance in the ranks, and none more so than his own section mates, half of whom thought he and the sergeant had been captured by a Jerry patrol, while the other half guessed he'd run off alone in search of women and wine – not that anyone was willing to reveal to which camp he belonged.

'You have to admit it looks pretty odd you turning up out of the blue, after disappearing without a word. Not to mention the whole business with Battersby,' said Dinesen, with his characteristic bluntness.

'So is that what's eating Wiles? He's on the bleeding warpath.'

'What d'ye think? He felt pretty stupid when he had to report to Captain Tighe that two of his platoon suddenly disappeared. Can't have been much better when you arrived back in fine fettle with a wild story, and then informed him his platoon sergeant was missing in action.'

'I'm hardly in fine fettle. I've had maybe two hours sleep in two days. And it wasn't a wild story; it was the truth.'

'Quiet in the ranks,' growled a voice, a few heads further.

'Who's that?' whispered Archie.

'Our fearless leader, Lance-Corporal Last Chance.'

'I'd forgotten about him.'

'Lucky you.'

Mount Crapuzza, Agira, Sicily

Of the march Archie recalled little afterwards. If anything, it was worse than the march with Major Bury and Lieutenant Dougan. At least those two knew the way. The regiment moved in a sweeping left arc heading northeast, inevitably encountering hills but no paths, and deep ravines where the only choice was to double back in the dark and find an alternative way forward. And climbing, much climbing was required. The night was clear but Archie shuffled forward in his own personal fog, no interest in the others or the surroundings, concentrating only on the truly necessary; setting one foot before the other in the footsteps of the fellow ahead.

It was well past midnight when an artillery concentration came thundering down to the east, much like a sudden summer storm. Judging from the consternation of the officers it appeared that the storm had been intended to support their assault. But there was no question of an assault. The assembly point lay ahead, somewhere in the dark hills.

Approaching 0300, they finally reached that first objective. Captain Tighe stood apart, marshalling "A" Company aside, instructing the officers and NCOs on how the attack would proceed.

'Archie?' It was young Postlethwaite tapping him on the arm. He was smiling broadly, his cheeks flush from the exertion and the excitement. 'Welcome back.'

'Thanks.'

'I just wanted you to know. I never for a moment believed that you took off and left us.'

Archie was on the verge of turning it into a joke when he saw Postlethwaite's face. It was deadly serious. 'No?' he replied.

'No.' Conspiratorially, Postlethwaite glanced left and right, and his voice dropped a tone. 'None of the others did either. They were just pulling your leg, Archie.'

'Thanks, Steven.'

They were okay, thought Archie, looking at his section mates. He could have done worse than end up with this bunch.

'But "D" Company, Archie?' Postlethwaite was talking again, a goofy grin on his face. 'Jeez. None of us could believe you'd gone and taken up with the "dog-eared and dumb"?'

Wearily Archie smiled. It was something he'd said, apparently several times too often, and to several times too many people. 'I was wrong about that. "D" Company's okay. Don't you go believing everything I say, young man.'

Postlethwaite grinned.

Suddenly the night erupted in a loud screeching, as if something was ripping and clawing its way across the sky. The heavens themselves seemed to be torn asunder. But as quickly as it came the noise disappeared.

'Archie?' Postlethwaite's eyes were bulging.

'A Moaning Minnie,' breathed Archie, suddenly very awake. 'It's gotta be. I heard one near Nissoria. Essentially a six-barreled, mortar-like contraption that fires rockets. They're real buggers.' If there was one thing that sent a shiver up Archie's spine, it was a Moaning Minnie.

But Postlethwaite was of other thoughts. He nodded eagerly. 'Oh, yes, I read about them: *Nebelwerfers*. Was that really a *Nebelwerfer*? I heard they were loud, but… my gosh!'

Then "A" Company began to move. 'We're attacking Mount Crapuzza,' someone called. Archie and Postlethwaite hurriedly fell into file.

'Crap Hill. I should have known they'd leave the worst for us,' opined some unseen wit.

However, the wit's prediction fell well wide of the mark. For once this campaign the Germans obliged by their absence – a surprise to all, a disappointment to a few, and a relief to those like Archie who knew what an attack uphill portended.

'Thank heavens for small mercies,' he said, when eventually they made it to the top, and it became clear that while Monte Crapuzza was an imposing hill, it was free of any enemy presence. 'I don't think I was up to another gun fight.'

Lachance, having slept well and been in no such clashes, bobbed his head in agreement. He may not have had much in the way of aptitude, drive, or intelligence, thought Archie, but he wasn't a complete fool. This would have been his first action as section leader; a role he must have realized he wasn't up to. Christ, he wasn't up to leading himself. On the other hand, recalling the memory of him and Battersby holed up like rats in Leonforte, perhaps he was simply a coward.

A few minutes later he'd forgotten Lachance as a sudden chatter of MGs and rifles, accompanied by the steady thud of mortars broke the stillness of the night. The fireworks came from 600 yards southwest of them, corresponding to the location of Cemetery Hill, an altogether more ill-omened name than Mount Crapuzza, all agreed. Brigadier Vokes was determined that Agira should fall. "B" and "D" Companies had drawn the short straw this time.

The noisy fury of the assault lent a tangible seriousness to the company's work to dig in. It was an effort in which Archie was only cursorily involved, requiring as it did considerable toil to dig slit trenches in the hard-baked and stony ground, including a waist deep-hole for Roberts and his Bren gun – none of which he had the energy for. No one paid him much attention as he tapped away for appearances sake. He found it difficult though not to think of their old platoon sergeant, Matt Evers, who at that very moment was presumably rallying the boys as they charged up Cemetery Hill in the dark.

Quicker than Archie would have guessed possible, Roberts got his hole. It was not deep, nor was it wide, but it accommodated him, his Bren, and a big satchel with ammunition with some room to spare.

'Say, Ben, do you mind if I crawl in there with you? I'm dog tired.'

'Fine by me, Archie,' responded Roberts. 'Just don't let the Lieutenant see you.'

The lieutenant didn't, and barely had Archie curled into a ball than he was fast asleep, his head coming to rest against Roberts's leg not long after. The sounds and flashes of the nearby battle were no impediment, and he slept as he had seldom slept before. Unfortunately, his rest proved of short duration.

Dawn arrived as scheduled well before 0600. At a few minutes past the hour, as a frisky yellow sun was preparing to spring from behind the line of craggy hills to the east, two things happened. The first was that Lieutenant Wiles appeared. He may not have intended it to be a surprise, although he may well have. Regardless, the first Roberts was aware of him was a jovial 'morning' spoken to his back, followed by: 'Is that Atwell there beside you? Atwell!?'

Roberts darted a glance over his shoulder to see who it was, even if the list of candidates was a short one. Without replying he turned back to stare at what he had noticed a moment before. This was the second thing. 'Look sir,' he said, pointing. Archie slept on.

Scattered groups of German soldiers were fleeing down the slopes of Cemetery Hill. It was clear that their intent was to make for Agira's northern outskirts. Sprawled over the conical form of a much larger hill immediately southeast of Cemetery Hill, was the jumble of greyish stone and bleached rooftops that made up the town.

Roberts could scarcely believe his eyes. The tan figures were as plain as could be, no more than a few hundred yards distant, lit by the sun and moving without care for cover or concealment – not that there was much to choose from. Their sole concern seemed to be to leave Cemetery Hill behind.

'By Jove, they've done it,' said Wiles, smashing one fist into the other. 'They've taken the hill.'

Roberts was already busy with the Bren, deftly moving it into position on its bipod, and settling the butt up against his shoulder. 'Sir?' he asked, looking up. His hand was pulling back the charging handle. 'Shall I?'

'By all means,' said Wiles. 'Don't let me get in your way.'

Meanwhile Archie was twitching and turning, his carefree dream becoming a nightmare. The Panzer grenadier officer, his face fixed in a savage rictus, had his pistol out and was blazing away at him.

Roberts pulled the trigger of the Bren gun. The noise was deafening.

Archie bolted upright, his heart racing, a lump in his throat. Then he saw Roberts bent over the LMG, and he felt the relief wash over him. He shook his head to dispel the last vestiges of the dream, only to hold his breath once more when he spotted the gangly silhouette of Lieutenant Wiles a few feet away. He was behind their position, erect, a pair of binoculars trained to the south. Archie dove for the haversack with magazines and retrieved one. Then, when the short bursts of fire ceased, and Roberts looked up, he motioned to offer it to him. Roberts nodded and thrust out his arm.

Roberts wasted no time in resuming fire. He was single mindedly focused like that; set an objective and Roberts was the sort who would keep going until he reached it. Archie returned his attention to the haversack with magazines, but then some instinct instructed him to look up. The lieutenant, binoculars dangling round his neck, stood watching. Archie ignored him, and quickly returned to an examination of the magazine held in his hands. After an awkward moment the lieutenant turned and left.

By now what sounded like all of "A" Company was blazing away. On the undulating, grassy ground in the lee of Mount Crapuzza, dozens of enemy soldiers were fleeing in total disarray, like a herd of wildlife panicked into a stampede by the arrival of a predator.

'Archie?' Roberts said it without moving his head, or removing his finger from the trigger.

'Ready when you are. It's a real turkey shoot, eh?' When the time came Archie passed him the fresh magazine. He could have picked up his own rifle and taken a few shots as well, and perhaps even hit something, but keeping the Bren in action with Roberts behind it was far more efficient. One glance at the bodies strewn over the yellow fields was proof of that.

The order to cease fire came not much later.

Thereafter the morning was dedicated to holding the ground taken, and keeping the road east of town under watch. Until the news came. It spread from man to man, and it was not long before the entire company was in the know, Captain Tighe making a point of strolling past each position to confirm it in person; the Patricias had entered Agira from the west. They were said to be mopping up. The small arms fire they still heard testified that the result was not entirely a foregone conclusion.

It was therefore with a nagging foreboding that Archie heard Lieutenant Wiles call out to him.

'Yes, sir?'

'Lieutenant Swan needs a few extra men for the patrol he's leading. I've offered you.'

While the lieutenant didn't explicitly mention that this offer was intended to be sacrificial in nature, his expression didn't rule it out either.

CHAPTER 25

28 July, 1943
Agira, Sicily

Like almost every other Sicilian town of Archie's acquaintance, Agira was built on the highest hill for miles around. This came about as a result of the island's history, which had known countless centuries of conflict and occupation dating all the way back to the Greeks. During which time the Sicilians learned to construct their villages on towering cliffs to ward off the invading barbarians. In the case of the Wehrmacht these measures hadn't worked as planned; the Germans simply motored in at their convenience, with invitations from the Fascists in Rome stuffed in their breast pockets. Getting them out, however, was another matter entirely.

Lieutenant Swan was busy with his map. Apparently aware of the men clustering round he folded it neatly in half, and did so again for good measure, before tucking it away. 'The Colonel wants us to take a peek at Agira,' he announced, 'and see if Jerry is still up to his tricks. Follow me, boys.'

Swan's patrol was section strength, although he must have lost a few to sandfly fever and the Jerries, for Archie noticed one or two others from Lieutenant Wiles's band of misfits.

'You in the shit too?' he asked one of them.

The man frowned. 'No, why?'

'Oh, no reason. Say, do you suppose this is it?'
Again the man frowned.

'What I mean to say is, you heard the Lieutenant. Colonel Jefferson instructed him to have a look around town. I don't know about you, but I saw an awful lot of Jerries from Cemetery Hill rushing towards Agira. And my guess is there was an ample crowd to begin with. And Patricias, or no Patricias, seems a lot to handle for one patrol, that's all.'

'I see your point,' said the man. 'Let's hope they've all buggered off.'

Once they had made their way down the nearly barren slopes of Mt. Crapuzza – tufts of dry grass, the occasional stone, and a smattering of lonely trees were all that adorned it – the patrol proceeded along a winding path across the parched little valley in the direction of Agira, where they began climbing a slight incline. Reaching the base of the hill proper, Archie looked up and saw the town clinging precariously to the rocks towering above.

Lieutenant Swan led them round the hill until they came to a road on the northeastern side of Agira. This appeared to be the road the lieutenant had set his sights on, for they followed it uphill, a straggling line of fifteen-odd soldiers in tin hats and bayoneted rifles. Buildings appeared as they entered the town proper. Soon the street came to another, this one heading east, and they turned on to it. It may even have been the continuation of the no. 121 that they'd been doggedly following going on two weeks. Swan would have known for certain; he had the map.

This part of Agira appeared to be deserted. The street was eerily still. To either side, the buildings of worn stone with their typical, sagging iron balconies were empty by all appearances. The lieutenant halted next to one such building, motioning for the platoon sergeant to come forward. After a brief discussion, the sergeant and a couple of men pushed through the heavy wooden doors with their flaking red paint redolent of better times a century before. The patrol stood waiting. When the sergeant reappeared on the balcony, he glanced about before shaking his head. Contentedly, Lieutenant Swan nodded, and waved for the patrol to move on.

After a few minutes there was a break in the wall of buildings. To the left, a dazzling panorama of the Salso Valley basking in the sunshine hove into view. On the far left of this tableau the prominent bulge of Mt. Crapuzza was visible. Abruptly the lieutenant retreated a step and pressed himself into the façade of the last building before the gap. He stood looking, not at the view, but rather down the road at a large ramshackle house set apart from the others, on the opposite side of this open space. Archie squinted as he followed the lieutenant's example.

His every instinct tingled. There was someone there, was there not? As Archie watched he saw a shadow in one of the upper floor windows flit past. Suddenly two men appeared by the front door. They stood for a moment, glanced casually around, then disappeared back inside.

An elderly Italian man appeared on the far side of the street. He was bent over, furiously gesticulating with a walking stick that was as crooked as he was. '*Tedeschi*,' he whispered, stabbing the stick in the direction of the building. Archie unslung his rifle. He knew what that meant.

Swan did too for he made a shuffling retreat of a few steps. 'Jerries,' he hissed. 'I'm going to have a look. The rest of you stay here.' To Archie's way of thinking this was foolhardy, but the young lieutenant's face was set in stone. In his hands Swan now gripped the Tommy gun he'd been carrying.

The lieutenant walked warily forward. The rest of the patrol stood unmoving, watching. Archie stepped forward into the spot vacated by Swan at the corner of the building. There he went down on one knee, and raised the Lee-Enfield to his shoulder holding it ready. Behind him he heard the scuffle of boots as others took up position. The lieutenant kept walking.

He had almost reached the house when a little further down the street a soldier appeared. He was German by the look of him, and at the sight of Swan he barked an impatient command. Lieutenant Swan kept walking and the man, cottoning on to his mistake, reached for the machine pistol that hung over one shoulder by means of a swivel sling. He stepped a little further into the street and brought the gun to bear.

Archie didn't hesitate. He already had him lined up in his sights. He held his breath in and gently squeezed the trigger. *CRACK*. Caught between the buildings to either side the sound reverberated long and loudly. A pair of pigeons bolted into the sky trailing indignant *clucks* and falling feathers. Archie threw the bolt open, and the empty casing went flying. Then it was only a question of shoving it forward again and down, before it locked into place, his finger reaching for the trigger. But the German was on the ground, going nowhere. At that the tension seemed to ebb out of him.

Then the lieutenant disappeared through the doorway of the house.

'Damn it,' said a gruff voice behind Archie. 'Look at him go.'

'We should follow,' opined another voice.

'No. We'll wait here. That's what he told us to do.'

'Don't be such a bleeding stickler. The Lieutenant needs help.'

'Look, I'm the corporal. It's my responsibility.'

'Have it your way, Pete. But I always thought Swan was okay. I guess we'll just have to hope the next guy's not too bad.'

Pete, the corporal, groaned. 'Fine. We'll give him two minutes, then you can play cavalry. Satisfied?'

The lieutenant met this deadline handily, however.

Archie was staring down the rifle barrel, moving it slowly from left to right, hoping to catch some glimpse of the lieutenant through a top floor window, when there was a commotion. At the sound of the hubbub he raised his head to look better. What appeared to be an entire platoon of Germans, hands buried deep in their pockets, was spilling out onto the street from the building's doorway. The lieutenant emerged on their tail, the barrel of his Thompson pointing the way forward. 'I'll be damned,' muttered Archie. 'Swan's bagged every Jerry in Agira.'

'Not only that,' said the corporal who'd come to stand beside him, 'the Lieutenant's collected a few Eyeties too.' Pete and he were well acquainted; many a card game together and the odd pint over the years.

'Eyeties? Are you sure? Where?' Archie stood with renewed interest, staring at Swan's motley collection of prisoners. Even in the moment of their capture it was the Germans who were leading; it may not have been their island, but they were the ones firmly in charge. Admittedly they outnumbered the Italians seventeen to four and, regardless of uniform, all twenty-one looked uniformly scared out of their wits – survivors of the Cemetery Hill battle, no doubt. The Italians were shuffling along behind, their comportment decidedly sloppier, and altogether cheerier. Archie eyed the four of them keenly.

With his rifle resting in both hands across his waist, he began walking down the street towards them. He had made a promise that he would keep his eyes peeled. Besides, there was no harm in taking a closer look. Pete and a couple of others joined him. As Pete explained, the lieutenant would be needing some help in herding his flock back to Crap HIll.

'Nice shot, by the way, Archie,' said Pete. 'You got yourself a sergeant from the mortar platoon. It could have gotten pretty sticky for the Lieutenant with that Schmeisser he was carrying.'

Archie could see the man crumpled on the ground a hundred feet further, but as to his badges he would have to take Pete's word for it. 'Mortars, eh? Ain't that something? Can't stand the bleeding things, so it serves him right.'

Then before he knew it the Italians were in front of his nose parading past. Lieutenant Swan was looking straight through him at the rest of the patrol who stood waiting. Then he shifted his gaze to Archie. 'You take up the rear,' he said. Without awaiting a reply he addressed himself to Pete. Archie hadn't heard a word he'd said; he was staring at one of the Italians.

The dark hair was definitely the same. But there wasn't a Sicilian born who you couldn't have said the same of, differences of shade notwithstanding. But there was something about the angular lines of the face, the vibrant look in his eyes, and the lithe build of his body. It was unquestionably a handsome face. From his memory of the photo he would have known the face anywhere. Even here, shuffling along with his tan uniform in tatters, blood streaking his forehead, dark hair dirty and matted, and the laces of his boots missing, he was unmistakeable.

'Lazzaro?' he said to him.

The soldier blinked, and he stared back, his mouth half ajar.

'Lazzaro Parisi?'

Archie could only imagine his confusion. First a night of mortars and machine guns, blood-curdling cries in the dark, and the glimmer of steel amidst the flashes as maddened men overran their position; then the terror of the flight from the hill while Robert's Bren and a dozen like it nipped at their heels; and only a couple of hours later, an enemy soldier in helmet and shorts bursts into their refuge and stands grinning before them, his tanned arms wielding a sub-machine gun. And now this.

'*Si?*' mumbled the soldier.

Archie grinned from ear to ear. Lazzaro, puzzled, felt the outlines of a cautious smile coming to his own face. His three comrades, who'd been watching the scene as they marched, smiled more exuberantly. For this couldn't be bad could it, that this tall, fierce Tommy soldier was smiling at them so?

It was all Archie could do not to reach out and hug him. Throwing captor-prisoner etiquette to the wind he seized Lazzaro's hand and shook it. Glancing warily around for Wiles, Pete and the others, none of whom would understand a thing, he rummaged in a pocket before passing over the modest photograph he had studied so often.

Lazzaro grunted at his own likeness. He turned it over to read the inscription. Of course, he'd do that, thought Archie; he'd written it for her.

'Ginevra!'

Archie kept grinning. '*Si.*' The other Italians appeared only too pleased by their state of captivity, which was as well for Archie as he was entirely focused on Lazzaro. 'She asked me to find you,' he said. 'She told me the Tedeschi had taken you.'

Lazzaro nodded, but didn't say anything. He may have understood something of Archie's few words, but clearly he didn't share his sister's talent for languages.

'She'll be thrilled when she hears that you're all right,' Archie said, beaming. Lazzaro beamed back, and over his shoulder his three mates beamed in chorus.

Shortly after the lieutenant announced that they would head back to the battalion. No one, least of all Captain Tighe, could fault him for that. For Archie it was a relief. The prisoners outnumbered the escort, and if this past week had demonstrated anything, it was that overwhelming superiority was the only sure way of dealing with their foe. They certainly didn't want to get into a running gun battle whilst escorting twenty POWs. And Archie couldn't wait to get the Italians to safety.

They followed the same route as before but, in a departure from their normal marching order, Swan had the prisoners walk in double file, the men scattered around them. Archie stuck close to the Italians. While it may not have been the sheer size of this formation that attracted the enemy fire, it was likely not a coincidence that the tightly ordered ranks of the prisoners were the first to be targeted.

Somewhere behind, a sole machine gun began zipping its way through an ammunition belt. Archie was not the only one to feel a pang of fear at the sound. They were halfway down the slope of the Agira hill, its jumbled agglomeration of buildings at their backs, with the dry valley ahead and Mt. Crapuzza rising beyond. They were entirely in the open, not a tree or a shrub anywhere. One of the Germans fell.

'Run,' someone shouted. To the prisoners this must have seemed like some recurrent nightmare; only that morning they had fled down Cemetery Hill, across the valley, and up the incline of the hill to the safety of Agira while countless Brens and rifles spat fire at them. Now they were doing it again in the opposite direction and, in the very cruelest of ironies, their own comrades were the ones shooting.

Unbidden, the prisoners scattered. In many respects this was the only sensible course of action. Recognizing the futility and the danger, not one attempted to return to his own side. Instead, they ran with the Edmontons towards Mt. Crapuzza and the promise of safe harbour.

To Archie, the idea of running across the valley while the MG shot at anything that moved seemed lunacy. His first reaction was to dive into the straw-like grass and stare up at the jumble of buildings, trees and rock formations that made up Agira, hoping to spot the MG. But before he did so he tackled Lazzaro, pushing him roughly to the ground. He wasn't going to let Ginevra's little brother die – not now. Lazzaro's mates took the hint, and Archie found himself in sole command of the Italian detachment.

Carefully he scanned the hill for the machine gun nest. A thousand nooks and dark crannies, windows and small peepholes stared back at him.

In frustration he got to his feet, and helped Lazzaro to his. 'Spread out,' he yelled to the others, and flapped exuberantly to translate. A knot of men grouped together would present the German gunner with altogether too much temptation. It gave him a fresh regard for the men who had faced this terror that morning while he had blithely handed Roberts magazine after magazine.

The Germans must have been changing magazines themselves for their fire died out. It was strangely quiet. The rest of the patrol and their prisoners could be seen hundreds of yards ahead, on the valley plain. 'Dammit,' he cursed, and pulling Lazzaro along sprinted forward. The Italians ran too, feet thumping on the parched earth, Archie's kit rattling madly, his lungs feeling like they were bursting. Then it began again – a short burst to begin with.

Archie felt a pit in his stomach form. A look ahead confirmed what he already knew – they had hundreds of yards of open ground still to cover. It would probably come down to luck, he thought, and the skill of the Jerry behind the machine gun. Although at 500 rounds a minute, and presented with an entire menu of targets, the man could scarcely avoid hitting something.

At that moment something remarkable happened. A succession of sharp thumps went off, one after another, the first following the second as closely as a metal tooth in a zipper follows the one before. Overhead the air whistled. Then, only fifty perilous yards behind Archie and the Italians, the mortar rounds plunged to ground. They fell in as close a succession as they had been fired, a half dozen bangs or maybe more.

However, and this was the remarkable part, he could hear from the sound that they were not high explosive charges being fired. And to confirm, over his shoulder, he glimpsed plumes of dense, white smoke billowing in the field. They were from the small two-inch mortars that the company carried. Captain Tighe had come through!

Soon a thick and nearly impenetrable curtain was drawn behind them. Archie, never a big believer in miracles, found this hard to describe any other way. He would have crossed himself had the gesture been a familiar one.

Archie shepherded the four of them up the hill, the rest of the patrol already there. Their thighs ached from the climb, the sun was beating down remorselessly, but at last they came to the final few yards, the battalion's encampment ahead. Several men watched them from the cover of trees where they lazed in the shade.

They drew up behind the others. Pete was there, dabbing at a river of sweat on his lean face. 'Lucky thing about those mortars, eh?' said Pete, with a curious smirk.

'Say that again,' said Archie, wiping at his brow. He put his lips to his water bottle, tilted his head back and gulped at it. Then remembering his scathing words about the German with the mortar flashes he realized what Pete was getting at, and he laughed, water still dribbling from his chin.

'Come on, I reckon we're in time for lunch,' said Pete. 'What do you suppose is on the menu today?'

'If I was a betting man, I'd say compo rations. Which would be great. I don't know about you, but I could eat a mule. First, though, I've got to take care of my friends here.' He motioned at the Italians. Lazzaro was staring at the water bottle. With a grin he handed it over. 'Save something for me, Pete!'

As he stood there, wondering how further to proceed with the Livorno Division in his custody, a couple of military policemen presented themselves and explained they would take over. Archie turned to Lazzaro. 'You're safe now, Lazzaro,' he said slowly. 'I'll write Ginevra and tell her you're well. Do you have anything you want me to send her?'

Lazzaro just stared at him, and Archie could see he was hopelessly trying to decipher what had been said. 'Send her?' he finally asked.

Archie fished in his pocket and took out a fistful of money, some papers, and finally a letter from home, and waved them at him. Then he pointed at Lazzaro's pockets. 'For Ginevra?'

'Ah,' grinned the young Italian. He bowed his neck slightly, and proceeded to remove a thin chain with a silver locket dangling from it. Prising open the locket he showed it to Archie – Ginevra looked back at him in miniature black and white. She was smiling, and Archie couldn't help smiling at her, the pressures and exertion of the patrol forgotten. She would be so excited to get the letter, and hear that her brother was alive, well, and out of the hands of the Germans. He wished, though, he could see her face when she saw the locket. With an apologetic shrug Lazzaro handed back his own picture.

'Quite right. I wouldn't want my own mug either. I'll see she gets them, Lazzaro.' As the Italians were hustled away, he had time only to call out, 'good luck' before they disappeared from sight. All things considered it had turned into a far better day than he'd expected. Whistling a bar of "Pistol Packin' Mama" he set off in search of what might be left of the compo rations.

'Hang on, Atwell.' At the voice he groaned and closed his eyes. When he reopened them Lieutenant Wiles was beckoning to him from the shadow of a small tent.

'Lieutenant Swan said you did well.'

Archie shrugged. His feet were killing him, he suddenly felt dog tired, and he hadn't forgotten that it was Wiles who'd volunteered him for the lions' den in the first place – even if had worked out. If the lieutenant wanted to smooth things over he'd have to do a good sight better than that.

Only Wiles showed no such inclination. This was not to be a conversation of accolades. 'I thought I saw you dozing at your post this morning?'

Archie sputtered briefly, but he didn't have his heart in it.

'You know as well as I do what the Captain thinks of anyone sleeping on duty. Equally you know what he'd do if he ever found out.' Archie hadn't a clue what the captain would do, but put like that he wasn't anxious to discover the details.

'*If* he ever found out, sir?'

'That's right. I'm going to keep this little incident between the two of us. According to Swan you've earned it. However, that still leaves the matter of you being AWL. Look, I'll be honest with you, Atwell. I spoke with Captain Tighe, and things don't look so good for you.'

'But, sir, I wasn't AWL! I told you both what happened. Besides, as I also told you, Major Bury will speak for me. All you have to do is ask.'

'No. I'm afraid that's quite impossible.'

'Sir, the Major told me himself he would. He promised. All you have to do is ask him.'

Slowly Lieutenant Wiles shook his head. 'As I said, that's quite impossible. Major Bury was killed this morning by a mortar round during the attack on Cemetery Hill.'

CHAPTER 26

29 July, 1943
Agira, Sicily

What the divisional staff initially envisaged as a day's work, a mere eight miles down the road from Leonforte, eventually took two brigades five days of heavy fighting. But finally, on that fifth day, after countless battles, Agira fell.

In the absence of an invitation from the brigadier to establish barracks in the relative luxury of Agira's town centre, the battalion instead bunkered down on Cemetery Hill. It was not only the shortcomings in the accommodation that the men bemoaned about this arrangement. These past three weeks in Sicily had tried them sorely, and Agira held the promise of being the land of plenty, where all (or at least many) things a soldier desired could be had for a price – even if the lucky few reported that the price had risen dramatically from a day earlier when the townsfolk were still tickled pink by their "liberation".

For Archie and the others on Cemetery Hill the victory passed virtually unnoticed; they were simply content to hear that they would be out of it for a while, a welcome rest at hand. For no one was this truer than for Archie.

Lazarro's little silver locket with its precious photograph had kept unpleasant thoughts at bay all day, the day before. In the evening he took a pad, and with his pencil and a fine view of Agira before him, wrote a short but effusive letter to Ginevra. He'd been holding the chain above the envelope, fully intending to drop it in, when he hesitated. No, it was far too valuable to trust to the mail, he decided, re-clenching it in his fist. He let it coil slowly back into his breast pocket. That night he slept like a king.

Further associations with royalty evaded him this morning. The ground had proved as hard and unforgiving as stone, and there wasn't a bone in him that didn't ache as a result, while a cup of weak tea accompanied by some biscuits that were as hard as the ground constituted breakfast. All this might have passed unnoticed, as it had every other day previous, were it not that Archie woke to other thoughts. Thankfully Wiles had simmered down to his usual even-keeled self. But Captain Tighe! By the lieutenant's account Tighe was still simmering.

The curt 'morning' that the captain barked in his direction a little later appeared to confirm Wiles's take on the situation. Tighe had just finished reading aloud General Montgomery's personal message to his army. It contained a few nice compliments, even if the parting war cry of 'into battle with stout hearts' was of a more bellicose nature. Soon after, Archie heard the captain jovially engaging with a couple of others in the platoon. Then, if it were not already abundantly clear, the regimental paymaster sergeant cornered him.

'Atwell, the Captain has told me to dock your pay by two-thirds this month. I was also to tell you: "this isn't the end of it".' The sergeant raised a quizzical eyebrow.

Archie groaned. If the sergeant didn't know already, he wasn't about to tell him. Let him ask the captain if he was so bloody eager to know the gory details. 'So what does that leave me, fifteen bucks?'

'No. $13.42 to be precise.'

All things considered it wasn't much for almost three weeks fighting, plus a week at sea. On the other hand, it could have been worse. Although perhaps worse was yet to come. The captain's message was hardly uplifting in that respect. 'Well, one consoling thought,' Archie mumbled, '$13.42 should last forever here on Cemetery Hill.' Then a thought came to him. 'Say, Sarge, I need to post a letter, but it's not for home.'

'Who's it for, then?'

Archie grinned. 'A girl I met in Modica. I have a feeling I may not be seeing her for a bit, and I wanted to send her a message. It's not as if I can drop it in the bag with the others for the Postal Corps boys.'

'No, no, I suppose you can't. Modica you say?' The sergeant scratched at his head.

'I can pay if that helps.'

At this the sergeant smiled amiably. 'No, keep your money, Atwell. You've little enough as it is. I think I can swing it. I'll send it with one of the despatch riders, they'll get a kick out of something different. Do you have it with you?'

Archie nodded and passed it over. 'I left it open, for the censors.'

'I hope it works out,' said the sergeant. Naturally he meant with the girl, but his words could equally have applied to Archie's troubles with the captain.

Matt Evers had told him that his chance would come. After that it would be up to him. Up to a point those words were prophetic. He'd certainly seen his share of action. But it seemed whatever he did on this island, regardless of how hard he tried to do it, the same old reputation clung to him like Sicilian dust. As anyone familiar with the stuff knows, it almost never washes away.

Tall, dignified Cypress trees lined the walled cemetery that Archie was traipsing through on a mid-morning recce. They cast long shadows that offered the promise of relief from the stifling heat, if not an actual respite. The ancient cemetery was filled with a jumble of odd and irregular tombstones and vaults, which had suffered remarkably little from the battle days before. Of course, it was such a shambles of unkempt stone that a mortar bomb or two wasn't likely to make much difference. Then down on the hot, dusty road coming out of Agira he spotted action and hurried back to the others.

'A mule train? You have got to be kidding. This isn't the bleeding Crimean campaign,' Archie said when he saw what the support platoons were up to. In the blazing heat men were wrestling with saddles and harness, all the while sidestepping the odd kick of the more ornery animals, loading the beasts down with all manner of kit including a big no. 22 wireless set (which unlike the no. 18 reputedly worked), and the even bigger 3-inch tubes of the mortar platoon, which definitely worked. A large patrol was preparing to head out.

'Nothing wrong with mules,' protested Roberts. Roberts was a farmer's boy.

'Perhaps not,' said Archie, thinking otherwise, but wisely refraining from saying so. 'But seeing as they've finally found us some trucks, why don't they use those? Or a few carriers, for that matter? Seems a heck of a lot easier.'

'Because, General, where we're going there aren't any roads,' interjected a newcomer to the discussion.

'Hey Matt,' enthused Archie, extending a hand.

'Hi, Sarge,' said Roberts. Evers had always been a popular platoon sergeant, even without bringing his successor Miles Battersby into the picture.

Wearily Evers shook his head. 'Hear that, Archie? Roberts has the whole darned rank system figured out. But I'll let it pass… for old time's sake.'

Archie grinned. 'Sorry, Sarge. So where's the mule train off to then?'

'The same place we will be shortly,' Evers said. 'Look, I don't know all the details, but there.' He pointed to the northeast and what looked like an unbroken chain of steep hills and blue topped mountains stretching as far as the eye could see. 'The brigade is to cut the last roads north to Troina and Bronte, and shut down Jerry's escape routes.'

Evers was always a fount of new information, but at this Archie and Roberts looked at him as if he were speaking Sicilian.

'Don't you two know anything?'

They looked at each other, then back at him. They shook their heads.

Evers sighed. 'Well, you must know Regalbuto is the next village down the no. 121 after Agira?'

There were cautious nods.

'And of course you know we just cut the Agira-Troina road, the one heading north?'

Yes, they knew that.

'Well, five or six miles beyond Regalbuto, almost at Aderno, you come to one last road, a track really, heading north to Troina. So if any Jerries want to bugger out of Regalbuto in a hurry – and they might want to rather soon – that's the road they'll take. Then there's only one other road heading towards Messina this side of Mount Etna. That's the highway to Bronte. Every Herman Göring still on the Catania plain, or on the 121 ahead of us is going to need to use that road if he intends to get home. The plan is to close it before they do.'

'Hmm,' said Archie. 'So instead of following a road, the Eddies follow the mules over hill and dale – from the looks of it I'd wager primarily hill – and cut Jerry off from the rear.'

'Exactly! You've nailed it, Atwell. There's a general lurking in you yet. Of course, there may be an obstacle or two along our path.'

'Somehow I had a suspicion there might be,' said Archie, staring thoughtfully out to the northeast. The idea of mules suddenly seemed not so crazy after all. But revealingly no mention had been made of mules, or any other form of transportation for the men. The rationale behind Captain Tighe's recent admonitions to have their boots repaired was now blindingly obvious.

Had Archie been looking west instead of northeast he might not have been caught so unawares.

Virtually overhead a roll of thunder clapped and it began to pour. In sheer astonishment they looked at each other before their faces twisted in joy.

Billowing, dark clouds were sweeping across from the west, the sky even now darkening noticeably. The rain began to come down in a mad torrent.

Archie was already unbuttoning his shirt, and once that was off, he threw his arms out to the side, and lifted his face to the heavens as the blessed, cool water pelted down. Everywhere around him men were rushing into the open, as excited as little boys. Roberts, wearing a sloppy grin, had his water bottle open and was holding it skywards. Archie spotted Lieutenant Wiles, and soon after Captain Tighe, and many other officers. To a man they were stripping down. Some even had the presence of mind to bring a bar of soap with them, a surprise chance to battle the weeks of accumulated dust and grime.

After two full hours the rain abated, and as the clouds scuttled on eastwards the furnace of the sun cracked ajar once more. Archie was wringing out his clothing when one of the platoon walked up.

'Hey, Archie, the Lieutenant says to get yourself dressed. There are a couple of American MPs who want to speak with you.'

Archie groaned. Why would some American MPs want to talk to him? There was really only one possibility. And because of that his freshly washed cotton drill jacket was soon soaked in sweat. Fortunately, the American inquiries were largely confined to a single name.

'Battersby? Yeah, sure, I know the Sergeant,' he said, shuffling awkwardly in front of the two military policemen. Curiously, not a drop of water had fallen on either of them. They looked immaculate. 'I hope you're not looking for him? You probably haven't heard, but he's gone missing.'

'Yeah, we heard about it,' growled the stocky, rock of a sergeant. In his late twenties or early thirties, with closely cropped hair, unsmiling eyes, and two scars across one cheek, he was the kind that could quell a barroom fight singlehandedly. 'Your Captain Tighe tells us you were one of the last to see him.' His dark eyebrows came together and he fixed his gaze on Archie. This last statement was obviously intended as a question.

'That's right,' said Archie. 'I was on a fighting patrol to cut the Agira-Nicosia road, along with the CO of "D" Company. That's Major Bury… He, uh… well, he was killed yesterday.'

'Yes, we know.'

Archie gulped. The Americans were startlingly well informed.

Beside the sergeant, a lanky, young lieutenant observed silently, wearing eye glasses, pomaded dark hair, and a uniform pressed that very morning. He was of the sort that likely had never even seen a barroom, let alone a fight. Familiarity with a courtroom was a distinct possibility, however. Archie guessed he was the brains of the operation. Together, the two of them made an intimidating duo.

Archie coughed. 'So, anyhow, the Major and I caught up with Sergeant Battersby on the Nicosia road. We were heading back to the regiment, and the plan was to collect him as well. The Sergeant and a few men were out on a recce at the time, about a mile from the patrol's position when we found them. They'd managed to capture a Jerry truck.'

'Was it carrying anything this Kraut truck? Troops? Supplies?'

'As a matter of fact it was packed to the gunnels with hospital supplies. Oddly they seemed to consist mainly of brandy.'

'Brandy!?' The two Americans exchanged looks, and it was all

Archie could do not to smile. He knew what they were thinking. Then the sergeant turned back to him. 'Go on.'

'We'd barely reached their position when someone caught sight of a small German convoy approaching from Agira. You see at that point the Germans were actively using the road to pull back to Nicosia. Our orders were to stop them if possible. So before I even had a chance to speak with the Sergeant the whole thing erupted into a nasty little fight. But we were lucky, and we caught them by surprise. After bloodying their nose, they withdrew in short order. Honestly, I don't think they had much fight left in them. Once they left, we discovered that Battersby had gone missing, so we went searching. Couldn't find a sign of him anywhere though. Meanwhile the truck had gone up in flames. But he wasn't in the wreckage either. We searched that too. No one has seen him since.'

'And before this firefight, did you speak with Sergeant Battersby? The Captain says both of you were absent from "A" Company for almost two days.'

'Sure. A few times. It was a long march.'

'Did you notice anything particular about the Sergeant's behaviour? Did he say anything strange?'

'You have to understand, the Sergeant is not always an easy man.' Archie spotted what he thought was amusement on the American sergeant's face. Sergeants were accustomed to their reputation amongst the other ranks. 'He's not the sort who would confide in a private like me.'

'There's something I should tell you.' The lieutenant was speaking. His was a cultured voice from one of the northern states, with a precise and educated manner, and Archie would have put money on it that he was indeed a lawyer.

'Sir?'

'We are holding two men in the brig. Theirs is a long and complicated story, but the essence of it is that we suspect them of establishing a bootlegging organization here on Sicily, to supply the Allied armies with various contraband. We're quite certain there are others in the military involved, and very likely several from the local population as well. One of the men is of Sicilian extraction, and has relatives on the island in fact. Naturally both strenuously deny any such activity. Under questioning, however, one has let slip a name. According to him this man offered to supply them with a large quantity of wine, which he says they refused. He believes the man was a corporal, and he was very certain that he belonged to the Edmonton Regiment.' The officer raised an eyebrow.

'And the name he gave you was Battersby?'

The officer nodded.

'Wow. The Sergeant's not exactly a pleasant man, sir, but it's hard to believe that he'd be mixed up in something like that. Besides, sir, didn't you say the man in question was a corporal?'

'Sergeant Battersby was recently promoted, was he not?'

'Ah. Yes sir, he was. Not more than a couple of weeks ago. Still, it seems incredible. Although –' Archie frowned.

'Yes?'

'It may mean absolutely nothing, but right before the Major took us out on that fighting patrol, Sergeant Battersby was unusually agitated, nervous, as if he had something on his mind. He took me to task for a handful of things, minor even by his standards. If truth be told he was downright cantankerous. When I asked if he'd slept poorly, he snarled something about a couple of Wop Yanks he'd run into the day before. Which seemed a very odd thing to say. We run into you fellows all the time. Whoever they were, they sure weren't friends of his. He actually seemed afraid of them. And who was I to question him further? Captain Bury took us out on the patrol almost immediately after, and it wasn't the sort of thing you could discuss in the middle of that.'

'I see. Very interesting. It's a shame that Sergeant Battersby has disappeared. He could have been extremely helpful. I fear he may be dead, though. Don't you?'

'It's certainly a good possibility, sir. But surely, sir, if you've already caught these two, you don't need Battersby anyhow?'

'That too is complicated, soldier.' The lieutenant rubbed at his chin.

'Shall I, sir?' the sergeant asked.

The lieutenant nodded.

'Without that Sergeant Battersby of yours we've got nothing. Just a couple of soldiers who took off with a few trucks for a day without permission. And a list of suspicious circumstances the length of your arm. Worse, they know we're on to them now –' He shook his head.

'I'm sorry I wasn't better able to help,' said Archie.

The lieutenant smiled politely. 'No fault of yours. We appreciate your time. If the good Sergeant does turn up, you may see us again.'

As the two Americans walked away, Archie took a deep breath. If Battersby wasn't already dead he was going to wish he was. Archie smiled at the thought. Either the Sicilians were going to get him – Polowski had that angle figured correctly from the get-go – or the military was going to throw him into a deep, dark hole. No, for all concerned, it was best if Battersby was dead. Even if that meant the bastard was getting off easy.

But whatever had he been thinking with those two characters from the US Transport Corps? And the warehouse of wine? Even by his dad's woeful standards it had the hallmarks of great stupidity. On top of which, his dad's standards were not the ones he wanted to live by. Not anymore.

Now if only Captain Tighe and Lieutenant Wiles would see that.

CHAPTER 27

30 July, 1943
Near Troina, Sicily

At Weyers's question the lieutenant shook his head dismissively. 'No, sir, he's actually been extremely cooperative. This one may have a red patch like the others, but he's of different stock entirely. He's very rattled. You'll see for yourself, sir. He's quite willing to tell us anything. I think he'd offer up his own mother if he thought it would help. He's convinced we intend to torture him.' The lieutenant's broad mouth broke into a grin.

'Torture him!' Captain Weyers rolled his eyes in exasperation. 'What does he think we are? Monsters?' Then, in a harsher tone: 'You haven't threatened him have you?'

'No, sir. Absolutely not.'

'So what has he told you? Anything new?'

Lieutenant Baumgartl consulted a notepad. 'Sergeant Miles Battersby. Recently promoted. Platoon sergeant in "A" Company of the Edmonton Regiment, 2nd Brigade, 1st Canadian Division. He's given us the entire chain of command right down to the section leaders, and everywhere they've been: Ispica, Piazza Armerina, Valguarnera, Leonforte, Nissoria, Agira… It appears we've faced them many times. According to him their current orders are to work eastwards.'

At this last detail Weyers grunted. 'I could have told you that myself. In fact I think I did at the last briefing.' He smiled. 'Alright, Lieutenant, let's go have a talk with him. You've made me curious. Perhaps he has something of interest to tell us.'

Coming to the small hut on the hillside with its thick walls of stone, the sentry stood aside. Weyers followed the lieutenant's example, ducking low to pass through the narrow doorway. Inside it was dark and cool and, to his irritation, confined enough that he found he was forced to stoop, whereupon his arm began to throb. It had been a long day. Several long days, actually.

At the sight of them the prisoner scrambled back into the farthest corner, pressing himself against the rough-hewn stone blocks. Feverishly he began plucking at his moustache.

Weyers turned and frowned at the lieutenant. The man was more than rattled. 'Sergeant Battersby?' he asked. It had been some time since he'd spoken any English, but in the *Arbitur* his grades were the best of the class.

A pause. 'Yes.'

'My name is Captain Weyers. I am the commander of the unit which took you prisoner. I have a few questions.'

The sergeant eyed him warily. 'Sure. As long as you don't hurt me, I'll tell you anything.'

'We have no intention of hurting you,' said Weyers sternly.

The sergeant brought his arm back to his side and made an attempt to straighten his battledress. 'Thank you, sir,' he said. And he was as good as his word. Whatever question Weyers asked, the sergeant answered: about their commanders, their dispositions, their equipment, and their plans. Only the answers revealed nothing of any real importance, or that they didn't already know. This Sergeant Battersby was clearly a small fish in the scheme of things.

'There was another man from your regiment at the ambush,' Weyers said suddenly.

'Ambush?'

'At the truck, on the Nicosia road where we found you.'

The man nodded. 'Sure. All of us were Eddies. I was with some others on a recce when we caught one of your trucks. Then Major Bury and Atwell turned up out of nowhere.'

There was something odd about how he had spoken the last name. 'Atwell. Who is this?'

'Archie Atwell. A private. He's nothing.'

'Tall? Lean? About my height with sandy hair?' Weyers felt his heart beating faster.

'Yeah, that's him.'

The pulse in his temple began to throb. His arm began to throb even more. Piazza Armerina, Leonforte, the Nicosia road. It had to be the same man. It couldn't be a coincidence, could it?

'Is he a good soldier, this Atwell?'

'Atwell?' Battersby scoffed. 'He's a no-good, good for nothing, sir. If it had been up to me he would have been court-martialled long ago. No respect, no discipline. A terrible soldier.'

Weyers raised an eyebrow. He was certain that it must be him, though he'd expected a more senior man. He was all the more certain because of the sergeant before him. It was not because Battersby was an enemy, but rather because he was a disgrace of a soldier. It was all Weyers could do to conceal his disgust. 'The character of a man determines the quality of his judgement,' Captain Biederman liked to say, and that said all there was to say. But this Atwell... he would very much like to know more about him. Finally, he had a name for the man who had caused him so terribly much trouble.

'Sir?' The weasel was speaking. 'I was thinking. I happened to hear something between the Colonel and the Brigadier about closing the gap to Etna. It sounded to me like the plan of attack. If I tell you what it is, will you let me go?'

'Who exactly was speaking please?'

'Lieutenant-Colonel Jefferson and Brigadier Vokes. Only a few days ago.'

'And pray what did you hear, Sergeant Battersby?'

The sergeant smiled a crooked lipless smile. 'I can't very well tell you that, sir, without a promise on your honour to let me go, can I? But I think it would be well worth your while, sir. Might even save a good part of your army at Catania. In fact I expect it would. They'd probably make you a major.' The irritating knob of a chin bobbed up and down enthusiastically.

Weyers doubted that anything the man could tell him would change the campaign. On the other hand, battles were sometimes won by the smallest of margins. And it was entirely possible the sergeant had heard something. He seemed like the type to listen at doors.

However, before Weyers could properly consider the matter, he was called away. The field police had come calling; captain or not that required his immediate attention.

31 July, 1943
5 miles northeast of Regalbuto, Sicily

'There you are.' Lieutenant Wiles was facing him, a stern look clouding his youthful face, both hands resting on his hips and looking like the teacher he'd once been. Archie wondered if the pose was something he'd learned facing down a classroom of recalcitrant eight-year olds. Or maybe this was a trick he'd picked up more recently – twenty-year old privates being every bit as difficult as your average school kid. 'Charlie… that would be Lieutenant Swan… is taking a new patrol out tonight,' said Wiles.

'Let me guess, sir, he needs men?'

Wiles shrugged. 'The Captain was the one who suggested your name. There are a few others going as well, including Roberts. They figured a good Bren gunner would be helpful.' Then he smiled. 'Look at the bright side, Atwell. Swan knows you, and you know him, and you also know most of the rest of the platoon. That will save some trouble, and if it comes to trouble that's a good thing.' He looked past Archie to the northeast. 'My, you've gotten a properly stygian night for it.'

'A what, sir? Is that Latin?' Archie was actually a good deal more interested in hearing about the trouble Wiles foresaw than discussing the quirks of his vocabulary. But to ask about trouble would be to suggest that it worried him. Better to play the clod then. Playing the clod was a time-worn strategy for dealing with superiors.

'Very dark, Atwell. It means a very dark night.'

'Oh. Well, it's plenty dark, sir. Whether it's dark enough remains to be seen.'

'Yes, well, good luck then. If all goes according to plan I'll see you and the others again tomorrow morning.' Wiles was keen to move on.

Archie was surprised in light of his recent altercation with the lieutenant that Wiles was at pains to explain that this posting wasn't his idea. But, in an odd way, Archie didn't mind. Out in the Sicilian hills, far removed from the rest of the regiment, his superiors, American MPs, and Battersby lurking in dark corners of his dreams, a man could be himself. Proper manners and knowing Greek from Latin didn't matter one iota. And it wasn't as though hanging around in the rear was a true safe haven, not with trigger-happy American Kittyhawks on the prowl overhead. They'd already made a go of trying to bomb one of the other regiments only yesterday. Meanwhile, a few well-coordinated letters and numbers on a map grid was all some crack German artillery jockey required to send them all to Kingdom Come. No, a patrol wasn't so bad.

Earlier in the day, Archie had heard a few things that surely influenced his mood. The intelligence officer, Lieutenant Longhurst, was tasked by the colonel with establishing a new scouting and observation section for the regiment.

'Indian warfare,' Dinesen had muttered darkly, after telling them. 'Nothing more and nothing less. Skulking around behind enemy lines in the murk of the night! I tell you it's not something fit for proper soldiers.'

Archie snorted. He rather liked the ring of Indian warfare. As to the murk of night, that seemed to be the ideal time to take it to Jerry. Even Brigadier Vokes agreed. He was fond of the night attack. 'So Harry, you'd prefer to line up shoulder-to-shoulder in broad daylight in a crimson tunic, smile, and wait for the sergeant to tell you to fire? And don't forget to remove your ramming rod?'

'Come on, Archie. That's what they did a hundred years ago. I didn't say that.'

'Tell me this, then, Harry. Do you think before we attacked that we knew all we should have known about the Jerry positions at Nissoria? Or at Leonforte? Or anywhere else, for that matter? Knowing a little bit about our enemy seems to me like an excellent idea. If that requires a little skulking, well, then I'm all for skulking. Skulking is a most underappreciated skill.'

There were chuckles. 'You tell him, Archie,' said Borden with a laugh.

Dinesen rolled his eyes. 'If you're so darned keen why don't you go see Lance-Sergeant Ellenwood? He's commanding the outfit. Maybe they'll have you.'

'I might just do that. Of course, I'd have to leave you sorry geese in the hands of Last Chance while Jerry plucks your feathers. So that's a consideration.'

There were groans. Someone tossed a lemon at him; lemons and Jerries – on Sicily there was no shortage of either. But the scouting and observation section, that bore thinking about. If nothing else it would be a fresh start away from the likes of Tighe, Wiles and Lance-Corporal Lachance.

Lance-Sergeant Ellenwood, who he tracked down a little later in a tent near the cemetery, was not at first blush visibly enthralled with his offer of enlistment.

'Atwell, isn't it?' The sergeant frowned and scratched furiously at his brow, no doubt trying to recall how he knew the name.

'Yes, that's right,' replied Archie. The less said the better, he reckoned.

The scratching came to an end, but the sergeant was still frowning. 'We've more or less a full complement at the moment, Atwell. You see we've selected only a handful of men, all of whom have some skill the section will need. But I'll keep your name in mind. Good of you to come and ask – a little pip and vim, eh.' The frown withdrew in favour of a smile. 'And never say never I always like to say. I'll let you know if something comes up.'

Which sounded an awful lot like 'never ever' to Archie's ears, even if Ellenwood was gracious enough to put it more diplomatically.

After walking a mile or two down the rolling, twisting road towards Regalbuto, the patrol lazed under some trees while the sun set. They ate cold steak and kidney pudding, biscuits and a piece of half-decent cheese from the compo rations, all the while contemplating the chain of hills to the north. Around dusk Lieutenant Swan signalled they should muster.

'We'll follow the Salso east,' he told them, 'then cut north. The Colonel has ordered us to reconnoitre a route to Hill 736. A curious name, alright, but that's the height of this feature in metres, in case you're wondering. Highest peak we'll come to. We're to ascertain if there are any enemy in the area. If all goes well we'll slip away and report back tomorrow morning.'

'If all goes well.' This was the second time in a matter of hours that an officer had fallen back on an optimistic but open-ended forecast of how the patrol would proceed. It was the sort of thing that made a contrarian like Archie distinctly uneasy. When everyone was expecting the best, it inevitably went to hell in short order. But first they had a succession of gulches and canyons to navigate.

The River Salso, for all its prominence on the maps, was nothing more than a wide, rock filled, almost dry river bed nestled into what might best be described as a modest gorge. They hadn't made much progress along its bank, so the lieutenant took them down into it. It was devilishly hard walking, particularly in the dark, although their pace did improve. There weren't any mules along, but even Roberts admitted that the creatures would haven't fared better on the jumble of rounded stones. 'Forget about mules,' he muttered at one point, 'One of us is going to break a leg.'

Lieutenant Swan must have shared this assessment, for not long after he directed the patrol to seize its chance and climb back onto the bank. They came to a railroad bridge spanning the river, and cautiously picked their way over the wooden ties to the far side. Soon after the north bank was also abandoned, this time in favour of a rocky track that led up through a valley a mile north of the river.

After an hour's march steep hills began to take form, the hillsides closing steadily around them. Still the trail climbed. Soon it was clear that a passage to the north or to the east was all but impossible. If they were to reach this point called Hill 736, a new plan was required. Lieutenant Swan raised an arm, and within a minute or two the extended line of men shuffled to a halt. Edgily they glanced about. The night air had a welcome freshness to it. A stiff wind was blowing. But it was very dark amidst the looming hills, and eerily quiet; even the cicadas and the crickets were still. A whole foreign wilderness surrounded them in the gloom. While for most the back country was nothing new, the men were ill at ease.

Having had his share of night marches through the Sicilian hills of late, Archie was unimpressed. He turned to the man behind. 'I'll eat my boots if Jerry's here,' he began. 'Terrible spot to –'

'SHH!' hissed the man, and put a finger to his lips to underline it.

No one else spoke. Some drank silently from their water bottles, while the lieutenant a dozen heads further buried his head in a map. If the Germans were here they could be literally anywhere. But Archie was convinced they weren't. The Germans weren't stupid, and the absence of footpaths suggested even the Sicilians avoided the place. Unfortunately, the only foolproof method of finding the enemy was to have them find you first. So perhaps silence had something to recommend it.

The lieutenant thrust the map away and they turned south, back towards the river, following another dry stream bed. Periodically they would halt and listen. On each occasion they heard nothing except the wind, the rustle of the trees, the creaking gear and shuffling boots of some twerp at the rear who was slow to catch on that the file in front had stopped. Then they would move on.

They arrived back in the valley of the Salso, and followed it for a mile before turning north again, into the hills. Almost three miles and two hours later the lieutenant drew up. The ground at their feet was rising sharply. It had been a steady climb the past thirty minutes, and all the while the dark mass of the towering hill drew ever closer. Swan had been right; Hill 736 dwarfed every other rise they'd seen.

The lieutenant was busy consulting with the sergeant.

'I sure as hell hope the plan isn't to climb that,' Archie said to Roberts. 'Especially not in the dark. 736 metres the man said. From sea level I'm assuming, but still –'

'736 metres? That's half a mile high, for Pete's sake. Why the devil would we climb another hill?' asked Roberts. 'I've had more than my fill of climbing for one night.'

'To see if there's any enemy on it, of course. Why do you think we're here?'

'Oh. But there's another way to do that. It's a cinch, Archie.'

Before Archie could say a word, Roberts had taken the Bren in both hands and lifted the barrel so that it pointed at the summit.

'Don't' shrieked Archie, reaching for him.

But it was too late. Roberts had his finger on the trigger, and the surrounding hills seemed to echo with the deep rasping of the Bren gun. Then he fired a second burst.

A deep silence descended on Hill 736.

'What?' said Roberts, seeing the shocked expression on Archie's face. 'We wanted to know whether the Jerries are here or not, didn't we?' He chuckled. 'Guess they aren't. Those Panzer grenadiers won't have slept through that.' With a self-satisfied look he clicked out the Bren's magazine.

'No, but now every Jerry in a three-mile radius knows we're here,' muttered Archie. Even he had to admit that he sounded like an old sourpuss. And this was just Roberts being Roberts; he was a man for action above inaction. The only drawback was that in his desire to get something done, he seldom thought it through.

The sergeant, a fellow with the mildly suspect name of Hauptman, saw it in rather more stark terms: 'What the fuck do you think you're doing, you idiot?' he shouted, marching towards them. 'Did I tell you to fire? Did the Lieutenant?'

Even in the darkness Roberts had a pale look about him. 'Sorry, Sarge. I thought we were supposed to root out the Jerries,' he mumbled.

'Who told you that?'

'He did.' He twitched his head in Archie's direction.

The sergeant snapped a look at Archie that could have cut grass. His eyes were like coal, emotionless. How very different from a couple of days earlier when returning from the patrol into Agira he'd clapped Archie on the back. At the mixture of anger and disappointment on his face, disappointment especially, Archie dipped his head.

Sergeant Hauptman turned to Roberts: 'Just so as it's clear. From this point forth, I don't care if you have an itch in your ear, a sandfly up your nose, or a bloody great lizard nosing around your balls, you're to ask my permission before you do anything. Clear?'

Vigorously Roberts nodded his head.

The sun's glow was inching over the hills when they arrived back at the battalion. All things considered, barring the small misunderstanding with the Bren, the patrol had gone a good deal better than Archie expected. Roberts was likely of another mind.

He had a weary and dispirited look to him as he returned from his summons to see Lieutenants Wiles and Swan.

'You caught hell, I suppose?' Archie asked. 'I wouldn't worry about it too much. I try not to.'

'Ah, could've been worse. Lieutenant Swan was actually pretty gracious. Don't think he was any too keen on climbing that hill himself.' He yawned. 'I don't know about you, Archie, but I'm gonna bed down. I'm absolutely beat.'

Despite the light, sleep came quickly, and all too quickly so too did a disturbance.

'Rise and shine,' shouted a voice in a commanding tone.

Archie peeled open an eye. 'What d'ye want Ed?' He was too weary to even attempt a joke. Roberts, sensibly, was still waking the dead with his snoring.

'Get your clothes on, and bring your rifle and kit.'

'Don't tell me, peace has broken out. What time is it?'

Lachance looked at his wrist. 'Almost two o'clock. Come on you two bums. The Colonel's ordered the battalion to muster. And the Lieutenant's asking for you.'

Archie was awake. 'Asking for me?' he said warily.

'Count on it. And Roberts too. You and him were with Lieutenant Swan's patrol, weren't you?'

'Sure.'

'Well, now, the two of you are to help lead the Battalion to the hill. Seems we're to occupy it.'

'Oh,' said Archie. 'Is that all? The march is a bugger, but the rest shouldn't be too difficult. Maybe then we can rest.' He winked at Roberts, who had the dishevelled look of a man emerging from under a Panzer. An objective without Jerries ought to be easy enough. Then he remembered the endless steep slope of the hill, and sighed.

CHAPTER 28

1-2 August, 1943
Hill 736, northeast of Regalbuto, Sicily

CRUMP…

The shell fluted down behind them. For those who hadn't heard its approach, the concussion was all the more shocking. Smoke spiralled skywards a hundred yards shy of their position. Suddenly "A" and "B" companies were scrambling, men were on their feet, moving. It didn't so much matter where to, so long as they were far from the spot where the shell had fallen. A half minute passed in a heartbeat. A second shell came whistling in. Archie fell to the ground and buried his face in it, holding the rims of his helmet with both hands.

CRUMP…

The blast was loud and deep, and the ground shuddered. A hailstorm of rocks and shrapnel sliced through the air, until they too rained to earth, followed by a billowing storm of white dust. This one had been much closer than the last. A plume of smoke marked the point of impact. Archie looked up, searching for shelter. But where? The plateau they were on was virtually flat and, apart from some dry grass, a few withered shrubs and the occasional large stone, nearly empty.

CRUMP…

They'd set off promptly at 1445 in a scorching afternoon heat. Initially the going was easy, ambling down the metalled roadway of the no. 121, downhill. Sometime later the battalion assembled at the very spot, four miles down the road and a few hundred yards off it, where Lieutenant Swan had led the patrol into the river bed the evening before. Naturally this was not a coincidence; Archie had shared his recollections with Lieutenant Wiles.

There however the similarities with Swan's patrol ended. The business of packing an entire mule train was so onerous as to defeat the best efforts of the regimental support companies. The hours passed such that afternoon faded into evening, and evening darkened into night – and still no mules arrived. Before they knew it the day had passed altogether. At midnight, Lieutenant-Colonel Jefferson, his patience exhausted, announced that they would leave, mules or no mules. That this also meant no wireless sets, no 3-inch mortars, or even much in the way of food or water was regrettable. But the colonel had promises to keep.

Soon they heard aircraft buzzing overhead, and assumed that they were friendly. Only to reconsider when the first red candle flares were dropped. At intervals the men would hurriedly disperse behind rocks and trees, or lay still, as the droning enemy airplanes searched them out.

Following much the same treacherous trails as the night before, the marching line of men, with Able and Baker leading, eventually came upon high ground and a plateau. The map denoted it as square 5800. There they paused to reorganize ahead of the last stage. Easily visible to the northeast was the high, rounded cone of Hill 736.

It had been a long and exhausting night, but the arrival of dawn didn't help matters. As Archie now glumly noted, any Jerry on a nearby hilltop would need to be blind not to see them. Unfortunately, judging by the volume of the present shelling, the nearby hilltops were not only filled to the brim with Germans, not a one of them was blind.

CRUMP…

As the latest blast echoed away, the small stones came showering down again, clanking off his helmet. Over his shoulder a haze of dust was settling, the spiral of smoke from the impact a mere hundred feet away. While it was impossible to know exactly who had been hit, it was equally impossible to think no one had. Most of the platoon was behind him, and another platoon behind them. From the pattern of the shelling Archie was convinced that it was coming from the rear, somewhere to the south, so likely near Regalbuto which the Germans still held. Regardless, they couldn't continue lying here in the open. The next one would be on them. And if not that one, then the one after.

'They're firing from near the Salso!' yelled a voice that sounded like it knew what it was talking about. 'Move the men forward!'

'That's it,' murmured Archie, as he climbed to his knees, and up onto to his feet. Even in the few fleeting moments that he dared raise his head, it hadn't escaped his notice that this part of the ridgeline dropped sharply away on its northern flank. And seeing as the shelling was coming from the south… 'North!' he yelled. 'Go north!'

The others were also on their feet – all except one. A single man still lay in the grass and the dirt, his hands clamped fiercely over his ears. It was Lachance. Archie booted him hard in the thigh. 'Come on then,' he barked, and raised his head to face the others. 'Follow me!' He began to run.

At the sound of scuffling boots he glanced to one side, to see young Postlethwaite stumbling along at his side. 'What's north, Archie?' he panted.

'Reverse slope.' There was no time to explain, only to keep running, and to hope that the Germans were walking their rounds forward in their methodical Teutonic fashion. An overshot, or a straddle… a dozen men would be done for.

CRUMP…

With relief Archie heard the shell detonate behind. It was no louder than the last, and therefore no closer. They were now many strides underway, running for all they were worth, scabbards and water bottles flapping awkwardly, the strap of their rifles sawing at their shoulders. The northern extremity of the plateau was in sight, the ground already sloping down in anticipation. The slight incline became a steep incline, and then a rocky slope, and Archie bounded down it. A brown rabbit, startled, sprang from some rocks and went zig-zagging away at speed.

After a dozen awkward, sliding steps Archie reached an outcrop that jutted outwards from the slope like the bow of a ship. Promptly he dove underneath the overhanging rock. Postlethwaite and most of the section, plus a few others from the platoon, slid in beside him.

Postlethwaite looked at him. 'This is a reverse slope?'

Archie nodded. 'Their fire's coming from the south. So it's a piece of cake for them to hit the plateau. But on the far slope – this one – the only way Jerry's going to hit us is if he plunges it straight down on our heads. It's a question of ballistics. And that's a heck of shot, even for a Jerry. Of course it could happen, but it would be most unfortunate.' He grinned. 'Now, just don't ask me what it is that's firing at us.'

'Oh, but I know that already, Archie. It's a self-propelled gun. One of those Hummels I'd bet.'

'Oh?'

'Did you know that a Hummel is actually a variety of bumblebee in German?'

'No, that's interesting.' Archie's words were at odds with his tone, which suggested that the relation between German armaments and German insects interested him about as much as the colour of Lachance's underwear. But Postlethwaite was not to be waylaid.

'A big bumblebee, mind you. Of course, that fits with the gun they carry.' Now it was Postlethwaite's turn to smile. '150mm. That packs quite a sting, Archie. Lucky for us we have a *reverse slope*, eh.'

Archie sighed. He was only a kid, but occasionally a little too old for his own good, and altogether too smart.

As things settled down, Lieutenant Wiles spotted them a few minutes later. With head down he scuttled over. 'Swan reported there wasn't a Jerry to be found within miles,' he said accusingly. It may have been Swan's report, but Wiles's words were directed at Archie.

'He was right, sir. There wasn't a Jerry anywhere. We were all over this country. In fact, we stood at the bottom of that hill,' – Archie pointed for emphasis – 'and Roberts sprayed it with fire. Not a single bugger popped up his head.'

'Strange,' muttered Wiles. 'Very strange, suddenly turning up like this.' Shaking his head, the lieutenant lifted himself to his feet and moved off in search of the rest of his platoon.

Of course, it probably wasn't strange at all, thought Archie. He glanced over at Roberts who'd overheard the whole exchange, and now stared back, his face one of guilelessness. There may not have been *many* Germans within miles, but it only took a single one, and that one could scarcely not have heard a machine gun blasting off the better part of a mag in the middle of the night. Damn it. Now Jerry had the entire area under a flipping magnifying glass.

Only it was far worse than that. A machine gun on the heights to the north began to zip. The telltale whistle of mortar rounds overhead followed soon after. Then, to Archie's horror, a *Nebelwerfer* screeched. Six rockets went clawing their way through the air above their heads. At the sound, shivers ran through him. The self-propelled artillery piece, the Hummel, located somewhere south of the Salso, hadn't given up either. Clearly the Jerries had moved into the area of Hill 736 in number.

Archie wondered whether this was the moment to explain another invaluable military concept to Postlethwaite – that of the crossfire. Under the circumstances, he decided it was not. In addition to mortar rounds dropping every so often, the slope they were on was completely exposed to the hill opposite, and the gunners on it. Bullets were flying everywhere, digging little furrows in the hard ground, and glancing off rocks. There was a yelp as one of those flying pieces of shrapnel hit someone.

'On your feet,' yelled Lachance. He'd been observing the other sections and "B" Company. Suitably educated, he was bobbing about in an attempt to emulate their example. Which in this case was eminently sensible, even if his erect posture was not. Another MG started up. 'Follow the others!' he shouted.

Dispensing with any noticeable formation Archie and the section scrambled down the slope, running in the direction of the German machine guns and mortars that were tormenting them from the north. This was not the suicidal mission it at first appeared. They'd been taught to close with the enemy, so their reaction was very much an instinctual one. And if they were to have any hope of taking Hill 736, whose slopes could be seen rising a little ahead and less than a mile to the right of their current position, they would first need to deal with the northern ridge. From it, the German defenders completely dominated the approaches through the valley to the east.

What soon dawned upon Archie was that there might well be dead ground below, in the deep cleavage between the two hills. And if that were true, they would be out of sight of the cursed MGs and mortar observers.

This proved to be the case. They came to a breathless halt in the low ground, sheltering behind a rock face. However, the respite from the German fire was fleeting. The company OCs had their orders, the platoon commanders were apprised of them, and the section commanders heard theirs forthwith.

'The attack's on,' announced Lachance. Archie had seen him sharing a few words with the lieutenant.

'What do you mean the attack's on?' demanded Dinesen, indignantly. 'We were running like a flock of headless chickens two minutes ago?'

'Orders,' said Lachance. 'We're to follow 7 Platoon and "B" Company in.'

'We hardly need them to show us the way,' said Archie, 'the bloody ridge is straight ahead.'

'Could you for once just do what you're asked?' pleaded Lachance. The strain of high command was clearly taking its toll on him. Rivulets of sweat trickled down his face, his helmet was tilted at an unsoldierly angle to one side, and his eyes exhibited an almost rabid quality. Perhaps it *was* a matter of cowardice, thought Archie. No, cowardice was letting it show. And whatever he might be feeling he at least was trying not to let it show. That deserved a little respect… possibly… maybe…

Archie dipped his head in reluctant agreement and made a show of throwing the bolt of his rifle back and forth to chamber a round. 'Ready,' he growled, as he locked it down.

Able and Baker began climbing the incline towards the top of the ridge. Lieutenant-Colonel Jefferson, from a vantage point five hundred yards to the rear, could have been forgiven for thinking he was sending the Edmonton Regiment to its doom. For while the artillery fire from the south had all but disappeared, the sight of his soldiers climbing the barren slope towards them, elicited a fresh fury of German MG and rifle fire.

'Jesus,' murmured Roberts. An officer a hundred yards further up the slope was striding energetically forward when suddenly he stopped; as if hit by a hammer, he crumpled to the ground.

'Sniper. Got to be,' said Archie. He crouched over even further.

Having seen this land only by night, what surprised him most was how bare the hills were. In fact, apart from the dry grass that grew everywhere, there was scarcely a tree or any other vegetation. Only boulders, and the occasional steep rock face or overhang provided a modicum of cover from the withering machine gun fire pouring down from on high. Undaunted, they set about climbing further.

Initially some halting progress was made until the hill's slopes steepened. Every step became a trial in itself, while the machine guns positioned near the crest traced trails of dust in the ground whenever they dared move. "B" Company, which was leading, had ground to a standstill. They heard shouting.

'Hold up,' shouted Lieutenant Wiles. 'Hold up,' shouted Lachance. The entire platoon dropped to the ground. At that moment a stray bullet whizzed by Archie's upturned head and he planted his face in the dirt. "B" Company and the other two sections further up the hill were getting the worst of the fire, but that one had been awfully close.

By now the hillside was covered with men lying prone making it difficult to tell who was alive or not. That there were many wounded was obvious; every minute or two another cry for stretcher bearers came.

'It's sheer bloody suicide,' called out Doug Borden. He and his Bren gun were prone like the rest of them, in his case squeezed behind a small rock.

'You could fire that thing you're lugging,' Archie shouted back.

'At what?' As Archie scanned the heights, the futility of their efforts became starkly evident. Not only could they not advance, they weren't even able to return fire for want of targets. The Germans could see them, but not vice-versa. The only thing they could do was keep low, and hope the enemy would then be as blind as they were.

'Dig in,' shouted Lachance.

A few around Archie made valiant attempts to follow his instructions. They clawed fiercely at the ground in an attempt to dig slit trenches. While slit trenches were the saviour of all infantrymen, Archie didn't bother making the effort; he'd already concluded that the dry earth was baked into a form of concrete that was simply too hard and too stony to penetrate. The consequence of this was that every boulder of any significance, or sheer rock face, soon found one or more men crouched behind it, grim looks etched on their faces, rifles and machine guns held in sweaty palms. The attack had turned into a stalemate. It was a poor man's stalemate, however, for the Germans were the ones who held the high ground.

As the sun rose so too did the temperatures. By late morning the rocks of the slope were warming to the touch, and would soon be hot plates. The sun beat down with ferocious intensity. Meanwhile the state of Archie's water bottle, and his morale, were approaching the level of the Salso. Were events to continue as they had, both would be gone by nightfall.

'Hey, Ben, you got any water?'

Robert shook his head. The others nearby looked away. There was no water and no interest in conversation. Each was bracing himself for the long hours ahead.

The only thing Archie carried in substantial quantities were weapons and ammunition, neither of which were any damn good with his chin rubbing in the dirt. Like the others, he was squeezed in behind a rock far too modest for his build, and slowly baking to death.

So much for the bold plan of cutting cross country and sealing the Germans off, he thought. There was nothing particularly wrong with the plan, only the enemy willingness to cooperate. And yet again he reproached himself for not having stepped in earlier with Roberts the night before. If he had, just maybe the Jerries wouldn't have prepared quite so thoroughly.

He hoped someone would soon come up with a new plan. If they left it too long, there wouldn't be anything left of Colonel Jefferson's two companies.

Troina, Sicily

Seven miles to the northwest the 2nd Battalion of the 104th Panzer Grenadier Regiment was all but finished digging in on a ridgeline of its own.

Weyers was thinking of the battle being fought near Regalbuto. The enemy was pouring through the hills, precisely as the Canadian sergeant had said they would. A little flattery, a few flowery words accompanied by vague promises, stern glances at critical moments – the man quickly spilled what he knew. Before they had spirited the sergeant away, ignoring his words of protest, Weyers told all to the officer of the field police. Measures were taken, most unusually the Luftwaffe had even ventured out. Sadly, the information seemed a question of too little, too late. While perhaps there was nothing further to be gotten out of the prisoner, he would have liked to have determined that for himself. But it was not to be. The Canadians were now pushing across the hard mountain country in the direction of the volcano. It would be a close-run thing, he decided.

'How goes it, Weyers?' enquired Lieutenant-Colonel Ens, coming to his side. The question was asked with a startling informality. As it was, it was highly unusual for a regimental commander to appear thus, completely unannounced. When he first spotted the colonel in their midst Weyers had rubbed his eyes in disbelief. But these were unusual times, and there was no mistaking who it was. The colonel looked very tired. They were all tired.

'Fine, sir. We haven't seen much of the Americans today, apart from their aircraft.'

The colonel nodded. 'No, I hoped as much, but they will try again. They will most definitely try again. And I don't have to tell you what happens if they capture this ridge.' At this both men turned and looked east, across the narrow valley, towards the grey sprawl of the village of Troina sitting imperiously on its hilltop perch. A road from the west snaked up the hill towards it.

'What do you reckon? It must be two kilometres?' asked the colonel.

'If that, Colonel.'

'Yes, you're right – less. But if they take Troina…' Clearly this was the concern foremost in the colonel's mind. 'You know what that means, Weyers.' Resolutely he shook his head.

A small number of highways had become the German life blood: the two coast roads that came together like a funnel at Messina in the northeast corner of the island; the no. 121 that cut from west to east through the interior, and which they had fought along for nearly two weeks; and this parallel road a dozen kilometres north, linked to the former by a couple of small secondary tracks. Highway no. 120 was to be the main conduit for their withdrawal. Without it all their forces to the south, not to mention those at Troina itself would be trapped, the passageway to Messina closed. Then they would be stuck. It was no wonder that the Panzer Corps commander General Hube had decided to plant an iron stake in the ground here, and he had chosen the 15th Panzer Grenadier Division to do it. After this battle, mused Weyers, there would be little enough stake left to plant again.

'We've dug in as best we could, Colonel. They won't pass easily.'

Lieutenant-Colonel Ens raised his head and focussed two bloodshot eyes on him. 'You and the others did well last night pushing them off the hill. Of course, we should never have let them capture it to begin with. Two weeks ago we wouldn't have.'

Weyers grimaced. 'Two weeks ago we weren't fighting with remnants, sir.' It was a daringly candid reply, he realized. There were those in the Reich who would have pilloried him for such language, or worse, called him defeatist. But those who would do so were thankfully not in Sicily. In Berlin, in complete safety apart from the occasional RAF raid, one could concern oneself with such wordplay. He was confident Colonel Ens would understand.

'How many do you still have?'

'In my company? Pfff…' Weyers paused to consider, although he knew the numbers precisely. He'd walked along the survivors of last's night counterattack only this morning. It seemed every time he summoned the energy to count their numbers, they were less. 'Thirty men, give or take – those who are fit for fighting. Most have their scratches, naturally. With the extra men you assigned, the battalion has less than two hundred.'

The colonel nodded. Both men were aware that a normal complement was closer to seven hundred. 'And your own injury? How is that?' He nodded in the direction of Weyers's arm. 'You haven't been giving it much rest, Captain.'

'Better, sir. Thank you for asking.' There was no need to elaborate. If anyone knew why he'd had so little rest, it was the colonel.

Then, as they stood there, a voice shouted in alarm. Soon others took up the call with increasing urgency.

Weyers and the colonel whipped their heads round to face west, where the 16th American Infantry Regiment was licking its wounds on a low ridge a kilometre and a half away, and no doubt plotting revenge. However, it was not the 16th Regiment that was now on the move.

Low to the horizon a new threat was bearing down upon them very fast. A glance was enough to see that they were American fighter planes. Flashes rippled on their wings. Then, after a moment, they heard the stutter of the machine guns.

'Sir!' Weyers seized the colonel by his arm, and roughly pushed him into a nearby trench. It was all he could do not to land upon him as he hurriedly followed. The trench was one they'd dug only that morning.

The racket grew louder and louder, and Weyers ducked as the bullets tore at the ground nearby. Then with a *whoosh* and a roar of their engines the planes, flying very low, thundered past. As silence returned he pulled himself to his feet. He was in time to see the planes bank slightly, then pass gracefully off to the right of Troina, heading for hunting grounds to the south. He grunted when he saw their path. Colonel Fullriede's *Kampfgruppe* was in possession of a handful of Flak batteries on the hills north of Troina. Since their first mutual acquaintance, the Americans had become rather more cautious about the northerly approaches.

Lieutenant-Colonel Ens sighed and brushed himself off as he came to stand beside Weyers. Then he smiled. '*Danke*. It pays to be alert,' he said. 'They fly very fast.'

Sergeant von Steinen approached. His arm was bandaged.

'And?' asked Weyers.

'Only one,' replied the sergeant.

Another man down was no reason for celebration, but von Steinen clearly felt they'd gotten off easy. Which they probably had. Weyers knew that tonight or tomorrow might well be different.

CHAPTER 29

3-4 August, 1943
Along the River Salso, north of Regalbuto, Sicily

Perhaps his luck *was* changing.

He was certainly lucky to be here, and doubly lucky not to have so much as a scratch. Yesterday afternoon, near Hill 736, there'd been anxious moments as the bullets whizzed past. Listening to the heart-rending screams of a man overcome by pain further up the slope, he'd wondered if any of them would make it out. But right when he and the rest of the platoon had resigned themselves to a long and dangerous night with no food and little water, and the promise of a sniper's round or a machine gun burst to punish a moment's inattentiveness, they were ordered to pull back, to withdraw to the flats near the Salso. Even the more optimistically inclined of the battalion's officers must have concluded that to continue was a fool's errand. The really lucky part was that it didn't go ahead anyhow.

Over the backs of a half dozen mules Archie glimpsed the familiar features of Lieutenant Wiles in conversation with Lieutenant Swan.

'Your missing man, Sergeant Battersby, is missing no longer. The Jerries have him,' he heard.

Whoa! What was this? Quickly he sidled up to a chocolate brown mule with pointy ears. On the other side of it the two young officers stood exchanging their gossip. Now, if only the blasted creature didn't take a sudden dislike to him. 'Steady, old girl,' he whispered, a gentle hand extended to her neck. She looked as tired and dispirited as the rest of them. The mule train had only now caught up with the regiment, having had its own painful encounter with the German mortars.

'Yes, I knew you'd want to know everything. I spoke with a Brigade intelligence officer about it,' Lieutenant Swan was saying. 'The Yanks recently captured a German staff sergeant from the 104th Panzer Grenadiers up near Troina. During questioning it turned out that his bunch ran up against ours several times, including once on the Nicosia road not long ago. Which is why we got the report. But the important news is that it's virtually certain the Jerries have Battersby. This von Steinen seemed to know a lot about him.'

'I suppose there's some consolation in knowing what happened,' mused Lieutenant Wiles.

'Look at the bright side, at least he's alive.'

Archie failed to see the connection; Lieutenant Swan had evidently never spent much time with Battersby. But this was a shocker. He'd been utterly convinced the bastard was dead. Still, if the Jerries did have him in their clutches, he was out of everyone's hair for the duration of the war. So for all practical purposes he was as good as dead. And Miles Battersby deserved nothing less. A bitter smile came to his face.

'What else did you hear on your visit to the Brigadier?' Lieutenant Wiles was asking.

'Regalbuto has fallen.'

'Regalbuto, fallen – has it really? That's some good news at least,' sighed Wiles. 'But it's an awful shame about poor, old Bob Kellaway. He bought it in that action yesterday. Sniper got him. I saw it happen. One moment he was charging up the hill, the next he was down. You must have heard?'

'Yeah, I heard. A damned shame all right. Bob was a real white man if ever I knew one.'

There was a short break in the conversation. Archie guessed both men were shaking their heads in commiseration. After Captain Tighe, the three platoon lieutenants constituted the bulk of the senior ranks of "A" Company, and now they were two. Archie couldn't help thinking the shock would have been greater still had it come a month earlier when not a man amongst them, including the officers, had any experience with the harsh realities of war. It was astonishing how a couple of weeks changed a man.

'After yesterday I suppose the Colonel intends to send in the whole darned battalion?'

'No, actually not. But that's what I figured too. Apparently Jefferson believes "C" Company can clean up Hill 736 on their own, with "D" in support. Only they're going to attempt it from the south this time round. There's a whole three-step plan they've come up with, beginning tonight. So that leaves Able and Baker with time on their hands for something bigger and better.'

Archie heard Wiles groan loudly. 'Bigger and better? I hope you're joking, Charlie. You missed all the action. But the rest of us were up to our ears in it at Hill 736. That was plenty difficult enough, thank you very much. But don't keep me in suspense. What does bigger and better mean?'

'Here, look at the map, Andy.' Archie heard the rustle as Swan unfolded it. 'Hill 736 is not the only big hill in this country. There's a couple more before we reach Mount Etna. Mount Revisotto to start with; you can see it there on the right bank of the Troina, not far from the road, a mile or two north. Then there's Mount Seggio – that's the one a few miles further east. If we're going to cut off the Jerries like Monty wants us to, we'll have to take all three. Brigadier Vokes, in all his wisdom, has picked the Eddies to capture both Revisotto *and* Hill 736. The Seaforths get Seggio.'

Wiles whistled. 'Two hills!? You fellows may not have seen a Jerry when you visited Hill 736, but they've got the place topped in the meantime. I'll bet this Mount Revisotto is exactly the same story. Seems a mighty tall order to me.'

'Look, that's all I know, Andy. Maybe someone is pulling my leg, but that's what I hear.'

'Hmm,' muttered Wiles. From his tone he didn't sound altogether convinced of the brigadier's wisdom. Having seen what the Germans did to fortify Hill 736, Archie was equally unconvinced.

Suddenly, someone nudged him roughly. He felt a tugging at his breast pocket. In alarm he jolted a step backwards. A large, brown snout in dire need of his half bar of chocolate appeared in view. Initially he was too surprised to do anything but stare. With doleful eyes the mule stared back. 'Hey, stop that now, you,' he said sternly, momentarily forgetting himself. Which naturally the two keen-eared lieutenants heard, and promptly investigated. Awkward frowns followed. Fortunately, the two young gentlemen chose dignified flight over confrontation – a course of action that came as a relief to Archie.

Soon after, having taking his leave of the mule and the remains of a bar of molten chocolate, there was a commotion. A file of men and mules could be seen snaking along the river bed. 'Reinforcements,' proclaimed Lachance, with a confident air.

Archie stared at him. Normally Lachance could barely spell his name.

'How do you know they're reinforcements?' piped up McDonald.

Before Lachance could reply, Dinesen jumped into the fray. 'Can't you see, Aubrey? It's obvious from the look of them. They're planning on swapping you out for a mule.' It was a better excuse to laugh than any other they'd had of late.

Yesterday had been a new deep point. Not only was there little progress at the hill, the ranks of the two companies involved had taken a beating. After three weeks of continuous fighting the casualties in the regiment were mounting at an alarming rate. As such reinforcements were no laughing matter, not least because they were a reminder of those they were replacing. When it came to the new platoon sergeant, however, Archie had no such maudlin thoughts. New could only mean better.

'Haver,' the man growled, wiping at the sweat on his brow. He was in his early thirties, of stocky build with short dark hair. He wore the signature moustache that was as much a sign of his rank as the chevrons on his sleeves. Damn, thought Archie. Why hadn't he thought of that before? The mystery of Battersby growing hair on his lip last spring was hereby solved. Come to think of it, it pretty much coincided with the very day Battersby was made corporal. He'd been planning ahead.

'I'm Sergeant Haver,' continued Sergeant Haver. 'I'm sure we'll get to know each other better in the days ahead.' As introductions go it was short and sweet. Haver had sensed the mood; "A" Company was still licking its wounds.

As if to underscore the thought, a long file of walking wounded shuffled in. Sergeant Clarke was leading. A few had arms in slings, half were missing helmets and other kit, some clutching primitive walking sticks. All looked on death's doorstep.

'Do you suppose they were all hit, Archie?' asked Postlethwaite. 'So many!'

'That would be my guess, yes.'

'It took them all night to get here?'

'First someone bandaged them up. Then they had to assemble and wait for the others to join them. They probably didn't move any faster than a mile an hour – the fastest pace of the slowest guy. Work it out. You're a math whizz.'

'Jeez.' Postlethwaite was shaking his head, looking sombre. Until now he hadn't realized how bad it had been.

It wasn't only the rifle platoons that had taken it on the nose. The support companies and the mule trains were also hard hit. Harry Bannon, the amiable Company Quarter Master Sergeant, was killed. For some reason these thoughts made Archie think of the little brown mule, and he smiled. He was happy he'd treated her well.

Thankfully, Matt Evers of hard-hit "B" Company also survived. His verdict about the whole Battersby affair was considerably shorter than the American intelligence report. 'Poor bugger,' he said when Archie told him. 'Never much liked him, but still he was one of us.'

Archie groaned loudly. 'In theory, I suppose.'

'Come on, Archie, you can afford to be a mite generous. Especially seeing as you owe him one.'

'Owe him one! How on earth do you figure that, Sarge?' he sputtered.

'Simple. If you hadn't been so hell bent on proving you were better than Battersby, you'd be the same old deadbeat you were when we first arrived.'

It was a perspective Archie grudgingly had to admit had some truth to it. But that still didn't detract from the fact that the Jerries snapping up Battersby was the best piece of news he'd heard since coming to Sicily. His luck really was changing.

That night they slept in an orchard. Tomorrow, they were told, their marching orders would come. Tomorrow would take care of tomorrow, reasoned Archie, and with his head on his small pack, bedded down under a tree where he promptly fell into a deep slumber.

'Look!' came a shout early the next morning. Archie was already on his feet drinking some tea.

Brushing over the hills to the north a flight of three single-engine planes came sweeping towards them, heading south.

'They're ours!'

It was a fair guess they wouldn't be German. Barring a few nightly excursions, the enemy had long since given up flying over the island.

They watched from the shelter of the trees as the planes roared low overhead, large, cylindrical bombs hanging under their fuselages. Then, after they had all but disappeared, they saw the specks climbing sharply in anticipation of dropping their loads.

'Apaches. A-36s,' said Postlethwaite dryly.

'British?' asked McDonald.

At this witlessness Postlethwaite rolled his eyes. Aubrey McDonald may not have been top of his class, but even if one knew nothing of airplanes, surely Aubrey had noticed their roundels? 'No, they're American,' Postlethwaite replied. He turned to Archie. 'Where do you suppose they're heading?'

'Judging from their direction, somewhere they're not supposed to be.'

They had little time to ponder the possibilities as Sergeant Haver appeared in their midst and motioned for them to circle round. "C" Company's first attack towards Hill 736 was a success, he told them. And now it was their turn. The lieutenant had ordered the platoon to form up. The company was moving out.

They found themselves walking through a rolling countryside, and into an ever widening valley, filled with groves of orange and almond trees. Sampling the wares, as thirsty soldiers are wont to do, the oranges were pronounced to be too green to be edible. As a consolation prize Archie took a sip from his water bottle. He was conscious he should carefully husband what remained. He didn't recognize the irrigation ditches for what they were, until Roberts explained.

Coming to one such ditch, and seeing a water pipe beyond, Captain Tighe called a halt. Through some miracle the pipe actually contained water and so "A" Company set out about refilling its water bottles.

'What the devil are you doing, Atwell?'

Archie looked up. He'd finished retrieving his fingers from the mouth of the bottle and was now shaking it vigorously back and forth. 'Chlorine tablet, sir.'

Lieutenant Wiles screwed up his brow.

'You've never had Gyppy gut, sir, or you'd understand.'

'But it's from a water pipe.'

'And how long has the water been sitting in that pipe, sir?'

'Hmm. Put like that, I see your point. Not a bad idea, actually.' Wiles went fishing around in his pockets and pouches. It took a considerable while. He frowned.

'Here, sir, take one of mine.' Archie dropped it down the neck of the bottle for him. 'Quick swish, sir, and you're done. Tastes like crap, but your crap will thank you for it.'

'Yes, well, thanks Atwell.'

Archie pointed at the pair of binoculars which were hanging around his neck. 'Your glasses, sir… ?'

The lieutenant gave a half smile, and taking the cord from around his neck he handed them over. 'You're absolutely right, that's the famous Aderno there in the distance.'

Clinging to the lower slopes of the great Etna were the weather-beaten clay roofs of the town, bright in the glare of the sun. Aderno. They'd heard about it almost since they began this long slog through the hills of the interior. It was the end of the road, both literally and figuratively. The last village before Etna, and the final piece of the puzzle that was General Montgomery's strategy. Mussolini had renamed the place Adrano. Out of spite the army stuck resolutely with the old name. Although it may also have had something to do with every map labelling it thus.

'What's it all about, sir,' one of the men asked Lieutenant Wiles, as the rest of the platoon gathered round.

'Mount Revisotto,' he replied. 'On the far side of the River Troina. The Colonel has asked us to take it.'

Archie could see the faces, hot, sweaty, all of them grimy, all staring at the lieutenant. After Hill 736 their self-confidence was dented. Doubts had arisen. There were questions with no easy answers.

Lieutenant Wile's face turned grimly serious. He must have realized that above all what they wanted to hear was an assurance from their commanders that it would work out. A confirmation that *they* could do it. 'The Captain told him we could,' said Wiles. 'So I figure that's precisely what we're going to do.' Then the lieutenant grinned, a broad, teeth-baring, full-fledged grin. The grin was what did it – it spread like a contagion.

For all his pleasant manner, organization and undoubted intelligence, Archie had never thought much of Wiles as a leader of men. But on this occasion the lieutenant hit the nail on the head. Whatever happened at Mount Revisotto, the men would be ready.

CHAPTER 30

5 August, 1943
Near Mount Revisotto, Sicily

The sky was a brilliant blue. There were groves of fruit trees to enliven the countryside. Even the grasslands with their patches of corn had a colour and a life to them that was unusual by Sicilian standards. On the northern horizon the belt of hills, if not quite the soaring snow-capped mountains of home, had nevertheless a certain majestic quality. The faintest whisper of a breeze blew. Far overhead a crisp, perfectly white puff of cloud sailed past at its leisure, like a sailboat floating on the glassy-mirror of a lake. Archie looked up, and stared at it for the longest while. He wondered if ever in all his days he would see such a perfect cloud again.

Of course, that rather depended on how many days he still had, he thought. It was not that he feared dying; he'd seen enough friends and comrades cut down by a sudden burst of shrapnel or a bullet. Enemies, too, for that matter, several at his own hands. He was all too aware what that distant crack of a rifle, whistle of a shell, or screech of a mortar might signal. But that was the life of a soldier, the life he'd signed up for, and it was a life that strangely seemed to suit him. No, this peculiar soul-searching of his was more than that, he decided. Someone had once asked him – it may even have been Captain Tighe – if he found war all a game. Gamely, and with a brazen dishonesty, he had replied in the negative. He knew better now. And he was damned if he was going to go his grave as a private, meriting nothing more than a disinterested shrug from the captain or Lieutenant Wiles on hearing the news, before each turned again to his papers. Afterwards the boys might hoist a well-meaning toast to him. But better to let them see what he was worth when he was still around. Because if he wasn't around, it sure as heck wouldn't matter anyhow.

Captain Tighe was leading.

'Fall in,' commanded Lieutenant Wiles. Sergeant Haver repeated the order, the platoon dutifully obeyed, and lined up behind the captain. Soon they were marching.

The company was strung out in a long, extended line, snaking along for what must have been half a mile or more, with "B" Company following "A". For all concerned it was a formation they were well accustomed to; Sicilian paths uniformly calibrated to the width of a single goat.

They marched east along the north bank of the Salso, traversing the little orchards and the gravelly wheat fields of the valley. Tiny stone huts were scattered about, and about them were friendly, waving peasants and a host of barking dogs.

'Look!' someone cried, an officer. It was maybe even Lieutenant Wiles.

'By God, you're right. They *are* tanks,' said another officer. The man had binoculars to his eyes. Upon closer inspection it proved to be Lieutenant Swan. 'They're across the river! And moving uphill.'

Without binoculars the tanks were a little hard to distinguish at a distance of three miles, though the hill he was referring to was clear enough. Archie knew it must be Mount Seggio. The Seaforths had cleared the approaches yesterday, and today the PPCLI were to clear the hill itself. The reference to the tanks was equally clear. A day before there was no bridge to cross the Salso; the rickety old rail bridge with its steep approaches that they'd seen on patrol was utterly insufficient. But today, apparently, it had sufficed. Which meant that the sappers were busy indeed. If all went well the brigadier would have his way by day's end, and Vokes could lay down claim to the trio of Mount Seggio, Hill 736, and Mount Revisotto. It would make for a suitably impressive report to General Simonds. Although, on reflection, assuming all went well was rather a big leap.

Even more interesting than Mount Seggio was what lay to the east of it seven or eight miles distant, and startlingly clear: the massive dome of the volcano Etna. With the exception of the coast road on the far side of Etna, that gap of seven or eight miles that he was staring across was the only avenue of escape left to the Germans. For those on the plains near Catania time was ticking.

What had Wiles told them only yesterday? 'The noose is tightening on the Jerries, boys. "C" Company is moving on Hill 736, and Centuripe fell yesterday. But it's up to us to close it completely.' Archie had the impression this little talk was intended to be inspirational. What Wiles hadn't said, but was equally true, was that the Germans would fight tooth and nail as a result.

Closer to hand, in a northerly direction, was a peak of far more immediate relevance to the Eddies than either Mount Seggio, Mount Etna, or the heights of Centuripe with its medieval village. Archie could see the cragged, brown crenellations of Mount Revisotto jutting arrogantly above the rolling hills, high mountains beyond. The occupier of Revisotto dominated not just the Troina, but the road along the river, and a swath of ground that extended for miles – including the valley they'd just left.

'Is that it?' A nervous looking Lance-Corporal Lachance was at his side.

Archie nodded. 'Yep.'

'Perhaps the Jerries will have pulled out.'

'Don't count on it,' replied Archie. 'Would you, if you were in their boots?'

Lachance pursed his lips but didn't immediately reply. Then: 'Do you suppose we'll be able to… Take it I mean?'

Archie turned to look at him. 'Sure,' he replied. 'I don't see why not. If everyone does their bit –' He let the words hang.

Lachance looked away.

'Look at it this way, Ed. This is your big chance to be a hero. Are you up to it?'

Saunders turned and grinned at them over his shoulder. Archie could see from Lachance's drawn face that his words had hit the mark.

'Sure, Archie, sure,' relied Lachance, and fell out of step, dropping back to join the more congenial members of the section.

After another mile the deep ravine of the River Troina could be seen crossing their path. Fortunately a railway bridge appeared, which solved what otherwise would have been a nasty problem. As they stepped cautiously from tie to tie, Archie glanced down at the dry, boulder strewn course of the river forty feet below. The tanks they'd seen must have used the bridge as well, for a crossing was quite impossible otherwise.

Once on the right bank a rolling countryside, spotted with copses of trees and more orchards, opened up before them. In the midst of one such orchard they sank to the ground for a brief rest, and a dinner of tinned bully, hardtack and other delicacies plucked from the compo rations.

Then, on their feet again, Captain Tighe turned left and led the company north.

It was starting to grow dark by this time as they edged along the bank of the river. The embankment down to the river bed grew ever steeper as the ground steadily rose.

Ahead, a ridgeline loomed across their path. Seeing no way around they began to climb the slope.

'Spread out,' shouted Captain Tighe. There was no need to say more and they split into skirmish lines by section, one abreast of the other, followed at a respectable distance by the other two. Tighe was leading them towards the crest of the feature. Revisotto couldn't be far.

As they reached the top, which was barren save for a few stunted shrubs and gangly trees, Archie gulped as he spotted their objective across the small valley. The final rays of the sun were marking out the peak of Mount Revisotto in spectacular fashion, the blue-grey mountains of the interior behind it filling the horizon. Seeing the captain and the lieutenant pause, Lachance motioned that the section should draw up.

'Won't be long now,' said Lachance, staring across at Revisotto.

At this Archie was tempted to snipe, but he bit his tongue. He'd said enough already. Lachance was vain, dumb and cowardly, but he was no Battersby. And regardless of what Archie thought of him it was through no fault of his that he had the timing so absurdly wrong.

Barely were the words out of Lachance's mouth when the *tchick-tchick-tchick* of a machine gun erupted.

Bullets hissed around them.

At the first sound Archie instinctively fell prone. Someone else was not so quick, or perhaps not so lucky. He heard a cry and a thud. Damnit, he thought, an MG-42. Every machine gun was to be feared, but the muzzle velocity of an MG-42 meant that it was capable of shredding a man before he even heard the sound.

There were shouts. Confusion reigned. 'Where are they!?'

Archie thought he recognized Lachance's voice in the query, before more machine gun fire burst well off their right flank. It was from a second position, quite possibly from the slopes of Revisotto itself.

Archie lifted his head slightly. By now his rifle was unslung, and resting beside him. His eyes darted left, then right. Back and forth they went, every sinew in him concentrated, waiting for the instant that the enemy would again reveal themselves.

The MG in front began to zip. A man cursed. Someone else fired, though at what was unclear.

There! He saw it. The spark of a flash. At the second burst he was certain.

'Eleven o'clock,' he shouted. 'Three hundred yards out. They're on the knoll.'

Off his left he could see others looking. There were nods. A few fingers pointed it out to comrades.

Archie shot a glance to his right. Men were lying on the ground where they had dived. One or two had found a shrub or a rock or a bump in the ground that might somehow shelter them. They were all woefully exposed. He caught a glimpse of Lieutenant Wiles and Captain Tighe further off, crouching brotherly behind a lone boulder.

Once again the Germans had chosen well. The ground here fell away in front until a touch to their right, and a half mile away, it began to rise once more: the first gentle slope leading up to Revisotto. Looking a little left the ridgeline they were on curved away in the form of a sickle to the west, only to sweep back towards them a few hundred yards distant. The ridge wasn't as high at that point, but the rocky outcrop where he'd spotted the MG stuck out like a protruding knuckle, an effect accentuated by the stone ruins of something built on top. From there the Germans had a perfect view of the hilltop the company occupied, and the bowl in the ground that separated them. It was a clever man's version of a reverse slope.

Lieutenant Wiles was now looking their way, furiously jabbing his finger at the German position. 'Try to work around it,' he shouted.

Lachance waved an arm in acknowledgement.

'After me, boys,' he shouted. In no time he was on his feet and rushing forward in a straight line towards the knoll opposite. One arm was waving madly in the air. The other gripped the section's sole Tommy gun. It was sheer bloody suicide.

'No, you fool!' Archie roared. 'You'll get yourself killed. Wait!' But even as he said it, his voice dropped away. Lachance was already ten feet ahead, and of a mind that was pre-decided; blinkered visions of glory had moved in and settled down.

'Stupid, bloody bugger,' Archie muttered, his voice laced with a certain venom. He had no respect for a man who was supposed to know better, but then promptly led them over a cliff. He hesitated, knowing he ought to do something. But what? Perhaps it was simply meant to be. He and Lachance had nothing in common – well, almost nothing, apart from the regiment. Besides, Lachance had pretty much sat out every other battle they'd been involved in. No, he figured, if he wanted to take his chances running in the open towards a squad of Panzer grenadiers with a sited MG-42, then best of luck to him. And good riddance.

However, his stomach turned and so did his thoughts when he saw Steven Postlethwaite and Aubrey McDonald springing to their feet.

'Hang on,' he cried. Of course it was useless. The two youngsters of the section went surging after the corporal, fired up by his words, and with visions perhaps not of glory, but almost certainly of duty. They were too young to think of the folly involved. 'Oh, damn it to hell,' he cursed.

The German machine gun began to rip.

A hundred yards downslope in the direction of the knoll, Lachance collapsed to the ground near some trees. It was hard to tell if he'd been hit, or was simply taking cover. Either way, it was impossible for him to move.

Postlethwaite and McDonald had sensibly also gone to ground at the sound of the MG. As it abated they got to their feet and started to hasten forward again, heading towards Lachance. Here on the crest the light was good, but as they moved forward down the embankment it grew gloomier. And fortunately there were a few trees. But that was of little comfort; the Germans had the slope dead in their sights. There was another burst of fire.

The two soldiers reared up like stallions encountering not a gate but a brick wall. They dropped to their knees, and scrambled towards the safety of a tree, pinned down. The dry earth around danced with bullets. They were trapped. There was no way forward, and there was no way back. It was only a matter of time before the MG found them, or crossfire from the direction of Revisotto did. And heaven forbid if the Germans had a mortar.

Fire and movement. Fire and movement. They'd had it drummed it into them during what seemed like an entire winter, spring and summer in England. In fact there was a time when drifting off to sleep in a draughty hut Archie could think of nothing else. Now, instinctively, those were the thoughts that filled his mind.

'Roberts, Borden,' he shouted. 'Spread out and get those Brens going. Keep them busy. Saunders? Help them.' Which left only a single man to help him: Dinesen. The section was not what it had been. Dinesen stared at him.

While Archie had no position, and definitely no authority to be giving orders, he didn't think twice. He was simply doing what needed to be done. And the others seemingly recognized this, for they did as he instructed.

One of the Bren guns fired. A short burst. Good boys, he thought, that should distract them. He hoped that they'd be sparing in their fire, however. Between Borden, Roberts and Saunders they would be lucky if they had ten magazines between them. Which sounded like a lot until one considered that a single magazine held only 30 rounds, and a determined gunner could shoot off that many in four seconds.

'We'll pull back a little, then head west,' he said to Dinesen. 'Try to catch them on their flank. We'd better hurry.'

'After you,' replied Dinesen, with a grin. It was just like Dinesen to see humour where there was none. But then humour was seldom humorous without a little spice thrown in.

They got to their feet and made a stumbling dash to a cactus plant fifty feet behind. They could see the other two sections spread out in the grass. 'MG post,' Archie yelled at a couple of men nearby, and motioned with his arm to indicate the direction. 'We're going after them. We need some cover though. And ammo for the Brens.'

A reassuring wave.

'Let's go,' said Archie.

The terrain was almost exactly as he had hoped. Once off the high ground they were soon out of sight of the Germans on the knoll and Mount Revisotto, and free to work their way west and north around the crescent of the ridgeline until, eventually, they'd reach the MG post. They took off, half running, half walking.

The ground was dry and firm under their feet, the going even. Apart from trees every twenty feet or so, there were few obstructions. As they moved they kept a wary eye over their right shoulders from where the Germans might spot them.

'Hold up,' said Archie, after a minute or two.

Dinesen had already stopped. He'd seen it too. They were emerging from the rounding of a hillock. The craggy outcrop was a little right of centre, visible across the shallow valley. And so too was Mount Revisotto, further away, meaning they were visible to whoever was there. This was the tricky part, where the ridgeline curved back east. 'We'll go slowly,' said Harry. 'No sudden movement. Slip from tree to tree. What'd ye think, Archie?'

Archie grunted in agreement. 'I hope the boys keep 'em busy.'

The boys, since reinforced, were doing their best. One of the German MGs ripped. The gulping staccato of a Bren answered back. To and fro salvoes were exchanged, but to little effect he guessed. But that too was part of fire and movement. Better a pile of spent casings than a bullet in the head.

It took them several minutes to traverse the ground. With the knoll almost straight off their right, and Mount Revisotto looming up behind it, Archie felt a tug at his sleeve.

'Shouldn't we head east now? Can't be farther than a couple hundred yards.'

Vehemently Archie shook his head. 'Not yet,' he said softly. 'There's only two of us, Harry. Better to go a little further and try to take them from behind. You got any grenades?'

Dinesen went searching in his pouches. 'Two,' he said finally. 'You?'

'Six.'

'Six!?'

'I came prepared,' said Archie. 'But keep them handy. And let's fix bayonets. The Jerries are really not keen on bayonets.' Grimly he clicked his into place.

Dinesen looked up from his rifle. 'What else are you packing, Archie?'

'Some stripper clips, a very nasty Jerry sword knife, a pistol, water bottle... the usual things.'

'No PIAT?' Dinesen was wrestling to keep a straight face.

Archie rolled his eyes.

It was truly dusk now, dark shadows everywhere, hilltops tinged with the last light of day. The grass was very long, almost to their waist. Archie watched as a line of red tracer arced gracefully down from Mount Revisotto towards the ridge line where "A" Company was doing its best to fight back.

Fifty yards straight ahead, across a small dip in the ground, was the outcrop and the ruins that so resembled a medieval keep. Taking the long route they cautiously circled around the knoll until they reached the rear. The remains of a fence and a large iron gate abutted a road beyond. Archie crouched down, and Dinesen slipped in beside him.

'How do you want to play this?' asked Dinesen.

'Carefully, very carefully,' replied Archie. 'I'll go first, you follow. That looks like a path up from the gate, so there must be a rear entrance. I'll head for that. Cover me, then once you see a bit of an uproar, come in behind. There may be a Jerry or two hiding in the rocks so keep your eyes peeled. I expect the place is teeming with the buggers.'

'Uproar, eh?' Dinesen looked at him dubiously, then quickly agreed. 'Will do. Good luck, Archie.'

Archie laid a hand on his shoulder and slipped away through the grass, heading towards a tree just shy of the gate. He walked deliberately one measured pace at a time, crouched over, and listening attentively. His eyes swept the ground ahead; no sign of the enemy. At intervals, he heard rifle fire coming from the ridge and the front side of the ruins. The Lee-Enfield was slung over his shoulder, grenade in one hand, the German officer's pistol in the other.

What sounded like several thousand local crickets and cicadas had begun their nightly tumult. Distant machine guns were still duelling it out, too far away to be of concern. Then an MG-42 ensconced in the stone keep zipped into action, startling him momentarily. Somewhere else, the dull crack of a mortar firing. Yet for all the background noise, Archie was most conscious of the sound of grass swishing as he passed. As he neared the tree something underfoot cracked alarmingly. He pulled up, his heart racing till the moment passed. He moved on, reaching the tree. Throwing a quick glance in the direction of the ruins he saw that the path was no more than an avalanche of stones.

It might once have been a small church, he thought. A house seemed unlikely. The surrounding courtyard walls were tall and thick, and barricaded any entrance from the rear. Fortunately, he'd come at it exactly right. There was an open gateway in the wall, the building mere steps beyond. Reaching the stone wall he peered cautiously through the opening. A furtive glance to the left, and then to the right. To be certain he looked up at the roof, but saw nothing unusual.

The building itself was some two stories tall. A little higher on the left where what looked like a tower could be seen, covered by a steep slanted roof with a tiny square window high in the crown. To the right was an imposing doorway, under an archway of stone slabs with no door.

Archie strode forward. After only a few paces, he passed through the doorway. Inside it sounded hollow and echoing. He heard voices and pressed himself up against the cold wall. The MG-42 began firing again. He took advantage of the unholy din to rush towards it. As he came to a small open doorway, the firing died away as unexpectedly as it had started.

Peeking around the corner he saw four of them; three crouched over the MG positioned near the narrow window, changing barrels. A fourth man was standing off to one side holding binoculars. Roberts and Borden could have fired at this bunch all night and wouldn't have hit a thing. The window was tiny, the wall a foot thick. Hell, the entire regiment plugging away wouldn't have hit anything. With the Walther still in one hand, Archie pulled out the little metal ring from his grenade, reached forward and with an underhand toss he let fly. An instant later he was rewarded by the sound of a crisp bang. At the acrid smoke his nostrils twitched and he ducked around the corner to survey the damage.

Smoke hung in the air, the MG crew lay crumpled on the ground near their gun. The man to one side was not on the ground, however. He was an NCO, and by all appearances entirely unscathed. Worse, he was extracting a pistol from his belt and staring straight at Archie.

Their eyes met. Archie brought the Walther to bear and he squeezed off two hurried shots in close succession before ducking away. The man's pistol cracked in reply an instant later.

Five, thought Archie. He had only five rounds left from a 9-round magazine; two he'd fired at the German officer on the Nicosia road, and another two just now. Which was fine, were it not that the Jerry sergeant almost certainly had eight. The Lee-Enfield was terribly cumbersome in close quarters, and there was a chance that some of the gun crew might be coming round. As if to underscore this possibility he heard the man now moving around the room. Then his mouth slowly twisted into a smile.

Stuffing the pistol into his belt he reached into a pouch and came away holding two grenades.

From the room he heard soft voices. There were at least two of them, and perhaps more. Very soon they would come for him.

He pulled the pins from both grenades then tossed the first around the corner with his left. There was a satisfying bang. Quickly he transferred the second bomb to the same hand and rolled it into what he hoped was the middle of the room.

Archie's ears were still ringing as he plunged through the doorway, his hand pulling at the sword knife. But the German sergeant was down, lying on his back, his legs folded awkwardly behind. Clearly he'd taken the full blast from at least one grenade. Archie stood staring at him.

At a rifle shot behind he nearly jumped out of his skin.

'It's okay, Archie. It's me… It's Harry.' Rifle held in two hands Dinesen stood in the doorway. He jutted his chin forward. 'That one had a gun.'

Archie looked down. One of the MG crew lying on the ground

was holding a pistol. Only his mouth was now open, a dark blot on his forehead spreading rapidly.

'You okay?'

'Yeah, thanks. Thanks for that, Harry,' he mumbled.

Dinesen gazed round. 'Jeez. What a mess.' Then he saw the MG-42, and whistled. 'Good thing that's out of action,' he said, leaning over to peer through the window towards the ridge line where the two companies were presumably still holed up. 'They could see everything.'

They turned and left. Walking through the opening in the wall, they checked their step at the sight of the dark soaring rise of Mount Revisotto, literally in front of them.

'Did you check the rock face at the front?' Archie asked suddenly, taking the rifle from his shoulder. The sky was a dark purple. Night was falling.

Dinesen averted his eyes. 'No, no I didn't. I came in after you. I was worried as hell.' Slowly he shook his head. 'I'm sure it's okay Archie.'

CHAPTER 31

5-6 August, 1943
Mount Revisotto, Sicily

To their left a machine pistol opened up.

Dinesen went down in a hail of bullets, clutching at his stomach, his rifle tottering away down the rocky incline. Archie stepped back through the gate into the courtyard.

Cursing himself for his carelessness, he raised his rifle and twisted it awkwardly round the stone pillar of the gate. Without looking he pulled the trigger. Then retrieving it he threw the bolt back and forth to reload, and fired again in a similar fashion. Not because he could see anything, but for precisely the same reason he'd asked Roberts and Borden to fire their Brens at this knoll; an enemy ducking his head was an enemy not firing at them.

A potato masher came clattering down outside. Archie retreated a step further into the courtyard and pressed himself against the thick wall. A flash. The grenade cracked. Voices were shouting.

'You'll have to try a little harder than that!' he yelled angrily.

Hurriedly he propped the Lee-Enfield against the wall, only in his haste it promptly toppled over. No matter. He was rooting through his gear. When he found all three that remained, he bent his sleeveless left forearm at the elbow and cupped it against his chest. Then he laid the no. 36s out, one for one in their new nest. If they came they would come through the gate. And Germans being Germans they would no doubt be proceeded by a flurry of potato mashers to announce their entrance in spectacular fashion; tanks, MGs and potato mashers, the Jerries had them in wearisome abundance. A tactical retreat was called for. Slowly, cautiously, and above all quietly, he stepped further along the wall in the direction of the voices on the far side.

He looked up, gauging the distance. The wall was high. He figured probably close to fifteen feet, plus he would need a few extra feet to clear it. It was not that twenty feet was so terribly high – if he simply brought his arm back and pitched the grenade with a good throw it would be over. But if he did that it would fall far from the wall, certainly too far away to catch any Jerries. Dollars to doughnuts they were lined up behind each other, slowly advancing, keeping close to the wall for cover.

It was a lifetime ago, but a prank from his childhood sprang to mind. He and a gang of buddies from the fifth grade would gather daily after school and each would take turns attempting to be the hero that plunged a stone down Mr. Hobart's chimney. Which, if they timed it right, left them precisely enough time for a smooth getaway. It had not always gone well, but they persevered.

The trick eventually learned was that it lay not in the strength of the pitch, but rather in the trajectory of the stone. The others would cheerily line up on the sidewalk beside the white picket fence, a hopeless endeavour if ever there was one, akin to shooting a field gun at an MG nest on a reverse slope. But Archie would slip across the lawn, and ease up a few feet from the wooden siding of the old crank's house. Then Billy would give the signal. Archie usually got to go first as he was the one in the greatest jeopardy. Then, with an underhand toss, he'd throw it straight up, almost straight, but not quite. He had been rather good at it at one point.

The Panzer grenadiers were setting out their own plan amongst themselves. He heard their murmur on the other side of the wall. He figured they'd attempt a rush, maybe from one side, or even both. Not that it mattered. There was only one way in. However there were likely a half-dozen of them. He thought of Dinesen, lying in front of the gate, possibly dead, but possibly not. He gritted his teeth.

Seizing a grenade in one hand, he pulled the pin, and took a deep breath. Then, as if releasing a dove, he lobbed it upwards in a graceful arc.

By the time it was twenty feet in the air he had a new grenade in hand, and was pulling the pin. His mind was going through the motions. He heard the blast. Concentrate, he told himself. He sent the thing flying, a few feet closer to the gateway. There was a new blast, and voices, louder now. But he was oblivious to everything, everything except his next toss. Then there was but a single metal egg resting on his forearm. Determinedly he clasped his fist around it, and pulled the pin. Something made him hesitate, some sound or extra sense. A soldier's instinct was what some called it.

Down near the gate there was a flash and a bang, followed by a shuffle of feet and a rattle of gear. A figure rushed through the dark opening heading towards the church.

Archie tossed the grenade underhand, little league style, hoping to get it over the plate if nothing else. The flash lit up a soldier coming through the gate behind his comrade. The man threw his arms up, and recoiled backwards. A few steps in front the first soldier cried out, small shards of shrapnel tearing into his back.

Instinctively Archie went to reach for his rifle, then saw it lying near the gate. Only twenty feet away, but it might as well have been twenty miles.

The pistol, the Walther! He still had the Walther.

He reached for it, but another German was already pressing into the courtyard. The man saw him and levelled his rifle. Archie brought the pistol to bear. The man fired. A flash.

Archie felt the bullet hit him somewhere in the side. But he felt unstoppable and he extended his arm. Stepping forward he pulled at the trigger. A miss. He pulled again.

It too missed, for he saw the soldier locking the bolt down, the muzzle end bobbing briefly before it settled on him. Then a new flash, and a *CRACK*.

A searing hammer slammed into his right hand. The pistol went flying. He saw the soldier reloading.

Archie screamed his Indian cry, and with a startling speed ran towards him. His left hand was pulling at the sword knife fastened to his waist.

It was a long, gleaming dagger, a wicked looking weapon. The German opposite would surely have recognized it, for it was one of theirs. It was barely out of the scabbard before he was on the man, no time to raise it, or even to point in the proper direction. So he did the only thing he could think of and put his head down and butted his helmet hard into the man.

The soldier stumbled backwards.

Archie lifted his head, then his arm. The blade flashed in the twilight as he twisted it round.

The German raised his rifle across his chest, diagonally, preparing to parry the blow.

Archie kicked him hard in the knee. Then as the German gasped he kicked him again, then thrust the knife forward into his midriff. He felt it slide in, and he kept pushing until it would go no further.

At a sound he looked over the man's shoulder and saw another soldier behind. The man just stood there, staring, his mouth open. Archie pushed the soldier backwards, thereby pulling the knife free. The German toppled to the ground. Scowling he took a step forward. With a look of horror the second soldier turned and fled.

Archie followed him through the gateway, grasping the knife in one hand, his head darting from left to right. But he could see no one except the single German soldier frantically stumbling down the rocks to the road, Mount Revisotto beckoning. Apparently he was the last of the squad. Archie glanced around for a weapon with which to shoot him, but spotted Dinesen first. Harry was on his back, his helmet off, and a hand gripping his side. Despite his obvious pain, a most peculiar grin broke out when he saw Archie. Archie reached for his water bottle to offer him a drink, then paused. The bottle was wet. At the sight of the finger sized hole in it, he took a deep breath.

Not long after a section of men reached them. Archie had watched as they cautiously approached across the field in the dark. They were bent over, rifles held at the ready. The soldier in the lead was carrying what was surely a Tommy gun.

'We're up here,' he called out, when they were within hailing distance. 'The Jerries scrammed already.' After all that had happened he didn't want some trigger-happy clod from "B" Company to mistake him for a Panzer grenadier.

In pairs they clambered up the rocks towards the gateway, exactly as he had done an hour before.

Grimy, hot faces looked from side to side. Bodies lay strewn seemingly everywhere. Their corporal whistled at the sight. Then he stared at Archie. 'Archie?' Curtly Archie nodded. He knew him. It was Tim Smithers. 'I thought you said the Jerries "scrammed"?'

'The smart one did. The others are here. There's a few of the buggers lying in the church too. I expect a few may be wounded, but Dinesen here needs some help first.'

The corporal glanced at him. Dinesen was sitting propped up against the wall, a hastily applied field bandage marking out the problem. Archie was pretty sure he'd make it, but the sooner he had some proper help the better.

'We've no stretcher,' said the corporal, frowning. 'But don't worry, we'll carry him.'

'What about the wounded Jerries?'

Smithers shrugged. 'Leave 'em. Let them clean up their own mess. But you two better come with me. Captain Stone and Captain Tighe have decided to pull back. We're going to try again tomorrow. They say we need more punch.'

'More punch? We just took this bloody place,' exclaimed Archie. 'That's Mount Revisotto right there. We're at the foot of the damned thing. Don't tell me we're supposed to hand this place back?'

'Sorry,' said the corporal. 'Not my choice. Orders are orders.'

In a daze Archie followed Smithers and section. First back to the feature known only as point 333 on the map, then on to some woods a mile or so south. Captain Tighe had located stretchers for those who couldn't walk. There were a goodly number who fit the description.

Archie walked alongside Dinesen's stretcher. Once or twice Harry let out a moan or a grunt when the bearers stumbled, but was otherwise lucid, and in surprisingly good spirits. No one asked Archie to help, and that was fortunate, for it was all he could do to carry himself.

Night was hours old, the next day long begun when finally they arrived at their destination and were told they could rest. Nothing in the world would have pleased Archie more than flopping down under a tree and closing his eyes. However, on the verge of doing so, the lieutenant accosted him.

'Come with me, Atwell,' grunted an exhausted-looking Lieutenant Wiles.

Wiles led him to a small tent, one of several close to each other, not far from the steep bank of the Troina. 'We won't be able to transport the wounded to the rear until tomorrow,' he said. Then he threw open the flap of the tent. 'He keeps asking for you. He's insistent.'

'For me?'

The lieutenant nodded. 'Go see for yourself.' Archie stepped inside.

There were three men lying on a groundsheet, a medic attending to them. As Archie entered, one of the men raised his head.

'I ain't no coward, Archie,' said Lachance. 'I'm not. Really I'm not.'

Archie sighed, and took a deep breath. Then he shook his head. 'No, I was wrong about that. You aren't a coward, Ed. You may be as daft as a daffodil in spring, but you sure as heck aren't a coward.' A reluctant grin crept onto his face.

Lachance grinned back. Clearly Archie's opinion of him was something that had been bothering him greatly, at least sufficiently that it distracted from a sizeable wound in his right arm. He mentioned nothing about Archie's role in clearing the MG nest. Knowing the army he was probably still in the dark about that. Then again, knowing the army he'd probably get a medal and a promotion for having planned it as section leader.

All of which made Archie recall talk of a new plan for tomorrow. Oh, how he longed to lie down. 'I've gotta go, Ed. See ya round. And good luck,' he called out, as he backed out of the tent. Lieutenant Wiles was standing, waiting for him.

'Follow me,' said Wiles. 'Time for a nap. We'll be up early.'

At 0930, accompanied by a most accomplished barrage provided by the regimental mortars, the divisional artillery, an assortment of 17-pounders, a troop of Sherman tanks, and a platoon of Vickers medium machine guns, the Edmonton Regiment made its second assault on Mount Revisotto.

Once again "A" Company led, and once again "B" followed. They moved forward in bounds, one company covering the other. There was something of a textbook exercise to it. Only after they had climbed the slopes of the hill was it obvious that all the meticulous preparations were for naught.

'There's not a bloody Kraut in sight,' sighed Roberts, sounding very much as if he wished there was. 'They've buggered off.'

Which was indeed the only possible explanation. Even if to anyone who had seen the place yesterday this was entirely inexplicable.

'Quiet there,' growled the new platoon sergeant, Haver, all full of pip and vim and a drill sergeant's sense of how a proper soldier should conduct himself.

'He's been on a beach the past month,' mumbled someone. But no one had any problem with the sergeant. They were simply glad Jerry had packed his bags. Dinesen and Lachance were not the only ones heading to a hospital today. Astonishingly, Postlethwaite and McDonald had come through it unscathed.

Proudly Lieutenant Wiles led the platoon to the peak. Archie tagged along behind. Lacking a flag to plant, they just gawked at the view upon reaching the crest.

Lieutenant-Colonel Jefferson was suitably proud when he arrived and spoke a few words: 'Yesterday "C" and "D" Companies took Hill 736. And today "A" and "B" took Mount Revisotto. You've done very well.'

Then came the explanation for the enemy's abrupt change of heart.

'The Jerries have abandoned Catania. They're blowing their dumps. Army intelligence says a general retreat from the Catania plain is underway. They're fleeing while they still can.' A cheer went up. 'That's in no small measure because of what you've done these past weeks. The 78th Division has been given the task of pursuing them. The Americans will do the same to the north. But now, gentlemen, it's time for the regiment to have a well-deserved rest.' The men roared. Helmets were tossed in the air.

That this left the Edmonton Regiment and the 1st Division pinched out of the final glorious race to capture Messina was not of concern. They were only too happy to finally rest.

CHAPTER 32

10 August, 1943
Strait of Messina, Italy

It was an almost perfect night, Captain Weyers mused, staring up at the sparkling field of stars that was the sky. The inky waters to either side of the pioneer landing boat were calm, and he watched as the silvery froth from the bow wave bubbled out from under the gunwale and away to the stern, where it disappeared into the currents of the strait. They'd been forewarned of the likelihood of activity from the enemy air force and navy – a *Flakvierling* was placed aboard and manned for that very reason – but halfway to the mainland there hadn't been so much as a whisper of opposition. Of course, in anticipation of their evacuation, batteries of heavy artillery were stationed to ward off the Allied capital ships. Some said the anti-aircraft defences lining the narrow strait rivalled those of the Ruhr. Regardless of the truth of that, the preparations had been commendably thorough.

His eyes wandered back to the crowded deck aft. There he saw two trucks, small gaggles of men standing together talking, the remains of his company looking out as he was doing. Other landing boats and Siebel ferries carried the rest of the regiment. The 104th Panzer Grenadier Regiment was amongst the first of the units to be invited to embark. Why this was the case, he did not know, but after Troina it must have been obvious that little more could be expected of them.

He knew he should have been pleased about this development, but he was not. It felt too much like defeat for his taste. This had been his first independent command, and although it was for only the briefest of times, he had hoped for much more from it.

'It's a nice night, Captain,' said one of his young lieutenants, coming to stand beside him.

Weyers nodded agreeably.

'Our foe will not be pleased,' smiled the lieutenant.

He frowned.

'Slipping away like this under their very noses.' The lieutenant shook his head. 'Taking our trucks and all our gear. If only they knew!' He chuckled.

'I think you forget, Lieutenant, all that we're leaving behind on that cursed island,' snapped Weyers. 'Not least of which are our fallen and missing comrades.' Losing von Steinen had been an especially bitter blow.

Chastened the lieutenant looked away.

Weyers gazed out at the sea once again. There was something very peaceful about it. It was curious though how the lieutenant had made their retreat sound as if it were a victory, he thought. That surely would be the same approach taken in the official communique from Berlin. For those involved in the actions they described, they were typically not worth the paper they were written on. But if not a victory, this was perhaps not the total defeat he had made it out to be in his blackest moments. In that the lieutenant was quite correct.

Take Troina. It had been a shame, certainly. But despite the weeks of battle, and their weakened state, they had retaken Hill 1034 and they had held it against all comers. And they did so until Colonel Ens, on the afternoon of the 5th, had ordered them to withdraw that very night. Even Weyers had to concede, with the wisdom gained from hindsight, that it had been a sensible decision. The Americans were simply too strong. Eventually they would have overwhelmed them.

And that was equally true of Piazza Armerina, Valguarnera and Nissoria. It was even true of Agira. They had put up the good fight against the Canadians, and they had made them struggle for every metre. And that alone made it something more than simple defeat, did it not?

The Canadians. A scowl began to form on his face, but then with a start he suppressed the old ingrained habit. The Canadians were worthy adversaries. They were not the demons he had once imagined sitting as an impressionable boy on his mother's lap. Still, with that red rectangular patch they all wore, and their infernal talent for pressing on like madmen no matter the odds, it was no wonder the men had taken to calling them red-patch devils.

The sergeant they had captured, the one from the Edmonton Regiment, was of more pliable material. Alas, the chained dogs of the field police had gotten wind of his capture. Flaunting their tin gorgets, they'd whisked him away. Only, it now appeared, the entire party was captured themselves by an American patrol soon after. If it wasn't so infuriating it would be amusing.

He would have dearly liked to have learned more about that soldier, Archie Atwell – the one who had nearly done him in. Not once, but twice! Leonforte, in particular, he would not soon forget. It was there that he experienced the bitter taste of true defeat; a personal defeat that had coloured his thoughts ever since. All at the hands of a single man. He had told no one, but the humiliation felt none the better for it.

That one was a real, red-patch devil, he thought. A red patch *private* no less. The odds were infinitesimal that he should ever see him again. But he prayed fervently that he would. And there was always a chance. It was war after all. And should he do so – well, then he would put things right. The next campaign was yet to begin.

He felt his spirits returning.

Seeing his captain smiling, the young lieutenant summoned up his courage, and wet his tongue. 'Look, sir. It's the mainland. We're almost there: Italy!'

Mount Revisotto, Sicily

Saunders was bubbling over. 'It's true, Archie! Our fighting days are over. We've been placed in army reserve.' Archie couldn't think the last time he'd seen Dick so cheery. It had been several weeks at least; he recalled Saunders having just won a big hand at cards.

But he frowned at his words. This wasn't the first time he'd heard good news only to have it later emerge that it wasn't news, but rather some wildly optimistic rumour that spread faster than a wildfire on a Sicilian hillside. 'Says who?' he demanded to know.

'Lieutenant Wiles. They're moving us to a training area tomorrow morning.'

'I'll believe it when I see it,' grumbled Archie. It had been another scorching day, bivouacking on the arid slopes of their most recent conquest: Mount Revisotto. The promise of being able to refill their water bottles was as fleeting as a mirage, and to a man they were parched. There'd been a litany of jobs as the regiment endeavoured to whip itself into shape after too many fights, and altogether too many miles cavorting up and down the Sicilian hills. But the battlefield had indeed grown quiet.

'Yeah, well, if you don't believe me, you can ask him all about it when you see him yourself. You're to report straight away to Wiles and the Captain.'

Archie groaned. For a brief while he had entertained hope that his status as the black sheep of the company might finally change in the aftermath of the fight on the knoll. It certainly wasn't long before men were coming to him, bubbling over with words of admiration, doling out pats on the back, and laughingly enquiring about medals. Medals!... As if! Naturally there were a few jokes as well – the one about giving Lachance his 'last chance' was especially popular. Admittedly, Lieutenant Wiles had sought him out and heartily told him, 'well done, Atwell', before quizzing him about the details. But that was it. Captain Tighe was invisible. Life went on. One consolation was that Harry Dinesen would make it.

'What's it about?' he asked Saunders.

Saunders shrugged. 'Beats me. They probably want someone to show the reinforcements the ropes.'

Yes, that was likely it, he thought. The reinforcements who had arrived that morning were most welcome. Archie's section alone was half what it had been when the invasion began. It was no different for the rest of the company. And the new men, for all their training, could definitely use a few practical tips. Matt Evers spotted him walking down the hill and waved. He'd ask Matt about it later.

He found Captain Tighe slouched in a wicker chair, under a tarpaulin that had been tied to the rock face above to form a lean-to of sorts. He looked weary. Lieutenant Wiles stood beside him. The two had evidently been talking.

'There you are, Atwell. I've been meaning to speak with you.'

'Sir?'

'I have a confession to make. It appears I've made a misjudgement.'

'Sir?' The puzzlement on Archie's face must have been obvious.

'It may interest you to learn who I ran into. Ran into is perhaps not the best description. In fact he was lying on a stretcher at the Regimental Aid Post at the time. You see, the good lieutenant was unfortunate enough to be hit in both hands at Hill 736, and was on his way to a hospital.'

Archie frowned. For the life of him he couldn't figure who the captain was referring to. It was certainly not Wiles; he was fit as a fiddle. So was Lieutenant Swan, for that matter. As for the third platoon commander, Lieutenant Kellaway, there was nothing a hospital could do for him.

'Lieutenant Dougan sends his greetings.'

With that the memories flooded back – Dougan, of course! Why hadn't he thought of him earlier?

Tighe took his silence for confusion, and went on to explain. 'Surely you remember Lieutenant Dougan? It was his platoon, after all, from "D" Company that was out on the Nicosia road on that fighting patrol with Major Bury. He was in some considerable pain when I saw him. But he insisted on asking about you. In fact we had rather a long chat.'

'Yes, sir,' grinned Archie. 'I could hardly forget Lieutenant Dougan.'

'Well, that's a good thing because he remembers you quite vividly. In fact he told me a couple of rather colourful tales. One in particular caught my attention, about you holding a PIAT in a showdown with a Panzer at fifty paces. Both he and Major Bury were very impressed with your conduct. He said that it was fortunate they'd "press-ganged" you.' Tighe paused. 'I'm sorry I didn't take you at your word.'

Archie bowed his head. He didn't know what to say, so he said nothing.

'You'll receive your missing pay, of course. Almost twenty-seven dollars.'

'Thank you, sir.' Archie straightened, and was about to salute when the captain waved a peremptory hand to forestall him.

'Two more matters. The Lieutenant and I have been talking. Among other things we discussed what you did at point 333. It was a damned fine piece of soldiery, if I do say so myself.'

'Thank you, sir.'

'We've decided to put you in charge of the section. You've earned it. You'll be a corporal, of course.'

'But what about Corporal Lachance? He's the senior in the section.'

'Yes.' Captain Tighe nodded his finely formed chin at Lieutenant Wiles. 'That came up in discussion as well. Lance-Corporal Lachance's injury is fortunately not likely to keep him away for long, so that is a consideration. However Andy did have an elegant solution. Two stripes, Atwell! That should take care of that.'

Corporal Atwell. A full corporal. It did have a certain ring to it, Archie had to admit. It was a distinction that had never meant anything to him before. But that was back when they were only boys playing at war. The real thing was altogether different. He was different.

'There's one final matter. I intend to recommend you for a Distinguished Conduct Medal for your actions at Mount Revisotto. As a matter of fact, Lieutenant-Colonel Jefferson is quite insistent I do so. It appears the Colonel was of a mind to recommend you himself for a decoration for what you did at Leonforte. But in all the turmoil afterwards the Colonel says that he missed the deadline.'

Captain Tighe smiled. And with that all the grey weariness that had hung over him like a cloak, seemed to vanish. His eyes sparkled. Meanwhile, Lieutenant Wiles looked as if he'd been proclaimed the proud father of a new baby.

The captain lifted himself to his feet and extended a hand. 'Well done.'

Lieutenant Wiles stepped towards him, and one hand reached for his shoulder, while the other firmly grasped his. Then he moved away. His two superiors stood watching him.

'Well, what are you staring at Atwell? Reveille's at 0400. We're off to Militello in the morning.'

'Militello, sir?'

'It's south of here. Not so far from Licodia. You might remember the place?'

Archie was thinking. He did remember Licodia. He remembered it being a dump, but it had the undeniable merit of being a dump not far from Modica. No, not very far at all. He grinned from ear to ear.

The captain was looking at him with a bemused look. 'Now get going, Atwell. With your new responsibilities you've surely got work to do?'

'Yes, sir. And thank you, sir.' He smiled at Lieutenant Wiles, then turned to leave.

'Oh, and Corporal Atwell?' It was Captain Tighe.

'Sir?' His heart began to pound. Was something wrong?

'You won't disappoint me again, will you?'

While he wasn't entirely sure how he was going to swing it, he was going to be in Modica in a couple of days. He was a corporal now, so surely there were possibilities. Something would come up. They might even give him a day or two of leave if he asked.

'No, sir.' Resolutely Archie shook his head. 'No sir, I won't.' Whatever happened he was going to keep his promise to the captain. His days of being a private were over for good. The army was his home now.

AUTHOR'S HISTORICAL NOTE

The invasion of Sicily, often known today as Operation Husky, came to an end in the early hours of 17 August, 1943 with the capture of Messina in the far northeastern corner of the island. It was precisely one week after the 1st Canadian Division ended its operations in the Salso Valley near Mount Etna, and only five weeks after the invasion began.

The seaborne invasion itself was of a scale and complexity never seen before. The lessons learned would prove invaluable in the even larger D-Day invasion less than a year later. Archie as a cog in the machine catches only glimpses of the broader Sicilian campaign, but experiences at first hand the skillfulness and tenacity of the German defenders. Bereft of air and sea power, all but abandoned by their erstwhile Italian allies, and facing overwhelming numbers, the Germans took full advantage of their one key advantage: the terrain.

When the American General Patton followed his forces into Messina that August morning, the streets were empty of the enemy. The German commander, General Hube, mindful of the tradition that a captain should be last to abandon ship, had departed only hours before with the final remnants of his forces on the island. In the preceding week more than 40,000 German soldiers, nearly 10,000 vehicles, untold tonnes of fuel and supplies, and almost 60,000 Italian soldiers were successfully evacuated. Sicily was decisively an Allied victory, but it was by no means a decisive Axis defeat.

The final race to capture Messina was to end in an American victory. It was a near photo finish with a British reconnaissance unit entering the town mere hours after the first American forces. But in history, as in sport, it is the victor not the runner-up that takes the prize. And it is certainly not the runner-up to the runner-up. As was to happen time and again during the war the Canadians, though important enablers of the race, were not invited for a stab at the history books. Still, the stories beyond the headlines are interesting ones, and Archie's tale is intertwined with the narrative of General Montgomery's 'left hook', and the gruelling battle that resulted through the hills of the interior.

The Edmonton Regiment (later the Loyal Edmonton Regiment), and the 1st Canadian Division (which even today takes pride in its nickname of 'Red-Patch Devils') are, of course, real units. Many of the officers and men named in the novel did indeed fight in Sicily. So too did the 104th Panzer Grenadier Regiment, including its officers who are mentioned – with the notable exceptions of Captain Biedermann and Archie's adversary, Oberleutnant Manfred Weyers, who are fictional. Archie and his entire section are also fictional, as is his platoon commander Lieutenant Wiles, all parachuted into a regiment whose exploits are nevertheless much as I described them.

Amongst these exploits was the capture of a winery near the beaches on the first day of the invasion, together with a large contingent of Italian soldiers. While the regimental war diary notes the 'rather disastrous results' from sampling the 'vino', no mention is made of any attempt to distribute it to the thirsty allied armies!

Likewise the capture of Italian General d'Havet at Modica was certainly not the work of Archie Atwell. The details of the actual event itself are disputed, and even the official history struggles to provide a definitive account. So into this 'fog of war' marches my fictional hero.

One of the fun parts of researching the war is to discover how many of the historical details are either not known or, are open to debate – even in a conflict as well documented as World War II. Generally I followed the lead of sources such as unit war diaries, official histories, letters, and the like; yet for reasons mundane and otherwise the truth is not always to be found in such accounts. There are numerous cases where dates and facts are demonstrably false. For the novelist anxious to put forth his own story such opportunities are to be seized upon.

One such example of conflicting information relates to the events during the fighting patrol along the Agira – Nicosia road described in Chapters 21 and 22. Major Bury of "D" Company – who only days later was to die leading his company's attack at Cemetery Hill – would posthumously win the Distinguished Service Order (DSO) for this action, one of the highest medals in the British Empire. The medal recommendation describes him having 'personally led the bayonet charge…' Yet there appears to be doubt whether he was even present on the patrol. The official history pads around the issue – unusually so – noting in a later section the actions of Lieutenant Dougan, but patently not those of Bury. Whatever is the poor novelist to do other than write it up and call it fiction? The attentive reader will note my version neglects neither officer, nor indeed a certain fictional private manning a PIAT.

For those interested in such things, a WW II Anglo-Canadian infantry division was composed of three brigades. In turn, each brigade was made up of three regiments or battalions (the terms used interchangeably – technically the first regimental battalion of some 800 men was in the field, while the second remained at home), plus artillery and other units. The closest equivalent to a full strength 1943 Wehrmacht regiment such as the 104th Panzer Grenadier Regiment, with three battalions in the field, was a brigade. Meanwhile, an American regiment was typically some 25% larger than the Anglo-Canadian variant with roughly one thousand men.

One small mystery that may remain was the destination of the American airplanes spotted by Archie and mates in Chapter 29. They turned up at the headquarters of XXX Corps. Shortly thereafter, Lt.-Gen. Leese, in a brief telephone call with General Bradley, would ask what they had done wrong that Bradley's chaps would want to bomb them!

The Sicilian campaign was short but intense, the walls of Hitler's fortress Europe only a stone's throw away across the strait, and it will not surprise the reader to hear that a heavy price was paid. For the 1st Division – at war for the very first time – losses amounted to 2,300 men, of whom 562 were killed. Major Bury and hundreds more rest in the splendid Agira war cemetery, short kilometres from the coast and Catania. Many more fell in the American and British forces to either side. German and Italian losses were also very heavy, although the precise numbers remain vague. The invasion was to be but an easily overlooked prelude to the many campaigns, and the many, many months of war that still lay ahead.

Finally, what would an author's note be without a brief but heartfelt word of thanks: to Dr. Gary Grothman for pointing out the faults in navigation and ship construction; to Dexter Petley for doing it again, whilst shoring up the timbers compartment by compartment; and to Ian Forsdike for ensuring my little ship set sail without too many loose nails and infuriating leaks.

I invite you to visit my website www.darrellduthie.com to browse my other books, sign up for my email list (hear it from me when the next book is out!), or if you just want to get in touch. All are most welcome. As is a review online should you have the time and inclination.

Thank you for reading!

Darrell Duthie, 31 May, 2024

Printed in Great Britain
by Amazon